T0360282

HISTORICAL

Your romantic escape to the past.

A Duke For The Penniless Widow
Christine Merrill

Spinster With A Scandalous Past
Sadie King

MILLS & BOON

A DUKE FOR THE PENNILESS WIDOW
© 2024 by Christine Merrill
Philippine Copyright 2024
Australian Copyright 2024
New Zealand Copyright 2024

First Published 2024
First Australian Paperback Edition 2024
ISBN 978 1 867 29970 7

SPINSTER WITH A SCANDALOUS PAST
© 2024 by Sarah Louise King
Philippine Copyright 2024
Australian Copyright 2024
New Zealand Copyright 2024

First Published 2024
First Australian Paperback Edition 2024
ISBN 978 1 867 29970 7

MIX
Paper | Supporting
responsible forestry
FSC® C001695

Published by
Harlequin Mills & Boon
An imprint of Harlequin Enterprises (Australia) Pty Limited
(ABN 47 001 180 918), a subsidiary of HarperCollins
Publishers Australia Pty Limited
(ABN 36 009 913 517)
Level 19, 201 Elizabeth Street
SYDNEY NSW 2000 AUSTRALIA

Cover art used by arrangement with Harlequin Books S.A.. All rights reserved.

Printed and bound in Australia by McPherson's Printing Group

A Duke For The Penniless Widow

Christine Merrill

MILLS & BOON

Christine Merrill lives on a farm in Wisconsin with her husband, two sons and too many pets—all of whom would like her to get off the computer so they can check their email. She has worked by turns in theater costuming and as a librarian. Writing historical romance combines her love of good stories and fancy dress with her ability to stare out the window and make stuff up.

Visit the Author Profile page
at millsandboon.com.au for more titles.

Author Note

Since so much of this book is devoted to letters, I might as well tell you about the money-saving, letter-writing practice of the Regency. Since postage increased when more sheets were used, thrifty writers of the nineteenth century wrote the first page of the letter normally. Then, they turned the sheet ninety degrees and wrote the second page over the top of the first.

Cross writing was common in England and the US and was probably even harder to read than my handwriting!

Happy reading,
Christine Merrill

DEDICATION

To Amanda and Jeremy Olsen
and my new great-nephew, Griffin

Chapter One

Talk of the Ton

After a night of high-stakes play and heavy losses, the unfortunate Mr John Ogilvie returned home and succumbed to despair, ending his life.

Tragedy might have been averted if not for that final hand of cards played with the callous Duke of G., who is known about London for his rapacious appetite for gaming.

Mr Ogilvie leaves a widow and a seven-year-old son.

What will they do now?

And what does G. have to say for himself?

Alex Conroy, the Duke of Glenmoor, stared down at the morning's newspaper in dismay, his finger tracing the item in the gossip column and its veiled references to him. 'I am not callous. I am not rapacious. And I am not at fault. I was there when it happened, of course. But correlation does not imply causation.'

'Your students at Oxford might have been impressed by such a response. But you will have to do better than that to impress the *ton*.' His stepbrother, Evan, shook his head, obviously disappointed at Alex's handling of the situation.

Of course, nothing like this had ever happened to Evan. He had known he would be the Duke of Fallon from the moment he'd known anything. He had received a lifetime's training in navigating London society and had no trouble keeping his name from the scandal sheets, other than the brief hubbub created by his sudden marriage.

But Alex had never expected to inherit a title. The death of an heirless cousin had resulted in his sudden elevation to a dukedom, a move that had left him scrambling to keep up with the new expectations put upon him and the prurient interest of strangers in the intimate details of his life.

Alex tapped the paper again. 'This makes it sound as if I drove a man to his death. That was not what happened at all.'

Evan sighed. 'As you should know from my marriage, it is not what *happened* that matters. What people *think* happened is far more important. Since you are relatively new to your title and were not expected to be heir to it, everyone wonders what sort of a peer you will make. They will watch you and they will read the gossip.'

'But this makes me out to be some kind of monster,' Alex said with a weak laugh. 'You know I am hardly the sort to push a man into risky wagers just to see him suffer.'

'I know it. But others may not,' Evan replied with another shake of his head. 'Unless they were there, all people will know is that, after losing a card game with "the Duke of G.", Mr John Ogilvie went home and blew his brains out.'

Alex winced. It was an accurate way to describe what had happened. But he could not help but wish that Evan had chosen a more polite euphemism to screen the truth. 'I did not know that the man had a problem with gambling. I thought it was a friendly round of loo to pass the time.'

And it had been just that. There had been nothing to distinguish this particular game from hundreds of other hands he had played in his life. The stakes were not particularly high and the other men at the table good-humoured. Even Ogilvie had seemed in high spirits and not the desperate man that he must have been.

'Earlier in the evening he had been banned from another gaming hell for his erratic play,' Evan said, repeating a truth that was common knowledge now that the gossip rags had got hold of the story.

'I did not know he'd already lost his savings and his house,' Alex said. 'Why did he not stop at that? Why did he insist on playing with me?'

Evan shrugged. 'Perhaps he thought his luck would turn.'

'And it was not even that great a loss. Fifty pounds…'

'That is more than some of my tenants make in a year,' Evan said gently.

'It was more than I'd planned to bet,' Alex agreed. 'But the fellow kept raising the stakes.'

'Trying to win back enough to stall the inevitable. By the time he got to you, there was nothing left to cover his loss. Fifty was the same as a thousand fifties to him.'

'Had he but asked, I'd have torn up his marker and thought nothing more about it. It was only a game...'

'Pride prevented him,' Evan said with a sigh. 'And the same pride caused him to take his own life rather than admit to his wife and son what he had done.'

This was even worse. The knowledge that a family was suffering as a result of what he had done was almost more than Alex could bear.

'Since you were the only titled man at that last card game, you are the one to take the blame,' Evan said, heaping guilt upon guilt.

'It is not fair,' Alex blurted, feeling like a selfish fool as he imagined the widow and child and what they must be feeling.

'I said something rather like that when I was forced to marry last Season,' Evan said with a smile. 'And you reminded me that it was not about what was fair, it was about what was proper.'

'That was an entirely different matter,' Alex said quickly. 'People thought your scandal was romantic. But this?' He picked the paper up and threw it into the fire. 'They will think me a murderer.'

'Some will,' Evan agreed. 'But the rumours fade with time. I would avoid the gaming tables for a while to prove that you are not going to make a habit of leading men to their ruin.'

Alex nodded in agreement. 'And I must see if there is anything to be done for the widow Ogilvie. It is not right that she and her son are to be turned out into the street because of her husband's folly.'

'A measure of forgiveness from her would go a long way towards mending your reputation,' Evan said.

It would salve his conscience as well. Though Alex knew he was largely innocent of what had happened with Ogilvie, he could not say he was totally blameless. If he had cried off the game, perhaps the fellow would still be alive. But he'd had no reason to. Perhaps Mrs Ogilvie would find it in her heart to reassure him. 'I will go to her. At the very least, I can give her the damned marker back and release her from a small portion of his debt.'

Then he could come home and begin the process of forgetting that this tragedy had ever happened.

It was Selina Ogilvie's first real day as a widow.

Though her husband had died three days ago, those first days had hardly counted. A hush had fallen over the house in the minutes after the discovery of the body. But when it had ended, there had been a flurry of activity that had not stopped since.

First, the housekeeper had sent for a physician, which had been thoughtful but pointless. It was quite clear to anyone that looked that her husband was far beyond the need of one. All Dr Crawford did to help was to try to force laudanum on Selina, which was even more pointless. She was stunned, but in no way hysterical.

If anything, she was angry. The least John could have done before ending his life was to have written her a note of apology. Instead, he had used his final moments to make a record of his losses, a carefully annotated list of markers and IOUs that contained the deed to the house and all the money in the bank. Then, as if he could not decide what to do about the debts, he had put a pistol to his head and exited life's stage, leaving the problem to her.

If she was asleep as Crawford wished her to be, who would take control of the household? There was no family on either side that would help. She had been an orphan when they'd married. And by his erratic behaviour and requests for loans, her husband had destroyed any family bonds or friendships that might have yielded aid in this difficult time. Judging by his final ledger, there was not a person she could think of that he had not already borrowed money from.

So she had done the only thing she could think of and sent her maid to pawn her jewels to pay for the funeral and to keep the house in groceries for as long as she could. Then she had gone upstairs to explain to little Edward that he would never see his father again.

With the arrangements to be made and the visit to the church, there had been no time to think about herself and her new status as a woman alone in the world. But now the study was cleaned, the body was buried and quiet had descended again. All the emotions she had kept at bay for those few days had come flooding back, threatening to engulf her.

The worst part of it was the change in the quality of the visitors. At the start, there had been a thin trickle of bereavement calls from acquaintances making vague offers of help and looking thoroughly relieved when she did not ask for any. But today's callers were the men who held the bulk of her husband's debt. She had been asked how she meant to pay, when and how much and, worst of all, when she was planning to vacate this house, which she no longer had the right to inhabit.

Mr Baxter, the house's new owner, stood before her now, staring at her with an unctuous smile and patting the pocket that held the deed. 'It is an unfortunate matter, Mrs Ogilvie. Most unfortunate. But it is a debt of honour and I am sure your husband would want to see it paid.'

She was tempted to shout that if John had wanted to see it, he would still be here. But it was clear that a display of temper would do nothing to move this man. Perhaps she could appeal to his sympathy. 'I am aware of that, sir. And I do mean to make good on all my husband's losses. But the current moment is a difficult one. John has only just died and there were arrangements to be made and the funeral to think of. We have not yet had time to look for new lodgings.' She added a hopeful smile to hint that it was in his power to give them time, if he chose.

He returned a smile so reptilian she expected to see a forked tongue dart into the middle of it. 'I am aware that it has been a difficult week. But I am sure, if you are amenable, an arrangement might be made that would allow you to stay here as long as you like.' He blinked once, then stared at her, his expression unchanging, and added, 'As long as we are both satisfied, at least.' Then he waited.

She stared back at him, shocked. He could not be suggesting what she suspected. But there was something in the sibilant hiss of the word *satisfaction* that made his meaning clear.

'If you are worrying about your son,' he added, 'you needn't. There are many schools that take in indigent students as a charity. He would be away most of the year and would not need to know.'

'That was not what I was worried about,' she said, 'because I have no intention of taking your despicable offer. I cannot believe that you would come here, when my husband's body is barely cold, and suggest that I...I...' She could not finish the sentence with anything more than a shudder.

'I am only suggesting what others will suggest, when you tell them that you do not have the money they are owed,' he said in a reasonable tone. 'You are only angry with me because I am the first. But once you realise the depth of your troubles and once you have weighed the solutions available, you might feel quite differently.'

'I will not,' she said.

He shrugged. 'Then you must tell me when you plan to be out of the house. I could perhaps wait until the end of the week, if you can be packed in that time.'

'It will take at least until the end of the month to auction off the furnishings,' she said with a frozen smile. 'Unless you mean to take those as well.'

When he seemed to be considering the idea, she added, 'Since they are not listed as part of what you are owed, I will have them appraised and you can pay me by cheque.'

'That will not be necessary,' he said, his eyes narrowing at the prospect of parting with money over something that was not her. 'You may have until the end of the month, Mrs Ogilvie. And in that time, if you have reconsidered my offer, you may reach me here.' He reached into his pocket and withdrew a calling card, which he set on a side table. 'For now, good day.'

'Goodbye, Mr Baxter,' she said emphatically, sinking into the nearest chair as he left her alone in the sitting room. As much as it disgusted her to admit the truth, he was probably right. He would not be the last to suggest that she work off her husband's debt while on her back. She was still young, and handsome enough to attract unwanted attention. Some people would assume that, simply because she was a widow, she would be eager to have a man in her life, with or without the sanctity of marriage.

As if she would seek more trouble, after the mess her husband had left her in. The idea made her want to laugh, but she was afraid if she did, she might never stop. It was either that or cry from sheer frustration. Was she to be allowed no time to grieve at all?

But if she did not mean to bend to an unsavoury

offer, how was she to manage to pay off the rest of the creditors? This afternoon, she would have to contact an auction house, just as she had said, and begin the process of liquidating her life in the hopes that there was enough to balance the books. Then she would have to let the servants go and search for a place where she and Edward could start over, though she had no idea where they would get the money to do so. What was she to do?

The thought brought on the first tears she had shed since John had died, and she allowed herself the luxury of letting them fall.

'Mrs Ogilvie?' Her housekeeper appeared in the doorway.

'What is it?' she said, quickly wiping the tears away.

'You have another visitor.' The woman gave her a worried look. 'The Duke of Glenmoor.'

The man who had all but killed her husband had decided to collect his debt in person, just as Baxter had. Selina sucked in her breath, her tears forgotten in a flash of anger. 'Tell him I am not at home to him.'

The words were barely out of her mouth before she saw the man just behind the servant, waiting to be announced. He was standing between her and escape, in plain sight and hearing of her attempted snub. Now he was staring at her just as Baxter had done and probably thinking the same thing: that she was alone and vulnerable to improper suggestions.

She glared back at him, her despair turning to anger. She had no experience with the peerage. When she had ventured out into society, her acquaintances had been far more modest, limited to untitled ladies and gentlemen and a few moderately successful cits. But the man who stood before her now was everything she would have imagined a duke would be.

His tailoring was perfect, his linen immaculate. Together they framed a body that was impressively tall and in peak physical condition. His short hair shone dark and shiny against a face that was unmarked by sun or worry. His eyes were dark as well, a rich sherry brown, and their alert gaze was fixed on her as if she was a problem in want of a solution.

In any other circumstance, she'd have been impressed by his rank and cowed by his good looks, stunned into submission by the sheer elegance of him and too aware of how far beneath his notice she must seem. She would also have been more than a little flattered by the intensity of his interest in her.

But not today. She had no intention of bowing down to the man who had ruined her life, or blushing and simpering like some idiot girl at her first ball. 'What do you want?' She spat the words at him, taking the offensive to prove that she was not about to be taken advantage of in her lowest moment.

'I… I came to help,' he said, taking a half-step back as if to move out of range of her ire.

'You have done quite enough already,' she said with a bitter smile, reminding herself that, though his appearance was pleasant, he was also the man who had fleeced her husband. 'I have you to thank for my current position. What more could you possibly do?'

'I…' Was it her imagination, or had her accusation

hurt him? There was something in his dark eyes and the set of his too-perfect mouth that hinted at injury.

If so, he deserved it. Compared to her own pain, his was nothing. 'You,' she said, sneering back at him, 'have done quite enough, thank you. But I suppose you will be wanting me to settle my husband's debt to you. It is a matter of honour and I know how important that is to a man of your stature.' She let the last drip with irony, to remind him of what he had done.

Then she reached to her throat, her fingers grasping the jet cameo brooch she wore as a symbol of her mourning. 'Here.' She pulled it free. 'If this is not worth fifty pounds, it will have to do. It is all I have left.' Then she threw it at him with all the force she could muster.

He snatched it out of the air with a graceful swipe of his hand and said, 'I am sorry.'

'You should be,' she snapped back, feeling the unshed tears prickling the backs of her eyes, ready to fall at the least provocation. She would not show weakness. She did not dare to, or she would be preyed upon by every unscrupulous man in London.

And this one was the worst of the lot, because his offer would not be as obviously repellent as Baxter's had been. He had been a serpent, but this man was Lucifer incarnate, proud and beautiful and all too tempting.

Staring too closely into those lovely eyes or focusing too long on that perfect mouth would weaken her reserve. The proposition that he was likely to make would be surrounded by sweet words and delivered with a gentle smile and a soothing voice. If she was not careful, she would agree to the unspeakable and think herself lucky. She should get far away from him as fast as possible, before she forgot that she had nothing left but her honour and bartered it away.

She must not run, or he would know how he affected her and use that knowledge against her. Instead, she rose slowly and walked to the door with her head held high, pushed past him and mounted the main stairs, never looking back until she reached the safety of her bedroom and had locked the door behind her.

Chapter Two

Mrs Ogilvie was a startlingly attractive woman. Far too pretty to be alone for long.

It was a horrible thing to think at such a time. Her husband was barely gone. She was distraught and thought he was the cause of it. He was ashamed of himself for letting his mind wander in such a direction.

But as Alex had looked at her, he'd felt he was falling into her huge grey eyes, caught in them like the tears that trembled on their lashes. He wanted to gather her to him, to stroke her smooth blonde hair and assure her that he would take care of everything, if she would only let him.

He'd even buy her proper mourning attire, if that was what she wanted. Her lavender gown had been a cheerful day dress until someone had hurriedly tacked black ribbons to the ruffles to signify her bereavement and added the black brooch she had thrown at him as a final touch. But no amount of crêpe could dim her loveliness, her vivacity and her obviously passionate nature.

He shook his head, surprised at the insensitive thoughts in it. He knew it was the worst time for him to notice such things. A new widow did not want to hear that she would have no trouble replacing the man she was grieving for. She certainly did not want to hear anything of the sort from a man who held her husband's debts.

It was probably just as well that he had been stunned near to silence at the sight of her loveliness. He was normally very good with words, perfectly capable of speaking up for himself in any given situation. But today, as he'd stared at her, he'd been unable to string two thoughts together.

Judging by her response to what little he'd said, she had not wanted to hear anything at all and had assumed the worst about his character and his offer to help. Alex stared down at the cameo he held and wondered what sort of visits she had already been paid. Had men been making improper suggestions to her?

If they had not, they soon would be. She was far too pretty to end up in a workhouse or as a charitable ward of some church or other. Men often made discreet arrangements with widows, offering to fulfil both their physical and financial needs in one go. Judging by the reports in the paper and her current distress, her monetary problems would soon outweigh any qualms she might have about accepting such an offer.

His hand tightened on the brooch until the pin pricked his finger. It was unfair. A woman like that should be offered marriage.

Not by him, of course. He had the succession to think of and she had a son already. The last thing he wanted was to bring up some small boy the way he'd been brought up himself, as the unwanted spare in a house with a legitimate heir.

His own widowed mother had not thought twice about accepting an offer from the Duke of Fallon, leaving him in the curious position of having a stepbrother who was both younger and already a marquis. Though he had got on well enough with Evan, his stepfather had made it clear from the first moment of the marriage that Alex was worthless and unwelcome, not really a part of the family at all.

The old Duke had been long dead when Alex had inherited a title of his own. But he doubted, even if old Fallon had known his future, it would have changed the way he'd treated the superfluous son he had acquired along with his marriage.

But none of this mattered. Mrs Ogilvie would not have him, even if he asked. She loathed him for the part he had played in her husband's downfall and blamed him, just as society did. She had rushed from the room to avoid him, leaving him stunned and silent with her housekeeper, who was trying to raise the nerve to put him out of the house.

He looked down at the cameo in his hand, then fished his other hand into his pocket for the marker Ogilvie had given him just before he'd ended his life. He tore the thing in half and folded the pieces around the brooch, handing it to the servant with a sympathetic smile. 'When she is feeling better, give this to

Mrs Ogilvie with my assurance that she is free from this debt, at least.'

Then he let himself out.

His carriage was waiting, the servants jumping to attention at the sight of him, a fact he was not used to, though he'd come into his title almost a year ago. 'I wish to walk,' he said to the coachman.

'Very well, Your Grace,' the man said with a worried look.

Then he set out towards home, the carriage following just behind him. The wheeled escort spoiled the solitude he'd wished for, but that was the problem with a large staff. One could never be totally alone.

The distance to his home was over two miles, but that was nothing. Or at least it had been when he'd been a humble don at Oxford and his feet had been his only mode of transport. London life was making him soft. Slow-witted as well.

In the past, he was sure he'd have been able to come up with the words to placate the woman he'd just met. There had to be something he could do to make her life easier. He was, in part, responsible for the situation she found herself in. Not to the degree that society accused him of being and certainly not in the way she thought. But he was not blameless.

There had to be something he could do.

As he walked down the street, the words echoed in his head and, slowly, a plan formed. By the time he'd reached his home, he had decided on a course of action. He handed his hat and gloves to the doorman with a nod of thanks and went directly to his study, sitting down at the desk and searching the drawers for the right sort of paper. He needed something plain, not the fine stationery that he used for Glenmoor's correspondence. The crest on that would give the game away before it was begun.

With an unembossed white sheet before him, he began to write.

> *Dear Mrs Ogilvie,*
> *I am sorry to hear of the misfortune that has befallen you and offer sincere condolences on the death of your husband and the situation it has left you in.*
> *I consider myself a friend of your family and hope that the enclosed will be of some help. If, as I suspect, you are in greater need and wish further aid, write to me care of the General Post Office and I will be honoured to assist you.*
> *Sincerely,*

He paused. He could not very well put his own name on the letter or she would throw it away unopened. Worse yet, she would open it and form an opinion of him that was even worse than she already had. She would be convinced, as she had suggested earlier, that he wanted something more than absolution.

But if not himself, then who should he be?

He turned and glanced at the shelves behind his chair and the books arranged alphabetically upon them by author. The first had ABBOTT neatly lettered in gold on the lower spine. Did he know anyone by that name? Was there anyone involved in the Ogilvie matter who would answer to it?

He could not think of any. And he could think of no more innocent nom de plume, for this one had a monastic sound to it that might assure her of his innocent intentions. So, he signed with a flourish at the bottom of the letter.

Mr Abbott

He blotted the ink and unlocked the top drawer where he kept a money box, opening it and counting out a stack of ten-pound notes on to the paper. Then he folded them in and sealed the letter with a plain blob of red wax before setting it with the rest of the outbound mail.

He smiled down at it, satisfied. Perhaps this was not the best solution, but it would allow him to sleep at night if he knew the fascinating woman he had met today would be free, at least for a time, to make her first decisions as a widow without the immediate and overwhelming pressure of poverty.

Then he went back to his desk to take care of the usual day's business.

Selina waited in her room a full hour after her meeting with the Duke, not coming down again until she was sure she was composed. To maintain calm below stairs, there must be no sign of chaos above stairs. Since her husband's death, she had already lost two housemaids, one of whom had taken a pair of silver teaspoons by way of severance. Crying and panic on her part might lead to a mass exodus tomorrow. Since she was not sure of her future, she wanted to maintain a stable present for as long as she could.

She returned to her place in the sitting room, praying that there might be some small light in a future that seemed uniformly black.

When the afternoon post arrived, she looked at the stack of letters with dread. The morning's had contained more bills than she'd known they received, many of them past due. This was likely to be more of the same. But at the bottom was a surprisingly thick packet addressed to her in an unfamiliar hand.

She took the lot to the morning room and opened the strange letter first, surprised to see a pile of bank notes flutter to the floor as she broke the seal. She scooped them up again, counting the money and stacking it neatly upon the writing table. Fifty pounds. Enough to pay the household bills for weeks. Her problems were bigger than that, of course. But at least the servants would stop leaving and give her time to think.

She read the note, then read it again, searching for any clue as to the identity of the mysterious Mr Abbott. Her husband had never mentioned the name, nor could she think of any Abbotts in her own limited acquaintance. There was no close family living on either side and she racked her brain for distant cousins named Abbott, but there were none.

If this man was not family or friend, there was no telling who he was, or what his motives might be if they were not as compassionate as they appeared.

If she did not want to be in debt to a stranger, she could not keep the money. She should not. And yet...

She pulled a sheet of paper out of the drawer and began a letter of her own.

Dear Sir,

She stared down at the blank paper for a moment and then wrote what she thought.

I was stunned to receive your letter and your most generous gift. However, no matter how kind the intention, it is very improper and I cannot encourage it. Ladies, if they wish to think of themselves as such, do not take money from strangers because of the assumed reckoning that comes with such gifts and the fear of finding oneself beholden to a man with less than honourable intentions.

She stared down at the sentence for a moment, wondering what he would think if his motives were truly as innocent as he claimed. Then she added:

Not that I am accusing you of such. It is just that, should the rumour get around that I am taking money from gentlemen, it will attract the sort of men who see it as a weakness and wish to put me in the difficult position of refusing their advances.

She nodded in approval at this, for it sounded very proper, then stared at the stack of banknotes he had sent her. This was the point where she should close the letter and fold the money into it, before sending the lot back to him, whoever he was. But if she kept it, it would buy her enough time to find a new home and a new life. She set the money aside and started her concluding paragraph.

And that is why I can accept no further gifts from you. Thank you so much for your consideration, but I am sure, with time, things will get better for me.

It was a lie, of course. She had no idea how she would manage. But there was no reason to tell that to a man who she did not even know. She closed.

Sincerely,
Mrs John Ogilvie

If he was a stranger, he was not entitled to her Christian name. And though he was no longer living, the presence of John in the letter would tell him she was not already angling for a relationship outside of marriage.

Satisfied, she carried the letter to the hall table to go out with the next post.

* * *

Alex tried not to show his excitement as the servant he had sent to enquire at the post office handed him the letter, stacking it carefully with the rest of his mail and taking it to the study to read. She had written back. And she had done it quickly, for her answer came to him the morning after he had written to her.

He had known that there was a possibility that he would hear nothing from her, not even a brief thank you. He did not think there was anything specific in the rules of etiquette about replying to anonymous benefactors, but he suspected it was rather like encouraging the attentions of strange men and was frowned upon.

But it appeared that Mrs Ogilvie was both brave and curious. He liked that about her, just as he liked her fine grey eyes and trim figure.

As soon as the door was closed and he was alone, he moved her letter back to the top of the stack and tore at the seal to reveal the brief message within.

She did not think she could take the money?

He allowed himself a short silent laugh. He noticed she had not sent it back. It meant that, even against her better judgement, his instincts were right. She needed his help. She would accept further aid with a little more pressure and he could keep her safe from the inappropriate offers she feared, until she was ready to marry again.

But would it be wise to write her again?

Her letter had laid out the dangers of it and he could not contradict a word of it. If someone discovered that he was keeping her, they would assume the worst about her and about him.

As for his own reputation, he did not care. After the incident with Ogilvie it was clear that the papers would assume the worst about him no matter what he did.

And for her, surely it would be better to be thought a whore than having to become one in truth. If he was very careful and they had no other contact that might arouse suspicions, there would be no danger of either. He would simply watch over her for a time, make sure she was provided for, then fade from her life once she had found a new husband to care for her properly.

He sharpened a pen and pulled a blank sheet of paper out of the desk drawer to scribble out an answer.

My dear Mrs Ogilvie,
I completely understand your hesitance to ac-
cept my gift and reiterate my assurance that I
require nothing from you in return.

As far as society's suspicions when a gentle-
man attempts to help a lady that is not of his
family? In my opinion, they can and should
be damned for their wicked interpretation of
simple generosity. There are people who insist
on believing the worst in others. Pray do not
sink to their level.

If you are called by such people to explain
the sudden change in your fortunes, tell them
that an aged uncle has left you an inheritance
and say nothing more about the matter.

To make the disbursement of funds easier, I am setting up an account in your name at Barclay's. Feel free to draw on it as needed and write to me with further requests.
Sincerely,

He paused for a moment, then added,

Old Uncle Abbott

He smiled, nodding in approval. He rather liked being avuncular. There was something uniquely harmless about it. Friendly as well, though he could not remember anything particularly kind or helpful about his own uncles when they had been alive. Perhaps it was only imaginary uncles who exhibited those qualities.

He put his quill back in the stand and folded the letter, reaching automatically for the signet ring in his drawer before remembering to leave the wax seal blank. Then he dropped the finished letter in the outgoing post.

Chapter Three

'It has been a year since John died. That is more than enough time to grieve a man who treated you well and far too long to honour John Ogilvie. It is time you looked for another husband. You are not getting any younger.' Selina's friend Mary Wilson was giving her a candid look as if searching for signs of decrepitude. They were taking their daily walk in Hyde Park and the bright sunlight of the morning was sure to highlight imperfections in the complexion that were usually hidden.

'John did not treat me badly. At least, he did not intend to. And I am twenty-seven,' Selina replied with a laugh, tipping her face to the sky in defiance. 'Some men think that I am already too old for marriage.'

'Who has told you that you are getting old?' Mary said, outraged on her behalf.

'Other than you, just now?' Selina reminded her. 'No one in particular. But you must admit that the majority of women my age are already settled, one way or another, and have already given up on husband-hunting. If you look to the members of the Ladies' Mathematical Society, you will notice a pattern. The single women my age in those meetings are all confirmed spinsters.'

'But you are prettier than they are,' Mary said with a grin. 'And how did you find yourself in that crowd in the first place? You will forgive me for saying so, but your interests do not seem to lie with mathematics.'

'I received an invitation from an acquaintance,' she said, hoping that Mary would not question the identity of that person. 'Someone who suggested that it was time for me to break my solitude and re-enter society.'

'Well, I am glad that you listened, or we would never have met,' Mary said. 'Now, we must find other invitations that will bring you a step further out and into the company of eligible men.'

Though Abbott had been eager to see her seek friendships with women of her set, he had done nothing yet to relaunch her into mixed society. Perhaps he expected her to fend for herself when it came to finding a husband. Or perhaps it was because he was jealous and wished to keep her for himself. She hoped that was it for she certainly did not want to spoil the unique intimacy of their correspondence by seeking another man.

In the year since he had first written, they had grown quite close. And though he insisted that he was unwilling or unable to meet her, she could not help but imagine there might someday be something more between them than letters. The thought made her smile, as she so often did when she thought of him.

Now Mary was giving her an appraising look, as if she had revealed something without speaking. 'Do not tell me that there is someone already.'

Selina forced a laugh. 'No one but my dear little Edward.'

'Are you sure? Because for a moment, there was a look in your eyes that was quite…' Mary gave a wave of her hand to express the inexpressible.

'No one, I assure you,' she lied. No one she could point to, anyway.

Mary looked around them, changing the subject. 'And where is your dear little Edward, by the way? I do not see him on the path ahead.'

Nor was he behind, when Selina turned to look. At times like this she wished ladies were allowed to curse, for sometimes it seemed that was what her son wanted her to do. 'He is probably just out of sight,' she said with more confidence than she felt. 'Edward!' She raised her voice so that it might be heard from a distance, but kept the tone light to avoid frightening him into hiding.

When there was no answer, she turned around, scanning in all directions, hoping that there would be some sign of him that she had missed before. Then she increased her pace, hurrying up the path to search for him.

As they walked, she shot Mary a look of false confidence. 'I am sure we will see him around the next turn. He cannot have got far.' But the last time that he had wandered off, it had taken over an hour to find him. That time, he had been lost as well as disobedient, and when he'd managed to return to her, they were both quite frightened.

But today it seemed that there would be no such trouble. As they rounded a bend Edward was stumbling back down the path towards her, his eyes focused on something he held in his hand rather than where he was placing his feet.

'Where have you been?' she said, hurrying to his side.

'I followed a squirrel and when I looked up, you were gone.' Then he glanced up at her, smiling, oblivious to her panic. 'But this works.' He held out his hand to her, showing her the item he held.

It was a brass compass, about two inches in diameter. 'Where did you get this?'

'A man gave it to me,' he said with a grin. 'He asked me if I was lost and told me if I pointed the arrow to North and walked towards the SW, I would find you again. And I did.' His grin broadened.

'We must find him and return this,' she said, holding out her hand for the thing.

'He said I was to keep it, as it was so near my birthday,' he said, closing his fingers around it to prevent her from taking it away. 'And that when I wander off, like I did last week, I must use this to keep track of where I was going.'

Abbott.

He was the only man she could think of who would know Edward's birthday and had been told about his habit of wandering off. And, as with so many of her problems, he had found a solution before she could think to ask for it.

Her breath caught in her throat as she realised the most important thing about this interaction. He was here. Or, at least, he had been. She looked around at the other men on the path, wondering if he was still nearby. 'Where is he?' she said, gripping Edward by the shoulder, then forcing herself to relax so as not to alarm him. 'I wish to thank him for helping you.'

'He walked away,' her son said, more interested in the compass than he was in the conversation.

He had been so close, but he had gone before she could see him. 'This man,' she said, struggling to stay calm, 'what did he look like?'

'He was old,' Edward replied, without looking up.

She nodded, trying not to look disappointed by the fact. He had the wisdom of a man in later life. There was no reason to think of him as anything but the uncle he had first pretended to be.

'Old like you,' her son added, and her spirits immediately lifted.

'What colour was his hair? Was it grey?'

'Brown.'

She smiled. He was not too old, then. 'And his eyes. What colour were they? Was he wearing spectacles? Was he tall? Did he walk with a cane?'

At this rush of questions, Edward gave her a confused look, then said, 'He was just a man. In a dark coat,' he added, as if this would help. Then he held the compass out to her again. 'Can I keep it? Is it all right?'

She sighed, for it was clear that she would get no more information than she had already. Then she held out her hand. 'Let me see it for a moment.'

He handed it to her and she turned it over, surprised to see the initials *M* and *C* engraved on the back.

'He said it was his father's,' Edward said, shifting from foot to foot, clearly eager to have it back.

'That means the initials are not his,' she said. Of course, the second would be. He would share his father's surname. But there was no reason to suspect that either of his names was Abbott. He had admitted long ago that it was a pseudonym.

None of this should matter. When they had begun their correspondence, he had made it clear from the first that they would never be more than friends.

But after a year of writing, she had grown to hope.

Next to her, Mary laughed. 'So, there is someone, after all. Do not deny it, for I can tell by the light in your eyes that there is.'

'Perhaps,' she admitted, staring down the path at no one in particular. 'At least, there could be. But he has made no promises, as of yet.'

'Is he married?' Mary whispered.

'I do not know,' she whispered back. 'We have only written.'

But there had been so many letters. Never more than a week had separated them for the whole of the year and sometimes they had written two or more in a single day. 'And yet, we have never met,' she added, unable to stop the sigh that escaped from her parted lips.

'How romantic,' Mary said with a sigh of her own.

'Not really,' she said, trying to regain control of the conversation again. 'We are friends, that is all. We have never really discussed our feelings beyond that. And no promises have been made,' she added, lest Mary think he was dishonourable. 'Nor has he made any demands on me, if that is what you fear.'

Mary laughed again. 'I fear no such thing.' She glanced down at Edward, who was too busy with his new possession to pay any mind to their conversation. 'In fact, a few demands might be just the thing you need.'

'I beg your pardon?' Selina said, with a blush that proved she knew exactly what her friend was suggesting.

Mary gave her a knowing look. 'I am only saying that, should my husband die, there are some things that I would quite miss in his absence, especially if it had been a whole year.'

It had been some time longer than that, if Selina wished to be honest, which she did not. In the last months of his life, her John had been far more interested in cards and dice than he had been in any comfort she might offer. And Mary was right; she was lonely. 'But what you are talking about has nothing to do with the gentleman we are discussing. Our friendship is purely intellectual.'

'And these cerebral conversations are what puts that colour in your cheeks,' Mary said with obvious scepticism.

'Yes,' she said, in what she hoped was a convincing tone. Then added, 'It is simply rather exciting to know that he was so close.'

'Yet he did not bother to meet with you,' Mary concluded for her, as if trying to dash her hopes. 'Judging by Edward's description, he is not old, or infirm, or scarred in a way that would frighten a small child.'

'Hmm...' Selina replied, trying to pretend that she had not considered just those possibilities. Her favourite theory, that of a disfiguring war injury, had been discounted by today's meeting. Though she had often imagined that she would love him just as much if he were missing an eye or some other important part of his body.

'Even though there is nothing obviously wrong with him, he has made no effort to advance your friendship into a courtship,' Mary said, considering. 'I suspect that means he is a married man and should not be writing to you at all.'

That was her greatest fear. That the reason he had been so reticent in declaring himself was that he was permanently beyond her reach. 'Our letters are perfectly innocent,' she insisted. At least, the ones she had posted were. There had been others, ones that she had written but not sent, where she had expressed her true feelings. These she kept neatly folded in her empty jewellery case, a tidy packet of billets-doux to take the place of the ones she had never received.

Mary sighed again, ignoring her protestations. 'It is still quite exciting. Too exciting to be proper, of course. You must find out who the man is. Then you will know if you should continue writing to him.'

It was good that she had not mentioned the money she had been given, for she was sure Mary would not have approved of that. 'I will ask him to reveal himself in the very next letter,' she lied, then changed the subject.

Alex sorted through the afternoon post, tucking the expected letter from Selina into the pocket of his coat and walking slowly towards the study, where he could enjoy it in private. He was eager to see her response to the gift he had given her son, hoping she did not think him too forward.

It was one thing to provide her with enough money to run her household, but quite another for him to approach Edward in person without bothering to ask her permission. Of course, he had not asked her leave before he'd begun to provide for her and had ignored her initial refusals, allowing the desperation of her situation to wear down any arguments about propriety.

And, as he too often did when thinking about the details of their arrangement, he felt a growing sense of unease. No one had uncovered their relationship, as of yet. But it had been a year and his luck would not last forever. He should reveal himself to her before someone else did it for him and hope that she could find her way to forgive him for the part he'd played in her husband's downfall.

Most importantly, he must find a way to end their relationship without damaging her reputation. What he had done had not been at her suggestion and he would not have strangers thinking her mercenary or unchaste for accepting his help. The last thing he wanted was to leave her in a worse place than he had found her.

He would have to leave her. That was inevitable. She deserved a man in her life and in her bed and, given their past, he would never be able to give her more than money and this unusual friendship. But he could tell from the carefully veiled hints in her letters that she had developed a tendre for him and was hoping that there could be something more than there was between them.

He understood the feeling. When he'd met her, he'd thought her the most beautiful of women. But their correspondence had revealed a spirit that suited her looks. She was inquisitive, intelligent and made him laugh.

As he read her letters, he heard the resonant alto of her voice, soft as velvet against skin, murmuring the words to him. At night, when the letters were put away, he imagined them together in body as well as spirit, making love to exhaustion, then whispering their hopes and dreams to each other as the sun rose on a new day.

When morning came again, he would remember what 'the Duke of G.' had done to her and her family and how she had looked at him, the one time he'd tried to help in person. If they had been any two other people, he would have revealed himself by now and made an offer. But she was who she was and he was the very thing she hated in all the world.

He smiled sadly down at the letter in his hand. At least, for a little while, he could be someone else. He ran a finger along the edge of the paper in his pocket, sighing as he drew it out. Then he popped the seal and began to read.

My dear Abbott,

He smiled again, pressing a thumb over the words and imagining her writing them, smiling back at him.

I am just back from Hyde Park and I must know the truth. You were there, weren't you? You spoke to Edward and sent him back to me when he strayed. The gift you gave him was most kind and very practical. I have been regaled with the compass points of each room in our little house and he is now out in the garden, mapping the flowers as they orient to true north.

He could imagine that as well, for he had done something similar when his father had given him the same tool, at about the same age.

But the gift would have been even better if you had followed him back to me and come home with us for tea.

'Or so you think,' he said with a sad shake of his head, and read on.

> *My friend Mrs Wilson was with us and noted*
> *my excitement and I could not avoid telling her*
> *about our correspondence. She expressed con-*
> *cern that you are already married and avoid-*
> *ing me so as not to give offence. Please tell me*
> *honestly, is there a Mrs Abbott? Perhaps you*
> *could bring that fortunate lady with you when*
> *you visit, so I might know her as well.*

He reached for the paper that sat ready on the corner of his desk and sharpened his pen to craft a response.

My dear Mrs Ogilvie,

He whispered 'Selina' as he wrote.

> *It was, indeed, me at the park today. I saw Ed-*
> *ward's distress and could not resist helping him*
> *in a way that might solve future, similar prob-*
> *lems. He will not get lost again, since he will not*
> *stop checking his direction. I am sure you will*
> *find it quite tiresome sometimes, as my mother*
> *did with me.*

He chuckled at the memory.

> *As for Mrs Abbott,*

He considered and rejected inventing an imaginary wife to solve the problem of her interest in him. For one thing, it would create as many problems as it solved. And for another, no matter how little sense it made, he did not want her to give up hope. If he could not manage to do so, why should she?

He continued.

> *I regret to inform you that no such lady exists. That makes our meeting an impossibility. I fear society would form the wrong impression should I spend too much time in your company.*

He bit his lip, considering how to explain in a way that would not hurt her feelings.

> *Much as we both might wish it to be otherwise, a visit between us is quite impossible. I am not the man you think me, my dear, and after the briefest of meetings, you would call an end to our friendship. I value that connection more than you can understand and am loath to spoil it a moment before its natural end.*
> *I speak of the day, coming soon, when you will re-enter society and find that worthy gentleman who will offer you a relationship based in flesh and blood rather than ink and paper. Then you will no longer need me and I will have to relinquish you to a better man.*
> *But until that day, I remain,*
> *Your Abbott*

He sighed as he sanded the wet ink, staring down at the letter in regret. The truth hurt him, but it was a thing he had ignored for far too long. He did not want to be the illusion that stood between her and true happiness, but, in a year of writing, that was just what he had become. And he could not imagine that her opinions had changed much on the worth of the Duke of Glenmoor.

In the distance, he heard the sound of the front door opening and closing and the bustle of servants greeting a guest. A few moments later, his brother appeared in the doorway of the study, causing him to slip the letter into the desk drawer to post later.

Evan was waving a letter of his own as he entered the room, holding it out with a flourish and dropping it on the centre of the empty desk. 'A missive from my wife. It seems we are to have a ball. If I cannot avoid it, neither can you. But we can at least save the postage by settling the matter of the invitation in person.'

'I will attend, of course,' Alex said, opening the invitation with a smile. 'As long as Maddie does not waste too much energy in matchmaking for me.'

'That, I cannot promise,' Evan said with a shake of his head. 'She has taken it into her mind that you should marry and be as happy as we are. So if there is anyone in particular you wish her to invite…'

The words hung in the air between them as Alex considered. Then he replied, 'Perhaps not for the reason she expects. Would it be too forward to request that Ogilvie's widow be invited?'

'Are you still obsessed about that?' Evan said, raising an eyebrow. 'It has been a year. The *ton* has moved on and you are all but forgiven.'

'Not by everyone,' Alex said, frowning as he thought of the dark looks he sometimes received when he entered a card room. 'There is still a faint pall hanging over my name in some circles. But it is not for my benefit that I wish you to invite her. The last year has been difficult for her.' He paused and added, 'Or so I suspect', since there should be no way he would know the truth.

'And you wish to give her what advantages you can, as you did with the invitation to my wife's Mathematical Society,' Evan concluded for him.

'It will do her good to be out in mixed company,' Alex agreed. 'Once she is married again, the scandal can truly be laid to rest.' And he would solve the problem he had created for her when he'd become Abbott.

'And what will happen when she realises that you are at this ball as well?' Alex asked, giving him a sceptical look.

If he was not careful, he would reveal his feelings by staring at her like a parched man near a glass of water. Even now, he felt a tickling excitement at the thought that they might soon be in the same room.

He forced it away and said, 'I do not know. For myself, I mean to make no trouble for her. I hope she will avoid me as well. Surely there will be other diversions to occupy her attention and other men who wish to speak to her?'

'That is probably true,' Evan agreed. 'I hear she is quite pretty.' Was he now looking at Alex with undue interest?

It did not matter. He could not help but answer honestly. 'Too beautiful to be a widow for long.'

'I see,' Evan replied. There was a pause before he added, 'And what of your plans for the future? Are there no other ladies you would like to see there?'

Alex gave a nervous laugh and shook his head. 'When there is someone, you will be the first to know. But at the present time there is no one with a claim on my heart.' At least no one he could reasonably offer for.

Evan gave an exasperated shake of his head. 'Very well, then. My wife will have to content herself with finding a match for Mrs Ogilvie. But do not think you can escape for another year. There will be no peace in my house until you are married.'

'Perhaps later in the Season,' he agreed. When Selina had married and he'd lost all reason to hope for the true happiness he imagined with her.

Chapter Four

It was Selina's first society ball.

When she had been young and unmarried, there had been no time or money for a London Season. Her father had said it was just so much nonsense and that a marriage could easily be arranged without it. Then he had died, as had her mother, and the point had been moot.

But he had been posthumously proven right when John Ogilvie had appeared in the neighbourhood to visit an old friend from school. It had taken little more than an introduction and a few meetings before he had offered for her, promising a glamorous future as mistress of a large London house.

It was not until they were married that she had discovered how precarious that life with him would be. Their house was fine enough, but not as grand as he'd described to her. Money that might have been spent on other entertainments was eaten up by her husband's vices. And the men John met in card rooms and gambling hells were not willing to invite him into their homes after emptying his purse.

But tonight, it would all be different.

As she was announced by the footman in the doorway of the Duke of Fallon's ballroom, she ran a hurried hand down her skirt, making sure that the moss green silk hung in even folds. Then she advanced into the room, smiling at the people who looked up to notice her arrival. She knew a few of the women from the Mathematical Society and offered a gracious thank you to the Duchess for thinking of her.

That woman responded with a mischievous smile of her own and pronounced herself happy to welcome her, now that her year of mourning was over. 'You cannot live in the past,' she said, gesturing out into the crowd on the dance floor. 'And there are many of us here who are eager to see you find your future.'

'Thank you,' Selina replied, wondering at the words. She suspected that *many* was an exaggeration, for none of those supposed friends had visited her after her husband's death and few had offered help in the months that followed. But she had one true advocate and she suspected he was behind this invitation.

The Duchess must know Abbott. But they were certainly not close enough for Selina to question her on the matter. She must hope that he revealed himself in some other way. He might be in the room with her even now. Perhaps this would be the night they met.

She smiled and looked around her, immediately catching the attention of Mary Wilson and some of the other women of her acquaintance. They hurried to introduce her to gentlemen and Selina was surprised to see her dance card filling with eager partners.

When only a few spaces remained, a shadow fell across the card. She looked up to find the Duke of Glenmoor standing beside her, staring down at it as if it was his business to do so. 'Mrs Ogilvie,' he said in a strangled tone, and offered her a stiff bow.

For a moment, she was too shocked to say anything at all. Then a host of rage-fuelled possibilities rushed to her lips. What right did he have to bother her after what he had done? Did he think that a bow and a quadrille would make up for the mess he had made in her life? Did he have to spoil the only evening she'd had out in a year?

Fortunately, her retorts stayed safely locked inside her as courtesy took the reins of her temper. She stared at him, for only a moment. Then she looked through him, offering nothing more than icy uninterest. If anyone in London deserved the cut direct, it was this man.

He shifted ever so slightly, trying to catch her eye. When it was clear that she did not plan to yield and recognise him, he murmured, 'Good evening', and moved away again.

When he was gone, she let out her held breath and heard the murmurs of gossip swirling about her, spreading like tendrils of fog through the room. Soon, everyone would know that a humble widow had cut a duke. It would likely be in the scandal sheets tomorrow. To court such notoriety would be either her making or her doom.

Then she heard a slow, soft clapping and Mr Baxter announced, 'Well done.'

If Glenmoor was the last man in London she wished to see, then Baxter was the second to the last. But she could not cut two men in a row. Even her friends would call her mad. So she offered him a chilly nod and made to walk away.

He stepped in front of her, blocking her path. 'So good to see you, Mrs Ogilvie, after so long.'

'Mr Baxter,' she said, then tried to move again.

'Is that an opening I see on your dance card? And for a waltz. You must not sit idle for that.' The card dangled from a ribbon on her wrist and he reached for her hand to take it.

'On the contrary,' she said, pulling away. 'It has been a long time since I have been out and I do not want to become overtaxed. But at the present, I am promised to another.' She smiled past him at the gentleman that had come to claim her for the first country dance.

Baxter stepped aside with an annoyed smile. 'We will talk later. But we will talk.'

Not if she could find a way to avoid it. For the moment, she was relieved to be able to occupy herself with dancing. One set followed another, which was followed by a glass of champagne and a visit to the buffet. After that, she spent some time conversing with friends. Before she'd realised, two hours had slipped by and she had forgotten all about him.

It was a delightful evening and she had not had such fun in well over a year. But by midnight, the room had become stuffy with the press of so many active people and she passed through the French doors along the back wall and out into the attached rose garden, seeking to cool herself in the night air.

But she was no sooner out of the house than Baxter came up behind her on the path, linking his arm in hers and walking at her side as if they were old friends.

She started, trying to pull away from him, but he held her fast and in a position of such casual intimacy that anyone observing would only remark on it if they saw her struggling to get away from him. If she wished to avoid more gossip, there was nothing to do but endure.

'Mrs Ogilvie,' he said with a note of triumph in his voice.

'What do you want from me?' she whispered, trying and failing to regain control of her arm.

'Only to get answers to a few simple questions.'

'Then ask them,' she said, giving him a frosty smile. 'And when you are through, leave me alone.'

'That I will not do,' he said softly. 'I have been thinking of you for over a year. And wondering how it is that you have managed to survive when you did not have a penny to your name after your husband died.'

'I received a bequest from an uncle,' she said, reciting the words that had been suggested to her by Abbott so long ago.

'How interesting,' he said, his fingers tightening on her arm. 'I was well acquainted with your husband before he died. When Ogilvie spoke of you, he was quite clear on the fact that he had married a woman with no family. You, my dear, are alone in the world. And yet you have managed to land on your feet, rent a home in a nice neighbourhood and secure an invitation to the Duke of Fallon's ball.'

'I am not alone,' she said, trying to keep the quaver out of her voice. It was a lie. Right now, when she needed help, she was very much alone and had no idea how to deal with this man.

'I am aware of that. And that brings me to my next question. Who is really helping you? And what were you willing to do to secure that help?'

She jerked her arm, trying to dislodge his grip. 'I did nothing untoward. It was an inheritance.'

'Do not lie to me,' he said softly. 'I will find out the truth, sooner or later.'

She had to fight to control her panic now. Her breath came in shallow gasps and she could feel her body beneath her gown slick with a cold sweat. Even if she told him the truth, Baxter would not believe it. The truth was far too unlikely to be believed. He would say she had given her favours to a man in exchange for security. It was what he was thinking, after all, and what he wanted for himself.

Then, before she could form an answer to his questions, his arm tensed against hers and she felt the jerk as he started in alarm, just as she had done when he'd grabbed her. When she glanced to her side, she saw a hand resting on Baxter's shoulder, the long white fingers sunk into the wool of his coat in a grip that must be painfully tight.

Then a voice came from just behind them. 'Baxter, isn't it?'

The man beside her nodded.

'The lady appears to be uncomfortable. Let her go.' There was a brief pause followed by the single word, 'Now.'

Baxter's arm slithered away from hers and he took a deliberate step to the side, away from her.

'Very good.' The hand on his shoulder gave a re-assuring pat. 'I suggest you give your regards to our hostess and say your goodbyes. It is either that or I will tell her that you are annoying one of her guests and have you removed from the premises.'

Baxter muttered a curse and said, 'This is not over.'

'I think it is,' said the man behind her.

There was a moment where she thought Baxter might be ready to argue. But the shadowed man behind them was large and as unyielding as a granite monument. So, with a final huff of irritation, Baxter retreated and the other stepped forward and took his place at her side.

He rested his hand gently on her arm and murmured, 'Come, Mrs Ogilvie. Let us take a seat while you regain your composure.'

'Glenmoor,' she said, staring up at him in horror as he guided her towards a bench set against the ivy-covered garden wall.

'I am not much of an improvement,' he said with a sympathetic smile. 'But needs must when the devil drives.'

'What did you hear?' she managed to say as she sank down on the seat.

'Nothing I care to repeat or remember,' he said, sitting down beside her. He stretched his legs out in front of him and adjusted his posture until he was near enough to her that she might feel the warmth of his presence, even though he was not touching her.

She tried not to lean into him, for after Baxter's threats there was a part of her longing to seek solace wherever she might find it. Things had been going so well. Now she felt as she had right after the funeral, when Baxter had paid his first visit, weak and vulnerable, wishing she could lay her head on someone's shoulder and cry.

She straightened, summoned all her resolve and leaned away from him. If she broke down now, she was likely to descend into uncontrollable hysterics, and she refused to do that in front of the man who'd ruined her life, no matter how annoyingly gallant his recent behaviour had been.

'This changes nothing between us,' she said, rising from the bench to get away from him.

'You're welcome,' he replied, remaining where he was. 'I recommend that you return to the ballroom, which is just up the path to your right.'

'I can find it myself,' she snapped. 'I don't need—'

'—a compass?' he concluded.

'Your help,' she corrected, giving him a final glare.

'Of course not,' he said, giving her a gesture of dismissal as she turned and hurried back to the house.

Chapter Five

*At the Duke of Fallon's ball last night, witnesses
were treated to a most interesting sight. The
lovely Mrs O. met with the man who made her a
widow. The fairer sex might not be able to wield
a sword, but that did not prevent her from staring daggers at the Duke of G.*

Alex sipped his breakfast coffee and stared down
at the gossip column in the morning paper, unsure
whether to be amused or frustrated. It was another
black mark on his smudged reputation. But at least a
point had been scored in favour of the brave widow
Ogilvie, who had stood up to him. People would
be looking for her at future events, eager to see the
woman brave enough to snub a duke.

Much as it had hurt to see her response to him, he
was proud of the way she had handled herself and the
way she had maintained composure, even in the face
of Baxter's pestering. He had watched her closely all
evening, counting the times she had danced and the

times she had sat out, making mental notes of the men who had paid her particular attention. It was almost as if he was launching a sister on her first Season.

At least, he had told himself that she should be like a sister. But when he had seen her standing in the entrance of the Fallon ballroom, stunning in a green gown that brought out the grey of her eyes, he had not felt the least bit fraternal. And seeing the dazed looks on the faces of the men around him, all clamouring for her attention, he had felt a most unbrotherly jealousy and the desire to pull her away from the crowd and keep her all to himself.

It had been stupid of him. For a moment, he had been thinking of all the fond letters that passed between them and imagining that, somehow, she knew that it was he who had written and understood that he meant no harm to her or her family. It was why he had approached her, unable to resist offering her a welcome back to society as his true self.

She had responded just as he'd known she would, with contempt and disdain. Before they had parted, he had not been able to resist a final hint at the truth and mentioned the compass, smiling at her and hoping to see some glimmer of recognition in her eyes.

It had fallen flat. What could he do to get her to see past her hatred of him, even for a moment? And why did he want to? It was not as if she would fall into his arms once she discovered he was Abbott. She might loathe him even more for his intrusion into her life.

But for a little while longer, he could still be Abbott for her, that undemanding paragon who was worthy of her regard. As he expected, there was a letter from her in the afternoon post, asking his advice.

I thank you, dear Abbott, for arranging the invitation, but fear that I have managed things very badly. I've got my name in the papers over the way I handled meeting that odious Glenmoor.

Alex winced. If he was still odious, he had been foolish to hope for forgiveness or to imagine that there could be anything more between them. He read on.

And now I have Mr Baxter to contend with as well. He insists that he will discover the source of my support, which cannot be good news for either one of us. Since you have remained anonymous thus far, I assume that you have your reasons for secrecy. I will understand if the threat of discovery makes you rethink our arrangement.

It should. It really should. A sane man would find a way to give her up. He got out his plain paper and crafted an answer.

My dear Mrs Ogilvie,
Do not worry yourself about the appearance of Baxter and his threats. We will find a way to defeat him together.

Lord knew what that was. But there must be something he could do that would decrease the scandal rather than making it worse.

> *And do not think for a moment that I would leave you in your hour of need, or run from idle threats, especially coming from a grubby little nothing like Baxter.*

And what was he to say about the odious Glenmoor? What could he say? He decided to ignore the insult and move on to happier things.

> *For now, you must focus on the obvious successes of the evening. You look stunning in green. You were very popular and danced frequently. Surely you took some pleasure in that? There will be other invitations, I am sure, and events that have no clouds hanging over them.*
> *Until then, know that I am,*
> *Your devoted Abbott*

Satisfied, he blotted, sealed and set the letter with the outgoing mail.

Selina rushed to the door when the next morning's post arrived, half dreading the response she knew would be there. She had done the right thing in offering Abbott a way out of their arrangement, for it was not fair to drag a good man down with her, should she fall from grace.

But all the same, she prayed that he would refuse

her suggestion. She wanted him. She needed him. She could not imagine a life without him, even though he insisted one must soon come. The men she'd met at the Fallon ball had all been charming enough. All equally well-mannered and attentive, and all but one had been good dancers. But in the day and a half that had passed, the memories of them seemed blurry and unimportant compared to Glenmoor and Baxter and the shadowy presence of the man who wrote the letter she was about to read.

She scanned it quickly, taking in his vow of loyalty with a sigh of relief and his promise that they would best her nemesis somehow.

Then her eyes caught on a single line and she shook the paper as she would shake Abbott were he to appear before her right now.

You look stunning in green.

He had been there. He had been in the same room with her, perhaps even danced with her or spoken to her without giving himself away.

How else would he have known the colour of her dress, or how much she had danced?

But had he seen Baxter harassing her? Obviously not or it would have been Abbott that came to her rescue and not the Duke. He would not have left her unguarded, would he? She tried to remember the men that had been in the garden when the incident had happened, but when Baxter had laid his hand on her arm, her mind had gone blank.

And after Glenmoor was through with her, she had fled for home, unable to stand another moment. Even now, the thought of the man aroused a strange mingling of hatred and curiosity. He had removed Baxter from her presence as if he was flicking a fly from her sleeve. Then he'd sat down next to her and behaved in a way he probably thought was comforting.

In truth, it had been more unnerving than anything else. It had been hard enough to stand up to him in a crowded ballroom. But alone in the dark she was aware of the size of him, the sheer masculine power and the same confidence that he had used to dispense with Baxter.

She shook her head, trying to relieve herself of the memory. She would do as Abbott had said and think of the rest of the ball, and the fact that he had been there. That was all that mattered. She hugged the paper to her heart, her problems momentarily forgotten.

She decided that they had danced, because, if she was to have a fantasy, it must be the best one possible. Their conversation had been banal and forgettable, but all the while he had been laughing to himself at the trick he was playing on her and admiring the way she looked in candlelight.

And he had held her in his arms.

That was a lie, she was sure. She had not danced the waltz, for she had not been prepared for the intimacy of such a dance with men she had just met. But in her imagination, she waltzed with Abbott, laughing and spinning and dipping.

And if she had not? Then perhaps at the next ball, or the next. He was out there, moving through the *ton* like a fish in water. She had but to find him and allow him to win her. Then they would be together just as she hoped and everything about her life would come right.

Chapter Six

'What do you know about a man named Bernard Baxter?' Alex was sitting in his brother's study in the Fallon townhouse, enjoying an afternoon brandy.

Evan's brow furrowed. 'When we were at school together, he was an evil little toady.'

'Then what was he doing at your ball the other night?' Alex asked, honestly curious.

'Because he is as lucky at cards as John Ogilvie was unlucky. Half of London owes him money and the other half owe him a favour.'

'And you?'

'I invited him as a guest of Lord and Lady Ellerby, who fall into one of those two categories,' Evan said, refilling his drink. 'Why the sudden interest in him?'

Alex frowned. 'I was surprised that he was there. I caught him bothering a friend of mine and threatened to put him out.'

'A lady friend?' Evan said with a sly smile.

'That is of no importance,' Alex said hurriedly. 'I

was simply surprised that Baxter would be among your guests.'

'You will not see him here again, if that is really your concern. He has no strings on me, nor will he ride into my house on someone's coat-tails, now that I have heard he was causing trouble.'

'That is good to know,' Alex said. He still had no clue as to what to do about the man, but at least his assessment of the fellow's character was correct.

'Now tell me more about your female friend,' Evan said, leaning forward expectantly. 'Is she, perhaps, above stairs right now, attending my wife's Mathematical Society?'

'Why would you think so?' Alex said. It was not quite a denial; therefore, it was not a lie.

'It is not unusual for you to visit here, but it is co-incidental that you convinced me to come back here during the meeting. Normally, I avoid the house when it is packed with my wife's friends and do my drinking at White's.'

'I did not want to discuss Baxter in public,' Alex said, any more than he wanted to discuss Selina in private.

But it did not appear that Evan was ready to let the matter drop. 'If you really have no favourite, you will find any number of eligible young ladies attend my wife's salons,' he said. 'And, occasionally, gentlemen, if they are interested in mathematics.'

'Or young ladies,' Alex said, setting down his glass and backing towards the hall, which already held a stream of departing females. 'But since all I wanted was information, I will be on my way.'

Selina sat towards the back of the room in the crowded nursery of the Fallon townhouse, a notebook in front of her, dutifully scratching the examples on the pages and struggling to understand the equation that the Duchess had chalked on to the blackboard in front of them.

The usual occupant of the nursery, little Frederick, was in the corner of the room with his nurse, chewing on an amber teething bracelet and staring at his mother with the same confusion that Selina felt.

She had no passion for mathematics, as some of the women in the room did, and was often confused by the puzzles and enigmas in the *Ladies' Digest*. But she had to admit that the biscuits and teacakes served here were better than her cook made at home and the conversation with the other ladies was excellent. She smiled at Mary, who occupied the seat on her left, and glanced at the clock, just as the Duchess of Fallon announced an end to the lesson for the day.

All around her, notebooks shut with snaps and, in the front, she heard a few disappointed sighs. But then the footman distributed tea and petits fours and the work was forgotten.

An hour later, the women thanked the Duchess and dispersed.

'I love these gatherings,' Mary said enthusiastically, then whispered, 'And I do not mind catching a glimpse of the Duke as well. The man is quite handsome, don't you think?'

Selina offered a 'Shh' and looked around to see if they had been overheard. 'You are married and so is he, if I need to remind you.'

Mary laughed and nudged her playfully in the arm. 'I am well aware of the fact. But it does no harm to look. In my opinion, you do far too little of that. Was there not someone from the ball that you would not mind seeing again?'

'From the ball?' she said with a blush. They were headed down the stairs towards the ground floor now.

'Someone other than your mysterious friend,' Mary clarified, her hand skimming the marble banister. 'If he has not come forward in a year, it is probably not wise to favour him with your full attention. If you choose another champion, he will either go away or be shaken loose from his reticence.'

The former was exactly what she'd feared would happen. That was why it was so difficult to focus her attention on other men. She did not want to risk losing Abbott.

'I met no one in particular,' she said at last. At least not anyone that she had wanted to see again. Baxter had been all too eager to see her and she dreaded his next appearance. 'But it is early in the Season and I have only been to one gathering. And there are hundreds of men in London. And…'

And one was right in front of her at the foot of the steps, oblivious to the women passing behind him. The Duke of Glenmoor stood, back to the chattering crowd, talking to someone down the hall and out of sight. It was probably the Duke of Fallon, for everyone knew they were as close as blood brothers and often seen together.

Why, of all people, did it have to be him?

Selina hesitated for a moment, unsure of how to get past without being noticed. Then she composed herself and continued down the stairs. She would simply walk, head held high, and do her best to ignore him. If she did not call attention to herself, he might never notice her.

Of course, given her luck, that was a desperate plan that could not possibly succeed. As she reached Glenmoor's side, he turned and stepped directly into her path and she ran into him.

He was solid in a masculine way that she wished she could ignore. And so very tall. And he smelled of sandalwood with a fresh green scent of soap underneath.

Her breath left her in a relieved sigh as if her body recognised, though her mind did not want to, that it had been a long time since she had been this close to a man, even closer than dancing. His hand came out immediately to steady her and the touch on her arm tingled.

For a moment, he seemed as shocked as she was. Then he said, 'Mrs Ogilvie.' And nothing else, as if the impact of their bodies had knocked the sense out of him.

'Your Grace.' She must be senseless as well for she could not even manage her usual indignation.

'I beg your pardon.'

They said it together, apologising in a choral unison that would have made two other people laugh in shared recognition of the absurdity.

Instead, there was an embarrassing pause, as each waited for the other to speak, or at least to move.

Then the Duke said, 'A lovely day we're having.' He paused again, as if noticing that they were not outside and that it was cloudy and spitting rain, so the conversational opening was wrong. He tried again. 'You were at the Mathematical Society, I suppose.'

She nodded, still too shocked to draw her arm out of his grasp.

'I was visiting with Fallon,' he said, stating the obvious. Then he turned, remembering his manners, and his hand slipped away. 'And this is your friend, I suppose.' He waited for an introduction.

She had forgotten that she had no intention of speaking to this man. She should snub him again and walk out the door and into the rain without looking back.

But before she could manage it, Mary elbowed her in the ribs to force more words out of her.

'Mrs Mary Wilson, may I introduce the Duke of Glenmoor.'

'Your Grace.'

'Charmed.' He bent over Mary's hand. Then he straightened and gave her a smile that made her giggle almost as much as she had at the thought of Fallon. 'May I offer the two of you a ride to make up for this inconvenience I have caused?'

'No.'

'Yes, thank you.'

This time, she spoke in unison with Mary, who drowned her out, leaving her refusal ignored, as the Duke signalled a footman to call for his carriage to take them home.

It was nothing, really. It meant nothing. But if that was true, why could she still not catch her breath? It was probably her smothered anger at his presence that was causing this upheaval. Her every muscle tensed as he handed her up into a seat, and she sat in silence as he made polite conversation with Mary, asking after her husband, her children and her interest in the Duchess of Fallon's latest enigma.

Was he flirting with her? It would be just like him to seduce someone else's wife. Was that better or worse than setting his sights upon an unmarried girl and offering her unchaperoned rides? Selina was not sure. And it was not as if the two of them were alone now. Selina was here as a third, if one was needed.

Mary responded, hesitantly at first, then with more enthusiasm, chatting amicably until the carriage rolled to a stop in front of Selina's home.

This was the moment where she ought to thank him for his consideration. But the words stuck in her throat. He must know she wanted none of his help. But if that were true, why hadn't she refused the ride and left Mary to her own devices?

She got out of the carriage, leaving her friend alone with the Duke as the horses started off again. Selina stared at their retreat, wondering what had just occurred. The peer had been doing his best to appear ordinary and non-threatening. It was obvious that he had won Mary over with a few kind words and a seat in his carriage.

But it would take more than that to convince Selina, especially after the uneasy way she felt whenever she was close to him. No one who aroused such strangeness in her could be trusted. It would explain his moment of awkwardness as well, for he'd needed a moment of preparation to put on a false and friendly face for her.

But what was his purpose with Mary? Had he made a point of taking her home last, specifically so that he could be alone with her? She was married, of course, and should be off-limits to predation. Was the man devoid of honour, or had it been an innocent courtesy? She must write to Abbott, tell him of these latest developments and ask his opinion.

The next letter from Selina arrived as Alex was sitting down to supper and he took it into the dining room with him, unable to wait until after the meal to read it.

The afternoon had been both a catastrophe and a triumph. After an unconvincing attempt to justify his presence in the house to Evan, he had literally run into Selina in the front hall. He hoped his brother had not heard him stammering about the weather like some awkward schoolboy smitten by his first love. If so, he would never hear the end of it.

As usual, she showed no desire to talk with him. Luckily, her friend was in awe of his title and had been desperate to prolong the conversation. It had given him an excuse to offer them a ride.

He'd sat across from them in the carriage, so he might stare at Selina at leisure while carrying on a conversation with her friend. She had been wearing a gown of soft rose that gave her complexion a healthy glow and made her eyes shine like moonlight. But she'd stayed prim and silent for the whole of the trip and he had dropped her off first, not wanting to press his already thin luck.

When she was gone, he had enquired gently after her, admitting that he did not think Mrs Ogilvie had enjoyed herself, but thanking Mrs Wilson for allowing him to assist them.

'I am sure that is not the case,' the woman had said, lying to save his feelings. 'She was complaining of a megrim before we ran into you. But it was most gracious of you to offer to drive us home. It saved us from having to walk in the rain. I doubt she is so stubborn to allow herself a soaking rather than a ride in a fine carriage such as this.'

And then, the conversation had turned to the weather, and he had learned nothing more. But surely this letter would give him insight. He popped the seal and scanned the contents as he started on his soup.

His spoon froze halfway to his mouth, then clattered back.

I could not avoid another interaction with that horrible Glenmoor...
He drove us home from Fallon House and he

*would not stop talking to my friend Mrs Wilson.
He showed no respect for her married state and
flirted most shamelessly with her for the whole
of the ride.*

She thought he was angling after Mary Wilson.
What had he done to imply that? Did she think him
incapable of common courtesy? Apparently, he was
a villain through and through.

He re-read the passage describing their meeting,
where she described him as *lying in wait in the hallway.*

Perhaps that had a note of truth in it. He had known
that she would be there, with the rest of the ladies for
the Mathematical Society. And he had timed his exit
from Evan's study to occur when they were leaving,
hoping to catch a glimpse of her.

But walking into her had been an accident. He was
sure. Or almost so. There had been nothing preda-
tory about it. And he had only spoken to her friend
because that woman had been willing to converse.
It had made for a handy excuse to spend a few moments with Selina.

But to think he had designs on Mary? She was
clearly married. He was not about to seduce her. He
crumpled the letter in one fist and slammed the other
on the table, making the china jump in response.

Behind him, a footman shifted nervously, probably wondering if there was something wrong with
his meal.

Alex took a deep breath to calm himself. Then he

deliberately folded the letter and slipped it into his pocket, eating mechanically as he formed a response in his mind. He waited a full five minutes after pudding before taking his port to the study and sharpening a quill.

Mrs Ogilvie,
I am sorry to hear of your trying afternoon and hope that it has not put you off attending the Duchess's little meetings, as I know how much you have enjoyed them in the past. I would hate to hear that you avoid the Fallon house in the future, just because of a chance encounter.
As for Glenmoor, and his attentions to your friend, I am sure he meant nothing by them and that she is far too sensible to have her head turned by a few kind words, even if they come from a duke. Do not think so little of her, even if you cannot think well of him.

There. He smiled and nodded in satisfaction. It did not precisely redeem his attempt to meet her, but perhaps it minimised the damage.

He paused and dipped his quill again, staring at the blank space left to fill. There had to be something he could do to soften her feelings towards him. Perhaps the admirable Mr Abbott could spare him a kind word or two.

Personally, I pity the gentleman. I think it is far more likely that Glenmoor behaves strangely

*because he is stunned by your beauty and loses
all sense when he is around you.*

*You are likely shaking your head at the idea,
but that is only because you underestimate the
effect you have on the gentlemen around you.
When it comes to matters of the heart, peers
are no different than other men, susceptible to
beauty. And yours is such a unique loveliness
paired with such a charming nature that I am
sure he is quite overcome by you.*

He signed, blotted and sealed the letter, then walked
to the hall to set it with the outgoing post. Now he had
but to wait to see her response to the suggestion that
the Duke, whom she held in such low esteem, might
be utterly besotted with her. His letter might do nothing to minimise her hatred for him and her general
distrust of every overture he made, but at least he had
admitted the truth.

Selina stared down at the latest letter from Abbott,
deeply unsatisfied with his answer. It seemed to her
that he gave too much credit to the Duke and too little
to her suspicions of his character.

But then she re-read the last paragraph and read
it one more time, smiling. He thought her handsome.
No, more than that, if he thought she was the sort of
woman to render a man insensible in person.

The motives that he attributed to the Duke were
clearly his own. It was another tentative proof that

he shared the attraction she felt for him, a love that he seemed to think could never be consummated.

Perhaps this explained why he only communicated by writing. He was too intimidated to meet her in person. It was ridiculous, of course. She had been married for eight years and had heard no such compliments from John, nor had he been awed by his good luck in catching her. She could not even muster enough allure to keep him at home.

But, apparently, Abbott was a different sort of man. What could she say to encourage him to overcome his shyness and meet with her? Whatever the words, they must not be sent in a letter, for it only reinforced the idea that she was unreachable. They must meet in person and she could think of one place to look.

Chapter Seven

It was a week to the moment since Edward had come to her with the compass and Selina was back in the park, pacing nervously on the path. Today, she had forgone the company of both friend and son and come alone for her walk. It was probably a vain hope. But perhaps Abbott kept regular habits and walked at this time each day, or each week. In case it was not his plan, she had hinted in her last letter to him that this was her usual time for a walk. Maybe he would come to watch for her.

If he was here, he might gather his nerve and talk to her. Or perhaps she would catch sight of a familiar face and be able to guess the identity of the man who so intrigued her.

But it seemed it was not to be. She could not see anyone who seemed the least bit interesting, nor did anyone seem to be interested in her. And she did not want to stare at strangers, lest she draw the sort of inappropriate attention that she was getting from Baxter.

It had been a mistake to come out here at all. She was making a fool of herself over a man who had made no promises. A few guarded compliments were nothing to build a future on. She dropped down on the nearest bench, overcome with defeat.

Then she saw someone she did know and it made her feel even worse. Baxter was heading down the path towards her at a pace that was almost a trot. For a moment, she had the terrible idea that he had been Abbott all the time and had used the letters as a way to get close to her.

But that could not be right. He'd have used the money against her by now or gained some advantage by all the insight she had given him into her life and her mind. The fact that he was in a public park with her was merely an unfortunate coincidence.

Her legs tensed as she considered rising, then rejected it. To get up and move away she would have to run from him. And there were no shadows and moonlight to hide what was happening. All would see her and note the interaction and she would be back in the scandal sheets again. It would be better to hold her place and hold her tongue, waiting for him to give up and leave her alone.

But before he could reach her, Glenmoor dropped into the seat at her side, offering a smile and a nod. 'Mrs Ogilvie, how are you today?'

Why was the man everywhere that she wanted to be? And why would he not leave her alone? As usual, he was the epitome of elegance in a blue coat, buff breeches and tasselled Hessians that gleamed in the sunlight. 'Your Grace,' she said, deliberately jerking her skirts away from where they settled against his leg. Then she looked straight ahead, refusing to meet his gaze or acknowledge his question.

As usual, her rudeness did not seem to bother him. 'I know that the situation is not ideal. You do not want my company. But then I doubt you wanted Baxter's company either. It is a difficult choice, is it not? So, I have made it for you.'

There was the hint of a breeze and the scent of his cologne reached her, mysterious and seductive, making it even harder to pretend he was not there. Why did such an awful person have to smell so thoroughly inviting? 'Go away,' she murmured, still staring straight ahead and trying not to breathe.

Oblivious as always, he sighed and stretched out his legs, settling in rather than offering to move. 'I do not think that is a good idea. Let us just sit here and enjoy the view together, shall we?'

She gave up and turned to acknowledge him with a glare. 'I will find it more enjoyable once you are gone.'

'And then Baxter will take my seat and insult you,' he reminded her in a pleasant voice. 'And you will have no good way to rid yourself of him. Better that he has to fight his way through me. I doubt he will bother, as it is exceptionally bad form to argue with a peer.' He gave her a sidelong look. 'You should learn that as well, I think.'

She sucked in her breath through her teeth. 'I did not seek you out. I go out of my way to avoid you.

And there is nothing that you can do to earn my for-giveness.'

'Not for want of trying,' he said in the same mild tone.

Was that what he was doing by trapping her like this? Trying to gain some absolution? If so, it would not work. What he had done was beyond forgiveness. But that did not mean that she could forgo his help at the moment. She sighed in resignation and watched as Baxter approached. Glenmoor was right. He did not dare leave her now. 'You are the lesser of two evils,' she agreed.

This seemed to amuse the Duke, who let out a small laugh. 'I knew you would see it my way.'

Baxter had reached them now and paused in front of the bench, staring from her to the Duke and back as if expecting Glenmoor to yield his position.

The Duke stared placidly back at him and did not move an inch. 'Mr Baxter? Is there something I can help you with?'

For a moment, she thought he would slink away without another word. Then he rallied and said, 'I wish to speak with Mrs Ogilvie.'

'She does not wish to speak to you,' the Duke replied.

For a moment, she was tempted to argue that he had no right to speak for her. But she was at a loss as to how to get rid of Baxter on her own, so she remained silent.

'She does not want to speak to you either,' Baxter said with a triumphant smile.

'But I, at least, am a gentleman,' Glenmoor responded. 'I am content to remain silent and not make any overtures that would offend her. If the same can be said of you, then you will have no problem conversing with her while I am present.'

Baxter let out a low growl and stared between them, unsure of what to do next.

'You might as well move along,' the Duke said, giving him his answer. 'I will not yield, if that is what you are expecting. And Mrs Ogilvie will not send me away to make space for you.'

Baxter shifted from foot to foot, obviously annoyed. Then he said, 'You will not always be here, Glenmoor.'

'Perhaps not. But I am here now and that is enough.'

Baxter looked to her now, as if she would stand up for him and send the Duke away so they could be together. It was time that she spoke for herself. 'Whatever the question, the answer is no. The next time you find me, the answer will still be no. The answer will always be no to whatever you want from me. Go away.' She followed this with her sternest look, holding her breath and hoping it would finally convince him to leave her alone.

He took a step back, as if the force of her rejection had driven him off balance. Then he caught himself again and said, 'I will leave you. For now. But I will be back and we *will* talk. Whatever you are doing to stay afloat without a husband, you cannot keep it up forever. When your plan fails, I will be there.' He gave her a final look, a gaze of pure avaricious de-

sire. Then he walked off down the path as if nothing
had happened.

For a moment, she could not breathe at all. There
was no reason to believe that Abbott would leave her
to this man's machinations. But Baxter had been so
certain that she could not help her doubts.

The Duke sensed the silence and filled it. 'It is nothing more than empty talk. He wants to frighten you.'

'He succeeded,' she said, then added a laugh, trying to show a confidence she did not feel.

'You must never forget that you have the support
of your friends,' he said, then added awkwardly, 'And
me, of course.'

'Why?' Though she did not want to encourage the
man, she could not stop the question from escaping
and the nagging memory of Abbott's letter and his
assumptions about the Duke's motives.

'I do not like bullies,' he said, staring down the
path after Baxter and frowning. Then he looked back
at her and smiled. 'And if you need help avoiding that
one, I am at your service.'

'Your help will not be necessary,' she said, trying to gain control of a situation that had got quite
out of hand.

His smile turned ironic. 'Of course not.'

'I am going home now,' she added, rising and heading towards the entrance to the park.

'I will give you a ride,' he said.

'It is not far. I mean to walk.'

'Then I will walk with you,' he said, refusing to take
the hint.

She sighed. 'I cannot prevent you.' Then she set out, taking care not to glance to her side where he was keeping pace. Behind them, she heard the clatter of his carriage, following them in case he changed his mind and decided to ride. It felt as if she had wandered into a parade and somehow become the leader. She quickened her pace and he did as well. Behind her the harnesses jingled and the coach horses walked faster.

She stopped suddenly and he stopped as well, looking at her expectantly as she blurted, 'This is unbearable.'

He gestured back to the carriage. 'We could always—'

'No!' She glanced around her in all directions and said, 'Baxter is not following. We are alone. There is nothing wrong with the neighbourhood. No one is bothering me, except you.' She followed this with a withering stare, hoping to dent his confidence.

He blinked at her, unmoving.

She waved her hands at him in a shooing gesture. 'Go away. I am fine without you. I do not need you.'

'I do not think that is entirely true,' he said, pausing to wet his lips, and inhaled, as if there was something important that he needed to say.

If he was about to lecture her about her problems with Baxter, she did not wish to be reminded of them. And she certainly did not want to hear an offer of any other sort. What was she to do if Abbott was right and the man had romance on his mind?

'You have helped me enough for the day,' she interrupted. 'Now, I wish to be alone.'

He let out the preparatory breath he had taken, obviously deflated. Then, as if he could not take no for an answer, he added, 'If you are sure.'

'Very,' she said, pointing to the carriage.

'Good day, then.' He offered a deep bow and turned to his carriage, not looking back. A footman hopped down from it to get the door and he disappeared into the body. The door slammed, the footman hopped back into his seat and the vehicle set off, turning at the next corner.

She watched it until it was out of sight, then set off on her way again, hurrying to get home. Even after the door of her house was safely closed and locked, she was still shaken from her latest interaction with her two adversaries and unsure of what was to happen next. But there was one thing she could do now, the thing that she always did with each new change in her life.

She went to the desk, sharpened a quill and began to write.

Dear Abbott,
Baxter found me in the park today and tried to insinuate himself into my day. And once again, it was only the intervention of the Duke of Glenmoor that saved me from his company.

I am well aware of what Baxter wants from me. He has been bold enough to say it directly. The Duke is another matter. His intentions are murkier and he has not yet made them clear. But it is only a matter of time until he issues his proposition, which I will, of course, refuse.

What am I to do if these men will not take no for an answer?

She closed the letter, sanded and sealed it, then sent it out with the afternoon post, instructing her housekeeper that she was not at home, especially not to any supposed gentlemen that might call.

After Selina dismissed him, Alex rode the rest of the way to his home, relieved to be alone in his embarrassment. He had gone to the park during her usual walking time, hoping to catch a glimpse of her. He had not been prepared to speak with her. And as usual, he had managed it badly.

It was easiest to play the hero when he had Baxter to deal with. Baxter was inherently unlikable and Alex could not resist goading him. Aside from that, opposing him created a reason to speak with Selina and things to say. He enjoyed protecting her. It felt right, somehow.

But once the little toady was gone, she had been eager to get rid of Alex and they'd fallen back into the awkward silence that was a hallmark of their interactions.

Or at least, he had. She had been most loquacious, and her chosen topic had been how much she wished that he would go away. There had been a moment when he had nearly confided the truth to her. He'd gathered his nerve to the sticking point and was searching for the right way to begin when she'd cut him off, with a disavowal so firm there was no gentlemanly way to ignore it.

She'd continued in the same vein in her next letter to Abbott and he grimaced as he read her attributing Baxter's motives to him when he was entirely innocent.

As he sat down to write his response, he was tempted to remind her of her words on the street and tell her that the only reason she had managed at all was because of the Duke's help. But that would be petty and unfair.

He did not mind helping her and would continue to do so as long as he was able. But it was impractical to be Abbott when dealing with Baxter, and Glenmoor could not follow her everywhere, imposing himself on her and demanding that she accept his help. There was only one thing he could think of to do.

He began,

My dear Selina,
Do not worry yourself about Baxter. As I promised, a solution is at hand.

I am sending you a new servant, a footman of prodigious size, who may guard your door by day and follow you about on errands, if you so choose. He will be instructed as to Baxter's unwelcomeness and will escort the man off the premises should he try to call on you when you are at home.

As for the Duke, it is possible that he dislikes Baxter even more than you do and is following that man about for some reason that has noth-

*ing to do with you. Perhaps that is why he seems
ever present in your life. But...*

Alex paused, forming his words carefully. She
needed looking after and Glenmoor was in an excellent position to do so. He was a duke in need of an
heir. He would have to marry, eventually.

Why could it not be her?

If he could come to her as himself, he might never
need to reveal his deception as Abbott. Or at least
he could wait until so much later that it was nothing more than an amusing anecdote and not a fresh
source of betrayal.

*...it is also quite natural that he would be
interested in you. Unlike Baxter, I have heard
Glenmoor is a decent man and not likely to
make unseemly requests to a lady who has been
a guest in his brother's house.*

*Have you considered that his attraction to
you may be an honourable one? He is, after all,
unmarried and must seek a wife sooner rather
than later. I can think of no reason he would
not be drawn to someone as fine, as charming
and as noble as you.*

He smiled, warming to the idea. He could imagine
her beside him in bed, soft skin and smooth hair, the
scent of her, like spring flowers after a rain. He would
be the happiest of men.

And there would be advantages to her as well.

Baxter would not dare touch the wife of such a powerful man. And you would have power in your own right. You would be a duchess in a great house, dressed in silks and jewels, with servants to wait on your every need.

The idea was insane. But it was the best solution, the happiest outcome for both of them. If only he could make her see.

He finished the letter quickly, sealing it before he could change his mind and retract the offer she would not know he was making. Then he put it in the outgoing post and sat back to wait.

Clearly, Abbott had gone mad. Selina stared down at the paper in her hand, re-reading it carefully to make sure she had understood correctly, for he was suggesting the unsuggestable.

Of course, he had begun with her Christian name, which was endearing, and extolled her virtues as a woman and wife. But no amount of flattery would make up for the fact that he wanted to give her away to the abominable Duke.

She ran to the morning room writing desk and took up her pen.

My dear Abbott,
First, I must thank you for the offer of a footman, which does seem like a good temporary solution for these incursions into my life.
But as for the rest...

Even if I believed that the Duke's intentions were honourable, there is no way I would consider a marriage to him. Have you forgotten the role he played in the death of my husband? The idea that I could link myself to such a man is unfathomable. Even sitting next to him for short periods of time is enough to make my skin crawl.

She paused for a moment, tempted to strike the last line and write something else. Her interactions with the Duke had indeed raised strange sensations in her, though they were not quite as she had just described them. But she was not sure how to chronicle the conflicting emotions she felt when looking at him, especially not to Abbott. She certainly did not want to give the impression that she had taken a physical interest in the man.

Though there was nothing particularly unnatural about such an awareness. He was handsome, after all. And she had been alone for a long time. But it did not signify.

She shook her head, trying to clear it of wayward thoughts, and continued her letter.

He is the last man on earth I would marry, even if he should offer.

Please, if you must make suggestions for my future, come up with something better than that.

Then, to remind him of the better thing she hoped for, she closed with

Yours, always, Selina

What had he expected?

Alex stared down at the letter, particularly the lines that described her reaction to him, remembering the expression of suspicion and loathing on her face each time they met. Her assumptions about her husband's last night were unchanged, even after a year.

In the few times they'd talked since, they'd exchanged only a handful of words, mostly about Baxter. He had never managed anything near to an explanation or an apology, or an assurance that she was mistaken about his part in any of it.

Unless things changed drastically in the future, there was no chance that he would earn her friendship, or even ambivalence. The idea of gaining her love was far beyond the realm of possibility.

He sighed. His wants were not part of this equation. She had asked him what she was to do about Baxter. There was one, easy solution that would make the man give up and go away. She needed someone who could protect her, not just occasionally, but always.

That man would not be him. He could not have her for himself no matter what he wanted. Nor could he expect her to stay a widow for the rest of her life. She was a flesh-and-blood woman who had needs.

At least, he assumed she did. When she wrote to

him, she seemed so full of life and passion. It was a crime against the universe that she should live with an empty bed and only a few tepid letters for company.

He took her latest letter to his study and sat down at his desk to pen his answer.

> *My dear Selina,*
> *It is clear that my first idea met with a poor reception. Forgive my impertinence for the suggestion. I only want what is best for you and that is to see you placed in society at a rank that suits you.*
>
> *But I am afraid the only true solution I have found to your problems is that you marry someone suitable who can care for you in ways that I cannot.*
>
> *That should be your ultimate goal, should it not? To find a husband who might keep you company and who would be a good father for your son. May I suggest a few gentlemen you are sure to meet, if you are invited to the Duchess of Melton's ball next week?*

He paused.

After an hour, he was still staring at a blank sheet, at a loss.

Evan would have been perfect had he not married. He was unequalled in character and good sense, just the sort of man Alex wanted for her. Perhaps it would be better to choose someone who was already a widower, with an heir who could be company for Edward. As long as the man was better than his own stepfather had been. He did not want to sentence the boy to a childhood like his own.

But that was not enough. The perfect husband must not gamble too much or drink too much. He must be healthy in mind and body. He must be attentive to her in all the ways John Ogilvie had not been. He must have enough money for her to live comfortably and enough sense to plan for the future so that she might never be thrown back into poverty.

He sat with his pen poised over the paper as he rejected name after name as unworthy, finally settling on three fellows in whom he could find no obvious flaws. He scribbled their names down, then signed and sealed the letter before he could change his mind.

Then he reached for the brandy bottle to numb the pain that would accompany the impending loss of the woman he could not help but love.

Chapter Eight

How dared he?

Selina crumpled the letter with frustration and headed towards the fire, ready to rid herself of it for good. At the last minute, she changed her mind and carried it back to the writing desk to read again.

It was one thing to suggest the Duke as a possible husband. He could not have been serious when he'd written that, knowing how she felt about Glenmoor. She had decided that it must have been meant as a joke between friends, though one that was not very funny. And it had been a little flattering to know that he thought her worthy of being a duchess, even if it linked her with a man she could not abide.

But this latest letter was serious and reasonable. Too reasonable. Logical to the point of coldness. Did he really mean to organise her future without a thought as to where her heart might lie? To suggest that she would marry one of these strangers and let that man take his place in her life as lover and protector? It was impossible.

She wrote back.

Do not say that this is the only way. Of course I would like to marry again. Sometime in the future. But I would rather face a dozen Baxters than marry without love.

She sent the brief missive off and waited for his response.

And waited.

When two days had passed, she wrote again.

I hope I have not offended you with my hasty words. It is unfair of me to imply that I am avoiding marriage for any reason. The alternative is to live on your charity and I realise I cannot do that the whole of my life. It was the height of selfishness to reject your suggestions out of hand.

If you wish to rethink your generosity, please tell me honestly and I will find another way to support myself.

Just the thought of that sent a chill through her, for she had no idea what she would do without him. But there were things far more important than money, his continued friendship foremost among them.

* * *

When another two days had passed with no word, she wrote again.

> *My dearest Abbott,*
> *What has become of you? I have never gone so long without a letter and you have me worried. Was it something I said? If so, I retract it and apologise.*
>
> *If it is just a matter of those gentlemen you suggested, I will dance with them at the ball tomorrow night and do my best to befriend them. We shall see what comes of it.*
>
> *But do not cut me out of your life without explanation. Just a line or two to assure me that you are not angry. Or something far worse.*
>
> *My mind runs wild with dire possibilities. If you are ill, tell me where I might go to tend you. I fear you are hurt and alone, or perhaps dead and beyond my reach forever. What shall I do if that is the case? Cannot someone answer me so I might lay a wreath and offer my prayers?*

Her fears were probably ridiculous, as were the tears she was shedding as she wrote the last words. It was much more likely that he had grown tired of their correspondence and decided not to respond. Or that he would write again in a day or two and tell her she was being silly and had no need to worry.

But being without him, even for a short time, had become unthinkable. Even more incomprehensible was the idea that she should marry and leave him behind. Her plan was to remain a widow until he came forward to claim her, or until death, whichever came first.

She could not tell him so. It was too forward, especially while she depended on him for her livelihood. He would think she was using him for the security he provided. But would it be any worse to use some other poor man, letting him take her to wife, while her heart had no room for anyone but Abbott?

She hurriedly signed, folded and sealed her latest letter, praying that it would move him to contact her. Was he really gone from her life without even saying goodbye?

Or was he simply waiting for her to come out and say the words of love that were always just beneath the text? How would she get him to make himself known to her, in person and not just in pen and ink?

There had to be a reason that he did not want to come forward and, as with the current absence, her thoughts raced trying to understand it.

Perhaps he was war-damaged, and unable to stand and fight for her. Of course, it spoiled her earlier belief that he had been at the ball with her. She could not remember seeing a crutch or a sling on any of the men who had attended that, and Edward had mentioned nothing of the kind. But there were disabilities to the body, mind and spirit that were not easily visible. He might be afflicted with one of those.

Or perhaps he was older than Edward had thought. An old uncle, just as he had pretended to be at first.

It made the most sense, but she could not bring herself to believe it. She had invested far too much of her heart and mind in believing that he was young and robust. Perhaps not handsome. But that would not matter to one who loved him as much as she did.

Or suppose that he had hidden himself among the three men he had chosen as her suitors? There was something so resigned in the paragraph of his last letter that she doubted it. It had sounded as though he was giving her away. And she could not remember meeting any of these three at the Fallon ball that she was sure Abbott had attended.

But if there was the faintest chance that he was offering himself as a possibility, she must be open to it. The idea was rather like a fairy tale, where the heroine had to pass a test to prove herself worthy of a prince. If she could not recognise him when he was standing right before her, then perhaps she was not deserving of his love.

She would go to the Melton ball as he wished her to and meet the men he recommended. If he was one of them, she would discover which and make him drop his disguise and admit the truth.

If he was not? Then he was sure to be somewhere on the guest list. She would be so charming, so beautiful and so witty that he would regret that he was giving her away and reveal himself.

Alex sipped his brandy and stared out over the crowd at the Melton ball, disgusted with himself and everyone else there. Since his last letter to Selina, he had been drinking far too much, and tonight was no exception. He had smuggled the spirit out of the card room and brought it out into the ballroom, where polite people were drinking champagne or lemonade.

But he had needed something to fortify himself if he was to watch Selina dancing and chatting with the men he had selected for her. Once she had made her choice and set a date, things would be easier. He would not have to see her at all if he did not want to. And he certainly would not write to her.

Except, perhaps, once. Just to congratulate her and to know that she was well.

No. Not even that. One letter would lead to dozens, just as it had before. If he wanted what was best for her, he had to give her up. Her recent letters had proven the fact, if nothing else had. She was as dependent on their correspondence as he was. The end of the last one had been blurred by tear stains, at the thought that he might be beyond her reach forever.

He had grabbed for his pen and scribbled two pages of assurances before catching himself and throwing the papers into the fire. Since nothing could ever come of their relationship, it was not healthy for it to continue. And if he set her free before she discovered the true identity of Abbott, he might at least know that she continued to love the part of him that had been her friend. That would be far better than letting things go until secrets were uncovered that would make her hate every fibre of his being.

There would be no more letters. But tonight, he could at least watch her from a distance and assure himself that she was well and having a pleasant time with other, more worthy men.

He took another sip of the brandy and stared across the ballroom at her, trying to be pleased at the way the evening was going. She looked happy, which was what he'd wanted, after all. And more beautiful than he had ever seen her. She was wearing an ice-blue dress, trimmed with silver embroidery that glittered when she moved as if she was floating on a field of stars.

At the moment, she was dancing with one of the men he had suggested to her, smiling radiantly at him, hanging on his every word.

Lord Stanhope had seemed like a good choice when he'd written the name down, neither too young nor too old, and with a decent income. Also, a squint, which Alex had forgotten when he'd suggested the man.

But Selina did not appear to be bothered by it. She stared up at him, her face alight, laughing at some inane comment he had made as if he was the wittiest man in the room.

Alex stared out at the dancers, forcing himself to look at other couples instead of focusing on each move she made, each time she stepped close to Stanhope, each time they exchanged a touch or a word. This was what he'd wanted. The plan was working. Why was it so vexing?

He felt a nudge on his arm and looked beside him to see his brother staring at him with an exasperated grin. 'Are you with us this evening? Or somewhere else entirely?'

'What do you mean?' Alex said, looking back at the dancers. The music was ending, and Stanhope was walking Selina back to a chair near the door.

'I have been speaking to you for a good minute and you have not heard a word.'

'Sorry,' Alex replied, losing sight of the couple and forcing himself to look at Evan. 'What were you saying?'

'Nothing important. Just that the evening is delightful, the company good. And you are scowling at the dance floor as if every person on it has given you offence.'

It was then that Alex noticed the pain in his jaw, probably caused by his clenched teeth. He took a sip of brandy and forced himself to relax.

'And how much of that have you had?' Evan said, staring at the glass in his hand.

'Obviously not enough,' Alex said, taking another deliberate drink.

Evan held out his hands in surrender. 'Do as you will. But it is not improving your mood, if that is your object.'

Alex sighed and handed the glass to a passing footman. A glance at the dance floor proved that Selina was standing up with another of his candidates, the unobjectionable Mr Henderson, who had more money than Stanhope and two good eyes. He turned back to his brother, forcing himself to ignore them. 'I apologise, my mind is elsewhere tonight.'

'Really?' Evan said with a knowing smile. 'Because

it appears to be out there.' He pointed to the crowd of dancers. 'Who is she?'

'She?' Alex frowned.

'Normally it takes a woman to bring out such a dark mood in a man.'

'There is nothing wrong with my mood,' he insisted.

'Like Byron on a bad day,' his brother chuckled. 'I have never seen you like this.'

'It amuses you?'

'To no end.' Evan patted him on the shoulder. 'Take heart. Whoever she is, she is bound to succumb to your charms in time. If you do not frighten her away with your sour looks first.'

In the distance, he was sure he heard Selina laughing at something Henderson had said. When he caught sight of her again, her smile was even more brilliant than before. 'There is no woman,' Alex said emphatically.

'Of course not,' Evan said, obviously pleased with himself.

'And even if there were…' Their eyes met.

She had caught him staring at her and she did not look away. His breath stopped in his lungs, his thoughts froze, even his heart did not beat, as everything about him tried to hold the moment for as long as he could. Then it was over and he turned back to look at his brother, struggling to complete the sentence he had started.

'You would not be in such a state over her?' Evan suggested.

'Exactly,' Alex replied, trying to see through the crowd that now separated them.

'Liar,' Evan replied. 'Fortune favours the bold and five years at Oxford have done you no favours.'

'What do you mean by that?'

'That you are out of practice in wooing ladies. Go dance with her, whoever she is, or someone else surely shall.' Then he walked away, leaving Alex alone.

She had been wrong.

If the first two gentlemen were any indication, this was not a test to help unmask Abbott. Mr Henderson and Lord Stanhope were pleasant enough, but there was no feeling of familiarity when she met with them. They did not laugh at what should have been shared jokes and hints at previous conversations. They merely looked puzzled.

They were impressed by her, of course. She had flattered and flirted, and did everything in her power to charm them. If Abbott was here, watching her, she hoped he was well and truly jealous.

And well he might be. Perhaps it was her imagination, but she thought she was being watched. As she spoke with Mr Henderson after their dance, she could feel a tickling at the back of her neck, like the breath before a kiss. Surreptitiously, she scanned the room, searching for the man who did not look away when she caught his eye.

The guest list of tonight's gathering was similar to that for the Fallon ball, and she was not surprised to see many of the same faces here. But though she danced with many of the same men both nights, none of them sparked the sense of recognition she had expected to find when she met Abbott.

Where was he?

At least she did not see Baxter when she searched the crowd. Whatever she might do tonight, she would not have to spend the evening dodging his attentions. But there was still the Duke of Glenmoor, whom she could not seem to escape. It was hardly a surprise to see him here. He was an eligible peer and could not avoid the attentions of the matchmakers.

Without meaning to, her eyes lingered on him, taking in his dark good looks. At well over six feet, he was much taller than her husband had been, with long legs and arms and a musculature that hinted at continual activity. It was strange because she'd heard that, before ascending to the title, he had been teaching at Oxford. She associated men of learning with a scholarly stoop, but he stood straight and wore his extra height with a relaxed confidence.

His hair was dark brown, almost black, and thick, worn short and tidy as if he could not be bothered with too much brushing. And his eyes...

They were looking directly at her now. She felt an embarrassing shock of connection.

She looked away, doing her best to pretend that she had not just been staring. It was not as if she wanted his attention, after all. She loathed the man, yet there was a certain something about him that drew her.

Sensing that she had lost interest, Mr Henderson found an excuse to depart, leaving her alone to wait for her next partner. She wished she felt something other than relief at his going. She could not marry the fellow, no matter how suitable Abbott might think him.

She spared a quick glance in Glenmoor's direction, then looked away again. He was coming towards her. It was as if she had accidentally summoned a demon or had pulled the cork from a djinn's bottle. What was she to do? It would cause a scandal if she ran from him, inciting even more comment than her snub at the last ball. She must steady her nerves and stand her ground and hope that he would go away again.

'Mrs Ogilvie.'

His voice matched his eyes, deep and rich. She would probably not be thinking such things if she had not had too much punch. In their last meetings, he had seemed polite but distant. But tonight, there was something in this ordinary greeting that spoke volumes.

She nodded in response, glancing up at him and then looking down at the floor again, suddenly unsure.

'You look lovely this evening.'

She could feel herself colouring at the compliment, which was even more confusing. She did not want to be flattered by this man, so why was she responding to his words? Suppose Abbott had been right and the Duke was in some way enamoured of her? He would think she was encouraging him with lingering glances and blushes.

'May I have the next dance?'

'No,' she snapped, trying to regain control of herself and the conversation. She held out her dance card to show him. 'I am spoken for.'

But the Duke was not interested in her carefully made plans. As usual, he meant to be in the way. He responded to her refusal with a non-committal 'hmm'. Then he reached for the little pencil attached to the card and struck through the name of the gentleman and wrote in his own above it. 'Problem solved. I claim the waltz, which is next.'

She stared down at the card in shock. The line he had crossed out, Mr Anthony Belleville, was the last of the men that Abbott had wanted her to meet. She should be outraged that he had spoiled her chance to question the fellow, but all she could feel was relief.

It served Abbott right. If he had been here, where she needed him, he could have protected her from Glenmoor and danced with her himself. She would write and tell him so when she got home.

But he probably would not answer.

And now her next partner had arrived and she was trapped between Belleville and the Duke like Charybdis and Scylla.

Before she could speak, Glenmoor chose for her, giving Mr Belleville a stern look. 'Apologies, sir, but I need a moment of the lady's time. You will have other opportunities to dance with her, I am sure.' Then, before she could object again, he took her arm and led her out on to the floor.

As he took her into his arms, she was surprised at his gentleness. When she had read of the reason for her husband's death, she had imagined Glenmoor as a brute. But as she looked back on their interactions, he had given her no reason to. He had been a perfect gentleman each time, offering aid and strength and asking nothing in return.

Tonight was no exception. His lead was commanding, but his hands were gentle, holding her as if she were as delicate as a butterfly and might be crushed by a moment's carelessness.

She had been strong enough, a few moments ago when she had been dancing with Mr Henderson. But with Glenmoor she felt shy and as fragile as glass. A sudden move, or an unexpected word, and she might crack. And who knew what might rush out of her if that accident happened.

Probably an embarrassing truth. What if she admitted that she had not wanted to dance with Belleville at all? That she was sure that none of these men was the one she was waiting for, that she was alone in the world and even more frightened of that than she was of him.

She closed her mouth tight against that possibility and forced herself to follow his steps. But not to smile, for that was quite beyond her.

He smiled back at her straight-lipped grimace as if she was the most charming woman in the room.

'There,' he said softly, so that only she could hear. 'It is not so bad to waltz, is it? I assume you have danced this before, for you are very graceful, even under difficult circumstances.'

She said nothing in response to this for, in truth,

it was still a shocking new experience to be so close to a stranger. Her husband had had little interest in dancing and even less in dancing with her. And she was not about to admit to that. 'Thank you,' she said, through gritted teeth.

'She speaks,' he said with a chuckle, and she felt a slight squeeze of her hand. 'You're most welcome. And it would be remiss of me if I do not tell you that you are the loveliest woman here.'

'You needn't bother with flattery,' she said, finding her voice again.

'On the contrary, this is just the time for it,' he replied. 'I often say such to the ladies I waltz with.'

'All the more reason not to bother.' It was nothing but an empty comment and without meaning. Strangely, this was disappointing.

'If you prefer, I will comment that the music is most fine this evening. And then you may tell me that you have heard better, if only to be contrary.'

'If you wish to hold down both sides of the conversation, it is not necessary for me to say anything at all.'

At this, he laughed again. 'Too true. It is tempting to do so since it is difficult to get a word out of you.'

'Because I do not wish to argue,' she said, glancing around her, still half afraid that this interaction would be reported in tomorrow's paper.

'Then I will give you no reason to. I am quite willing to agree with whatever outlandish stance you wish to take, if only to keep the peace. And as for my past with your husband…'

'I do not wish to speak of it,' she said, trying to pull away.

He spun them deftly, turning her moment of resistance into an elegant twirl. Then she was back in his arms again, held more tightly, so she could not escape.

'Well, I do. And now is as good a time as any, since you cannot run from me without causing another scene. While I have you here...'

'Captive,' she said with a frown.

'If you say so. But only for a minute or two. And before I lose you, I wish to apologise for what happened. It was not my intention to cause pain to a man who was already wounded, or to drive him to the action he took.'

When she did not respond, he continued.

'When we played, he gave no sign that it was anything more than an innocent game.'

'But it was,' she said, unwilling to give him credit.

'I am aware of that. And I know that it is not enough to apologise, and I do not expect absolution. But the words need to be said. I never meant him harm and would not have gambled that night had I known what the result would be.'

They made another turn of the floor in silence and she stared out over the sea of faces around them, wishing for anyone to rescue her.

No. She wished for one in particular, though she doubted that he would interrupt, even if he was here.

'It will be over soon,' the Duke said with a sigh. 'Too soon, perhaps. I suspect this will be our only dance and I cannot help but wish that it would last a little longer.'

'There is no point in wishing for anything,' she said firmly. 'In my experience, wishes do not come true.'

'How very sad,' he said with surprising feeling. 'Then, if I wish for anything, it will be that your opinion on that matter will change. After all that has happened to you, you deserve to have at least one dream come true.'

'That is an exceptionally sentimental thing to say,' she said, surprised.

'You were expecting that I would be otherwise?' he asked with a smile.

'I was expecting…' the worst. She had expected him to be like Baxter. But he was so very different and, for a moment, she almost felt…

What? Was it sympathy for this man, who had accidentally changed her life? Or was it something else? She felt a strange sort of kinship arising out of this stolen dance and she did not want it. It was too confusing and far too complicated. 'Never mind,' she said, and looked resolutely past him, over his shoulder and into the crowd, trying to focus her mind on anything else.

Next to her, he sighed. Then the music ended and he released her, before taking her arm again to lead her back to her seat. Once there, he held her hand, bowing stiffly over it, and said, 'Thank you again for favouring me with a dance. Better days are ahead for you, Selina Ogilvie. And if there is anything I can do to help, you have but to ask. I want the best for you. I always have.'

And then, before she could think of a response, he was gone.

Chapter Nine

After dancing with Selina, Alex made his excuses to the hostess and called for his carriage, not wanting to spoil a perfect evening by staying too long. Once he was away, he settled back into his seat to relive each second of the last few minutes to fix them permanently in his mind.

It had been paradise.

If he was to have only one partner in his life, he would have chosen her. And if he could have chosen only one dance, it would have been a waltz.

When he had finally worked up the nerve to go to her, there had been no verbal stumbles. He had not muttered about the weather or forgotten what to say. He had swept aside her objections and scuttled the competition in a way that would probably horrify him tomorrow, but at least he had achieved his goal and had a normal conversation.

Better than that, she had heard his apology. She had not accepted it, of course. But with time, the seed might grow in her mind that he was not the villain she assumed he was. Even in the short time they'd danced, he had felt some small change. By the time the music had stopped, she'd moved with ease, as though some of the weight she'd borne at the beginning of the waltz had been lifted. After a few minutes in his arms, she had almost seemed to be content.

He must find a way to ask about the Duke, in his next letter.

Then he remembered that he had sworn not to write to her. And did he really want to read her answer, if she sent one? The truth of her current feelings might be so far from his that it would spoil the glow of this moment and the feeling that, if he continued these tentative attempts to win her, he might ultimately succeed.

He smiled to himself and shook his head. If another letter arrived, in a day, a week or a year, he would read it immediately, just as he had all the others. It was one thing to deny himself the pleasure of answering her and quite another to deny her the help that he had sworn to give her. Abbott would always be there for her, whether she wanted the Duke or not.

It was nearly dawn when Selina arrived home from the ball and she was exhausted and yet unable to sleep. She had done what Abbott had asked of her and spoken to the men on his list. Before the night had ended, she had even managed a dance with the one that Glenmoor had frightened away.

Unfortunately, that man had been as disappointing as the other two. All were well-spoken and handsome, yet when she talked to them, she felt nothing other than a slight megrim from straining to be polite. Perhaps if she wrote to Abbott about them, he would have something more to say.

But when she sat down to do so, she was lost for words. It had been so easy to converse with him before he had sent his cursed list of names.

What was she to say now? That she could not tell one from another? Then he might tell her that she should let the men vie for her hand and let the winner claim her, as if she was a prize to be won and not a feeling human being. If she claimed she did not like them, she would be called too particular, for were they not all likable men?

The brutal truth was that, while they were likable, she did not find them lovable. She would not wait eagerly for their homecoming, as she waited for the latest mail, now. She could imagine becoming the rigidly obedient wife she had been for John, the happiness or sadness of her days measured by her husband's moods and her nights spent dreaming about a man she could never have.

She was still sitting at her writing desk with a blank sheet before her when the morning post arrived. And, as she had for nearly every day of the last year, she rushed to the front hall to receive it, hoping for just one more letter. As she sorted through the stack, she found nothing from Abbott. But there was a strange letter written in a businesslike hand with no return address.

Her curiosity piqued, she carried it back to the writing desk and cracked the seal.

My dear Mrs Ogilvie,
If you are interested in protecting the identity
of your mysterious benefactor, meet me in Hyde
Park at ten o'clock at your usual bench.
A friend

She turned the paper over again, searching for any indication of its sender, or who this mysterious friend might be. But the paper was unmarked and the seal was plain.

And did she have a usual bench? There was the place she'd sat when Glenmoor had interrupted her. If he had written the letter, why would he not have signed it properly?

It did not matter. If there was a chance that she might learn Abbott's real name, she could not help but take it. She set the letter aside and rang for the maid to help her into a walking dress.

When she arrived at the park, she went straight to the bench where she had met Glenmoor, trying not to look as excited as she felt. Finally, she was about to learn the truth about the man she loved. She smiled and it felt like the first natural expression she had worn in a full day.

'Happy to see me. That is an excellent start to our relationship.'

Her smile faded as Mr Baxter dropped into the seat beside her and stared at her expectantly.

'I was waiting for someone,' she said, hoping he would take the hint and go away.

'A friend,' he confirmed. 'Someone who sent you a letter just this morning.'

'You,' she said, her hopes falling.

'Me,' he agreed, grinning back at her. 'You don't have the Duke to protect you today, I see,' he added. 'Nor have you brought that strapping footman to turn me away.'

She was regretting that very fact. But it was probably time that she learned to defend herself against this man, since she could not count on anyone else to help her. 'You will have to take my word that your attentions are not welcome,' she said, keeping her head high and defiant.

At this, he laughed, and showed no sign of budging from the spot next to her. 'Then it is about time that you learned to be less particular. You are a woman without means, after all, and dependent on whatever man is willing to give you charity.'

The description was too close to the truth for her sake. But how was she to respond to it? 'I have friends who are concerned for my welfare.'

'Is that what you call the man who assists you?' he said, giving her a sidelong look. 'And what do you do to maintain such a close friendship? There are rumours about that you have a line of credit at a bank and yet you have no family to leave you an inheritance, nor did your husband.' He gave her another revolting smile. 'Unless you have become a shopgirl in secret and are earning your own way, you must be doing something to reciprocate for the generosity of your benefactor.'

In his letter, he had claimed he knew about Abbott. And he spoke with the air of someone who had more details than she did. Was there a way to get information out of him, without giving any more of the truth away? 'You seem to think yourself well-informed as to the details of my life,' she said, choosing her words carefully.

'I make it my business to be,' he said smugly.

'And why is that?'

He rolled his eyes. 'Really, my dear Selina, you must be aware of how I feel about you. I was captivated by your beauty, even before your husband died.'

At the idea that he had been observing her before her widowhood, she could not help a shudder. 'I had never spoken to you. I did nothing to encourage such an interest.'

'And your late husband did nothing to protect you from it. He gambled your life away without a second thought.'

'I was not a part of his wagers, to be bartered to a stranger,' she said, glaring at him.

'You might as well have been. If he had cared what was to happen to you, he would have left you something to live on. And your current protector is doing very little to help you, other than placing that enormous footman at your door.'

'He is not my protector,' she blurted. 'I have not even met him.'

'If he truly cared about you, he'd have made some honourable offer, instead of leaving you open to rumours.'

Were there rumours? She had seen no sign of them last night at the ball, nor had she read anything in the papers. But perhaps people had begun to speculate, as Baxter had. She felt a flash of annoyance towards Abbott for putting her in this position, before remembering that, without him, she would likely be in the workhouse, or living off the charity of the church. Or, worst of all, accepting Baxter's first offer of protection.

There was nothing she could do at the moment other than to look blankly at him and say, 'You are hardly one to judge what best I am to do with my life. Nor do I wish any more letters from you, nor any more insidious hinting about my future.'

'Then you had best make a break from the man who is supporting you,' he said with a mocking shake of his head. 'Because I have uncovered the details of your little arrangement and the name of the man who is caring for you. If you continue to resist me, I will share them with all who will listen, and what is left of your reputation will be forfeit.'

He knew Abbott. Or at least he claimed to. For a moment, the thrill of that blocked out her fear of the revelation. If he told the world, she would learn the truth as well. Then she realised that he was bargaining to keep the secret rather than reveal it.

She took a breath to steel her nerves and said, 'I will never give in to you, no matter what you threaten.'

'Are you sure your friend would be so cavalier if his name is made public? If he leaves you over this…'

'He will not leave me,' she insisted. But was that true? She had not heard from him in over a week. It was possible that he'd left her already.

'Are you sure? If you are wrong, he will leave you with nothing. And then you might not be so particular about the next man in your bed.'

'He is not sharing my bed,' she blurted, then looked quickly around her to be sure that no one had heard.

'Am I to believe he helps you from the goodness of his heart?' Baxter laughed. 'He wants the same thing I do. If he has not yet collected his debt, then it is only a matter of time.'

None of his suppositions proved he knew anything more about Abbott than she did. There was only one way she would know for sure and that was if she let him reveal the truth he claimed to have. 'You don't know him as I do,' she said firmly. 'He will not leave me. And I will never accept you even if he does.'

Baxter's face darkened. 'If I cannot get affection, I will settle for revenge. Come to me willingly or I will see to it that no one else will want you. Not for anything proper at least.' Then he deliberately laid his hand on hers, offering a squeeze before withdrawing it and rising. 'I will give you until this evening to make your decision. If I do not hear from you, you will see your own name in the scandal sheets tomorrow.'

Then he turned and walked away.

She sat there alone for a moment, trying to hide her shivers, forcing a false smile on to her face lest passers-by wonder at her pallor. What was she to do?

She must write to Abbott, of course, to tell him that Baxter was aware of his help and meant to interfere in their arrangement. He must not be caught unawares by the revelation of his identity.

But would he write back? His answer the last time she had complained of Baxter was that she must marry. But even he must know that could not be done in a week. Would he find the motivation to intervene when his own name was in the paper alongside hers?

She rose and walked home slowly, greeting the very large footman whom Abbott had installed at her front door to prevent just the thing she had gone off to do on her own. She smiled up at the fellow and said, 'If a Mr Baxter comes, I am not home to him. Now or ever.'

The servant grinned and cracked his knuckles. 'Of course, Mrs Ogilvie.'

Then she went inside, went up to her room and did not come down until supper.

Chapter Ten

It had been two days since her meeting with Baxter and she had not slept well on either night. It was clear that he meant her harm and, if his threat was serious, there was nothing she could do to stop him from destroying her reputation.

Half a dozen times she had started and abandoned a letter to Abbott, explaining the danger they were in. It was possible that he was married, or perhaps a member of the clergy, and public association with her would be embarrassing to him as well.

But he was the one who had started this. He was the one who had abandoned her, of late. It served him right if he was shocked to find himself uncovered by Baxter and without a plan to fix things.

There was also a niggling, unworthy fear that if she told him what was about to occur, he would abandon her again, deny everything and throw her to the wolves. She had trusted him for so long that her heart did not want to believe it was possible. But there was a chance that he was a man as unworthy as Baxter and she was better off without him.

In any case, she would know the truth if and when Baxter carried out his threat and told the world that Selina Ogilvie was a kept woman.

She came down to breakfast, tired and wan, to find a single letter awaited her in the morning post. As usual, it bore no return address. She thought of the letter she had sent, begging for news from Abbott. What if her worst fears had come true? He was dead and some solicitor was writing to tell her of the fact.

Then she recognised the hand from Baxter's cryptic note earlier in the week.

She opened it and read.

Have you seen today's scandal column? There is an item that may interest you.
Bernard Baxter

For a moment, she could not do anything more than stare at the words, frozen in place. The moment had come. Then she came back to herself and rang for the maid to bring her a copy of *The Times*.

She laid it flat on the dining table and stood poised above it, gathering her courage. Then she turned to the society page, her hands trembling against the paper.

She was ruined. But at least she would finally know who Abbott was. And if he was the man she hoped he was, he would come to her and make this all right. Her three suitors had not been the fairy-tale test she'd hoped for, but this was. She was in danger, for all the world to see. And now was the time for her knight in shining armour, her handsome prince, her clever hero, to come to her rescue.

It has been discovered that a certain gentle-man has been providing for the widow of the late Mr O. for almost a year now. Apparently, it was not enough that he forced her husband to suicide. Or perhaps that was the reason be-hind the act. For Mrs S. O. is said to be quite beautiful...

Her name had been abbreviated to give the illusion of privacy, but it was no better than a fig leaf for that. Everyone would know who the on dit was referring to, even her friends. She read on.

...and since the Duke of G. is a notoriously devious man, we can guess what he wants from the poor widow.

She stared down at the newspaper in disbelief. It was nonsense of course. Baxter had it wrong. Of all the people she had imagined, it could not be him.

She was halfway to her writing desk before the wording of the item penetrated her consciousness. There was no point in writing to Abbott ever again. Her lover had been an illusion and her love for him a sick joke.

If she had been supported by the Duke all this time, then the letters had come from him as well. He had not just ruined her reputation; he had tricked her into revealing her innermost thoughts. He'd let her pour out the contents of her heart to him, sometimes two and three times a day for months.

And her most recent letters had been the most revealing of all. She had begged him for another letter, prostrated herself over his departure from her life. She had wept for him.

Thinking about it, she felt naked, vulnerable. She had not wanted anything to do with the man, but he had found a way into her life and upended it. She had thought that he could not do anything worse to her than he had already done, and now? This.

She owed him. Money and more. She did not have a penny to repay him, nor would there be a marriage to release her from his grip. No one would want her.

'The Duke of Glenmoor is here for you, madam.' The housekeeper made the introduction in an awed whisper, happy to be announcing a member of the peerage, even one as reprehensible as this.

If someone saw him coming or going from the house, the gossip would only increase. She raised a limp hand to her forehead and closed her eyes. Then she said, in the strongest voice she could manage, 'Tell him to go to perdition.'

'I am afraid it is too late for that, Mrs Ogilvie.' He was standing in the doorway of her tiny dining room, blocking the way to the stairs. She could not escape him. And, damn him, his voice was as deep and velvety as it had been at the ball. It showed no sign of the panic she was feeling at the most recent turn of events. 'You need me here.'

'Your Grace,' she snapped, pulling her hand down from her face, straightening her spine and wheeling on him. 'Or should I call you Mr Abbott.'

There was an awkward pause where his mouth worked, but nothing came out. Then he smiled weakly back at her and shrugged.

'Tell me it is not true,' she demanded, staring at him for what seemed like the first time.

'I cannot,' he said, holding his hands out helplessly before him. 'When I first saw you, a year ago, you clearly needed help. But I knew you would not accept that help from me.'

'So you created a whole new identity to trick me into depending on you,' she said, disgusted with him and with herself for being foolish enough to fall for the ruse.

'To help you,' he repeated. 'It was not a trick. It was...' He shook his head as if he could not tell her what his motivation had been. 'I meant no harm.'

'Given your history with my family, do not dare claim to be unaware of the damage you cause,' she snapped. 'That is just an excuse you use when you have done something unforgivable.'

His eyes darkened for a moment, as if he stifled some sharp retort. But when he spoke, his voice was as mild as it ever was. 'I did not mean your husband harm and I certainly have nothing against you. I tried to tell you, you know. Each time I saw you. When I could not find the words to say it, I hoped you would guess on your own.'

'More the fool you,' she said.

'I know I have made a muddle of things and I mean to make them right.'

'I don't know how you can,' she said, frustrated. 'You have rendered me utterly dependent on your aid. The world now views me as your whore. No man will offer anything but that.'

'But what if you could marry?' he pressed. 'Would you do it?'

'To one of your insipid friends?' she said with a scoff. 'Of course I would. It is that or accept Baxter the next time he comes sniffing at my door.' Or she could simply become what the world already thought she was: Glenmoor's mistress.

She shuddered at the dark surge of emotion that accompanied that thought. Would it really be so horrible to give up and become a creature of pleasure? She could imagine herself naked, fists balled in the satin sheets as she awaited her true fall from grace, fingers opening in shock at the wave after wave of satisfaction that would follow it.

She blinked the fantasy away and stared at the Duke, who was having no such dreams. His eyes were dark and his mood unreadable. 'Baxter,' he said in a cold, hard voice. 'He will pay for what he has done.'

'Do you mean to call him out?' she said, worried. 'That would render me infamous, if I am not already. It will make things even worse than they are.'

'I will find another way to hurt him,' he said. 'A way that does not punish you as well. But he will pay. You can be sure of it.'

She sighed in frustration. Why did it always seem that men could not see further than their own pride when things were darkest? 'How wonderful for you. For both of you, in fact. Go enjoy your vengeance and leave me alone.' She pointed towards the door, hoping he would take the hint and leave.

'But that is not all,' he insisted, and his mood changed again. He was shifting from foot to foot like an embarrassed child.

'Then please, finish what you have to say.' *And leave.* She left the last unspoken, indicating it with a roll of her eyes and a wave of her hand.

'I mean to put you beyond Baxter's reach,' he said with a nervous smile. 'Mrs Ogilvie...' He paused and wet his lips. 'Selina. If you would marry, then marry me.'

She could not help it. She laughed. 'You can't be serious.'

'I am,' he assured her.

'You are the man who ruined my husband,' she said. 'I cannot... I would not... The two of us?' She shook her head. 'I would never.' But hadn't she just imagined something even worse?

'I understand the damage I have done to you and your family. I know I have done nothing to deserve your affection, or even your respect.' His words were coming faster now, as he warmed to the topic. 'But if we were to marry, you would be permanently safe from Baxter and any other man who might think to abuse you.'

'I would be married to you,' she reminded him.

And he would own her until she died, body and soul, in a way that he would not, should she simply become his mistress.

'You would be a duchess,' he said in a coaxing tone.

'An honour I never sought,' she reminded him.

'But an honour, nonetheless. No one would dare think less of you. And your son...'

'Do not dare to mention him,' she said, shocked.

'I have to consider him and so do you,' he said. 'Edward would have advantages that you could never give him as a humble widow, or even the wife of a lesser man. No door would close for him. He will have the best education, his choice of careers. His choice of bride.'

'Because people seek a connection to you,' she said, trying not to sneer.

He nodded and stared down at the paper in front of her. 'Yes. Despite the villain the gossips have tried to make of me, the title is all most people care about. It is not fair, but it is the way of the world. The same will be true of you, when you become my wife.'

He spoke of it so casually that it made her even angrier to be forced to agree with him. He was miles above her socially. And at the gaming table, he had squashed her untitled husband like an ant, totally oblivious to what he had done.

Now he was giving her the devil's own offer. A chance to sacrifice herself to get what she could out of him. Without knowing it, she'd already taken his money. With marriage, she could use his social status to her advantage as well.

People would be horrified at her mercenary nature. She would be in all of the gossip columns as a woman willing to forsake her husband and marry his murderer.

'You are already linked with me in the newspapers,' he reminded her, as if he could read her mind. 'They are calling you my mistress. I can think of no better way to change that than to marry you.'

He was right. She could not forget that her reputation was already forfeit. No man would want her as wife now that it was assumed she had been with Glenmoor. Baxter was still expecting her to weaken and take him in.

There had to be another way. She had but to think of it. But she could not do that with him standing in the doorway, staring at her with those dark eyes, as if he knew the contents of her mind when she did not herself. 'I cannot think,' she said, shaking her head at him and backing away so that the table was between them.

He took a half-step forward, then stopped. 'It is very sudden,' he agreed, in that soft, soothing voice that seemed to vibrate along her nerves like the pull of a bow on violin strings. 'You do not need to tell me now. I will wait as long as you need.'

She did not need time. She needed to be able to say no. But the words would not come.

'I will go now,' he said, and set his calling card on the table. 'Send for me when you have made your decision.'

'Perhaps I will write you a letter,' she said, and saw him flinch. Then he turned and left her.

* * *

When Alex left her house, he glanced back only once, half expecting to find Selina in the window watching his departure. But the curtains to the dining room were shut and there was not so much as a hand resting on the edge of them.

He walked on, all the way to Hyde Park, where he paced the length of the Serpentine, trying to burn away the frisson of energy coursing in his blood at the enormity of what he had done.

He had proposed. Finally.

On one hand, it had been inevitable. Abbott had wanted to do it many times. It was what she had wanted to hear from him. She had hinted often enough that she hoped they were more than friends and he'd known it was true.

He had written the letters suggesting marriage and he had not sent a single one of them. He had one of the better ones in his pocket at the moment, to inspire him for the conversation he had known he must have. He should have simply read the thing to her. It was much more glib than the blunt delivery of facts that he had managed just now.

He had known that the very idea was a disaster. No matter what he'd tried to do to make matters better between them, the best he had managed was to reduce her outright loathing to a mundane, simmering hatred. Even that small achievement was gone now that the world knew he'd been supporting her.

The papers thought the worst—that this had been some kind of insidious plot that involved driving her husband to his death so he might take the widow as his own. The idea was positively biblical. He'd had a good mind to write a letter to *The Times*, informing them that he had never met the woman, or her husband until the night of his death.

He could not explain what had happened after that. Her beauty had dazzled him from the first moment. But she was so much more than that. He had seen it in her letters. That was the woman he had fallen in love with. The one who spoke freely to him, who had shown him her unguarded soul.

Now her spirit was slammed shut tight against him and he might never see that inner light again.

The thought stung. Though she had mocked him for it, he knew someone who deserved to pay for the breach between them. He left the park for an address on Jermyn Street, an upper flat that belonged to Baxter.

The valet announced that his master was out and directed Alex to a tiny sitting room, where he waited for almost an hour before Baxter returned home and greeted him with a smug smile.

'Your Grace. This is an unexpected pleasure.'

'For one of us, perhaps,' Alex said, staring back at the fellow until he looked away.

'I assume you are here about the item in the paper?'

'Which I know came from you,' Alex said. 'May I ask how you came to the conclusion that I was supporting Mrs Ogilvie?'

'It was nothing more than an educated guess at first,' he said, still grinning. 'You always seemed to

be there when I wanted to talk to her. It was very con-
venient.'

'I see.'

'But then, I happened to be playing cards with a
clerk at your bank.'

'And I suspect he bet more than he could afford,'
Alex said with a disgusted shake of his head.

'It is not my fault that the men I play with are not
more circumspect,' Baxter said with a shrug. 'But I
was graciously willing to accept information in lieu
of payment, and this banker was there when you set
up the line of credit for Mrs Ogilvie.'

'I see,' Alex said again, thoroughly annoyed. 'And
you used this information to ruin her.'

'I warned her that this would happen, two days
ago,' he said with a shrug. 'It was within her power
to stop the revelation at any time.'

'By yielding to you,' Alex said, repulsed. Or she
could have come to him. Why had she not written
to Abbott?

Baxter smiled. 'This is really none of your affair.
It is between her and me.'

'There is nothing between her and you,' Alex
snapped.

'Yet,' Baxter said with far too much confidence.
'You will tire of her eventually. I will be there when
you do.'

'On the contrary. I mean to marry her,' he said,
with more confidence than he felt that a wedding
could come to pass.

At this, Baxter laughed. 'You have persuaded her of that, have you?'

'I will,' Alex said, firmly. 'Know that if you bother her, you will be harassing the future Duchess of Glenmoor.'

This, at last, seemed to affect Baxter. His eyes widened and he let out a small, frustrated puff of air. 'You would not…' he said, too confused to finish the sentence.

'Marry her? You think that because you attribute your motives to other men,' Alex said with a smile. 'It is a weakness men like you often have. You try to drag the rest of the world down to your level. Let me add something I think you will understand. Once I marry her, if you come anywhere near her, I will make your life hell. And do not think I am threatening something as tawdry as a duel.'

He thought for a moment and added, 'If the papers are to be believed, I am notoriously devious. I will focus that part of my nature on the best way to bring about your ruin.'

This, finally, seemed to have an effect. Baxter went white and mumbled, 'I mean no harm.'

'No further harm, you mean,' Alex said, voice dripping with irony. 'Now that you have a view of the future that awaits for troublemakers, I am sure we will have no more need to speak to each other. Stay out of my way, Baxter. And leave Selina Ogilvie alone.' Then he called for his hat and stick and left the man shocked into silence.

Chapter Eleven

Once the Duke had left, Selina declared to the servants that she was not at home to visitors and went back to her room, where she threw herself face down on to the bed and wept. Her tears began soft and fast like spring rain. Then they came faster, accompanied by a storm of heaving sobs. She buried her face in the pillows to hide her wailing, for she did not want Edward to hear her. He, of all people, must not see what a fool she was being over a broken heart.

She had not cried like this since her husband had died.

And even that was not true. She had cried over John, of course. It was normal to grieve. But many of the tears she'd shed had nothing to do with his death and everything to do with her fears for the future and the baffling road ahead. She'd cried for herself when he died.

His absence, if she was honest, had not plagued her much. He had been gone from her for a long time already. Death had just made their parting irrevocable.

But for Abbott, she felt as though she would cry her heart out of her body. He had been her friend. And John, poor John, had never been that. He had been her husband and her lover, but he had never seemed particularly interested in her as an individual. He had not asked after her day or her feelings as Abbott had. He had not laughed at her jokes or amused her in response. And he certainly had not cared enough to rescue her when she was in desperate straits. He had created the problem and then he had left her.

Then Abbott had appeared out of nowhere, to save her.

Now she knew why. It had just been Glenmoor, trying to make up for his part in the disaster. The rest had been lies and nonsense. He had made her believe that Abbott was real. In a way, he had been, for he had lived whole in her imagination.

Now he was dead. She could not conjure him up, as she had so many nights in the last year, when she had dreaded being alone. She could not imagine his arms around her without thinking of the Duke. He had been her one true love for almost a year, and now he was gone.

And her heart was gone with him. Now that the tears were slowing, she was an empty shell, as if her soul had poured out of her like salt water. Her future was just as barren, a winter landscape where there had just been spring.

There was a cautious knock on her door and a maid delivered the afternoon post, offering her an encouraging smile as if there might be something there that would bring her back to happiness.

No letter from Abbott, she thought bitterly. But there was a note from Mary, a reminder that they were to take a walk in Hyde Park the next day, as they had planned. The knowledge that her friend was willing to stand beside her in this difficult time was the only bright spot in Selina's day, the only proof that there was a reason to get up and keep going.

When she went to the appointed spot, Mary was there on the bench, ready to meet her. At the sight of Selina, she stood and reached out to take her hands, pulling her down to sit beside her. 'Oh, my dear. What are we to do with you?'

'You have read the newspaper?' Selina replied with a worried frown.

'My husband did not want me to come to you because of it,' her friend replied. 'I told him that it was nonsense. I know for a fact that you were not Glenmoor's mistress and that there was nothing to the rumour.' Then she gave Selina a long, silent look, waiting for her to confirm that as the truth.

'I am not,' she agreed, feeling foolish. 'He was sending me money. But I had no idea who it was really coming from. He called himself Abbott in his letters. And I thought, eventually...' She bit her lip, unable to explain what she had expected.

'You thought there would be an offer of some kind,' Mary finished her sentence. 'An honourable one, of course.'

'Of course,' Selina said hurriedly. She had wanted marriage. But when it was dark and she was alone in her bed, she had wanted other things entirely. She was embarrassed at the amount of time she had spent fantasising about nights of passion with the mysterious Abbott. If he would have come to her, she would have given him anything he wanted.

But he had never asked. And now the Duke was trying to take his place.

'And all the time, you did not know who he was,' Mary marvelled. 'He is your secret correspondent, is he not?'

'No. I mean, yes.' Selina took a breath. 'I mean, I would never have accepted the money had I known who it was from.'

Mary gave her a baffled look in response, which suited her contradictory feelings on the matter.

'And now he has offered to marry me, as if that will make everything all right again,' Selina concluded, with a disgusted frown.

Mary stared for a moment, still confused. 'The Duke?'

'Glenmoor,' Selina confirmed. 'He came to my home and proposed.'

There was yet another pause, then Mary's face split into an amazed grin. 'But that is too wonderful.'

'It is not,' Selina insisted, staring back at her friend.

'All this time, he has been writing to you and you have harboured a tendre for him,' Mary said, giving her a gentle shove.

'I have not,' Selina said. 'I do not like Glenmoor at all.'

'But you liked him when he was writing to you,' Mary said gently.

'Well, I do not like him now,' Selina said firmly. 'I was sharing my innermost thoughts with someone I thought I knew.'

'But you did not know him,' Mary said, even more confused. 'You told me yourself that he was anonymous. Now he has revealed himself.'

'And I do not know what to do,' she said with a sigh.

'That, at least, I can advise you on,' Mary said with a bright smile, patting her hand. 'He is young and rich, and he is offering to save you. You must accept this offer of marriage and clear your name. The Duke has taken care of you before and he will take care of you now.'

'But...' Selina shuddered. 'He was the one who was responsible for what happened to John. I cannot imagine myself lying with a man who would ruin another like that.' But that was just another lie. When she looked at the Duke, she felt strange, expectant and very, very guilty.

'You will learn to feel differently in time, I am sure.' Mary wrinkled her brow. 'The title will make up for any scandal involving your late husband. And if you do not like lying with him, it need not be forever. Once you give him a son, he might not bother with you any more. You could pursue someone who suits you better. Many couples take lovers of their choosing, after the succession is secure.'

It would be just like Glenmoor to cast her aside when he had what he wanted from her. Considering the elaborate ruse he had concocted to force her into marriage, there was nothing she did not think him capable of.

But that did not mean she should disrespect John's memory by choosing this man, out of all the men in London, to be her next husband. 'I won't,' she said at last. 'There is no way I can go through with this. Not with him.'

'Well, I could,' Mary said firmly. 'I am sure, once you have had time to consider the situation, you will come round to thinking sensibly about this.' Mary was patting her hand again, this time in encouragement. 'There are many marriages in the *ton* that are little more than business arrangements. Perhaps yours will be one of those. That is, if you wish. If it were me?' Mary giggled and raised her eyebrows suggestively. 'The Duke is quite handsome, really. And rather dangerous.'

'It is not exciting to have a dangerous husband, if that is what you think,' Selina said with a disapproving sniff. 'When I married John, I made sure that there was nothing objectionable in his character.'

'Well...' said Mary with a small shake of her head, as if to say, *And look how that turned out.*

'My marriage to him was not all bad,' Selina continued, though the statement sounded weak, even to her. 'And what will happen to Edward?' she added.

'Did the Duke speak of him?' Mary asked.

'He promised to take care of him,' she said.

'Then you must trust that he will do that. Some men are far less accommodating when it comes to children from previous marriages. If he is already thinking of what is best for Edward, that is a very good thing.'

Selina sighed. Perhaps she should do this for Edward. But what of her own future? There was more to being the wife of a duke, she was sure. More advantages than disadvantages. But she could not think any further ahead than the wedding night and the marriage bed.

When she did not respond, Mary nudged her and said, 'Do you even know what you would do without his help? If you refuse him, whom would you turn to?'

That was just the problem. She could not think of a single person that would care for her. She would not even have Abbott, who might as well have vanished now that she knew his true identity. It was quite possible that the Duke would cut her off without a penny, if she refused him.

But there would always be Baxter.

'I have no one,' she said with a shudder. 'And I doubt that I will get a better offer, now that the *ton* thinks I am the Duke's whore.' Which they would not have done, had he not decided to meddle in her life. But if he had not...

'The whole thing makes my head ache,' she said at last.

'Living in a great house and having dozens of servants and no worries about money will do much to clear your mind,' Mary said with a reassuring nod. 'Say yes to the Duke.'

'Who I hate,' she added.

'And who will be bound by God and law to keep you for the rest of your days. You will have ample time to make his life miserable, if that is what you choose.'

And he did deserve some misery, after what he had done to John and after the trick he had played on her by inventing Abbott. Normally, a duke was above the law and far out of reach of the censure of ordinary mortals. But as his wife, she would be inside this bubble of protection.

She would be able to pay him back.

For the first time in two days, she smiled.

Mary nodded back in relief. 'You are coming around to sanity at last. Do not brood on things you cannot control. For now, think of the ways that this can make your life better.'

And ways that would make his life worse. She would accept him, if only for that. He would live with a thorn in his side for the rest of his days and he would know that it was his own actions that had caused the pain.

'I will marry the Duke,' she agreed, with an emphatic nod. 'And I swear I will be the wife he deserves.' She smiled again, satisfied with her plan. Then she rose, reaching to help Mary to her feet. 'And now, let us walk and talk of other things.'

'Certainly, Your Grace,' Mary said with a giggle, and changed the subject.

* * *

A day passed. And then another. And still he heard nothing from Selina.

Alex's palms itched to write a letter, as he used to, before she'd known who he was. The habits of a year were hard to break, especially habits as pleasant as writing to Selina had been.

Now that he'd stopped, he felt like an opium addict who had given up the pipe. He was adrift and alone and with the growing fear that she would never contact him again. If she spurned him, what would he do? Would he have to watch her founder without his help, to see her reputation tarnished by what he had done to it?

He would not allow that. He did not know what he would do if she did not accept marriage, but he would never abandon her.

In any case, it was too late to go back to the happy time they'd had together when they'd exchanged letters. The part of his life where he had been Abbott was gone, just as his time as a don at Oxford had ended.

He'd been happy then, too, even though he had expected a future without wife and children, his life devoted solely to learning. There had been something very satisfying about having nothing but the higher calling of philosophy to guide him. He no longer had to measure his success against the impossible standards set by his stepfather, the old Duke of Fallon.

When that man had deigned to notice him, it had been to compare Alex to his own son and to find him

wanting. Fortunately, Evan had had none of his father's prejudices and had embraced him as brother
from the moment they'd met. He had been totally
supportive of his plans to teach, other than a fit of
laughter when Alex had entailed the requirements
of the position.

'Celibacy?' Evan had said, doubling over with
mirth. 'You?'

'I admit it will be a change,' he'd said, for in his
early years he had never wanted for female companionship. 'But I will have my books for company. And
friends, of course.' His life would be ruled by a search
for wisdom and he'd been secure in the knowledge
that it would never hurt him the way people could.

'How very satisfying,' Evan had responded, still
laughing. 'You must tell me how it works out for you.'

It had worked well enough for five years. And
then his cousin had left him the coronet and he'd
been reminded that the rules for a peer were the very
opposite of those for a don. The goal was to be fruit-
ful and multiply. To create and procreate, and leave
something behind when one died, other than scholarly writings.

And if she said yes, he would do that with Selina.

He sat down at his desk, surprised at how moved
he was by the thought of being with her. It was more
than he'd ever imagined, yet everything he wanted.
In a few days, he might come to her as a worthy sup-
plicant. He would break the long, romantic drought
he'd been experiencing to hold her in his arms. He

would be able to kiss that white throat and bury himself in her body.

He was awed. He was honoured. And he was most definitely aroused.

'Your Grace.' When he looked up, the butler stood politely at the door of his study, awaiting his acknowledgement.

Alex nodded, wiping the silly grin from his face.

'A Mrs Ogilvie wishes to speak to you.'

His passionate reaction withered as quickly as it had grown. His mouth went dry and his hands became clammy. He eyed the brandy bottle and rejected it. Whatever she had to say, he must accept it in cold sobriety. 'Show her to the red salon. I will be there directly.'

He waited five minutes, until he was physically and mentally in control again, then made his way to the room where his future awaited.

When he entered the salon, she was standing by the fireplace, her hand on the mantel as if she needed the marble shelf for support. Their eyes met in the mirror above the fireplace and he saw her look of worry replaced with resolve as she stared back at him.

He walked to a chair by the fire and gestured to the sofa.

She shook her head and walked to the centre of the room, but did not sit.

This did not bode well. But he nodded in agreement and shut the door behind him, standing with his hands behind his back. 'Have you reached a decision?'

She nodded, pausing for so long that his nerves were near the breaking point before she spoke.

'I will marry you.'

He breathed a sigh of relief.

'On one condition.'

Condition? He was the one saving her reputation. If anyone was to set a condition on the terms of their union, it should be him. But it was Selina he was marrying and there was nothing on earth he would not do if it meant being near her.

He took another breath and said, 'Go on.'

'It will be a marriage in name only. I will never love you. And I will never lie with you.'

She could not be serious. He waited, expecting her to admit that she was being unrealistic so that he might bargain anything else away but the thing she had just said. But she stayed silent, staring at him with those magnificent grey eyes. 'And what of all the things you wrote to me?' he said. 'Your feelings were quite different in your letters.'

'I made no promises,' she said, straight-faced. 'And the man that I wrote to made no offers.'

'Me,' he reminded her. 'You wrote to me.'

She shook her head. 'I would never have said those things if I had known it was you.'

He had known that was true. But to hear her say it still hurt. 'The man you expected to find did not exist.'

'I am painfully aware of the fact,' she said, staring at him in disgust. 'Because of your deception, I have no choice but to marry you. But I am not doing so willingly and I will not let you forget the fact.'

What had he expected? If he'd thought that she would dismiss all that had happened and forgive him, he had been a fool. He had only wanted to help. But she was right—he had left her no choice but marriage.

But could he accept the union she demanded? Even if he could live without the marital act, to forgo children went against all his title required and all he had wanted for himself. When he'd left Oxford, it had pleased him to know that at least he would have a family, a dream he had given up when he'd begun teaching. Now he must give up that dream again.

But he could do it. He would do anything she asked, if it meant that her reputation was restored and she remained safe from Baxter and men like him. It would be like being a don again. Then he had been a celibate follower of knowledge. Now he would be a monk, worshipping at the feet of an unfeeling goddess who longed to see him suffer. And he must never let her know. If he did, she might find a way to make his life even worse.

He schooled his face to show none of the turmoil he was feeling and said, 'As you wish.'

'You agree?' She seemed honestly surprised by the fact, as if she had come to him expecting to be refused.

'You have my word,' he said, staring back at her, daring her to look away.

'When must I…? Will we…?' She was flustered now. Apparently, she had made no plans as to what would happen if he accepted her offer.

'I will take care of everything. An announcement of our engagement will be posted in *The Times*, and a special licence will be procured. The wedding will be at St George's. The whole matter will be settled inside a week.'

'But all my things...'

'Will be brought here. I will explain the situation to my servants, and footmen will be dispatched to help you with the move. Positions will be found for your staff in my household. There is nothing to worry about.'

He waited for a moment to see what other excuses she might make. When there were none, he said, 'And now, if you will excuse me, I have other business to attend to.'

'Of course,' she said in a faint voice, as he escorted her to the door and out of his house.

When she was gone, he went back to his study and sank into the desk chair, stunned. He had agreed to the impossible. He was going to marry the most beautiful woman he'd ever known, the woman whom he had dreamed of since the first moment he saw her. And he was to remain apart from her, living as strangers.

There would be no family, no heir, no days full of children and laughter. For hadn't that been what he'd imagined as he'd written to her, that she might some-day care for his son as she did her own? Instead, she meant to deny him that, to give him a house as cold and empty as the one he'd grown up in.

He slammed his fist against the desk, so hard that

the inkwell jumped. Then he unclenched his fist and released the anger along with the tension. If this was what she thought she wanted, then he would do it. Because there was a chance, the slimmest of hopes, that once she knew him better, she might change her mind and love him. That would be worth risking a lifetime of misery.

Chapter Twelve

A week later, with his brother as witness, Alex stood by the altar of St George's Church, waiting for the woman who would change his life.

He stared at the door, trying to control the tapping of his foot as he waited for Selina to arrive. He was not impatient as much as he was nervous. He would not be surprised if she changed her mind. He could picture her writing to tell him so. It would be the height of irony for her to crush his hopes with a letter.

In another life, before she had learned his identity, they would have laughed about the idea that she might someday leave him. She would have assured him that there was nothing he could do that would ruin their friendship.

He would have known it was a lie. But he'd have chosen to believe it and smiled as he wrote back to her, calling her foolish, but dear. Now all that was lost to him, and he had not felt so alone in years. Not since his father had died and he'd had to face his mother's new husband, a man who hated his very existence and took pleasure in reminding him of that fact.

'It is the bride who is supposed to be nervous, not the bridegroom,' his stepbrother reminded him, with a smile.

'As I remember it, you were not worried that your bride would show up for the wedding.'

'I was secretly hoping that she would not,' Evan said, shaking his head. 'I have since learned how foolish I was. And how fortunate that she agreed to marry me.'

'I already know that I am fortunate,' Alex said, staring at the church door and wishing it would open.

'But your bride does not,' his brother reminded him.

'I am sure the idea of marriage will grow on her,' he said, hoping he was right.

'Most women would be satisfied to become a duchess,' Evan replied.

'Selina is not most women,' Alex said, and could not help but smile. 'She is not interested in being a duchess. At the very least, I know I am not getting a title hunter.'

'But are you getting a helpmeet?' Evan asked. 'It is not too late to call off this farce and find another way to deal with the gossip.'

'You know that is not true,' Alex said firmly. 'As long as she is unmarried, her reputation will be suspect. It is because of me that she is at risk from Baxter. I cannot allow that.'

'Very noble of you,' Evan said, in a tone that made

the word *noble* sound like *foolish*. Then he added, 'I do not wish you to be taken advantage of.'

'I am a grown man and older than you,' Alex said, scoffing. 'I know what I am doing.'

'And that is why you have got yourself into the papers over Ogilvie's widow,' he said with a shake of his head.

Then the door to the church opened and Selina entered, accompanied by her son.

Alex felt himself leaning forward, unable to disguise the yearning he felt at the sight of her. Then the move was cut short by an elbow in his ribs.

'I see the problem now,' Evan muttered. 'It is as I always expected—you have feelings for her that go far beyond honour.'

'And what if I do?' he said, staring at the woman approaching up the aisle towards him.

'That is both the best and the worst reason to marry,' his brother said. 'It all depends on the feelings of the woman involved.'

Now they both looked to Selina, and Evan sighed. 'And this does not bode well.'

His bride was wearing a grey dress and had not bothered with flowers.

'It could be worse,' Evan said. 'It could be black.'

'With the special licence, she had very little time to buy a gown,' Alex said. But she'd been out of mourning for some time and had other more cheerful dresses in her wardrobe. It was hard to see her current choice as anything other than a display of ambivalence.

'I am sure that will change, once you are married,'

Evan said with a barely perceptible roll of his eyes. 'If she discovers she can hurt you with shopping, she will spend every waking moment on Bond Street. If not that, she will look for another way to wound you. She will lead you a merry chase and your life will be misery.'

'Thank you for telling me this now,' Alex said, eyes fixed straight ahead. 'I would never have realised it on my own.'

'It is only to remind you that it is not too late to back out.'

That was a lie. It had been too late from the first moment he'd met her. He had always wanted it to end like this, with the two of them at an altar. But he had imagined the smile on his bride's face and not the dead-pan stare she was giving him now, as if she was walking to her own funeral.

She approached cautiously, pausing at a front pew to install her son, who sat, legs swinging, watching him with curiosity.

He gave the boy a nod and a smile, hoping that their brief meeting in the park a few weeks ago had instilled some small amount of good will. Edward smiled back and patted his pocket, to assure him he still had the compass.

Then Alex turned back to Selina and felt his smile slip in the face of her obvious disdain. She reached his side, her expression unchanging, then looked up at him with resignation, as though she had also decided that it was too late to stop what was about to happen, and announced, 'I am ready to begin.'

'I brought Fallon and his wife to serve as witnesses,' he said, stating the obvious.

'We are family to Alex, after all,' Evan said in a warm and welcoming tone. 'We will be your family as well, now. If you need anything, do not hesitate to speak up.'

'Or forever hold my peace,' Selina supplied, probably aware of what everyone was thinking.

Evan's wife stepped into the gap in the conversation and smiled as if she had not just heard Selina's ambivalence, holding out a bouquet to her. 'I did not know if you had time to find flowers. Alex says you live in a small house with no garden. But ours...' She shrugged.

For a moment, Selina softened, smiling back at the other woman. 'The Fallon roses are very well known. I visited the garden myself when I attended your ball.' She took the bouquet, which was a marvellous arrangement of pink and white blooms, held it to her face and inhaled deeply. Then she handed it back to the Duchess to keep during the ceremony. 'Thank you for your thoughtfulness.'

She turned to Alex again, her face hardening, and said, 'It is time to begin', negating the doubts and stepping towards the altar.

Evan gave his brother a sympathetic smile and Alex stepped forward to take his place at her side.

He had heard the ceremony often enough at the weddings of others, but had paid it little attention. Now, as he was reciting the vows in the empty church, there was a solemnity and importance to it that he had not expected. He wondered if Selina felt the same, or if she was merely repeating the lines as they were fed to her and waiting for the service to be over.

She had been through this once already, with John Ogilvie. And she'd said surprisingly little about that marriage, even after all the letters they'd exchanged. Had she loved him? he wondered. Or had that marriage been as empty as this one?

As she said her part, her expression never changed from that grim frown that she had worn when entering the building. During the bishop's sermon on procreation, she stared at him with such intensity that the man lost his place and looked to Alex in confusion.

Alex offered him an encouraging nod, as if he had not noticed his future wife's foul mood, smiling hard enough for both of them until the officiant continued.

A short time later, the rite was done, the licence was signed and he was declaring them man and wife and encouraging Alex to 'kiss the bride'.

He had never been so nervous in his life. The kiss might be the last one he gave her, if things remained as he'd promised they would. He did not want to waste the moment on a peck on the cheek. But a church was no place for intimacy and he did not want to embarrass her or himself by giving her the kiss he wanted. So he turned slowly, placed his hand on her shoulder and pressed his lips to hers.

As he did it, he could feel her flinch.

He paused for a moment, to mark the solemnity of the event, then pulled away and let his hand fall to his side. 'There,' he said softly.

She blinked at him, her frigid demeanour cracking for an instant, and he could see something like real surprise in her eyes and perhaps a touch of fear. Then it disappeared again and she was as cold as ever.

With the ceremony over, the Duke offered his arm and Selina took it, along with the bouquet of roses that the Duchess of Fallon had been holding for her. The flowers gave her something to focus on other than the touch of the man at her side. She was strangely conscious of it, after the intimacy of the kiss.

She had known he would kiss her. There was always a kiss at the end of a wedding ceremony. But the knowledge was purely academic. She had not expected to feel anything from it, sure that it would be brief and polite, more a symbol of something than the thing itself.

But there had been a moment, when his lips had touched hers, where everything had changed. She had felt a spark of life striking her dead soul like tinder.

And then it had been gone again.

She gripped the flowers tightly and resisted the urge to touch her lips, longing for a mirror to see if there was anything showing in her eyes or face that would tell the others of the difference inside her.

Had he felt it, too?

He looked the same. But then, she did not think that men felt as deeply as women did about small things.

He escorted her out of the church and led her to the same splendid carriage that she had ridden in when they had met after the Mathematical Society meeting, taking her elbow to help her into her seat. Before she could climb up, Edward scrambled up between them, taking a seat on the far side and leaning out the window to wave at the passers-by.

'Edward,' she whispered, ignoring the Duke's hand and hauling herself up in an unladylike lunge to get to her son. 'Where are your manners? You have ridden in a carriage before and needn't make such a scene.'

'Not in one so grand as this,' he insisted, bouncing on the seat and making the springs creak, then he looked back at the Duke. 'You did not tell me that you were marrying the man who gave me the compass.' He favoured her new husband with a wide grin of approval.

She tensed as she waited for the rebuke that was sure to come and the reminder to keep the child in line and out of sight. She should never have brought him to the church, but leaving him alone with the housekeeper as she did something that would change his life had not seemed the right thing to do either.

But instead of demanding obedience, the Duke smiled back. 'You have it with you?'

Edward nodded. 'Mother said I could not have it out during the service.'

'And I will tell you that you cannot have it out at the wedding breakfast,' the Duke agreed. 'But we are in neither of those places now and it might be interesting to know the direction to my house.'

At this prompting, her son pulled the compass out of his pocket and carefully aligned the needle with true north, watching it turn as they wound through the streets towards the Duke's townhouse, where a meal had been set out.

The Duke leaned back in his seat, content, and looked across the carriage to Selina. 'The ceremony went well, I think.'

'Weddings are all the same,' she said, trying to remember what it had been like to marry John. There had been a similar feeling of panic. But then, it had been because of all the things she had not known about married life. Now it was because of all the things she did know. Was this man serious when he had agreed that this would be a marriage in name only? Or did he mean to fall on her like a ravening wolf the first time they were alone together?

More importantly, why did the idea hold such fascination for her? When she closed her eyes, she could imagine those long-fingered hands gripping her skin and those deep brown eyes boring into hers, as he demanded her surrender.

She glanced across the carriage at him and then quickly looked away.

'I am glad you brought your son,' he added, smiling at Edward again. 'It is easier to understand life's changes when one feels one is a part of them and not just flotsam in the tide of others'.'

Edward looked at him, confused. 'What is flotsam?'

'The things that break off a ship during a wreck,' the Duke provided.

'So, weddings are like a shipwreck?' Edward said, wrinkling his nose.

'That remains to be seen,' Selina said, glaring at

the Duke. It did not help that he was speaking the truth in front of her son for she'd had trouble enough explaining to him how things had come so far, so fast.

'Not all of them,' the Duke said, still smiling. 'Some of them are more like rescues. It is easier for people to survive when they cling together rather than floating alone.'

'And even better if one of them has a compass,' Edward said, totally missing the point.

The Duke nodded, trying to stifle a laugh.

'What the Duke means,' Selina said with an exasperated sigh, 'is that we were poor and now we will not be. We will be living in a great house with him.'

Edward's smile faltered. 'What will happen to my things?'

'As we speak, they are being boxed up, and will meet you in your new home. It will all be just as it was,' Selina said, forcing a smile.

'But better,' the Duke added.

Edward stared at him, unconvinced.

'And first, there will be a breakfast. With cake,' the Duke added.

The idea of cake for breakfast seemed to cheer him and he went back to watching his compass.

She stared at the Duke, annoyed that he had found a way around the boy so easily.

He looked back at her, smiled and shrugged. 'Everyone likes cake.'

In his defence, the cake was very good, as was the rest of the food. If she had to be the head of a household, it would not be a hardship to be mistress here. It would be ideal if it weren't for the man who she had married.

He sat at her side, smiling and polite, making sure that her glass stayed full and she wanted for nothing. She ate in silence, turning away from him to be sure that Edward was happy, his plate heaped full of delicacies and his compass properly stowed away.

He was still smiling from the carriage ride and looked down the table at the Duke, his gaze one part curiosity and one part awe. She wanted to shout at him that he must beware. That the man he might grow to idolise was in truth a betrayer who had made him fatherless.

Then she bit her tongue and sipped her wine and said nothing. She was doing this for Edward, after all. The Duke's promise of a school and a future for her son was more than she could have got for him on her own. Even with the monetary help of Abbott, she could not have been sure that she could have opened the doors for him that would swing wide for a boy sponsored by the Duke of Glenmoor.

When the breakfast was over, Fallon and his wife rose to go and the Duchess paused to assure her again that if she needed a friend, she would find one ready. 'We are both most fond of Alex and eager for him to be happy,' she said, as if totally unaware of the reason for the marriage. 'We want you to share in that happiness as well.'

'Thank you,' Selina said.

'And I am sure, given his past, that he will be an excellent stepfather to your son,' the Duchess added.

'His past?' She struggled to remember what she had heard of the Duke that might have brought about such a comment.

'He was a stepson himself, once,' the Duchess said with a nod in his direction. 'It was not a happy time for him and I am sure he vows that life in his own household will be different. When you have children of your own, he will know what to do.'

'Children,' she said in a numb voice. The Duke was unlikely to tell even his closest friends of their arrangement. When they did not have a family, the world would think him sterile.

Then she reminded herself that whatever unhappiness or embarrassment befell him, he had earned it by his duplicity to her.

She turned to the Duchess with a forced smile and said, 'That is good to know.'

'We will leave you alone now,' the Duchess said with a smile and a blush. 'It is your wedding day, after all. I am sure you are eager for us to be gone.'

Selina resisted the urge to grab her hand and beg her to remain. What was she going to do in this great house, alone with Glenmoor?

He came to stand at her side now, smiling at Fallon and his wife, his expression unchanging until their carriage had pulled away from the kerb. Then he turned to Selina, his smile fading. 'If I might see you in my study for a few minutes?'

She followed him down the hall into the room.

He gestured her to a chair and closed the door behind him.

She took her seat and waited for the storm to break. His polite façade could not last forever. Then she would pay a reckoning for pushing him to anger with her stubbornness.

Instead, he took his seat as well and looked at her enquiringly. 'How much do you know of the duties that will be yours, now that you are Duchess of Glenmoor?'

Why could she think of nothing beyond the fact that she was supposed to provide his heir? That could not be what he was speaking of. They had already settled that matter, hadn't they? For the moment, all she could do was stare at him blankly and wait for him to speak again.

'You will be responsible for managing the servants and running the household,' he reminded her. 'I assume you are somewhat familiar with those jobs, but on a smaller scale.'

She nodded.

'There is this house and the manor where we will go in summer. There, you will have tenants to visit and I will wish you to see to the more personal side of their care...'

He rambled on about visiting the sick, tending to the still-room and other harmless duties that did not seem particularly daunting. The idea of playing Lady Bountiful was much more comforting than being the recipient of charity had been. Perhaps Mary had been right and this was to be a business arrangement and not a union at all.

'And while we are in London, you will be responsible for our social life,' he concluded.

'Our life?' she said, surprised.

He was looking at her with a matter-of-fact smile. 'Our life. We are united now, in ways that you have obviously not considered. When we receive invitations, they will come to both of us and acceptances will need to be written. A schedule must be kept and I wish to leave that to you.'

She blinked, thinking of her limited acquaintance with the women of the *ton* and wondering what they would say about her sudden rise in stature.

'Unless, that is, you intend on hiding in my home, afraid of what the papers might say next of you.' He was staring at her now, waiting for some proof that she understood. 'The gossip will not stop. But if you wish to avoid the more salacious speculation about our marriage, I recommend you accept these.' He pushed a pile of invitations across the desk towards her.

She stared at them for a moment, then scooped them into her lap. 'Very well.'

'And we must throw a ball by the end of the Season,' he added. 'People will assume that you want to show off your good fortune in bagging me.' His face had not changed as he'd spoken, but for some reason, she felt he was laughing at her, somewhere deep inside, in a place she could not see.

'A ball. I have no idea how...'

'You will have to learn,' he said. 'Ask Maddie.' At her baffled look, he clarified, 'The Duchess of Fallon. She will tell you everything I have forgotten, I am sure.'

Silence fell between them. When it was clear that he had nothing more to say, she rose, automatically resisting the urge to drop a curtsy to him in deference. Why did she feel so meek? He had not ordered her to do anything. All the same, she found herself falling easily into the role of obedient wife and servant, when she had meant to cross him at every turn.

How had he done it? Was it some ducal trickery? Or was it simply that the requests he'd made were all too reasonable to refuse?

He smiled at her, as if aware of her confusion, and said, 'It is the title, I think. And this damn desk and chair. It is hard not to be intimidating when sitting here and equally hard not to be cowed when sitting on the other side.'

'I am not frightened of you,' she said, frowning at him to prove it.

'That is good. Because there is nothing to be frightened of,' he assured her. 'Despite what you think of me, I am not an ogre. And our marriage need not be unhappy, unless you choose to make it so.'

'This union was forced upon me,' she reminded him. 'It was this, or ruin. I am little better than a prisoner in this new life. Do not expect me to be happy in captivity.'

'You made the cage as much as I did,' he said, and she saw the slightest of furrows in his brow, hinting

at unexpressed anger. 'You made no effort to contact me when you knew Baxter had discovered the
truth. I might have stopped him, had you written to
tell me of his plans.'

It was true. She had been so eager to discover Abbott's identity that she had been willing to risk anything. She had gambled and lost, just as John had.
And now that it was too late to do anything, he was
throwing her mistake back in her face. 'I am well
aware of my mistake,' she snapped, and turned to go.
'And now I am dismissed, Your Grace?'

Behind her he added, 'Dinner is at eight. After, on
nights we do not leave the house, we will spend the
evening in the sitting room, as a family. I expect Edward to join us. And I do not expect any friction between us to be witnessed by him. Is that amenable?'

The last was delivered in a tone unlike the other
statements. There was a weight to it that turned it into
an unavoidable command.

'We will see,' she said, without turning back to him.
Then she left before he could issue any more edicts.

As the door closed with a firm click, Alex slumped
in his chair, drained. He should have spoken to her
in the dining room, or the morning room, anywhere
but this damned study, which was the most pompous
and uncomfortable room in the house. He had meant
to be approachable and friendly, and to have a perfectly ordinary conversation about the expectations
of their marriage and her place in it. Instead, he had

been pedantic and dictatorial, not at all like her beloved Abbott, who had listened more than he'd talked.

Like it or not, they would have to work together to repair the damage he had done to her reputation by his heavy-handed generosity. He meant to ensure that she was not just accepted as a member of the *ton*, but placed at the pinnacle of the social hierarchy. She was a duchess now, after all, and he would be damned before he saw her slighted by her inferiors.

None of his plans spoke to what she wanted. It was the same mistake he had made by helping her. He had only compounded it by forcing her into marriage.

He closed his eyes and took a deep breath, trying to calm his nerves and focus his mind. The past could not be changed, but the future could. He would do better by her. He must. If he was ever to have the life he wanted with her, he must take the time to regain her trust.

Chapter Thirteen

After leaving the study, Selina threw herself into her duties, if only to distract from the long night to come. She toured the house with the housekeeper, spoke to the cook about supper, approved a week's worth of menus and went to the morning room to answer the invitations the Duke had given her.

Despite herself, she felt excited at the prospect of managing the house and was relieved to see that the servants were devoted to the Duke and eager to help her adjust to her new role. This life could be a good one, were it not for the husband she would have to share the house with.

Then she went to the nursery to visit with Edward and found her son was as enchanted by the prospect of a man in the house as she was appalled by it. He was having his dinner early in the rooms that would be his own private kingdom since there would be no brothers or sisters for him to share them with.

He left his plate to show her the toys that the Duke had assured him he was allowed to play with and the maps and globes and astrolabe that were in the school room, and added the promises of the Duke that they would be even more interesting than the compass if he was inclined to use them.

'He has been here?' Selina said, frowning back at the stairs and wondering what reason he had for coming to visit with her son.

'He says the astrolabe is for sailors,' Edward continued, his eyes wide. 'And I told him that I would like to be one of those.'

'You did,' she said, feeling a moment of panic at the thought. He was only eight now, but she had heard of boys no older than fourteen who left their mothers and went to sea.

'He said that if that was the case, I must study very hard. And he said that I would have a tutor and go to a fine school when I was a little older,' Edward said, showing no fear at the thought of abandoning his mama to see the world.

'When you are older,' she agreed, resisting the urge to pull him to her and to tell him that she would never let him go.

'He said that he would discuss it with you at dinner and that I could come down after and be with the family for a while in the sitting room, until it was time for bed.'

'Did he?' She could not keep the flat tone out of her voice at this. Her plan had been to ignore the Duke's demand for ceremonial togetherness and dine upstairs before an early bedtime.

'You do not want me to?' Edward said, his eyes

wide with worry. 'When we were at home, you always let me stay in the sitting room.'

'It is not that,' she said quickly, not wanting to hurt his feelings. 'It is just that I do not yet know how the Duke wishes his house to be ordered.'

'But he said...' her son interrupted, undercutting her argument.

She sighed. 'If he says you are to come down after your dinner, then you most certainly may.'

Edward smiled at her and then hurried back to his table so that he might be ready to come down when he was called.

Since she did not intend to leave her boy alone for the evening, she would have to go downstairs as Glenmoor wished. It was already too late to eat with Edward and she could not simultaneously shut herself up in her room and keep an eye on her son. So she went to her room to dress, thoroughly annoyed.

Her maid, Molly, was already aware of her feelings about the Duke. She'd made no effort to disguise them while she'd lived alone. But tonight, there was something in the girl's eye that hinted at disapproval of Selina's position.

Had she been talking with the rest of the staff? Were her quarters and pay better here than they had been when Selina had been both master and mistress to her? Or was she under the impression that Selina's opinions had changed as easily as walking through a door or signing a marriage licence?

Tonight, she dressed Selina with as much care as she had for her first ball, taking extra time with her hair and fussing over each ribbon of her dinner gown to make sure that the bows were perky and pressed, so she might make the best possible impression on her new husband.

For Selina's part, she did not care what that man thought of her. But it was easier to face him knowing that her appearance was unassailable. She descended the stairs to the ground floor slowly, as if she were making a grand entrance that required ceremony. But if she was honest, she was simply prolonging the inevitable. From the foyer, it was just a few feet down the hall to the dining room, where a footman hurried to open the door to admit her.

As she entered, the Duke looked up from the book he had been reading, hurriedly slipping it beneath the table to sit on the chair next to him.

'Excuse me,' he said with a wry smile. 'Reading at the table is a bad habit I've got into in the months since I came here. It is very rude, but it made the room seem less empty to me.'

She said nothing in response, but took the chair opposite the one where the book rested, glancing down the long table at all the empty seats and noting that her place had been deliberately set beside his and not at the far end, as she'd imagined.

'It will be less running about for the servants if we share the end of the table,' he said with another smile. 'And less cold food for us, I assume.' He stared at her, waiting for a response.

She unfolded her napkin and placed it in her lap, then stared back at him, silent.

'This is going to be a long evening if you leave all the talking to me,' he said, still smiling. 'I was a philosophy professor before I came into my title and my friends assure me, if I am allowed to ramble on the subject, I become quite tiresome.'

'Do as you will. It is your house, after all,' she said, staring down into her plate.

'And yours as well,' he reminded her. 'You are mistress here and not some sort of prisoner, no matter how you choose to imagine yourself.' His smile tightened somewhat, as if he was still hiding his annoyance from earlier in the day.

She could not help the flush of joy she felt at finally being able to hurt him, even a little. His most irritating feature was his unperturbability. 'It was never my intention to become so,' she reminded him. 'I was happy enough where I was.'

'In a house that I paid for,' he reminded her, his voice crackling with tension. 'If you are content to have me run your life, it is much more economical to do it here than at a distance.'

It was as if they had been fencing and she'd finally drawn blood. She felt a moment's triumph, tinged with a strange bitterness, and the desire to do it again. 'I never asked you to take over my finances,' she snapped back. 'I did not want or need your help.'

'Because you were doing so well on your own,' he replied with a sarcastic smile. 'Perhaps you have forgotten how it was when I came into your life. You were destined for the poorhouse.'

'Thank you for reminding me,' she said with equal

sarcasm. 'I also recall that you were one of those men who helped land me there, by taking my husband's money.'

'Aha!' he said. 'That again. I suppose I should be grateful that you at least admit that I was not the sole cause of his demise.'

'If it were not for you...' she began to say.

'Then your husband might have found some other reason to end his life,' the Duke said. 'A man who would gamble away his fortune as your husband did was clearly not happy with himself or his lot.'

'He had no cause to be unhappy,' she countered quickly. 'He had reason enough to stay alive.' Suddenly, it felt as though she was the one who had lost control of the conversation. He was probing old wounds that she'd hoped to hide from him.

'He had a wife and son,' the Duke agreed with her in a gentler tone. 'For most men, that is more than enough.'

But it had not been for John. It was one of the things that kept her up nights, wondering. Had he even thought of them in the last moments of his life? Apparently, when the time had come to write that note, he had not, for there was nothing in it for her. No advice. No words of love or comfort. He had been thinking of nothing but his debts and how to escape them.

The man beside her at the table was quiet now, as if he knew what she was thinking. Then he said, 'I should not have prodded you just now. If I have forced you to remember something you would prefer not to, I am sorry.'

She shook her head, surprised that the hurt was still as fresh as it had been on the day John died. The feeling that, somehow, she had not been enough.

'It was not you,' the Duke said, his voice even gentler than before. 'There was nothing you could have done that would have made a difference.'

'You can't know that,' she said, staring down into her plate.

'I did not know your husband, but I have known other doomed men,' he replied. 'If they think of others when making that final decision, they convince themselves that what they are doing is the best for all concerned.'

'But if...' She had been about to admit the truth before stopping herself. If she had loved John, perhaps it would have made a difference. He must have known. He must have realised how she felt and acted upon it.

And why she would tell such a dark truth to this man, of all men, was beyond her. She stiffened to hide her vulnerability and glared at him, angry at herself for being so weak. 'I did not ask you for consolation, any more than I sought your interference before.'

He straightened as well, chastised. 'As you wish.'

'And what right do you have to tell my son that he should go into the navy?' she added, remembering the conversation from before.

'I did not suggest it,' the Duke said blandly, picking up his spoon and tasting the turtle soup they had been served. 'But he was put in mind of it by the playthings in his nursery. There are instruments of navigation there and a fine model of a frigate with tiny lead sailors. When I was his age, I had thoughts that were the same.' He looked thoughtful for a moment. 'Nothing came of it.'

'It is not his nursery,' she snapped again. They were still strangers here, after all.

'Is it someone else's?' he asked, locking her gaze with his own. 'Have you decided to give me a child of our own who will supplant him?'

'Certainly not,' she said, unable to help the shudder that ran through her at the thought. She hoped it would appear to him that she was appalled by the idea. But strangely, his suggestion had been like a fingertip run over bare skin, leaving her tingling and expectant.

'If there are to be no other children, the nursery is Edward's,' the Duke said, in a tone that was surprisingly final. 'And if you wonder at my authority in speaking to him of the future, it came to me when we married. I am head over the household, over both you and him.'

'You cannot force us to obey you,' she said stubbornly, before remembering that there were men like Baxter who viewed such words as a challenge.

'Do you intend to rebel against anything I might wish, or only the things you do not agree with?' he said, giving her a searching look.

She did not intend to rebel at all. She simply wished to have some say in her life. Between John and this man, it felt as if that might never happen. And if marriage meant that she would lose Edward... 'I have no intention of allowing you to pack my son off to school or the navy, or whatever you intend for him, just because it inconveniences you to have him here.'

This elicited a sharp bark of laughter. 'And I suppose you intended that he would stay in your shadow forever? It is an indication that he needed some man in his life. If he wishes to make anything of himself, he will need schooling. Sending him off to Eton is hardly a black-hearted scheme to get him out of my sight. It is merely what happens to boys of his class. He will go away to school and, when term ends, he will be welcomed home to see his loving mother wherever she might be at the time.'

It was better than she could have hoped for Edward with no money or connections. And if the offer had come from anyone else, she would have been grateful. Instead, she said, 'You should have discussed it with me first.'

He gave her a sceptical look. 'So that you could refuse me? I suppose you mean to fire the tutor I am hiring, so that he might keep up with his studies while in London.'

A tutor was a thing she had meant to hire with the money from Abbott. But while she had been in mourning, it had seemed like an unnecessary stress to add to their already confusing lives. Now that they were to be settled here, there was no reason that he should not be properly educated and prepared for school. But she had not planned to turn the raising of her child over to this stranger. 'I wish to speak with the tutor, before you hire him.'

He shrugged and took another sip of his soup. 'I see no reason why not. But I assure you, I would not choose anyone who was not suitable.'

'He is *my* son,' she said firmly.

'And my responsibility,' the Duke countered. Then he went back to his soup.

The rest of the courses proceeded in silence, with her smouldering over her food and trying to ignore the presence of the man she loathed. It was a shame that he was there, for it was the only thing spoiling an otherwise excellent meal.

Alex busied himself with his food, trying not to wonder what his bride was thinking. Dark thoughts, he suspected, for though the roast was tender, she sawed at the meat as if it gave her pleasure to stab something.

Tonight's conversation was, if not better than previous attempts, at least longer. He wondered if all interactions between them would be battles for supremacy, as this one had been.

It rather reminded him of his mother and stepfather. They had argued constantly when they were together and it had set the whole house on edge. When they'd chosen to live apart, it had been almost as bad, for he and Evan had had to contend with one or the other of them, still bitter but with no one to shout at but their combined children.

This was not the way he meant to run his own household. If she must hate him, she should learn to do so civilly. And he must not rise to the bait when she was not. They must find a way to get along, if only for the sake of the child.

When dinner was finally over, he led the way to the sitting room. As they left the dining room, he could hear Edward at the head of the stairs, as fidgety as he had been in the coach after the wedding. Before he could be summoned, the boy came galloping down the stairs to join them.

Selina gave a warning 'shush' as he arrived, as if awed to quiet by the grandness of the hall. He had to admit that he had felt the same when he had moved here. The house had seemed as staid and elderly as the previous duke had been, unaccustomed to little boys and their ways.

But that was about to change, or so he hoped. It was to be a home now, for the three of them, and not just a showplace. He turned as the child approached and said, 'It is all right.' Then he gestured him on ahead to a door on the right-hand side of the corridor.

They entered before him and he paused in the doorway, waiting to see their response to the size of the room, the ornate decoration of it and the comfort of the furniture. It was an impressive sight, with blue wallpaper and thick rugs over the gleaming white marble of the floor.

Selina lifted her head in defiance and drifted into the room, as beautiful as a swan, claiming her place by the fire as if she had belonged here all along. She reached for the basket of needlework that had been brought from her old home, selecting an embroidery hoop and some coloured silk, then set to work.

She might be fine, but there was nothing in this space for a boy to entertain himself with. Edward saw that immediately and lost his nerve, bumping into the Duke in his effort to get out and go back to the nursery.

Alex nudged him forward again. 'Go on. There is nothing to be afraid of. It is only family here to-night, after all.'

Selina's eyes narrowed as if she wanted to argue that they were nothing of the kind. Perhaps they weren't. It was not as if a few magic words said at the altar had made them compatible.

But they would have to find their way somehow. From her letters, he knew that she longed for this sense of family and stability. It was only him that she objected to. At the moment, she was staring at her embroidery with a deliberate intensity, as if she could make him disappear simply by ignoring him.

He turned to Edward, whose loyalty had been bought with a compass and a carriage ride. The boy had gone to the game table by the fire and picked up one of the delicately carved chess pieces from the board, turning it over in his hand. A knight, Alex noted with a smile. It had been the little horses that had fascinated him, when he had first seen the game.

'Do you play?' he asked.

The boy shook his head hesitantly.

'Let me show you.' He pulled up a chair to the table

and gestured to the opposite side of the table for Edward, then showed him the movement of each piece, spotting him several pieces at the beginning of the game and offering gentle corrections to prevent any egregious, game-ending mistakes.

At what age had he learned to play chess? He had known it when his mother had remarried and been the one to teach Evan when they were twelve and ten, respectively. That meant that his own father had taught him, though he could not remember a time when he had not known the rules.

Apparently, John Ogilvie had been too focused on games of chance to teach his own son. The fact annoyed Alex, as did the slavish devotion that Selina showed to a man who had neglected and betrayed her. He did not have to look up from the board to feel her disapproval of him now. He could hear the uneven tempo of her breath and the soft stabbing of her needle as it struck the stretched linen she was working on.

Was she thinking of him? he wondered. Comparing him to Ogilvie? If so, why was he found wanting?

Edward went to bed after three games. He had lost all of them, but did not seem bothered by the fact, kissing his mother and smiling proudly at Alex, who promised him they would play again soon.

Of course, his absence left Alex alone with his wife again and she seemed ready to argue. He ignored her and stayed at the board, painstakingly setting up the pieces for various gambits, running through a game against himself to pass the time.

'Speak,' he said at last, when her silence became too oppressive to stand. 'I know you have something to say. The air is pregnant with it. You might as well get it out and save us both the suspense.' Then he looked up at her and waited.

'I do not want you to talk with my son,' she said, bristling like an angry hen.

'I am aware of that,' he replied, watching her.

'You are responsible for rendering him fatherless and have no right to his company.'

'Perhaps,' he allowed. 'But now that I have married you, I am responsible for raising him, for paying for his education, his food, his clothing and his entertainment. I have no intention of doing that in silence for the next ten years.'

'I would never have married you if it were not for the article in the newspaper, and I certainly did not do it to burden you with the care of the two of us.'

'Having a stepson is not a burden,' he snapped, surprising himself with the vehemence. 'At least it should not be.' Then he looked at her directly, his fingers deliberately knocking over the white king with the piece in his hand. 'I speak from experience.'

'In what way?' she said, watching him closely.

'I was that boy,' he said. 'Or one very like him.' Now his fingers closed around a pawn, squeezing until his hand ached. 'The unwanted stepson of a powerful man. Evan's father would not acknowledge me when we were in the same room together, much less care about my future. It was fortunate that there was money from my late father to cover my education, for I doubt old Fallon would have paid for it.'

'I did not know,' she said.

'I have lived the life you would choose for your son and know that he will not understand the disagreement between us. He will think that there is a deficiency in his own character that renders him somehow unlovable. Is that truly what you want for him?'

When she did not answer, he shook his head. 'Then I misjudged you, for I thought that, of all things, you wanted what was in the best interest of your son.'

'But not to be raised by his father's murderer,' she snapped, still resisting.

'If that is what you still think of me, then there is little to be done to mend the breach between us. But there is no such division between Edward and me, and I refuse to create one. Like it or not, his real father is no longer here and it is better that someone step up and take over his job. I mean to do so, whether you like it or not. And now, if you will excuse me, I am going to bed.' Then he set the chess piece aside and left her alone.

It was exhausting to be cross all the time. It was giving her a megrim.

As her maid prepared her for bed, Selina rubbed at her temples, trying to relax the tension that had settled there. She was tempted to announce to the girl that there was no point in laying out her best nightgown or adding ribbons to her braided hair. No one would be seeing it. Nothing was going to happen.

This was not the wedding night that she was imagining for her mistress.

But that would embarrass her more than it did the Duke. He seemed to have adjusted to their loveless marriage with little comment. It was Selina who could not seem to manage her emotions.

She still did not know what to think about the way Glenmoor was treating her son. All her instincts cried out that she must protect the boy from the man she had married. But what reason was there to save him from chess lessons and the promise of an Eton education?

She dismissed the maid and climbed into her bed, staring up at the hangings, waiting for sleep and thinking of her last wedding night, which had been even more difficult than this one. With John, she had been totally unprepared for what had been expected of her. He had looked at her as if she were a fool, then pushed her on to her back and spread her legs, and a few moments later there had been pain and, with it, understanding.

The act had grown easier with practice. But his treatment of her had never been what she had imagined when she'd fantasised as a girl. She had learned how best to seek and find pleasure in their times together, and, in the end, had found it quite pleasant.

But there was no guarantee that it would be the same with a different man, especially one as selfish as she had assumed the Duke was. And why was she even considering it, since he had given his word that he would not come to her? The thought of lying with him was terrifying, and something else as well. Something undefinable, part-dread and part-excitement. She had to admit, he was an attractive man.

But then the devil was reported to be so as well. And the Bible was quite clear that temptation was something to be resisted, not brooded upon.

She rolled over, trying to clear her mind of the possibilities and get some sleep. Whatever was to happen between them, it would not be tonight.

Then, in the distance beyond her bedroom door, she heard a thin, reedy voice calling, 'Mama?'

With the instincts of eight years of motherhood, she was out of bed and into her wrapper, heading towards the door before Edward could call again. The last thing they needed was for the boy to wake the Duke and anger him. She did not want this odd union of theirs to be any more stressful than it already was.

'Mama?'

She was out in the hall now and could see her son, his nightshirt a ghostly white as he stumbled down the hall towards her.

'Here,' she whispered, hurrying towards him with a finger to her lips, urging him to silence.

'I cannot sleep,' he said in a normal tone, ignoring her warning.

He must have been too loud, for beside them the door opened and the Duke stepped into the hall, staring at the pair of them in curiosity. 'What seems to be the matter?'

'Nothing,' Selina said hurriedly, laying a protective hand on her son's shoulder.

'I miss my old room,' Edward said, ignoring her again.

'I see,' the Duke replied.

'There is nothing wrong with the nursery,' she said, almost over the top of his comment. 'It is better than your old room.' Bigger, at least. Of course, that was probably part of the problem. The whole house was large and the two of them had been swallowed up in it.

'We had to move when Father died and I did not like it. And now we are moving again,' Edward said, tired and cranky and hearing none of her assurances.

'It must be most difficult for you,' the Duke said in a surprisingly reasonable voice. 'Let us go back to the nursery and see what can be done to make it better.' Then he turned down the hall and led them back to the open door.

Edward hesitated on the doorstep, staring in with dread.

The Duke walked into the room, clearly unfazed, and went to the window, pulling the curtains wide to let the moonlight into the room. 'Does this make it better, or worse?'

The boy took a hesitant step over the threshold. 'I can see better.'

'With a candle, you could see even more,' the Duke reasoned, and lit a taper off the embers of the fire, fixing it in a holder on the mantelpiece. 'There, not so bright that you cannot sleep, but bright enough so that the room does not seem so strange. Do you need your mother to sit with you for a while, or should I send for a maid?'

The boy gave him a speculative look, then raised his chin. 'I am fine, now.'

'That is good to know.'

'Are you sure…?' Selina said, drawing closer to him, only to see him draw away.

'The boy says he is fine,' the Duke said firmly, giving Edward a smile and a nod.

'I will be better now,' Edward assured her, giving her the same closed-mouth smile.

'Very well,' she said with an exasperated sigh. 'But if you need me again, you have but to call.'

The boy climbed back into bed and the Duke shut the door, wiping one hand against the other as if pleased that the matter was settled. Then he looked at Selina and said, 'Do not worry about him. He just needed a moment's reassurance.'

'From you,' she said doubtfully. 'And what do you know about children?' For someone who had never been a parent, he had done surprisingly well.

'He is a boy. As such, he will not want to show weakness in front of me.'

'It is not weakness to be afraid in a new place,' she said, narrowing her eyes.

'Of course not. But that does not mean that he was not embarrassed that I came to see what was wrong.'

'Then you should have stayed in your room,' she said. 'He is my son, after all.'

'Are you telling me what I can and cannot do?' he said with a smile.

'Of course not.' Her eyes fell and she found herself staring at his bare feet on the carpet and travelling slowly up the expanse of equally bare leg that was showing beneath the hem of his dressing gown.

'Because I meant what I said earlier about being a father to the boy.'

He was talking to her now, but she could not seem to concentrate on the words. Her mind and her eyes were still focused on the sight of his legs and the fact that he seemed to be wearing nothing beneath the robe. She continued her inspection of him, following up the length of his body to note the satin belt slung low on his hips, tied in the most casual of knots, and the few inches of fabric that lapped below it, lending decency and saving her from the ultimate embarrassment.

She should not be staring there. She should not be showing any curiosity at all. But then, he was her husband and this was her wedding night. If things had been different, curiosity about his naked body would be perfectly natural.

But that was not what she had wanted. He was not that sort of husband, nor was she that sort of wife. He certainly was not ogling her in the manner that she was looking at him and she must do him the same courtesy. She dragged her gaze from his legs, only to find that she was staring at the vee of bare chest displayed by the same half-open robe.

As she watched, his words stopped and he sighed, clearly frustrated by her lack of response. 'It is late. Let us return to our rooms and to bed. I think your Edward is settled for the night, but if you fear not, there is no reason that you cannot go back to check on him and undo the damage you think I have done.'

'No,' she whispered in a hoarse voice. 'He will be all right, I think.'

The Duke gave his head a little shake as if he was surprised that she had yielded so easily. 'Goodnight, then.' Then he turned and went into his room, shutting the door behind him.

She hurried to hers and did the same, only to find herself staring at the connecting door between their rooms. Was he really naked, just on the other side of the door?

The question shamed her. She hated Glenmoor. The fact that he was a virile man should not alter her feelings in any way. But there was something about her newly married state that had awakened unexpected feelings. A carnal interest that aroused something in the depths of her, an urge that pushed her towards that connecting door. She approached silently, dropping to her knees in front of it, pressing her palms against the wood panel and putting her eye to the keyhole to stare into his room.

He was standing by the fire, the robe discarded at the foot of the bed, and he was naked, as she had expected. His back was to her and he stretched his arms above his head, giving her a view of the sinews of his shoulders, muscular arms, a narrow waist and the taut curves of his hips, the thighs and calves flexing and relaxing as he turned to sit on the bed.

She stifled a gasp as she saw the rest of him, the sculpted muscles of his chest and abdomen and lower, the place where she should not be looking, but from which she could not seem to look away.

The muscles of her own body tightened at the sight of him and the memory of what a man like that could do for her, if she allowed him to. One of her hands dropped to her belly and pressed tightly against it, smoothing down to touch between her legs.

Then she closed her eyes and turned away. This was not just any man she was spying on. It was Glenmoor, who had tricked her into dependence and into marriage, just as he had tricked her husband out of his life.

She clambered to her feet and crept away from the door again, waiting until she was well clear of it to throw herself on the bed and turn her face and body from the keyhole.

But she could not force herself not to imagine him. When she closed her eyes, she could still see the magnificent figure on the other side of the door, as if the image was etched on her very soul. At last, she could stand it no longer and pleasured herself, stroking until a fire rose within her and burned away the uncontrollable urges. When she was spent, she pulled the covers high and fell into a fitful sleep.

Chapter Fourteen

Alex had never been the sort to hold romantic notions about marriage, since he had never intended to have one. He had given even less thought to his wedding night. He had decided, long before Oxford, that if he desired companionship in bed, there were any number of women willing to oblige. It was a pleasant pastime, but there was nothing particularly sacred about it and no need to obsess about any one occasion.

Of course, that was before he'd met Selina. In the last year, he had spent far too much time imagining what it would be like to be with her. The first time would be a profound event, the beginning of their life together.

He had never imagined that he would spend the night reading in bed, trying to distract himself from the delectable woman sleeping just a room away. When he had seen her in the hallway, tending to her son, she had been wearing a nightgown of lace, her long blonde hair bound in a thick, beribboned braid that hung down her back, swaying as she walked.

The ensemble had been beautiful, but rather fussy for his tastes. He'd wanted to undo the ties and loosen the braid, to see the beautiful woman underneath.

But last night had not been the right time. He had married a widow and he had known there would be a child to care for. But he had not expected she would be so protective of her son, when he'd made it clear that he meant the boy no harm. It was not as if he had beaten the boy, or locked him in his room, as his own stepfather had done to him. He had been gentleness itself.

But by her snapping in the hallway after, she would have preferred discipline to kindness. Apparently, she would not be satisfied with him until he became the villain she imagined him to be.

If that was so, she would be sorely disappointed. He had no intention of compromising his values by becoming a tyrant.

Though the night was nearly sleepless, the next day passed easily, because he had reason to avoid her. He was up early for a walk in the park and took luncheon at his club, before the afternoon session of Parliament.

Evan was waiting for him at White's, the table set for two and his glass of claret ready. He smiled as Alex approached, and set down the paper he was reading. 'You are in the gossip columns again, brother.'

Alex winced. 'That was what I tried to avoid by marrying.'

'It is the marriage itself that is the topic. This time,

you are the "fortunate Duke of G." and your story is proclaimed to be "romantic".'

He winced again and hoped Selina had not seen it, for he doubted that she shared the view of the writer.

'And is it?' Evan said, his smile fading to one of polite enquiry. 'Romantic, that is.'

'It is as I expected it to be,' Alex said, dodging the question.

'That bad,' Evan replied, shaking his head.

'Last night, I played chess with the boy,' Alex said, evading again.

'Have you explained to him about the succession?' Evan asked. 'And about your connection to his father?'

'He has just come into the household,' Alex said.

'He has to be told. If his mother has not...'

'I do not know what his mother has told him.' But whatever it was, he could guess that it was not good. 'I will talk to him in time.'

'And what do you mean to do about the fact that his mother hates you?'

Alex started in surprise. 'Is it so evident?'

'Clear enough to those of us who were at the wedding.'

He sighed. 'She has reason enough to do so.' Then he told Evan about Abbott and the letters they'd exchanged.

In response, he received the derisive laughter that he so richly deserved. When Evan had wiped away the tears of mirth and regained control of himself, he said, 'I swear, you were much smarter about some things before Oxford. Never lie to a woman and expect her to love you afterwards.'

'I never expected her to love me. At least, not at first. But things got out of hand.'

'They certainly did,' Evan said, smirking. 'But to your credit, you write very compelling letters.'

'Abbott does,' Alex said, sullenly.

'And you are Abbott,' his brother replied.

'Abbott is a fiction,' Alex said, shaking his head. 'As such, he has no flaws and makes no mistakes. Of course she fell in love with him. But I?'

'You are a mere mortal,' Evan stated.

'I have created my own worst enemy,' Alex said with a frown. 'And I do not know how to get rid of him. I cannot help but think that she compares me to the man she expected and has found me wanting.'

'This is a conundrum,' his brother agreed. 'How do you intend to make her settle for a man who is merely young, handsome, rich and titled?'

'I have no idea,' Alex said, and took a sip of his wine. 'For now, I mean to have lunch. After that, who knows what will happen?'

By the time the Duke returned home from Parliament, supper was finished and Selina and Edward had already gone to the sitting room. Edward was entertaining himself with the chess pieces, marching them around the board and sighing over the absence of his new friend.

Selina had her needlework and a growing feeling of dread. It was a lie to say she was waiting eagerly for his homecoming. But without his presence in it, the house seemed even larger and emptier than it had the day before. She did not belong here. Pretending she did put a strain on her nerves.

When he finally arrived, he came straight to the sitting room to join them, offering a deep bow to her and a smile to Edward, who looked at him hopefully, glancing to the chessboard and away as if afraid to ask for attention, lest his request be refused.

'It is rather late for that,' the Duke said. 'But...' He went to the drawer of a side table and pulled out a deck of cards and offered it to the boy with a smile.

Her son tipped his head to the side, considering. He was no more familiar with them than he had been with the chess set on the previous evening. The Duke was probably wondering what, if anything, the boy was allowed to do when in her care. And what, if anything, his father had taught him while the man was still alive.

The answer to the second question was close to nothing. She had not noticed it when they were alone together, but Edward seemed starved for male attention, soaking up the Duke's favour as a parched plant took in water.

Why did that man have to be so deceptively charming?

He was smiling as he dealt out the cards quickly to the two of them, as if he had been just as anxious to see Edward as the boy had him.

But why did it have to be this pastime? She had shielded Edward from his father's vice thus far and had no desire for him to take up the habit now. She looked up from her embroidery and gave a sniff of disapproval.

He ignored it and said to the boy, 'This game is deceptively simple. But you will discover, after a time, that it can be quite challenging.'

'Can Mama play as well?' Edward said, looking across at her with longing.

She gave a slight shake of her head and glared at the Duke.

'Perhaps another night, once you have learned the rules and she is not busy with her needlework,' he said, smiling to put the boy at ease. Then he went on to explain the rules.

The hour passed quietly, as Alex taught the boy casino and vingt-et-un and she sat on the other side of the room, stabbing her sampler and waiting for the night to be over, so that she could talk to the Duke without Edward hearing.

When he had kissed her goodnight and was gone from the room, she stared at Glenmoor, her eyes narrowed. 'I do not want you playing cards with my son.'

'My stepson, you mean,' he said, staring back at her with a placid smile. 'In time, you will see that there are things I can teach him that you, as his mother, will not know.'

'But those things will not include cards,' she said, equally firm.

He picked up the deck from off the table, fanned it effortlessly, then shuffled, his long fingers riffling through the cards with a dexterity that enthralled her.

'If you deny him this, you will create just the un-healthy fascination you seek to avoid. You are far more likely to turn him into his father than to keep him from travelling the particular path you most want him to avoid.'

'And what do you mean by that?' she said, know-ing perfectly well what he meant.

'There are card games that require luck and those that require skill. Your husband had neither luck nor skill, nor the intelligence to know the difference,' the Duke said, his smile disappearing.

'How dare you?' she said, eyes blazing.

'Speak ill of the dead?' he replied, setting the cards aside. 'I dare because, at least in this case, someone must. Your husband made many mistakes in life—the greatest of them was how he treated you and Edward. If he could not keep himself from gambling, the least he could have done was told you the truth and stayed alive to face the consequences of his losses. But he left you to do that, didn't he?'

'He did not know what he was doing,' she said softly, not wanting to be reminded of it.

'He knew exactly what he was doing,' he pressed. 'He left you a list of his debts. You told me so your-self.'

'In letters that were not addressed to you,' she countered, relieved that she could turn the argument back on to his faults and away from John's.

'You were willing to confess the truth to a man you had never met,' he reminded her. 'And to take money from him when it was offered.'

'I had no choice,' she replied, trying not to think of how desperate she had been in those first days.

'Because of your husband,' he reminded her. 'And what would you have done if I hadn't offered to help you? Would you have gone to Baxter, or some other man?'

It would have been that or the poorhouse. And wouldn't it have been better for Edward to have had some stability, even if it meant sacrificing herself and her pride? 'I went to you, which was bad enough,' she said, hoping to wound him.

'And you have again,' he reminded her.

'Because you forced me into this marriage.'

'Baxter forced you into it by revealing our arrangement.'

'You did, by your previous actions. If you hadn't meddled, there would have been no scandal,' she insisted.

'If you would have remarried someone else when I suggested it, there would have been no scandal either. But instead, you were waiting for an offer from Abbott.'

'I…' she said, unable to bring herself to deny the fact.

'And now that you have got one, you are not happy with it,' he declared. 'It was only me, all along. And you cannot abide that, can you?' He stared at her, his expression one part pity and one part frustration.

He reached for her then, taking her upper arms in the gentlest of grasps. 'You must understand why, in my letters, I was careful not to lead you on. I knew you would hate me when you learned who I was. I knew it was hopeless. I did not want to hurt you. But I could not stop writing.' His voice was rough, but soft. And now his hands stroked her arms, grazing the sides of her breasts.

At the slightest touch, she felt a growing yearning deep inside. Her body tingled and, without meaning to, she leaned into him, stepping closer.

He responded, his breath low and shaky. 'I could not leave you, even when I knew it was best for both of us. And now, here we are.' His arms wrapped around her, stroking her back as they had her arms, moving slowly from nape to the small of her back, where they settled, pressing, urging her close to nestle against his body.

It was wrong. But Lord, she wanted it. It had been so long since she'd been touched and he was so gentle, coaxing, not demanding, waiting for her to make the next move.

She took a breath and forced herself to forget who he was, tipping her head up to his and closing her eyes.

His lips met hers, surprising her with their hunger. He paused for only a moment before opening her mouth with a lick of his tongue, kissing her in a way meant to banish the last inhibition, his tongue teasing hers, bringing her to life until she could not help but kiss him back.

It was beyond good, like life itself pouring back into her with each stroke of his tongue. She balled her fists in his lapels, pressing herself into the solidness of his chest, breathing in the sweet, spicy scent of him and letting her mind drift. This was what she had wanted, when she'd read his letters, a strong man to lean upon. Someone who would hold her as if she meant the world to him.

One of his hands stole up to cup her breast through the fabric of her gown and she felt her nipples, already tight with desire, puckering, eager to be kissed. His other hand, which was still at the small of her back, slid lower, moulding her against the bulge of his erection.

If he wanted, he could have her here and she would not stop him. Even with closed eyes, she could picture him as he had been last night, large and naked and virile in a way that was nothing like John had been.

Then she remembered who he really was and the promise that she had exacted from him that their marriage would be cold and barren. She pulled away, out of his grasp, hurriedly patting her gown as if to assure herself that she was still decent. She felt naked before him, even though fully dressed.

He stared at her, panting, expectant. But he did not reach for her again.

'You should not have done that,' she said automatically.

'I?' he said with a sardonic raise of an eyebrow. 'I suppose now you will tell yourself that you were forced into it.'

He had not forced her; she had gone to him willingly and she hated her weakness. 'Whatever it was, it will not happen again,' she said, stepping back to put some space between them.

He was staring at her now, searching for…something; she was not sure what. He nodded, as if he'd found it, and said, 'You know that is not true. What will happen between us is inevitable. But when it happens, you will be the one to come to me.'

'Never,' she said, but the word had no real strength to it.

'Soon,' he replied, with even more certainty. 'The door to my room is unlocked, should you choose to use it. Goodnight, Selina.' And then he left her alone.

Chapter Fifteen

She'd let him kiss her. And it had been every bit as good as he'd hoped. Her lips were like honey, her response eager. And her body pressed against his had been the sweetest of tortures, hinting at a future that he didn't dare hope for.

But he did hope. He had been up most of the night, staring at the door that connected their rooms, willing her to open it and come to him. It had remained stubbornly closed. Eventually, he had fallen into a fitful sleep of erotic dreams and woken alone and disappointed.

But perhaps tonight would be different. They were to make their first public appearance as a married couple at the Folbroke ball, an invitation she had chosen to accept without his prompting. He hoped that meant she did not intend to embarrass him. It would be impossible to do so without shaming herself, and he did not want that. She might have married him out of spite, but he had more than enough love for both of them and did not want to see her hurt.

After a light breakfast, he went to the study and put daydreams aside in favour of the stack of bills that were accumulating on his desk. He had been there for nearly an hour before he noticed a shadow lurking in the doorway. He tried to ignore it, but after a few minutes gave up and called, 'Come.'

A moment more passed before the boy appeared, toeing the edge of the carpet, staring at Alex, as if considering.

'It's all right,' Alex said in a softer tone, gesturing him to come closer.

'Mother says I am not to bother you when you are working.'

'Then you do not have to worry. I will tell you when you are bothering me, and you are not.'

There was another moment of hesitation, then Edward stepped into the room and climbed up into the chair in front of the desk. He stared in silence at the papers stacked there and then back at Alex. 'What are you doing?'

'I am going over this month's bills for my estate.' Then he added, 'I have a house in the country that is much bigger than this with miles of land around it.' He thought for a moment, remembering the things about the property that had fascinated him when he had visited as a child. 'There is a stream for trout and many trees that are good for climbing, and a Roman ruin as well. Sometimes, I would find coins in the garden.'

The boy's eyes grew round with wonder. 'And can I go there?'

'We will all go there, once the Season is done.' At least, he assumed that they would. Perhaps his wife meant to remain in town as his mother used to, when she was avoiding her second husband. It would not hurt if he gained an ally in Edward, to encourage Selina to make the trip.

'I would like to see the ruins,' he said. 'And I will take the compass, so I do not get lost.' He patted his pocket.

'That is very wise,' Alex said, nodding in approval. Then he sobered. 'How much has your mother told you about our marriage, Edward?'

'That we were to come and live with you now and that you would be my...' he paused as if trying to remember the word '...my stepfather, which is not like a father at all.'

Alex stifled his wince. 'It is different, yes. But did she explain to you how?'

Edward shook his head.

'When I die, most of my property, the money, the title of Duke and the great house that we will live in will pass to my son, if I am blessed to have one.' Now was not the time to explain how unlikely that seemed right now. But he went on. 'It will not go to you, since you are my stepson and have, or had, a father of your own.'

'And he did not leave me anything,' Edward said with surprising bluntness.

'Should I pass, you will be taken care of,' Alex said hurriedly. 'I will set up a trust for you and, while I am alive, I will see to your welfare, your education and guide you to a career, if you wish to have one. Your father would have done the same, if he had not died when he did.'

Edward blinked at him, thinking. Then he announced, 'Father shot himself. My mother does not like to speak of it, but I heard the servants talking.'

'Did your mother tell you that I was with your father, the night he died?' He held his breath, afraid of the answer.

The boy solemnly shook his head.

'I played cards with him. He lost money to me,' Alex admitted. 'But when I played with him, I had no idea...' How was he to explain this? 'But it wasn't my fault that he died. Your father was a very unhappy man,' he stated.

'Why?' Edward said, a strange cloud passing over his face.

'Not because of anything you did,' he said hurriedly, and watched the boy slump in relief.

Had Selina really told the boy nothing? 'And not just because of the game he played with me. He was unlucky in cards. He lost all the money he had and was embarrassed to tell you.'

'We had to move houses,' Edward said with a frown.

'Because he lost the house to a man named Baxter,' Alex supplied.

'Mother was very sad,' he replied thoughtfully.

'I imagine she was.'

'And angry as well,' the boy said, still frowning.

'But never at you,' Alex assured him.

'At my father?' he said, his voice trembling a little.

'At the way things turned out,' Alex said, allowing himself a small lie. 'Life has been very difficult for her since your father died.'

'But it is better now,' Edward said, beaming at him. 'She has you to take care of her.'

'Of course,' Alex said, feeling the guilt rising in his throat like bile. He forced it back down again and added, 'I will take care of her.' Whether she wanted him to or not. 'We will take care of her together.'

Edward responded with a solemn nod. Then asked, 'What do I have to do?'

'Continue to do what you are doing,' Alex said, relieved to be back on solid ground. 'Keep up with your studies and obey her when she asks something of you. She is very proud of you and happy that you are with her. She has told me so herself.'

Edward nodded again, content with the answer, then stared at him as though afraid to ask his next question.

'And I am happy, too,' Alex said, watching the boy relax again. 'I do not have time for games today. But if you wish, you may sit in the chair by the window while I work.'

The boy climbed up into the seat, watching with interest as Alex returned to his accounts.

Selina stared into the mirror in her bedroom as her maid fastened the back of the new ball gown she had chosen for the night's outing. She'd made a special trip to Bond Street and begged the poor modiste to rush so that it might be ready for tonight's ball. And now, though she could not see anything wrong with the construction or trim, it seemed to be missing something.

The whole shopping trip had seemed rather strange to her, for she had never been in a position where money was no obstacle to the purchase of a gown. Of course the dress could be ready on such short notice for *Her Grace.* The seamstresses had thrown aside their other tasks for a chance to sew for a duchess. They had been excited to do so.

And if truth were told, Selina was excited as well. She had gone into the shop wondering if there might be some way to annoy Glenmoor with her purchases. John would have been appalled at the price she had paid for a single gown.

But Alex Conroy was nothing like her last husband. When she had remarked in passing that she would need new clothing for all the events he'd wished her to accept, he had simply nodded and told her to send the bills to his bank.

She had toyed with the idea of buying something ridiculous that would embarrass him, but hurriedly put the idea aside. If she made a cake of herself with too many ruffles, or garish colours, the gossips would announce that the new Duchess had no sense of fashion.

And, if she was honest with herself, she wanted to look beautiful, even if it was only for herself. There was no indication that her wearing grey to the wedding had insulted him. But it had made her feel shabby and elicited some odd looks from the Duchess of Fallon. She would not go through that again.

So now she was wearing emerald green silk, with a bodice cut dangerously low. Perhaps that was the problem with it. She had no jewellery to wear, beyond the jet brooch she'd worn after John died. And even on a green ribbon, the little cameo was inappropriate for evening.

Perhaps there was some piece of Glenmoor family jewellery she could borrow for the night, so she might not look so plain. But that would require her asking her husband for his help and nothing could induce her to do so. It would be hard enough to walk at his side tonight without knowing that she was even deeper in his debt.

Then there was a knock on the bedroom door. When her maid opened it, His Grace's valet handed her a blue leather case, delivered with His Grace's compliments.

She could not help the gasp of shock when she opened it. It was a parure, complete with necklace, hairpins, ear-drops and shoe clips. Gold leaves and stems intertwined, ending in a complicated arrangement of floral sprigs where each blossom was set with an emerald at its centre.

She should refuse it. She had sworn, when she decided to marry Glenmoor, that it was only to spite him at every turn. But she could not bring herself to close the case, much less send it away.

Her maid had even fewer scruples and removed the necklace from the case, draping it around her throat and fastening the clasp at the back. 'Oh, madam. I mean, Your Grace. It is perfect. Sit down and let me do up your hair with the pins.'

Selina sank into the chair at the vanity table and watched as Molly put up her hair. The girl was right. It suited the dress perfectly.

You are stunning in green.

The words popped into her head, seemingly out of nowhere. Then she remembered them from one of Abbott's letters, received after the Fallon ball. She had been so excited to think that he had seen her there. And all along, it had been Glenmoor, flattering her and forcing his way into her company.

But then, she touched the necklace at her throat and wondered aloud, 'How did he know?'

Molly giggled. 'He asked me what you would be wearing. He said the family jewels were hopelessly out of style and that there was no time to reset them. So he bought something new that would suit you.'

'Oh.' She went back to staring in the mirror as Molly curled her hair and then piled it high on her head. What was she to do about this latest development? She should thank her husband for the gift. But she had not asked for it, nor did she like the idea that she was beholden to him in this new and surprising way.

But it was strangely touching to see a necklace glittering at her throat, after a year with nothing there. Even when she'd had jewels, they had been simple ones: a strand of pearls and an amber cross that had belonged to her mother.

John had promised to drape her in diamonds, when he was courting her. But even then, she'd known that he was exaggerating. After they were married, the promised gifts had never materialised. If there was money to spare for luxuries, it had been lost at the gaming tables. Afterwards, there was always a promise that next month, or next year, when he was winning, everything would be different.

She shook her head, trying to escape the memory, only to receive a frustrated sigh from Molly, who was affixing the last of the pins to her curls. John was gone and she needn't think about the unhappy times in her past.

Things were better now.

The fact hit her like a slap. It was undeniable that the last year, she had been happier than she had been with John. There had been no worries about money, no loneliness and no broken promises.

Then she remembered the enormous lie that her whole life had balanced upon. Perhaps things had not been better. Perhaps Glenmoor had only found a different way to hurt her. The parure was a peace offering, trying to make up for that. And, she had to admit, it was an impressive one.

She must not allow herself to be bought. If their relationship was only about money, she was no better than the newspapers said she was. She would wear the thing because it suited the dress and because pulling the pins from her hair would make unnecessary work for Molly.

But she would not allow the presence of a few stones to change who she was. She would not be in awe of the thing, or of the man who gave it to her. She would be true to herself tonight, whatever that turned out to be.

Molly was finished with her hair and Selina rose and turned towards the door. After a final brush to the folds of her skirt, she went out into the hall to find her husband.

Chapter Sixteen

Alex was waiting at the foot of the stairs when Selina appeared at their head, and he allowed himself a moment to admire her.

She was magnificent. The jewels he had bought her were a perfect match to the green of her gown; her skin was luminous beneath the gold, glowing pink and flushed with an excitement that she could not conceal.

She did not smile when she looked at him, but that was not unusual. At least she did not look haughty. He did not think he could abide having the kind of duchess his mother had been. That woman had been arrogant in the extreme, aware of her power and not above using it against people she felt were inferior to her.

In contrast, Selina looked elegant but approachable. She had reached him now and he took her hand, relieved that she did not pull away from him as he escorted her to the carriage and helped her to her seat. She was quiet, which was also not unusual. She rarely spoke to him when she did not have to.

But tonight, it felt different, as if there was something she wished to say that she could not manage.

He understood the feeling. There were frequently things he could not manage to say to her, although conversing had grown somewhat easier since their marriage. Perhaps it was because they were so frequently arguing. And why was it easier to find words for that?

He smiled.

She noticed and was unable to help a small sound of enquiry.

'I was thinking that we are often sniping at each other when we are home. I hope we shall not do it tonight,' he said in explanation.

'I hope you do not give me cause,' she said, still unsmiling.

'I am not planning anything unusual,' he said. 'We must share a dance, of course. But I do not mean to monopolise your time. This evening is for you as much as for me, and many people will wish to congratulate you on your recent marriage.'

'Oh.' She sounded small, which wasn't like her. Was she worried about being a focus of attention?

'There will be a stir about you in the papers, tomorrow. For when is there not gossip about someone bagging a title?'

'I thought we married to prevent gossip,' she said with a sigh.

'Perhaps if you'd married some minor lord, that would be true,' he said. 'But a duchess cannot avoid notice.'

Now she looked nervous, but said nothing.

'Do not worry,' he said quickly. 'They will find no fault with you. You are...' Now his words were starting to fail him again. He looked away, out the window of the carriage so that he did not become confused. 'You are a goddess. Men will be clamouring for your attention. And women will flock to befriend you.'

There was a pause as she absorbed the words. Then she muttered, 'Thank you.' And added, 'And thank you for the gift of the necklace.' The words seemed to come grudgingly, but they were there all the same and more than he'd expected from her.

'You are most welcome. You deserved some sort of wedding gift.'

'People might have wondered,' she declared.

'That is not why I did it,' he replied. He had been almost childishly eager to give her something, to prove himself worthy of her. It was disappointing to think she felt it was only from obligation.

They arrived at the Folbroke residence and he helped her down from the carriage, doing his best to ignore the weight of her hand on his arm and the warmth of her body beside his. She was rarely this near to him for long and he savoured the moment, keeping her close as he introduced her to the Earl and his Countess.

Then he led her to the dance floor. 'Will you join me?' It was nothing more than a country dance. But he thought that, if she allowed him this, perhaps he could convince her to save him the waltz later.

They moved through the steps, bowing and weaving among the others in their set, advancing and re-treating as the music called them to do.

She smiled at him. Nervously at first, then with more feeling as the spirit of the dance took hold of her. Perhaps she was happy. Or perhaps it was merely too much work to remember to scowl at him and smile at the other men in the row.

Either way, he had the pleasure of looking at her, of touching her hand and of watching her body as she moved. Was this what courtship would have been, had she allowed him one? Sighing over each smile she imparted and waiting for the next brush of her fingers against his?

The music ended all too soon and he walked her back to the side of the room, procuring her a glass of champagne and holding his breath as she allowed him to tie the dance card to her wrist. Then, when he could think of no other reason to remain at her side, he bowed and said, 'If that is all, my dear, I cede the room to you. I will be in the card room, if you need me.'

'The card room,' she said in a shocked voice, her smile disappearing. 'You certainly will not.'

He dipped his head to hers so they might seem more like a bride and groom and less like a fractious couple about to argue in public. 'It is either that or spend all my time with you. If you do not want me playing cards, I will dance every dance with you and hang on your every word. Does that suit you better?'

She hesitated for a moment, and he wondered if her hatred of cards was even greater than her hatred of him. Then she stepped away and made a vague gesture in the direction of the hallway. 'Go if you must. But when you lose, do not come to me for the money to pay your creditors.' Without thinking, she touched her necklace as if fearing that he might take it away at the end of the night.

'I never lose,' he said with a smile. Then, before she could pull away, he kissed her quickly on the lips and left for the card room.

When he arrived, Evan was already there, taking in a hand of loo between dances. He slid his chair to the side to make room. Then, to his dismay, Baxter took a seat opposite them, offering an unctuous smile. 'Shall we play, gentlemen?'

Alex glanced around the room, considering and rejecting the possibility of finding a chair at a different table. Then he said, 'Since there is no good way to avoid it, I suppose we shall.'

Baxter laughed at the insult and helped himself to the deck, dealing out the cards. 'It is either that or one of us must go out and dance with your wife,' he suggested. 'But I suppose she is used to being abandoned for games of chance.'

'She will be glad of it, once she learns that I spared her your company,' Alex said, picking up his cards.

The play proceeded and, unlike most nights, the game would not go his way. He began to regret his glib comment to Selina about always winning. Things went no better for Evan and they watched pot after pot going to Baxter.

When Alex's purse was empty, he pushed away from the table and made to leave.

'So soon?' said Baxter, grinning.

'I am played out,' Alex said, trying to hide his annoyance at his bad luck.

'You needn't stop. I am willing to take your marker.' He paused and then said, 'Your word is good, isn't it?'

Alex felt his temper rising and was ready to retort that his honour was not a matter of question. Then he remembered whom he was talking to and reined in his temper.

Loo was not the only game Baxter was playing. Each word and action he offered was meant to elicit a predicted response from the other players. There was something in the manner of the man before him that seemed too confident in the outcome of the game and the reactions of his opponents. If Alex wished to best him, he should not be playing along.

So he smiled and pushed away from the table. 'Unlike some men, I know my limits.'

'Unlike John Ogilvie, perhaps,' Baxter said, staring up at him. 'You were much slower to end the game the night he died, weren't you?'

Another taunt. To what purpose? Alex stared back at him, wondering. 'I am beginning to see why so many people owe you money, Baxter. But I am not going to be one of them. And now, if you will excuse me, they are tuning up for the waltz and I must go and find my wife.'

In the ballroom, Selina sipped her lemonade, curling her toes in her slippers to stretch her tired feet.

'How do you like being a duchess?' Mary Wilson asked, from a seat at her side.

'Very well,' Selina said, trying to ignore the pang of guilt she felt at the admission. Now that she had the protection of her husband's title, her glass and dance card were full and everyone in the room seemed eager to greet her, meet her and be her friend. 'I must not allow my head to be turned by flattery,' she added, 'for there has been more than a little of that. I suppose I shall see what people really think of me, in tomorrow's papers...'

Mary laughed. 'Do not read them. You should know by now that the tattle sheets print nothing but nonsense.'

'Probably true,' she replied, still doubting. They certainly would not print the truth about her marriage for they did not know how she truly felt about the Duke. Even she was not sure of that, any more.

'And here comes your husband,' Mary said, nudging her and grinning. 'Is he not the handsomest man in the room?'

'You say that about any man with a title,' Selina said with a laugh. Even so, she could not help the way her heart lurched at the sight of Glenmoor, who was resplendent in a dark blue evening coat and buff breeches.

'Do you feel differently about him, now that you are married?' Mary whispered from behind her fan.

'I...' Selina stared at him as he approached, trying to decide how to answer the question. Then she remembered that he was on his way back from the card room and her resolve stiffened. 'I do not wish to speak of it.'

'Of course not, Your Grace,' Mary replied in a hurt tone.

She turned to apologise, but it was too late, for her husband had arrived at their side. As usual, he was courtesy itself to Mary, bowing over her hand and smiling. 'Mrs Wilson,' he said, as if greeting an old friend. 'I hope you don't mind that I have come to claim my wife for the waltz.'

Then he turned to Selina and gave her a smile different from the one she had received at home. Tonight, he was brilliant and flirtatious, playing the part of the gallant young lover and inviting her to play along for the sake of the crowd. 'If, that is, her card is not already full.'

She did not have to look at her dance card to know that the waltz had remained empty. The eager men who had sought her out for other dances had left that space free as if they'd known the Duke would be back for it. She smiled at Mary then, rose and turned to Glenmoor, offering her hand. 'Of course, Your Grace.' Then she allowed him to lead her out on to the dance floor.

It was easier than it had been the first time they'd waltzed together, as this time there was no fear of his touch.

It should not be so. She should have resisted or refused his request. She might have claimed to be too tired and no one would have questioned it. Hadn't her plan been to fight him in all things?

But she liked dancing with him. Surely allowing herself this small pleasure was not a surrender? If she closed her eyes and let the music take her, being with him was like walking on air.

He let out a soft laugh and whispered, 'Pretending that I am someone else?'

She opened her eyes again, her smile faltering as did her step.

He caught her and brought her back to the rhythm with his body. 'We move well together, whether you want us to or not. I do not think we can help it. We are alike, Selina, mated in all the ways that matter.' Then he added, 'All the ways but one.'

The reminder sent a tremor through her, like the ring of crystal when the rim was struck. She did not want to feel this answering chime and the tingle of desire that came with it. This wanting to know what it would be like to be with him and what they would be like together. Would it be like dancing?

'Remember,' he said softly, 'the door is unlocked. It is only your stubbornness that keeps it closed.'

'I am not stubborn,' she said, latching on to the only thing she dared comment over.

'Of course not,' he said, his voice like velvet against her frayed nerves. 'You are merely resolved. But I knew that about you from your letters. You have needed to be strong to survive. But it is not a weakness to change your mind.'

Before she could think of an answer, the dance had ended and he was leading her back to her chair and relinquishing her to her next partner, who stood ready for the Sir Roger de Coverley. Her mind was whirling as she danced and, without meaning to, her eyes searched the room for Glenmoor, whenever she turned.

He was standing to the side, talking with his brother, Fallon. And often, when she looked to him, his eyes met hers as if she was never far from his thoughts. She looked away again, trying to remember the promises she had made to herself, and to John. And for a time, she was resolved.

But then the ball was over and Glenmoor collected her again, still painfully polite, but somehow, more confident than he had been before. He led her to the carriage, helped her up into it and took the seat across from her, stretching his legs out before him. 'Did you enjoy the evening, my dear?'

'I am not your dear,' she said automatically.

He ignored the retort and said, 'Is that a yes, or a no?'

'It was very pleasant,' she said in a more polite tone.

'I am glad,' he said, then turned to stare out the window, allowing her to ride in silence. Strangely, this was even more difficult than talking to him. There was a tension between them that was different than before.

In previous trips, she'd felt wariness, and repulsion. It had been easier to keep her distance and remain apart from him. But now there was a magnetic pull drawing her eyes to his face, his body, his hands, his lips. It was probably the flush of excitement, having danced all evening and drunk too much champagne. Tonight, she had not been someone's mother, or someone's widow. She'd been a wife. And, though she was not sure how such evenings ended for others, she knew what her imagined ending might be.

But not with him. Never with him.

Someone like him, perhaps. Someone tall and handsome and polite. Someone who smiled at her and danced with her as if he already knew her body and what it would take to pleasure it.

They arrived home and he was as solicitous there as he had been at the ball. He waited at the doorway for her to pass and slipped the cloak from her shoulders, allowing his fingers to brush the skin of her throat as he did so.

Then they went upstairs to their respective bedrooms, calling for servants and preparing for bed. But when her maid left her, she did not feel truly alone, knowing that he was there, just on the other side of the unlocked door, waiting for her.

The feelings she had for him were purely physical and there was no way to control that. Perhaps what some people said about widows was true and they were too knowledgeable to ever be truly proper. When she was a green girl, she certainly would not have had the nerve to peek in at him as she had done on the first night, to catch a glimpse of his nakedness. Nor would she have known what to do with what she had seen.

Of course, even clothed, he was a formidable sight.

There was something about the quirk of the corner of his mouth that fascinated her. It was as if he was aware of what his lips could do to her after that interlude in the sitting room and the thought amused him to an almost smile.

Or he might have been thinking of something else entirely and the idea of carnal bliss might be totally in her own mind. That was why she could not stop looking at his hands. She could imagine those hands on her breasts, squeezing until her breath caught in her throat. And one of his long legs hooking casually over her hip to pull her close as he entered her.

She sat up in bed, hands twisting nervously in the sheets. If she closed her eyes, she could almost feel him moving inside her. It was better if her eyes were closed, for she could forget who it was she was thinking of, forget where she was and who she was and who she had been, and focus only on the pretended sensation of a man hard for her, taking her.

That was what she had done for Abbott, after all. She had read his letters before bed and used her imagination for the rest. And for a time, that had been enough.

Her eyes popped open again and she stared at the door, just a few feet away. It didn't have to be a dream. She could have what she wanted, if she had the nerve to open the door and walk through. It did not have to mean anything more than the scratching of an itch. It was not as if it would mean more to him than that. It never did, to a man.

She needn't fear rejection. He had made it very clear

that she was welcome in his bed. She just had to go and present herself and nature would take its course.

She threw back the covers and swung her feet out of the bed, shivering in the night air for a moment, feeling her breasts tighten with the chill and, surprisingly, with anticipation.

Then she walked towards the door, grasped the handle and paused for only a moment before throwing it open and walking into the Duke's room.

Chapter Seventeen

He was lying on the bed with a book in his lap, the sheet draped at his waist and his bare chest exposed, oblivious to the coolness of the room. At her appearance, he looked up from his reading, not so much surprised as curious. His head tipped to the side, considering, but he said nothing, simply waited for her to explain herself.

She wished she could oblige, but her mind was blank. The sight of him rendered her mute. He was even more formidable up close than he had been in the peek she had taken through the keyhole, his upper body well-muscled, his chest flat and hard in a way that made her fingers ache to touch it. And the memory of what lay still hidden beneath the sheet...

She wondered if she was quite right in the head. Surely women were not supposed to be the aggressors in the bedroom. She had never been before. But since it seemed he was a man of his word, he made no move to rise and help her. She would have to be the one to start this, just as he had said.

She took a step forward, into the room, and undid the buttons of her nightgown, shrugging out of it and stepping clear as it dropped to the floor.

His only response was a raised eyebrow and a tensing of muscle as his breathing increased. Then, slowly, he closed the book in his lap and set it to the side.

What had she expected? An announcement giving her permission to continue? Or perhaps she had hoped he would send her away. There was no sign of either. He was letting her decide what was to come next and she knew what she wanted that to be.

She walked to the bedside and slid the sheet down his hips and out of the way. Then she drank in the sight of him, bare and still before her, waiting. But not unresponsive this time, for he grew aroused beneath her gaze, unable to hide his interest in her.

In an act of supreme courage, she reached for him, tightening her hand around his manhood and stroking it to full erection. His breath quickened now and he shifted on the bed, reaching for her.

She stepped clear of his hands, not ready to feel his touch in response. She did not want to be coddled and held, to have him turn this into something that she knew it was not. She longed for something base and primal. She wanted release.

She took a breath and stepped forward again, batting his hands out of the way.

He deliberately folded them behind his head, leaning back into the pillows to watch her touching him. His breath hissed between his teeth as she stroked, but the pace of each exhalation was carefully controlled, as if he did not want to admit to what was happening to him, lest it cause her to stop.

He was hard beneath her fingers and she was aroused by the sight of him, wet with anticipation of their joining. She climbed on to the bed, straddling his hips, pressing him tightly against her belly before smoothing the single drop that had formed at the tip down his shaft. Then she slid forward and rose up, hovering over him for a moment before easing down to take him into her body.

'Hell's teeth.' The exclamation slipped out of his mouth and then he was silent again, closing his eyes and then opening them slowly, as if he expected she might vanish if he looked away.

She pursed her own lips, refusing to explain or apologise, or, worst of all, to lean forward for a kiss. She did not want tenderness. She wanted the hard, tight, full feeling that she had now and the mad rush of sensation as she began to move on him.

He seemed to sense what she needed, for when he reached for her again, it was to seize her hips to steady himself as he thrust, finding the rhythm she had set and matching it.

She gasped as he pushed into her and again at the retreat and return, and the commanding pressure of his fingers on her flesh.

'Is this what you want?' he murmured on another thrust. 'To be taken hard? To be used, as you are using me?'

A week ago, she would have whimpered and rolled passively on to her back, afraid to admit the truth.

But then, she had not been married to her enemy and fighting these strange uncontrollable desires. Tonight, she closed her eyes and bit her lip, bucking her hips, grinding down on to him and letting him fill her.

'Very well, then,' he muttered, and drew back and took her again, even deeper.

She gasped and steadied herself as he thrust again and again. Her thoughts scattered, fear and disgust and sadness all fled until there was nothing left but the pounding of her heart and the pounding of his body into hers, demanding her surrender and release.

She tried to hold back, to make it last, but her reserve shredded like silk and she panted like an animal, shaking with the orgasm that tore through her as he finished with a curse and one last plunge into the depths of her.

The passion ebbed and they stilled, but did not relax. She was still trembling like a bowstring, ready to go again. It had been good in the way she wanted and better than anything she'd experienced in years. But there was the nagging sense that it could be so much more, if only she was willing for it to be so.

Sensing her hesitation, he sighed and withdrew, rolled away from her to take up his book again as if nothing had happened.

Perhaps nothing had. She had got what she wanted. What reason was there to remain? Refusing to be hurt by it, she climbed out of the bed and returned to her room.

Chapter Eighteen

It was an excellent morning.

Alex smiled down the table to the footman at the door of the dining room, overwhelmed with good humour. If he was honest, it was not the best possible of mornings. If it had been that, he would still be in bed, staring at the sex-tousled hair of his wife, spread across the pillows, tickling his arms as he pulled her close to wake her and take her.

There had been no romance in their joining, no wooing or ceremony. She had not come to him to be loved. He supposed he should be hurt by that fact, for he wanted more from her than a purely physical union. He wanted the joining of spirits that he'd felt in the letters they'd exchanged.

But it was hard to feel pain over what had happened when she had delivered pleasure in such an effective, no-nonsense way. God bless a woman who knew her own mind. She had taken him in her hand, worked him to the point of desperation and then provided the relief of her body, gasping out her own climax as he'd found his.

If the act had not left him spouting poetry and cloud-headed, it had certainly left him to sleep soundly and to rise with the urge to crow like a rooster, to announce to the whole world that he was King and had claimed his Queen.

There was the slight problem that his Queen did not want to be claimed. But she had brought that on herself by opening the door of his bedroom and climbing into his bed. She was regretting it this morning, by the look on her face as she sat across the dining table from him. It was unusually sour, as if daring him to mention their intimacy.

'Chocolate?' he said, lifting the pot and gesturing to her cup.

'Thank you.' The words were mundane, but icy.

Alex smiled back and handed the pot across the table to Selina.

Their fingers brushed on the handle and she withdrew her hand as if the contact had burned.

It was not the adoring sigh he might have wished for, but it was proof that she was not indifferent to him. She might not like that she felt something, but she felt it all the same.

He nodded and withdrew as well, ceding her the pot and watching as she poured it herself.

He wondered what she had made of what they had done. Women did not feel things in the same way as men, or so he had been told. But perhaps this one did. She had been hungry enough to come to his room.

There was no point in speculating if she would not talk. But it would have been nice to receive a letter from her today, telling him what she had really thought of the ball and what had happened after. She had not been afraid to speak the truth to Abbott, nor had she been angry at him for things he could not control.

As for Alex? He was going to read the newspaper and try to pretend that he did not want to lean over the table to kiss his wife good morning. He flicked open the pages, turning directly to the tattle page to see what had been said about the previous evening.

He scanned down the page and could not prevent an exclamation of shock when he found what he was looking for.

Selina startled like a frightened deer. 'What?'

'Nothing,' he said quickly, closing the paper again.

'Is it about me?' she said, reaching for it. 'Let me see.'

'No.' But that had been a foolish response. If she did not see it now, with him here, she would simply find it later when he had left the table. He took a breath and handed the paper across the table to her. 'The things that they publish are mostly rubbish. It is best to ignore them.'

Last night at the Earl of F.'s ball, bystanders were shocked to watch the Duke of G. lose a large sum of money to B.B. That man once took the house of Mr O. in a similar game, the first husband of G.'s lovely new bride. Does history repeat itself for the poor Duchess?

'You said you would win,' she said, looking up from the paper.

'I do not always. That is why it is called gambling,' he replied.

'I did not want you to go into that room.'

'Nor did you want me to stay with you,' he reminded her. 'And it is not all bad. They called you lovely, which you are.'

She growled in frustration.

He shrugged and added, 'And it was not a substantial sum. He took as much as I'd planned to wager for the night, then I left the table. I am not beholden to him in any way, as so many men seem to be.' He considered for a moment. 'Although he seemed to be eager for me to get in over my head.'

'Because he still thinks to have me,' she said with a shudder.

'Then he is a fool,' Alex said. 'I told him what would happen to him if he bothered you again.'

'And when did you do that? Or is that something that I will have to read in the papers, too?'

He sighed, for it seemed that he could do nothing right as it pertained to the woman he had married. 'I went to him before the wedding and told him he had lost and to go away.'

'As if I was the prize in a contest?' she said.

'Not at all in that way,' he said, regretting his words. 'I sought to protect you.'

'I thought that marrying you would do that,' she said, looking as frustrated as he felt.

'So did I,' he admitted. 'But it seems I will have to make good on my threat to him.'

'And how will you do that?' she said, her eyes narrowing, then added, 'And do not tell me you will duel. Letting blood might salve your wounded pride, but it would do nothing to help me at all.'

'For a moment, I thought you might be worrying for my safety,' he said, irritated.

She stared back at him, unflinching, waiting for a better solution.

And what would that be? When he had made the threat to keep Baxter away from her, he had thought that the words would be enough and had made no plan. That was his first mistake, but he would not make another.

He thought for a moment more and an idea came to him, but he immediately rejected it, for he was sure Selina would never approve or agree. But the thought would not leave him and he could not begin to persuade her if he did not voice it.

He gave her what he hoped was a winning smile and said, 'On our wedding day, I suggested we have a ball. But I think we should have a card party instead.'

'We most certainly will not,' she said, pushing away from the table and him.

'There is no better way to show that we are not afraid of Baxter and the things that the papers might say about us,' he said.

'But I am afraid,' she replied, her angry façade crumbling to reveal her true feelings. Her grey eyes were huge in her pale face and her lip trembled as if tears might be imminent.

He reached out a hand to cover hers. 'There will be nothing like your husband's gaming. I promise. The stakes will be low and I will eject anyone who is bidding outrageously.'

'John made promises to me as well,' she said, staring at him doubtfully.

'I am not John,' he said gently. 'I have never had a problem with cards.'

'Until the night you gamed with John,' she reminded him.

He took a breath and nodded. 'But though you blame me for what happened, there was nothing I did that caused his death. I happened to be the final straw in the heavy load he carried. But it could just as easily have been someone else.'

'And now you could be the bane of someone else,' she said, her frown returning.

'Baxter,' he reminded her. 'The man is a demon with a deck of cards and I mean to discover why. And to do that, I need to play him in my house, on my terms.'

'I am familiar with that madness,' she said, shaking her head. 'One game will become a dozen and will not end until he has fleeced you of everything you have.'

'One night will be enough,' he swore. 'If I fail, I will not ask you for more.'

She was hesitating now, as if she wanted to believe him. It gave him hope.

'Trust me,' he said, softly, urgently.

Those two words were a mistake greater than any he had made this morning. Her resolve returned and she smiled and shook her head. 'You are the last person in the world who should ask that of me.'

He wanted to remind her that she had awarded him with the ultimate act of trust, just the night before. But that would escalate the argument and do nothing to help his cause. Instead, he shrugged. 'As I promised, I will only ask this of you once. But I will have this game. Let me know when you have picked a date.'

She rose and pushed back from the table, her fists balled in frustration. 'Very well, Your Grace. It is obvious that I cannot stop you from ruin. But do not expect me to mourn you when you end up as John did.'

Selina hurried away, not wanting to hear another word of her husband's cloth-brained plan. If she'd had any hopes going into this marriage, it had been that her days of being a widow to a deck of cards were over. Her last marriage had ended long before John had died. His love of the game had killed anything that there had been between them.

Now the Duke meant to go the same way. She had not wanted him to duel, but she might have forgiven him for it, had he shot Baxter dead.

Of course, she did not mean to forgive him for everything. But then, she had not meant to go to his bed either. And even after doing that, she had not meant to be as affected by that experience as she'd been. She'd been seeking release, nothing more than that.

She had got that and returned to her bed. Then she'd dreamed. Whispered words of love. A man's arms about her. His lips kissing her hair. Flashes of sensation, glimpses of skin. The scent of sandalwood. She had woken feeling not just sated, but loved. It had frightened her.

But not as much as the suggestion of a card party. That was madness.

As she arrived at her room, ready to go in and slam the door, she heard the voice of her son from the nursery, reciting his Latin verbs for the governess whom the Duke had hired, in one of his more sensible moments. The ordinary sound calmed her nerves. Her fears were her own and she would not let them touch the boy in the nursery schoolroom.

She walked down the hall to him and stood at the open door of the room, soaking up the peace of it, exchanging satisfied smiles with the governess, Miss Gates.

Then Edward noticed her and stopped his declension, calling, 'Mama', and rushing to her side for the hug which she was eager to give him.

'My dear,' she responded. 'Well done. Are you enjoying your studies?'

He smiled and nodded, then cast a hesitant look at Miss Gates and requested, in his most formal voice, to be allowed to speak to his mother alone.

The governess nodded back and left the room, giving them their privacy, and Selina took one of the chairs at the schoolroom table, then gestured to Edward to join her, waiting for what he had to say.

'Mama,' he said in a cautious tone. 'Is it wrong that I like it here?'

'Not at all,' she said, relieved that this was their only problem.

'Because I think you do not.' His brow furrowed as he examined her face, searching for clues to her mood.

'Why do you say that?' she said, worried.

'Just now, you were arguing with the Duke,' he said.

She had been unaware that their voices had carried above stairs and wondered how many of her sharp comments he had heard in the last weeks. It made her ashamed.

'It is an adjustment for me, nothing more than that,' she assured him, wondering if that were true. 'Things will be different with time.'

'Because I like it better than I did at our old house,' he said firmly.

'That is what we promised you, when we first brought you here,' she said.

'And is it wrong that I like the Duke better than Father?'

This was a question that she had not expected. One that she did not know how to answer. She remained silent and allowed Edward to continue.

'I do not remember Father very well,' he said. 'He has been gone a long time.'

'A year,' Selina corrected, then remembered that for a child, twelve months was forever.

'And when he was not dead, I did not see him very often. I do not think he liked me very much.'

'Of course he liked you,' Selina said automatically, trying to think of an example she should give him. 'He was very proud when you were born.' And he had been.

Then she remembered her husband's words.

'Thank God it is not a girl.'

Perhaps pride was an overstatement. But John was dead and not all his words or ideas needed to live on in either of their memories. She gave her son an encouraging smile, trying not to think of how dismissive John had been of the idea that they might have a second child and his uninterest in spending time with her or their son. Nothing could compare to the lure of cards.

At last, she said, 'Your father was a troubled man. It did not always leave him time for his family.'

Edward gave her a knowing nod. 'But the Duke does not have troubles, does he?'

Of course he didn't. When he played, he usually won. And when he did not, he was eager for another game, just as John had been. Hopefully his pockets were deep enough to stand the madness he seemed eager to bring down on them. 'No, he does not,' she said, hoping that it was not another lie.

Edward smiled. 'That is good. Because I would not want to lose him like we did Father.'

'We will not lose him,' she said, and forced herself to give him an encouraging smile. 'We are a family now.' But was that true?

After last night, they were at least as much of a family as she and John had been. Perhaps more so, since the Duke seemed more interested in Edward's well-being than the boy's own father had been.

Edward seemed satisfied by her answers and called for his governess to come back, ready to continue his lessons.

Selina thanked the girl and left the room, still confused. Wasn't this what she wanted for her son? To see him happy and thriving?

Of course it was. But she had not expected to see him adjust so quickly or so well. Nor did she expect to feel the emotional ground shifting beneath her feet each time she was near Glenmoor. It had been easier to hate him unconditionally, as she had when she'd married him. But her feelings last night had been something else entirely. He had made her angry again at breakfast, but after talking to Edward, she did not know what to think.

She went to her room and shut the door, both relieved and frustrated to be alone. Then, the desk by the window caught her eye and she went to it, searching the drawers for paper and pen and sitting down to write.

Dear Abbott,

She shook her head at the madness of writing a letter to a man who did not exist. But she could not help the comfort she felt as the words describing the last weeks poured out of her and with them all the confusion and anger and fear.

In my heart, I know this is no different from
writing to myself. But I cannot help it, my love.
    I miss you.
    I need you.
    Tell me what I am to do.
Yours always,
Selina

Then she folded, addressed and sealed the letter,
kissed it once and threw it on to the desk.

Chapter Nineteen

Alex went to his study after breakfast, but left the door open so he might hear when Selina came back downstairs. He wanted to offer something in the way of an apology. He could have told her last night about the loss to Baxter, but had not thought it would matter, to her or to anyone else.

But that was what he'd thought on the night he'd won money from John Ogilvie. Somehow the gossips had made that into a major happening as well. And after seeing it in the papers, she had believed every word of it.

He smiled. The next time she read of him, it would be different. But first, she must be persuaded to accept the unacceptable and allow gambling in their home. And before that, he would have to coax her back downstairs. It appeared that she meant to spend the day in her room, hiding from him.

She avoided him at supper as well, having a tray sent up. But that night, they were to attend a musicale together, and he was relieved to see her appear at the foot of the stairs promptly at seven, in a white-and-gold evening gown, hair bedecked with some of the emeralds he had given her.

He raised her hand to his lips as he helped her into the carriage. 'You are lovely, as always.'

She blinked at him, face expressionless save for a faint blush staining her cheeks. 'Thank you.'

'And I am sorry I upset you this morning,' he added.

At this, she could not hide her look of surprise and, for a moment, her fingers tightened on his hand in what he hoped was gratitude.

'The amount I lost was a trifle and I did not think it would concern you. But you should not have read about it in the papers. I should have told you.'

'That is all right,' she said mechanically. The words sounded like a lie, but they were better than the alternative of a public row, so he accepted them with a smile.

'And as for the card party...'

'I do not wish to speak of it now,' she said.

They rode the rest of the way in silence.

When they arrived at the home of the Duchess of Danforth, they were ushered into the music room and seated side by side on the tightly packed chairs to hear a mediocre soprano warbling through a song about lost love.

Alex was usually immune to sentimentality, tolerating such performances rather than enjoying them.

But perhaps his feelings had been changed by marriage. Tonight, he found himself moved by the plight of the singer, hoping that the last verse would end in a reunion.

Or perhaps it was just the touch of his wife's arm that made him think of romance. She was close at his side, the bare skin above her long gloves brushing against his coat sleeve. Was it his imagination or was she deliberately leaning into him as she swayed to the music? Her eyes were closed as she lost herself in the song.

When it ended, she looked up at him, surprised at their nearness, and tried to correct her posture so they were no longer in contact. But the seats were so close together that there was no room for her to get away. After bumping against the gentleman on her other side, she shrugged and returned to leaning on Alex, nervous but resigned.

He smiled back at her, unperturbed. She might not admit the fact, but she was coming to accept him as her husband and to enjoy his company. It was like watching a plant growing, inch by inch. If he was patient, he would be rewarded by blooms.

In time, she would forgive him for the incident with her husband and forget the supreme mistake that Abbott had been, and they would have the marriage he had always hoped to share with her. But for now, they could sit together, as close as lovers. It was another hour and a half before the music ended and he escorted her back to the carriage for the quiet ride home.

* * *

Once there, they readied for bed. After checking on Edward, Selina called for her maid and sat in silence as Molly combed and braided her hair, still amazed at the changes that had happened in a few short weeks. Tonight's outing was one she'd never have been invited to, had she not married Glenmoor. The company had been august, the house grand, the refreshments elegant. The music had been sweet and sad and it had suited her mood.

It was not at all what she had imagined when she'd wanted to marry the mysterious Abbott. If she was honest, her thoughts on their life together had not strayed much further than the bedroom door. Once the lights had been out, there had been no need for talking. They'd understood each other perfectly. It had all been quite different than the awkward silences she shared with her husband, when she was never sure what he was thinking.

There certainly had not been other people in that fantasy. Nor had she needed to dress in fine clothes and act charming only to have her every move dissected and mocked in the papers the next day.

She missed the dream.

After writing to him this morning, she'd retrieved the stack of his letters that she had saved in her empty jewel case, pulling one from the ribbon-tied bundle and reading a random paragraph. Here, he was assuring her that Edward would be fine and that he had survived his own father's death, though his mother had not been nearly as caring as Selina was. Since he had become a duke, survival was an understatement and any similarities with Edward were hard to imagine.

In another he wrote that he had never owned a horse and much preferred to walk. It was a simple detail about his life, a casual admission that told much. She tried to imagine Glenmoor telling her such a thing, but could not. Surely the Duke had a stable in the country with many horses for riding and pulling carriages.

Perhaps the letter had been a lie. If so, she did not want to hear the truth. She liked the idea of a man who strolled through life at eye level rather than looking down on other people from his place in the saddle.

She had flipped back through a year's worth of letters, gorging herself on his writing for most of the afternoon, feeling her heart flutter as it had each time she'd seen his elegant script, especially when he had written her name. On the rare times he had called her Selina, rather than Mrs Ogilvie, she had been so overcome by the implications she had not slept for days.

Now she had married a man who should know her, but who seemed like a stranger. He called her Selina whenever he chose to. Perhaps there had been no special meaning to it at all.

Molly helped her into her nightgown, which they both knew had been found on the floor of the Duke's bedroom by his valet this morning. Selina could not decide how to feel about the fact. It was certainly not scandalous to visit the bed of one's husband. But then, everything they did now seemed to be of interest to the world.

She closed her eyes and sighed, then opened them again and looked at the door on the other side of the room. It was impossible to deny what she had done and how it had felt to be with him, which had been full of the wordless passion she had expected from the man who wrote her with such dedication. She was sure he would not object if she came to him again. Surely he would have said something if he had not liked what she had done.

She hesitated a moment more, then got out of the bed, stripping her nightgown over her head and dropping it at the foot of her own bed before opening the door and going into his room.

He was there as he had been on the previous day, naked beneath the sheets. But this time, the book had already been set aside and he was staring at her in the doorway, as if he had been listening for her steps. As their eyes met, he shifted, making room for her to climb in beside him. Then he threw back the sheet, revealing that he was already hard, as if the prospect of her arrival had been more than enough to excite him.

She climbed into bed and straddled him, but her position lasted for only a moment before he took hold of her ankle and rolled, trapping her on her back, under him.

For a moment, she was too shocked to do anything, not even breathe. He raised himself up on his elbows to look into her eyes and smiled in a knowing way that sent a tingle of expectation through her body. Then his lips came down upon hers in an un-expected kiss.

It was as heady and dangerous as the kiss in the sitting room had been. She felt her control disappear, her resistance to him evaporate as his lips touched hers and her mouth opened to let him take her fully, his tongue moving against hers in invitation.

This could not be happening. Last night, she had meant to keep herself apart from him, but after a day spent with Abbott and a night of love songs, her resistance was low and her surrender complete. She closed her eyes and focused her mind on the sensations rushing through her and not the man who was causing them, this stranger that she did not understand.

This was easier. She allowed her mind to float and the pleasure crest in waves as his hands found her breasts and took liberties that she had not allowed last night.

Why had she denied herself this? It had been so long since she had felt any touch other than her own. This was different. Unfamiliar, exciting and uniquely male. Possessive yet gentle. It was everything she'd imagined, when searching for hidden meanings in the mundane letters they'd shared. A man who knew her, body and spirit, had longed for her, held himself in readiness for the moment when they could finally be together.

The kiss continued, and she returned it, thrusting her tongue into his mouth and biting his lip and eliciting a low chuckle of satisfaction at her response. She had not touched him last night, other than to arouse him. But now she ran her hands over him, searching each muscle and sinew of his chest and arms, amazed at how hard he was and how soft it made her feel to be near him. Her legs relaxed, spreading for him, eager to accept all he had to give.

His hands smoothed down her sides before locking on to her hips, holding them steady as he rocked his erection against her, once, twice, three times, to remind her that she was not the only one ready for pleasure.

She remembered the feel of him filling her and could not help the eager sigh that escaped her lips as she kissed his throat, biting gently at the cords of his neck, rubbing her face against it, savouring the scent of him, soap and spice, exotic and intoxicating.

And then he was moving against her, sliding down her body, leaving a trail of kisses as he went, like a shower of rose petals, velvet soft against her body.

She felt a moment of surprise that was close to panic. In the past, with her husband, the act had been quick and a little one-sided. She had never experienced the feel of a man's lips making free with her.

She did not know, but that did not mean she had not imagined. In the past, she would take his letters to bed with her and pretend that they said so much more than they did. That he was there with her, as she stroked the paper lightly against her skin. She knew full well how to bring herself to life with her hands and she had imagined that, if they ever met, he would, too, teasing her with his fingers before he claimed her.

But kisses. So many kisses. Her breasts, her belly

and, oh, Lord, between her legs. She had heard whispers of such things, when married women had gathered to giggle over their lives. But she had not believed that it would happen to her, had been afraid to even suggest such a thing as seemed to be about to happen.

No. It was happening. He had spread her legs wide and was nuzzling her thighs, coming closer and closer to her most sensitive place before settling there with a nimble tongue and firm lips and soft breath. She was going to die, she was sure of it now, for no one could withstand a pleasure this intense and simply get out of bed and walk away from it. It was amazing.

It was everything she could have hoped it would be, from the letters he had sent her, kind and funny, always stopping just short of a promise that there might be more between them than just words.

But she had wanted more. And now, here it was, more than anyone had ever offered her. He was worshipping her, feasting on her, loving her as only he could.

And she was lost in it, spiralling tight as a watch spring, gasping and moaning, and finally crying out his name as the tension released.

'Abbott!'

He pulled away with a curse, leaving her cold and trembling as he demanded, 'Open your eyes.'

She had not realised they were closed. She opened them and looked up, thighs still quivering, and for a moment, she was baffled at the sight of Glenmoor, leaning over her, eyes dark with passion and rage.

Then she remembered the truth and turned her face away from him.

He put his fingers on her chin, turning her face back to his, staring into her eyes and daring her to look away again.

'My name is Alex,' he said. Then he laid a hand on her thigh, making the muscles jump with the remaining tension of her orgasm.

He slid into her then, hard and long, and it was as shockingly good as she had hoped it would be, as good as last night, even better than her imagination.

'Say my name.' His body was moving slowly against hers, but his voice was as tightly controlled as his movements.

She was silent, both excited and terrified, confused by the feelings that were raging in her. She wanted him, and yet she didn't. She wanted this. But she shouldn't.

'Say my name,' he said, in a tone that was rough with arousal.

'Alex,' she whispered, trying to look away.

'Again.'

Her muscles were tightening again, against logic and will. The slow hot friction was bringing her back to where she had been when his mouth had been on her, driving her wild. She stared at his lips, strange and yet intimately familiar, and felt the first shudder of passion wash over her.

'Again.' More urgent this time, his breath ragged with his own exertions.

'Alex,' she said, forcing the word out and gasping

as he came into her again. 'Alex.' But who was that, really? She did not know. But they were rushing towards something now that was impossible to stop and she would have said anything he asked if only to have that feeling again. 'Alex.'

He came into her, losing himself in one final thrust, taking her over the edge with him.

There was a moment of peace, then he rolled off her, on to his back, staring up at the ceiling.

She was afraid to look at him, yet she could not look away. He was beautiful, even if she did not want to admit it. He raised his hand, covering his eyes, and spoke without turning his head. 'You may go back to your room now.'

It was not a request. It was a demand, though spoken so softly that the pain it caused surprised her. After all that had happened, she did not think this man had the power to hurt her any more than he already had. She sat up and swung her legs out of the bed, and walked unsteadily to the door and through it, back to her own lonely bed.

She was not making love to him.

Alex wiped his face with his hand, as if he could wipe away the last few minutes, or perhaps the whole of the last year. Maybe, if he could begin again, it would be different. Or perhaps it would be better if he had never met her at all. But he was sure that he wanted to free himself of this thing he had created, this double who was so much more attractive to her than he could ever be.

It was against all logic, really. He was a duke, and a rich one at that. Educated as well. And, he had been told, more than moderately good-looking. To any other woman in the world, it would have been enough. But the one woman he wanted had to pretend he was someone else so that she could lie with him.

It was not fair. What they had just shared had been wonderful. At least, he'd thought they'd been sharing it. Instead, she had been thinking of someone else.

The fact that that someone else was just another part of him was the cruellest irony of all. He had created his own competition, a man who lived large in his wife's fantasy and was not beholden to the paltry rules of reality that chained Alex. Abbott had never hurt her. He did not gamble. He never made demands, nor did he drag her reputation through the mud. He gave and gave and never asked for anything in return. The man was perfect. There was no way to compete against that.

Why even try? From now on, the bedroom door would stay closed and locked, until she had a reason to seek *him* out and not some fantasy lover that he stood in proxy to. If they could not come together properly as man and wife, they would not be together at all.

Chapter Twenty

After a sleepless night, Selina came down to the breakfast room to find her husband in his usual spot, going through the morning post as if nothing had happened the night before. He was not smiling the secret smile he had worn yesterday morning, the one she had not appreciated when she'd had the chance.

Now she discovered she missed it and was not sure how to get it back. Did he expect her to apologise for what she had done last night? It had been an accident, but that was really no excuse for it. And it would not happen again. After how he had marked her with his lovemaking, she might never be able to close her eyes again, much less utter another man's name.

But had she really? It was a name he had chosen. It was him.

And yet, it was not.

Her hand trembled as she reached for the chocolate pot, for it was all very confusing and she was not ready to deal with it the first thing in the morning after worrying about it most of the night. But someone had to say something. The silence, which she thought she had grown used to, suddenly seemed too oppressive to bear.

'Do you have a horse?'

She sucked in a breath of surprise, for that had not been what she'd intended to say.

'I beg your pardon?' It had not been what he'd expected to hear either.

She cleared her throat. 'I said, do you have a horse?'

'No,' he said, looking at her as if she had just lost her mind.

'But you have carriage horses. And I assume there is a stable at your country home,' she pressed, unable to stop herself.

'There were horses there when I came into the title. Hunters, riders, carriage horses, dray horses.' He shrugged. 'I am unsure how many. More than are needed, I suspect. But there are none that I would call mine. I do not know their names or feed them sugar lumps and dote on them, as if they are large, stupid children. I have horses, but none that I hold any attachment to.'

'Oh.' That explained the letter, which was, in some sense, an accurate way to describe his preferences.

'Do you have any other questions?'

She had many. But the last was delivered in a way that said he had no desire to answer her frivolous queries, so she shook her head and went back to her chocolate.

He was silent, too, for a time. He helped himself to another cup of coffee, buttered a muffin and opened another letter, then spoke without looking up. 'Do you need any instruction in preparing for the card party? Have you chosen a date?'

She had not precisely forgotten yesterday's request. She had simply hoped that it might go away, especially after what had happened in bed. She wet her lips. 'I have done nothing, thus far.'

'It need not be large. Ten couples, more or less.'

It might as well have been a hundred for the dread she felt at the suggestion. 'It is not the size that upsets me,' she said, then challenged him. 'How large was the party where you met my husband?'

He looked up at her with an expression that said he'd said more than enough on this subject, then replied, 'It was not a party, nor was it at one of the seedy gaming hells you seem to think I inhabit. It was at White's. I have no idea how he gained entry there, as he was not a member. He must have been someone's guest. No one stepped forward to claim him, after what occurred. I am sure the person who led him to that final game was more than happy to see me get all the credit for it.'

'Oh,' she said softly. This was not what she had imagined at all.

'And he is not your husband,' the Duke reminded her. 'He is your first husband. Or perhaps your late husband.'

'I did not mean…' she began to say, then trailed off, embarrassed.

'Of course you didn't,' he said bitterly. Then he looked back at his plate, refusing to meet her gaze.

'Because of the location, I had no reason to distrust his marker, nor were the stakes so high that I meant to ruin him. It was a friendly game and in no way memorable.'

But he obviously remembered each detail of it. Perhaps she was not the only one haunted by what had occurred that night.

'I should have asked you before this,' she said softly.

'Yes, you should have,' he agreed without looking up. 'But from the moment we met, you have argued and misconstrued, and rebuffed me at every turn. You have spared no opportunity to remind me that I am not the man you wanted to marry.'

Why was she surprised at the pain in his voice? Hadn't her intent been to make him suffer in this marriage? But suddenly her plans seemed foolish and they were hurting her as much as they ever did him.

He pushed his plate aside and stood up, staring down at her. 'The fact that you do not want me no longer matters, nor will I torment you with my demands after this one. The card party will be my farewell to London society for the Season. After that, you and this city are welcome to each other.' Then he left the dining room, and she heard the front door slam behind him.

She sat in silence for a moment, unsure of what to do next. Last night, they had been as close as two human beings could be. Now he did not even want to be in the same city with her. The woman who she had been on the day of their marriage would have rejoiced at this news. Now she did not know what to make of it.

She finished her breakfast and went to the morning room, sitting down with her book of names and addresses, and prepared the guest list that he had asked for, paged through her calendar and found a date a week hence, then began writing invitations.

The mechanical process of putting words to paper was comforting, as long as she did not think of what she was writing. But that uncoupling was impossible when she reached the final sheet that was to go to Baxter. She had to force her hand to form the words of courtesy needed to invite him and she sealed the paper quickly and put it in the stack of finished letters, hoping that the toxic nature of the receiver would be dissipated by the company of the other invitations.

Once finished, she went back to her room, closed the door behind her and went to the writing desk to the stack of Abbott letters, paging through them, searching for something that would help her understand what was happening to her now.

But instead of the comforting passages that she usually found, she saw continual hints and reminders that, no matter how strong their friendship and her love for him, they could never be together. Abbott had told her over and over that it would not work. Apparently, he had been right.

She folded the letters, stacked them and retied the ribbon. Then she noticed the conspicuous absence of the letter she had written yesterday. She paged through the papers again, more frantically this time, then turned to her maid, who was straightening the gowns in the wardrobe. 'Where is the letter that was on the desk?' she said urgently.

'I put it in the post,' Molly said, blinking innocently back at her.

'You foolish girl…' But that was unfair. She was the foolish one for writing that letter at all to a man she knew did not exist. She shook her head in apology and said more calmly, 'I was not finished with it.'

'It was sealed,' the girl reminded her.

'That was my mistake,' Selina replied. 'Is it too late to get it back?'

Molly hurried down to the front hall and back again, shaking her head. 'It is long gone, Your Grace.'

Selina took a breath to calm herself. What was the worst that could happen? It would probably sit unclaimed at the post office that she had addressed it to, for what reason would Alex have to retrieve it? In case it did come here, she would watch the incoming post and snatch it back before her husband found it and opened it. The last thing she needed was this further proof that she was still dreaming of a man who would never come.

At his club, Alex sat with his paper, pretending to read and hoping that it would be enough to dissuade any of the other members from conversation. He should have gone to Gentleman Jackson's for some sparring instead. He felt like hitting something.

Or perhaps he felt like being hit. A few sharp jabs to his head might clear the fog and make it easier to

see a way forward that didn't involve running from
his wife like a coward. But was it really cowardice
not to stay in a place he was not welcome or wanted?

And what was he going to do about Edward? The
boy's mother might not want him, but the boy had
grown to depend on him in a few short days. He
would have to sit down with the child and tell him
that Alex's departure had nothing to do with him.
Perhaps he could teach the boy how to play chess by
mail and they could still have their games.

Evan dropped into the chair next to him, pushing
the paper away and staring at the wine glass on the
table next to Alex. 'You are here early.'

'No earlier than you,' he replied, giving the paper
a warning rattle.

'Responding to the invitation that was just hand
delivered to my house. We will be there, of course.'

Apparently, his wife had taken him at his word
and organised the event as he'd requested. 'The card
party? And when are we holding it?'

Evan laughed. 'Shouldn't you be the one to tell
me?'

'The calendar is Selina's purview, not mine.'

'Tuesday afternoon,' Evan replied, giving him an
incredulous look.

'Five days' time, then,' he said thoughtfully.

'And was this Selina's idea as well? Because I would
find that hard to believe,' Evan said, still staring at him.

'She arranged the party at my instruction.'

'And that is why you are out of the house now,'
Evan said with a nod. 'Go home and say you are sorry.'

'I have nothing to be sorry for,' Alex snapped.

'Of course not,' his brother replied with a laugh. 'You are merely forcing your wife to play cards after she watched them destroy her life. Why would she be angry with you over that?'

'There is little I do that does not make her angry,' he said, annoyed at the note of self-pity in his voice. 'And it is all the fault of Abbott.'

Evan shook his head. 'I blame Oxford for giving you misguided views of male and female relations. Even I did not make such a hash of the early days of my marriage and I was decidedly wrong-headed.'

'Thank you for your assessment,' Alex said, glaring and reaching for his wine glass. 'I could never have come to that conclusion on my own.'

'And now, what do you mean to do about it?'

'Travel,' he said. 'Now that the war is over, I thought, perhaps a trip to Paris…'

'You are running away,' Evan said.

'I am merely putting sufficient space between myself and the woman I married.' But would the Channel be enough to ease the hurt. 'I am considering the Americas as well.'

'Or you could stay and make up for what you have done,' Evan suggested in a gentle tone.

'She ignores my actions and will not listen to a word I say.'

'Then you must do the obvious,' Evan said.

'And what is that?'

'Why don't you write her a letter?'

Chapter Twenty-One

The few days before the card party passed quickly, and there was little to do to prepare other than to plan a menu of light refreshments and locate enough tables and chairs for the players. There were no regrets in the responses to her invitations, as far as she knew.

When the answer from Baxter arrived, she could not bring herself to open it. Instead, she tossed it into her husband's pile of mail on the breakfast table and told him in a curt voice that he must deal with any correspondence with that man as she simply could not.

The Duke looked up at her without speaking, then popped the seal and scanned the response. 'He is coming,' he said, then went back to eating his breakfast.

They spoke little to each other, these days. Two weeks ago, she would have preferred the silence, but now it bothered her. There were things she needed to say to him and she was still not sure what they were.

Things were different in the evenings when they were home, for Edward was there and they had declared an unspoken truce while in his presence. She stayed on one side of the room and busied herself with her needlework and the Duke stayed on the other, where he continued to teach her son chess, training him on the notation of the spaces so he might understand how best to describe the moves he was making. It was all very civil and she suspected that Edward was not the least bit fooled by it.

Afterwards, they went to their respective bedrooms and closed their doors without saying goodnight. Then Selina lay awake, staring at the connecting door, afraid to touch it, lest she find it locked. Even if it was open, she did not think she had the nerve to go through it, though her body yearned to be with him again.

If he was going away, as he had threatened, would it be so wrong to be with him, one last time? Perhaps she could make him change his mind. But with the card party looming ever closer, it was impossible to think. Her head ached. Her stomach roiled. She could not sleep at night or focus during the day.

When the day of the party arrived, all she could manage was a sip of tea at breakfast before going to the sitting room to oversee the removal of the furniture and its replacement with game tables. Everything was properly in its place and the guests would be arriving in the early evening. All that was left was for her to dress and be ready to greet them.

And when she did, she would have to sit down with them, to shuffle and deal and pretend to be happy. She had seldom played and was not particularly skilled at any of the games the Duke was planning. She did not know how or when to bet at loo, and to be partnered with anyone for whist would be a disaster, since there was no way she could keep up with the subtleties of the play.

She slowly backed out of the room, then turned and hurried down the hall and up the stairs, unable to face the prospect any longer. Before going to her room, she stopped to see Edward in the nursery and he greeted her arrival with a sulky glare. 'You promised,' he said, folding his arms in front of his chest in a gesture of defiance.

'What, my darling?' she said, crouching down beside him.

'You said that the Duke had no problems and would not go away. But he has told me that he is going on a long trip and that I cannot come along.' The words tumbled out of him, his face going red with anger and unshed tears.

'But we will remain in his house,' she said patiently.

'Where is he going?' Edward said, stomping a foot. 'Is he going to the country house? He said I could go there. He said that we would all go there in summer.'

She had no idea how to answer, for the Duke had said nothing of his plans to her. 'I do not know,' she admitted, placing her hand on her son's shoulder. 'But I am sure he would take you along, if that was all he planned.'

'What did you do?' Edward demanded. 'What did you say to make him not like us any more?'

The accusation hurt, probably because it was so accurate a way to describe what had happened, and her silence proved to him that he was right.

'Can't you say you are sorry?' he said hopefully. 'Then perhaps he will not go.'

She had not. Perhaps it would not be enough, but perhaps it would. 'I will talk to him,' she said at last, not wanting to dash the boy's hopes.

He smiled back at her, offered her a hug, by way of a reward, and returned to the book he had been reading, confident that she would solve all their problems with a simple apology.

She walked out into the hall and to her room, her feet dragging at each step as she thought of the night that lay ahead. She had not wanted to do this when the Duke had first suggested it and she liked it no better now that the event was upon them.

She turned to the connecting door and listened to the faint sounds of movement on the other side. He was preparing for the party, just as she should be. She walked forward and put her hand on the door handle, rattling it in frustration when she discovered that it was locked. 'Alex,' she called. 'I need to talk to you.'

There was a moment of silence and then a mutter, as the Duke dismissed his valet. The door opened and he stood before her, staring expectantly.

'I am sorry,' she said. When he did not respond, she continued. 'Sorry for everything. For the way I have treated you, for not trusting you. And,' she whispered, 'for the thing I said in the bedroom.'

'But?' he replied. 'For there is clearly more you want to say to me.'

'I cannot do this,' she said, then added, 'I am ill.' And she did feel sick. It was not a lie.

'We have guests coming in an hour,' he reminded her in a calm voice.

'You have guests,' she countered. 'You know I cannot abide gambling. Please do not force me to do it. Anything but that.' And, for the first time since they had married, she could not stop the tears that were welling up in her eyes. She reached out for the doorframe as the world seemed to pitch and rock beneath her and her knees buckled.

'Damn.' He caught her before she could swoon, scooping her into his arms and carrying her back into her room to lay her on the bed. He laid a hand on her forehead, then rubbed her wrists as if trying to force life back into her. 'You have worked yourself into a state over this.' His voice was rough and annoyed, but not totally without sympathy. 'What have you eaten today?'

She answered with an embarrassed shrug, for it was long past luncheon and she'd had nothing at all.

He let out an exasperated sigh. 'I will give your regrets.' Then he walked to the bell-pull and summoned her maid with a sharp tug. 'Her Grace is ill. Feed her and put her to bed.'

Then he left her, embarrassed and alone.

Alex went back to his room and called for his valet to finish with his cravat and coat, trying to ignore the creeping guilt at the thought of the woman in the next room. He had dismissed her protestations over this event, but had never imagined that she would work herself into a state of nervous prostration over it.

He was not so great a villain as to force her to entertain when she might swoon at any moment, though it would certainly add that touch of melodrama that would earn them a place in tomorrow's paper. Instead, he would have to manage the event himself. Once he was dressed, he informed the servants of the change, checking on the menu and assuring himself that there was sufficient claret for the gentlemen and ratafia for the ladies.

Then he went to the entryway to greet his guests as they arrived. The footman at the door turned to him nervously and bowed, reaching into the pocket of his livery and offering a letter to Alex. 'From the lady, Yer Grace.'

He stared down at it, surprised to see that it was addressed to Mr Abbott. 'Where did you get this?'

'The post office, Yer Grace. You said I was to check the mail every day.'

And he had never told the fellow to stop, even after he had married Selina. Somehow, her last letter to him had fallen through the cracks and was only arriving now. 'Thank you for your dedication,' he said to the footman, stuffing the letter into the pocket of his own coat. 'It will no longer be necessary to go to the post office for me. There will be no more letters.'

The boy looked vaguely disappointed that he had lost such a special duty, but he nodded in obedience and went back to stand at the door as the guests began to arrive.

As usual, Evan and his wife were first. When they heard that Selina was indisposed, Maddie offered to stand in as hostess for the evening. They asked no questions, but he could see by the look they exchanged that they wanted to.

The other couples trickled in, including Selina's friend Mary Wilson and her husband. But he was waiting for the one person that Selina had wanted to avoid. When Alex had almost given up hope, Baxter appeared, pausing in the doorway to rake the foyer with his eyes.

'You are alone?' he said with a sly smile. 'I expected that the Duchess would be here to welcome me.'

'She is indisposed,' Alex said, gesturing towards the sitting room.

'How unfortunate. I so looked forward to seeing her.' The comment was no different from ones made by other guests. But somehow, when Baxter said it, it was vile.

Alex hid his feelings of disgust beneath a smile. 'Another time, perhaps. But now, if you will accompany me, the games are about to start.'

They went to the sitting room to find two chairs open at a table with Evan and Mr Wilson. It was exactly the setting that Alex had hoped for when he had planned the party and he took his seat and watched as Baxter picked up the deck.

'Fancy a game of loo?' Baxter was shuffling the

cards with an easy dexterity and smiling in what he probably thought was a welcoming way.

Alex smiled back, trying to conceal his loathing. 'Don't mind if I do.' He glanced at the other two men, who nodded in agreement and reached for their purses to throw coins into the pot.

Baxter dealt the cards. Then the play began.

Alex's hand was near to worthless and Baxter was a clear winner. He fared somewhat better in succeeding hands, only to lose again when Baxter dealt.

It was probably a coincidence. But it led him to watch more closely when the third round happened with the same results. There was something in the way Baxter held the cards that seemed wrong. Awkward, yet incredibly smooth. Without warning, he switched from riffling the cards to an overhand shuffle. Then dealt out Alex another worthless hand and took the pot again.

When it was Alex's turn to deal, he took a moment to feel the cards in his hands as he shuffled. Was there a faint bend in this card? A scratch on the back of that one? The deck had been new at the beginning of the evening, but now they seemed worn.

When it was Baxter's turn again, Alex waited until the man was about to begin dealing and called, 'Halt.'

Baxter froze, looking at him in confusion.

'Turn over the cards. I wish to see them.'

Baxter ignored him, ready to deal again.

'I said, I wish to see the cards,' he repeated, standing up and reaching across the table for them.

The other man instinctively pulled them back

towards his body, laughing nervously. 'Don't you trust me?'

'That remains to be seen,' Alex said, smiling back at him. 'Turn over the deck, please, so that we may see the source of your good luck.'

'This is ridiculous,' Baxter said, shaking his head. 'I have never…'

'Just show us the cards and be done with it,' Wilson said, staring at Baxter expectantly.

'Don't be ridiculous,' Baxter said, reaching to drop them into his pocket and end the game.

But Alex was too fast for him, grabbing his wrist and closing his other hand over the deck before Baxter could throw the cards away and hide the truth. Alex plucked the deck from his fingers, turning it over and fanning it out to reveal the aces placed neatly at the bottom.

He glanced from man to man, around the table. 'I suspect, if we examine the cards, we will find that they are bent or marked in some other way to make it possible for him to stack the deck.'

Curses rang out around the table and hands gripped Baxter, forcing him back into his seat as he tried to rise. 'Explain yourself,' said Evan. Around the room, play stopped and heads turned to watch the drama unfolding before them.

'Gentlemen,' Baxter said with a weak laugh. 'It is a strange coincidence. Nothing more than that.' Then he looked at Alex, as if daring him to make an accusation. 'Unless someone would want to imply that it is not.'

Alex laughed. 'Imply is such a gentle way to put it. I am stating quite plainly that you have been cheating at cards.' He pointed to Evan and Wilson. 'I know that these men are innocent and the deck that is now marked was fresh when we sat down to play. My only question now is, how long have you been playing us false and how many men have you cheated?'

Now the whole room was watching, fascinated.

'These are dangerous accusations,' Baxter said with a huff. 'As a man of honour...'

Alex held up his hand. 'Do you think to challenge a duke to an illegal duel? If you strike me down, you will hang for it. And personally, I would not waste a bullet on you, for you have no honour to offend. Now leave my house, or I will have you removed.'

'I have never been so insulted,' Baxter said, rising to go. But there was no strength to his words and he was unsteady on his feet as he made to go.

Before he could pass, Alex leaned in and said softly so that no one could hear, 'I told you if you harassed my wife again, I would ruin you. This is for that embarrassing on dit in the paper the morning after we gambled. I expect to hear no more from you. Now be gone.' Then, with a glance in their direction, he signalled the footmen by the sitting room door to see the fellow out.

The room stayed quiet for a moment, then everyone began talking at once, amazed by what they had just seen and eager to analyse each word.

After exchanging a satisfied look with Evan, Alex stood and spoke. 'I apologise for the rather colourful interruption in our fun. Let us refill our glasses and I will ring for the sandwiches. Then we shall have time for another hand.'

The play went on for another hour and a half and everyone declared that it had been a most enjoyable evening and very entertaining.

As the room cleared, Evan grabbed the last cheese sandwich off the tray on their table and said around a large bite, 'How long have you known that Baxter was a cheat?'

'I only suspected. I needed proof. If I had hinted at it before and been wrong? You know how quickly rumours spread.'

'The fellow is well and truly ruined now,' Evan said, satisfied. 'And all his previous wins are suspect.'

'If he is smart, he will pack his tricks and travel to the Continent. He will not be welcome in London for years to come.'

Evan laughed and Maddie tugged at his sleeve. 'We must leave now, for I expect Alex will want to tell his wife the good news. This discovery will lay to rest that nonsensical rumour that you took advantage of her late husband. Now everyone will see Mr Baxter as the villain.'

Alex could not help the smile, for that had been his hope all along. He had assumed that she would be in the room for the unmasking. But a second-hand tale would have to do. Then they would see if she wanted him to carry out his threat to leave her.

He saw his brother to the door, then went to his

study, to rehearse what he would say to her. The words, when he spoke them, must be better than anything he had managed when he had pretended to be Abbott.

It was then that he remembered the letter still in his pocket. Would it hurt to visit that part of his life one last time, when things had been less complicated and their love unconsummated and pure?

He cracked the seal and read.

My husband is not the man I thought he was. But neither is he you, and I do not believe he can be. How can I allow a man to touch my body who has never touched my heart? I fear that this marriage will be no different than the one I shared with John, an empty imitation of the union I seek.

He thrust the letter into the drawer where he saved the rest of the letters from her and slammed it shut. Then he went upstairs to pack, just as he had planned.

Chapter Twenty-Two

The next morning, Selina rose slowly, exhausted from the day before. It was true that she had not wanted to attend the card party on the previous evening and was glad that she had missed it. But neither had she intended to collapse weeping and be put to bed like an invalid. It was embarrassing and not at all like her.

But now that the party was over, they would be alone to deal with their own problems. She hoped that there was still time to convince the Duke to stay, as her apology had been weak and confusing, and not at all the cogent argument she had hoped to put forth for trying again.

Her maid came to her room to dress her and she paused for a moment before choosing a green day dress, remembering how much he'd remarked he liked her in green. If she was to live with him in any kind of harmony, she needed all the advantages she could find.

With her toilet completed, she went down to the breakfast room, only to find it empty. Was he avoiding her, or was he sleeping later than she had? She came back to the bedrooms, then, and knocked at the door of his room, only to have it opened by his valet.

'He was up with the dawn, Your Grace,' the man said with a subservient bow of his head. 'Then he went out and did not say where he was going.'

For a moment, she thought of John, who had sometimes stayed out for days and come home when his pockets were empty, smelling of strange perfume. Then she remembered that the Duke was a different sort of man. Even if he was not, it was hardly her place to object to how he wanted to spend his time. She smiled at the servant to prove that she found nothing unusual about her husband's behaviour, fighting down the nervousness it had raised in her. 'When he returns, tell him I wish to speak to him,' she said, then went to the nursery to see to Edward.

It was early afternoon and she was considering a nap when she received a visit from her friend Mary Wilson, who rushed into the room and enveloped her in a sisterly hug. 'Are you better today? What was wrong yesterday? We all missed you.'

'It was nothing,' Selina assured her. 'I was overtired. Nothing more than that.'

'I enjoyed it immensely, as did everyone I spoke to. And, of course, the latest on dit in the paper has cemented you as the most interesting couple of the Season.'

'Oh, dear,' Selina said, thinking of the argument that she'd had with the Duke and the possibility that one of the servants might have heard. 'What are they writing about now?'

Mary looked at her with wide eyes. 'Surely you have heard.'

'Heard what?' Selina said with a smile.

'Your husband did not tell you what occurred? He did not speak to you after everyone had left?'

'Really, I have no idea what you are talking about,' she said, becoming annoyed. What had the Duke done to raise such a fuss and why had he kept another secret?

'It was in the paper this morning and is in all the scandal sheets,' Mary supplied, shaking her head in amazement. 'Rumour has it that Baxter has fled the country to avoid the shame.' Then Mary's lips snapped shut and she covered her mouth. She was practically bouncing in her chair with excitement.

Selina sucked in a breath at the mention of the man's name before the full meaning of the sentence reached her. 'He has left England?'

Mary nodded. 'My husband was at the same table with the two Dukes and Baxter and assures me it was far more dramatic than the paper can convey. Your husband took the deck from his hand and proved that Baxter was dealing from the bottom. Baxter tried to bluff, even after he was caught, and threatened a duel. Your husband laughed at him and said that such things were for men of honour and that he was not worthy of a bullet. And then Baxter slunk off like the miserable cur he is. All of London wonders how long he has been cheating and whether he gained any of his winnings honestly.'

Her nemesis was vanquished, in an act so dramatic that the whole *ton* knew of it. It was the sort of romantic gesture that she had dreamed her hero Abbott would make for her. A public humiliation that had preserved her honour and avenged John Ogilvie.

'And I am sure we will hear no more nonsense about Glenmoor ruining your first husband,' Mary said with a solemn nod. 'Personally, I never believed it and I am sure you did not either. Not really, or you would not have married him.'

A lie of agreement was on the tip of her tongue and she bit it back, as the shame of the truth washed over her. 'That is just it, Mary. I blamed him. I always have. When I married him, I think it was more out of revenge than anything else. I wanted to hurt him and thought this might be the easiest way to do it.'

'But he was so kind to you,' her friend said, surprised. 'And didn't you say when he was writing you all those letters that you were friends? And I thought perhaps something more.'

'I did not know what to think, when I found out. I was so foolish. I read and read them, but I never imagined his hand holding the pen.' Or his face, smiling as he wrote, just as he had smiled at her on their wedding day, no matter how foul she was to him.

But she could see him now, though the image wavered in the tears that were filling her eyes. 'I was a fool,' she said, wringing her hands.

'You must tell him so,' Mary said softly, offering

her a handkerchief before she could ask. 'Is he in the house right now?'

'No. He has gone out, to Parliament, I think.' But that did not begin until afternoon. He had gone far too early for that.

'It is not in session today,' her friend corrected her.

'Oh,' she said faintly. 'He is probably at his club then. I am sure I will see him at supper and he will explain everything. Then I can tell him how wrong I have been.'

'Of course,' said Mary, giving her a sympathetic nod. 'And thank him for all of us, for handling Baxter with such skill. The man is hated throughout London.'

When her friend left, she hurried upstairs to find the Duke's valet to enquire as to whether he had returned without her noticing. That man knew nothing, but admitted that two suits of clothes were missing and enough linen to last for a week. Wherever he had gone, he did not intend to come back anytime soon.

'And he would not have gone to the country without me,' the valet insisted, his brow creased with worry.

'I am sure it is nothing we need to be concerned about,' Selina said, experimenting with a brave smile to show that it was just a tiff that they would settle in time.

But was that the case? She did not think so. She had wasted so much time blaming Alex for John's death, no matter how many times he had insisted that it was not his fault. Why had she not seen Baxter for the villain he was? If he had won the house by cheating, he owned the lion's share of the blame for what happened after.

And John was to blame as well. The Duke had been blunt in his assessment of her late husband and she had felt the need to defend him. But what John had done must be viewed through the lens of his own affliction. There had been nothing right or fair about his treatment of her. Blind obedience to a dead man served no purpose, especially when there was a living man in her life who had done nothing but try to help.

She thought of the way she had treated him and she got a sick feeling in the pit of her stomach that only grew worse as she imagined each interaction and how desperately she had clung to John, though he had done nothing to deserve her devotion.

She had punished the Duke of Glenmoor unfairly. Even after she had learned how much he had helped her. Lord knew why he was so kind to her through it all. And, without her asking, he had continued to uncover what had happened on the night John had died, to bring the facts of it before the *ton*. How could she ever thank him?

For now, she had to find him, to talk to him and try to make right some of the things she had done wrong. She thought of them in bed together and the fiery passion they shared. If she could put her girlish fantasies aside, and stop longing for the man in his letters, she could be a good wife to him, she was sure. But first, she must find him.

She ran down the stairs, then down the hall and

into his study, hoping that he had left some clue behind there. His desk was orderly and spotless, though there was a pile of books on the shelf that had not been put away, as if he kept them out to refer to them frequently.

She ran a hand over the spines and read the titles. Philosophy, poetry, Shakespeare. Food for an enquiring mind with perhaps a touch of romance in the soul. They were the sorts of things she had imagined Abbott would have had in his study, for he had claimed to be a romantic at heart. Their presence made her smile, for, though he did not seem to want to be associated with that name, the spirit of his letters resided somewhere within him.

She opened a desk drawer, looking for other clues. The first was uninteresting, holding ledgers and unpaid bills, and correspondence with his man of business. But in the second drawer, the one at his right hand so the contents were close at all times, was a stack of crisp fresh paper, devoid of monogram or crest, a bottle of blue ink and a pair of freshly sharpened quills.

Her heart quickened at the sight, for it was as if she were looking into another desk entirely. Abbott's desk. She could imagine him taking out the makings of a letter to her, pushing his work to the side to indulge himself in the joy of writing.

Then she rejected the fantasy. She was far too guilty already of attributing motives to the man without asking him his mind. Maybe he had viewed those letters as a chore. He certainly seemed to think that the persona was unwanted baggage, now that she knew the truth. Maybe he was ashamed of the time he had wasted on her.

But perhaps there was something here that would tell her the truth. The stack of paper was not as flat and symmetrical as it should be. When she riffled through it, she could see several folded sheets tucked between the unused ones, as if he had wanted them out of sight even in the already private space they occupied.

She was not supposed to see them. But neither should she be in this room, going through his desk. What was one more sin on top of the first? She pulled the papers out of the stack and smoothed them flat, reading.

My dearest Selina,

This had been crossed out, then replaced with the same words again, followed by the admission,

That is what you are to me, though I have been too cautious to write the words before. You are dearest to me and grow dearer with each passing day. Your name is like a poem, a refrain that rings over and over in my head each time I see you, and each time I sit down to write.

How I long to say the word aloud, rather than hiding behind the courtesy of your married name. Selina.

By now, you know the reason why I have not

*come to you or made the offer I think you hoped
for. If you know, you hate me, which confirms
my need for secrecy.*

*Please believe that it was never my inten-
tion to trick you. Our correspondence began as
something simple and I intended it to be brief.
But I enjoyed your letters so much that I could
not seem to stop. A dozen times at least I wrote
a letter that I hoped would be the last, only to
write another the next day.*

*And a dozen times I wrote a letter proclaim-
ing my love for you, admitting all. And each
time, I tossed them into the fire. I was too great
a coward to confess and too self-indulgent to
give you up.*

*Now you are mine. And yet, you are further
away than ever.*

*What shall I do with you, Selina? You come
to me pale as a shaft of moonlight and offer
your body freely. But I fear your soul belongs
to another. That man. A man I can no longer
be for you.*

*Abbott was an illusion, a man without a past
that he needed to atone for. But I, my darling,
am all too human and I fear that will never be
enough for you.*
Your adoring husband,
Alexander Fitzgerald Conroy

He had written it recently, just as she'd written to
him. She ran her finger along the lines of text, hear-

ing his voice as she read. She stared at the script, the hand so familiar, like dozens of letters that she had received and cherished. She could set it beside the others and know that all the words had come from the same man. The only difference between this and the previous notes was the name at the bottom, the name of her husband, the man who would admit to a depth of feeling that Abbott had never claimed for her.

Why had she not remembered what he had said of the Duke while in his disguise? He had hinted that Glenmoor could not behave normally in her presence. That he was stunned by her beauty until he was unable to talk. And if she had to describe him, he was still a taciturn man, more comfortable with Edward than he was with her.

But what did he need to say? She knew him through a year of letters. If all he had said in them was true, then she knew him better than she had John. He was her soulmate, after all.

Another proof of that was the familiar bundle of familiar papers, tied neatly with a cord, that had been pushed to the back of the drawer. He had kept her letters to re-read, just as she had kept his.

And there, at the top, was the foolish note she had written to Abbott a week ago, when she had been sure that her marriage could never be happy. He had received it and read it, and now he was gone.

She had driven him away with her own words.

The bottom seemed to drop out of her world as it had yesterday, while she was poised in the doorway between their rooms and had been suddenly too weak to stand. She had needed him then to care for her and she needed him now. What would she do, now that he was out of her reach? How could she apologise? How could she make this better?

In the distance, the front door slammed and she heard footsteps pounding down the hall and her husband, Alex, her beloved, calling her name. He stopped in the doorway of the study and they stared at each other in equal confusion, embarrassed by the emotions that racked them.

'Your Grace,' she said in a shocked gasp.

'Selina?' The name was a question, as if he did not know what to do with her, now that he'd found her.

'You left without telling anyone where you were going,' she said, still breathless.

'I did not think it would matter,' he replied.

'You did not even tell your valet,' she reminded him. 'He is beside himself.'

'Harvey fears that I will travel without a clean shave and fresh linens. He always worries about me.' His lips quirked into a smile at the idea.

'And he is not the only one,' she said, pausing and wetting her lips.

'Really,' he said, eyeing her and waiting for any sign that she might say more. 'Edward, I suppose.'

'He is most fond of you and was overwrought to think that you might go away,' she said, blinking at him. 'I wanted to tell you that yesterday. But I failed.'

He took a step into the room. 'And was that all?' he asked, searching her face.

'And I heard what you did with Baxter. It will change the way society views you,' she said.

'If I cared about the *ton*, it would please me to know that,' he said, still staring at her.

'I care,' she said, and it came out in a whisper.

'I beg your pardon?' He cupped a hand to his ear.

'It matters to me that people think well of you. And that they understand that you did nothing wrong when you and John played cards. I know that now.'

He closed the door and took another step closer.

'I was wrong,' she said, her voice growing stronger. 'About so much. But my life changed so suddenly. And I did not want to blame John, because one should not speak ill of the dead. And to admit that there were problems between us was like admitting that my life had been wasted.' She hesitated, trying to find the rest of the words that would make him believe her. 'This would be better in a letter.'

'I think we have both had far too many of those,' he said with a sad look, and turned again.

'I read yours,' she said. 'The one in your desk.'

He flinched.

'And I know that you read mine. I was not myself when I wrote that. I never meant for you to see it.'

'You wrote it to me,' he reminded her, with a frustrated shake of his head.

'I was not ready to give up what we had together,' she said, struggling to explain. 'And I was confused. Because you were everything I had hoped for, Alex.'

At the sound of his name, something changed in

him. Though he did not move, he felt closer to her, more open to her words.

She went on. 'But I was afraid that you weren't telling the truth when you wrote to me. That you made it up, like you made up Abbott.'

'I have never lied to you,' he said softly.

'Then your last letter is true,' she said, smiling hopefully at him. 'You love me.'

'Always. Ever. Still.' He shook his head helplessly and took another step towards her.

'When I read it, I saw all of you,' she said, spreading her hands wide. 'Both Abbott and Alex. I saw you and I knew I loved you, too.'

He closed the last few steps between them, leaning over the desk to give her a kiss that was as possessive as anything she had imagined in the long months when she'd been falling in love with him. She surrendered to it, wrapping her arms around his neck, clinging to him, still half afraid that he would change his mind again and leave her.

When he pulled away, they were both panting and his eyes blazed into hers.

'I love you, Alex,' she said, smiling up at him. 'And when I was afraid I had lost you, I did not know what to do or how to find you. Do not ever do that again.'

'I was halfway to Portsmouth when I turned around,' he said, leaning down to kiss her again. 'I had some half-baked idea that I would board a ship for Boston.'

'I am glad you didn't,' she said, stroking his face and kissing his cheek, surprised at how familiar it felt, as though she'd known him all her life. 'But what made you decide to come back to me?'

'The item in the paper about us,' he said, smiling.

'About Baxter?' she said, confused.

He shook his head. 'The gossips seem to think that your absence last night was proof that you were in a delicate condition. And I thought, if it might be true, I could not leave you.'

She laughed, kissing him quickly on the lips. 'I suppose it is possible. But I would hope that I would know before the rest of the *ton*. And as yet...?' She shrugged. 'It is far too soon to assume.'

'But it is not impossible. We have, after all...' He was blushing and it made her laugh.

She stood up then and came around the desk to settle in his arms. 'You ought to know that you cannot believe everything you read in the papers.'

'True, I suppose,' he said. 'But since it is such happy news, I suggest we celebrate our good fortune.' He smiled and kissed her again in a way that left no doubt as to his intentions. Then he went to lock the door.

* * * * *

Spinster With A Scandalous Past

Sadie King

MILLS & BOON

Sadie King was born in Nottingham and raised in Lancashire. After graduating with a degree in history from Lancaster University, she moved to West Lothian, Scotland, where she now lives with her husband and children. When she's not writing, Sadie loves long country walks, romantic ruins, Thai food and travelling with her family. She also writes historical fiction and contemporary mysteries as Sarah L King.

Books by Sadie King

Harlequin Historical

Spinster with a Scandalous Past
is Sadie King's debut for Harlequin Historical.

Look out for more books by Sadie King
coming soon!

Visit the Author Profile page
at millsandboon.com.au.

Author Note

When embarking upon my first historical romance novel, I could think of no better setting than the wild and rugged Cumbrian coastline. It is a corner of England that, even nowadays, feels quiet, unspoiled and remote. The perfect place for a scandalised spinster to escape to and the perfect place for a brooding baronet to hide.

Lowhaven is based upon Whitehaven, a port town that grew exponentially during the Georgian period, with its busy quays receiving imports of tobacco, rum and sugar and exporting coal from the nearby mines. For me, settings become like characters themselves, and as a northerner, I was excited by the idea of exploring Regency life in a place that is not readily associated with the era in the same way as, for example, Brighton or Bath. Today Whitehaven is a lovely town to visit, with many of its fine Georgian buildings still extant, and its once-bustling harbour transformed into a peaceful marina, filled with boats. I hope to return soon—in the interests of research, of course.

Britain in the late 1810s was an unsettled place, emerging from war, grappling with extreme weather events and failed harvests, and similarly the hero and heroine of this story have been through a lot. At its heart, though, this is a story about seizing second chances and about finding happiness during one long and (occasionally) hot summer. It was uplifting to write, and I hope you find it as uplifting to read.

DEDICATION

For my family

Chapter One

June 1818

As the carriage rattled along the road towards Lowhaven, Louisa Conrad wondered what on earth she had been thinking. The sound of braying horses rang in her ears, and if she closed her eyes she could still feel herself tumbling down, could still feel her body thud against the coach's solid wood as it landed on its side and took her with it.

In her lap, her hands tremored. She clasped them together and pressed her lips into a tight smile, forcing calm where there was none to be found. Her gaze moved between the two brothers sitting before her, but only one of them returned her smile. The other did not even look at her, apparently preferring the country views offered through the small carriage window.

Briefly she furrowed her brow at him, before giving her full attention to his sibling as he struck up a conversation once again.

'I'm sure that you will find Juniper Street to your liking,' Mr Liddell said.

'I'm sure I shall, sir,' she replied crisply. 'And I believe that after the journey we've had I will appreciate it all the more.'

'Indeed, indeed. A wholesome meal and a good night's repose cures most ills, I find.' His eyes shone, almost teasing. 'You have both had quite an adventure.'

Beside her, Nan shifted, gripping the cushioned seat so hard that her knuckles turned white. Louisa couldn't decide what was distressing her maid more. The terror of the stagecoach accident, or everything that had happened since.

'I'm not sure I would describe it quite like that,' Louisa answered him. 'Those poor horses were dreadfully frightened after the coach turned over. I'm quite sure that the coachman was beside himself with concern for their welfare.'

'Of course—well, until the next time he's whipping them relentlessly so that he might travel at a dangerous speed,' Mr Liddell countered, a smile playing on his lips.

Louisa gave him a small nod, suppressing her own smile but finding that she could not, in earnest, disagree. Nan, meanwhile, chose that moment to clear her throat, no doubt to remind Louisa of the impropriety of their situation. They would have words later, that was for certain. Strong words about getting into the carriage of some unknown gentlemen, about reckless decisions and their consequences, about the manifold horrors which might have occurred.

Louisa had already prepared her defences. What else could they have done when they were stranded in the middle of nowhere, miles from the nearest inn? Were they not fortunate that the gentlemen happened upon them just moments after the coach had overturned?

Her hands trembled again, reminding her that she was not certain of her own argument. After all, Nan's undoubted reservations would be more than justified. Shaken and disorientated, the coach stricken and their luggage scattered on the ground, she could hardly claim to have been thinking clearly. No, instead she had allowed them to be swept along, embracing the notion of rescue without reservation. In those few moments she had been utterly unguarded. And Louisa, more than most, ought to remember the dangers inherent in letting down one's guard.

'Forgive me, Miss Conrad, I am making light of a difficult day, but you might have been seriously injured. I would urge you to consult a doctor once you are settled at your aunt's house. I can ask our physician to pay a visit to you, if you wish?'

'That's very kind of you, sir,' she replied, 'but I'm sure there's no need. We are, as you see, unharmed.'

She forced a smile, ignoring the ache in her ribs which served to remind her that she was not being entirely truthful.

'My brother is right.'

Louisa blinked, startled by the low timbre of the voice which had interjected. The other brother looked at her now, fixing his deep blue eyes upon her so intently that she almost wished he'd return to looking out of the window. Sir Isaac, Mr Liddell had called him during their fraught introductions earlier. Sir Isaac Liddell of Hayton Hall. As she stared back at him now, Louisa realised that this was the first time Sir Isaac had spoken to her in the several hours they'd been travelling together.

'My brother is right,' he repeated. 'We will send our physician.'

Louisa nodded her assent, sensing it was not worth her while to disagree. This appeared to satisfy him, as he said nothing more, but continued to look at her for a little longer than would be deemed polite. Louisa dropped her gaze, and after a moment she sensed him resume his interest in the scenery outside.

'What did you say your aunt's name was, Miss Conrad?' Mr Liddell asked, apparently keen to break the awkward silence which had descended in the carriage.

'I'm not sure that I did, but it is Miss Clarissa Howarth.'

'Miss Clarissa Howarth,' he repeated. 'I know that name. Is your aunt the rector's daughter from Hayton?'

Reluctantly Louisa nodded, feeling immediately guarded at this new line of questioning. 'That's correct, sir.'

Mr Liddell nudged his brother. 'Do you remember Reverend Howarth, Isaac?'

'Of course,' Sir Isaac muttered, not troubling himself to tear his gaze from the window.

From across the carriage Louisa found herself observing him, both offended by and grateful for his apparent lack of interest. With his striking blue gaze safely averted, she felt able to note his other features: near-black hair, a strong, angular jawline, and a sun-kissed complexion which hinted at time spent outdoors. He was dressed from head to toe in black, apart from the white shirt which she glimpsed beneath his coat, and it struck Louisa that he would not look out of place as a character in one of Mrs Radcliffe's gothic romances.

He was handsome, she concluded, but disagreeable. Not that either aspect of Sir Isaac Liddell mattered to her.

'It must be some time now since Reverend Howarth's passing?' Mr Liddell continued.

She nodded, returning her attention once more to the talkative brother. Unlike Sir Isaac, his features were fair, his hair the colour of sand and his eyes a pale blue-grey. In both looks and demeanour, it was hard to believe that they were related.

'Yes,' she replied, 'almost fifteen years.'

'And now your aunt lives on Juniper Street,' he said, in a way which seemed to be neither a statement nor a question.

'She does, yes.'

Now it was Louisa who turned to look out of the window, emulating Sir Isaac's aloof posture in the hope that it would signal an end to the conversation about her family history. Answering questions about Aunt Clarissa was all very well, but she was not keen to see where Mr Liddell's enquiries might lead. He'd already discovered where she'd come from, not long after they'd settled into the carriage.

'Berkshire…?' he'd pondered, before remarking upon how far she'd travelled and recounting a tale of some arduous journey south he'd previously undertaken.

She'd only half listened, and after a while he'd seemed to sense her weariness, smiling an apology and insisting that she needed to rest. Now, so close to her destination, she was determined that they would not revisit the subject. Louisa Conrad was a stranger here, and that was how it was going to remain.

Fortunately, it appeared she wouldn't have to deflect his attempts at conversation for much longer. Outside the carriage window, the wild Cumberland countryside had given way to a gentle townscape of smart grey and white buildings, and the streets were alive with coaches, carts and crowds, as people went about their business.

Her first glimpse of Lowhaven was a reassuring one, and she recalled the excitement she'd first felt when her parents had proposed this sojourn to her. A change of scenery, they'd called it. An opportunity to travel, just as she'd always wished.

She suspected there was more to their desire to send her away than mere broadened horizons, but she didn't care, and had loved the idea from the very first moment. Her eagerness had been dampened somewhat by the travails of the journey, but now, as it reached its welcome conclusion, it returned with renewed vigour. Even Nan looked happier, staring wide-eyed out of the window, her mouth agape at the town as it unravelled in front of her.

'Juniper Street is not far from the port,' Mr Liddell informed them. 'I do hope you won't find the noise and traffic too disturbing.'

Louisa thought about her family's estate, enveloped in rolling green fields and an almost unendurable silence. About the large country house, containing too few people and too many opportunities to ruminate on what might have been. Without doubt, she'd had her fill of living quietly in recent years.

'If it's near to the port then it is near to the sea, which will do very well for me,' she countered cheerfully. 'Besides, lively places can be very diverting.'

Mr Liddell let out a soft laugh. 'If diversion is what you seek, Miss Conrad, then I do believe you will find it in Lowhaven.'

The carriage drew to a halt on a dusty street, lined on either side by rather humble-looking stone townhouses, uniformly built, but with little embellishment. After a moment the coachman opened the door and Mr Liddell exited, offering Louisa his hand as she descended the steps, with Nan following closely behind her.

Louisa smoothed her palms over the crumpled, muddied skirt of her day dress as she took her first breath of Lowhaven's fresh sea air. *Yes,* she thought, *this will do very well indeed.*

'Our driver will fetch your luggage to the door for you, Miss Conrad,' Mr Liddell said.

Louisa turned to face him, realising then that Sir Isaac had not followed them out of the carriage. Instead he remained within, his sombre countenance visible through the little window to which he'd given so much of his attention throughout the journey. Briefly Louisa shook her head at his rudeness, before regarding Mr Liddell once more. There might have been two gentlemen in the carriage today, she thought, but really only one of them could be regarded as their rescuer.

'Mr Liddell, I must thank you most sincerely for coming to our aid today. Truly, you are a good Samaritan. I only hope we have not caused any significant delay to your own journey.'

The gentleman shook his head. 'None whatsoever. Our home is merely a few miles up the road. It was a pleasure to escort you, and to see you safely to your destination, and I will see to it that our physician calls upon you later. I hope that your stay in Lowhaven is agreeable. It is not comparable with the fashionable resorts of the south coast, but nonetheless it has its charms.'

'I'm obliged to you, sir. Will you not stay for some

tea? I'm sure my aunt would be glad to welcome you both,' she added, glancing warily once more towards the carriage.

'You're very kind, Miss Conrad, but I'm afraid we must take our leave,' he replied, tipping his hat briefly. 'Perhaps our paths will cross again, while you are here.'

Before Louisa could respond, Mr Liddell had climbed back into the carriage and closed the door behind him. Through the window he gave her one last broad smile, before his coachman cracked his whip once more and they were off.

For a moment Louisa just stood there, staring after that handsome carriage, surrounded by the luggage which Nan was frantically trying to put into order. After the ordeal of their journey, it seemed miraculous that they had finally arrived. In fact, it almost didn't seem real: the accident, the rescue, the kind gentleman, the rude gentleman—all of it.

Louisa let out a weary sigh. What a long and strange day it had been.

Then, behind her, a door opened and a voice she hadn't heard for years rang out in delight.

'Louisa! Oh, my dear Louisa! Is it really you?'

Louisa turned around and walked straight into the outstretched arms of her Aunt Clarissa, who embraced her quickly before stepping back to regard her niece. The woman looked older than Louisa remembered, her face heavily lined, her once blonde hair now silver and peering wildly from beneath a lace cap. Thinner, too, Louisa thought. She could compete with the minuscule Nan in terms of slenderness.

'You look well, my dear, all things considered,' her aunt said carefully, and Louisa couldn't help but suspect that she was referring to more than just the long journey. 'Your mother was right; you've grown into quite a beautiful young lady.'

Louisa laughed aloud, gesturing at her mud-spattered travelling clothes. 'I look far from beautiful right now, Aunt! And I don't believe I merit being described as "young" any more, either.'

Clarissa raised a curious eyebrow. 'Oh, nonsense— you're barely five-and-twenty; you're not allowed to deny your youth for a few years yet!' She placed a gentle hand on Louisa's arm and steered her towards the door. 'However, you do look as though you've become acquainted with our Cumberland countryside already. Come, let's get your luggage brought in, then we can have some tea and you can tell me all about it.'

'Tell you all about what, Aunt?'

'Your journey, of course—I'd say it's quite a story, judging by the state of your dress.' Clarissa smiled, a look of amusement sparkling in her keen blue eyes. 'But above all you must tell me—how on earth did you come to be accompanied here by Samuel Liddell of Hayton Hall?'

Chapter Two

Samuel Liddell patted his older brother on the back as they walked through the grand wooden door of Hayton Hall. 'I'd say that was a very successful trip,' he declared. 'A number of business matters put to bed, and we rescued a fair maiden in distress on the way home.'

Isaac grunted as he loosened his cravat and threw off his coat, wearied both by the long journey and his brother's endlessly cheerful disposition.

It had been only a short stay in Penrith, and that had been quite long enough. With every passing hour Isaac had found himself yearning to return to the peace and tranquillity of Hayton Hall. The bustle of towns had never suited him and, after spending so long away from them, he now found that he disliked them all the more. He'd never felt so relieved when they'd finally left the coaching inn that morning and begun the final part of their journey home.

A journey which had taken far longer than it should have, thanks to a stagecoach accident on the road and Samuel's insistence that they deliver that young woman and her maid to her aunt in Lowhaven.

'Related to the old rector, Howarth, and coming all the way from an estate in Berkshire,' Samuel remarked, mulling over the details he'd managed to prise from their unexpected carriage guest. 'A gentleman's daughter, to be sure.'

'The very reckless daughter of a gentleman,' Isaac countered as he marched towards his library. 'Getting into a carriage with us—we could have been anyone.'

Samuel followed, his amused chuckle seeming to echo down the hall. 'Well, fortunately for her, we were perfect gentlemen. Or at least I was. You barely looked at her.'

Isaac grunted again as he collapsed into his favourite armchair. Samuel was wrong about that: he had looked at her. Had observed the deep brown of her eyes, her pink pursed lips, and the way her striking blonde curls peered from the edges of her damaged bonnet. He'd noted the mud on her dress, and the way she'd winced and put her hand against her ribs every time the carriage met a bump on the road. He'd caught her frowning at him, more than once, and sensed that his aloofness displeased her. Not that any of it mattered to him.

He slumped back in his chair and closed his eyes as Samuel rang for some tea. No, he thought. Fair maidens and their opinions of him were of no consequence.

'You'd better make sure that you do send the physician to attend to her,' Isaac said. 'Despite her protestations, I do believe that she was injured.'

'Ah, so you are taking an interest in her?' Samuel teased.

Isaac's eyes flew open and he sat up straight. 'I'm merely concerned for her welfare after being in such a bad accident. And might I remind you that it was you who invited the lady and her maid into our carriage?'

'And you'd have left them stranded on the road?' Samuel scoffed.

'Of course not,' Isaac snapped. 'I am many things, but I am not heartless.'

Isaac watched as his brother sat down in the armchair opposite him, sighing heavily as he resigned himself to a lecture. It had been like this ever since Samuel had returned from his European travels, apparently determined to atone for his lengthy absence by seeing to it that his grieving recluse of a brother got his life in order.

Sometimes he was glad of it, content to have his morose moods offset by a dose of his brother's buoyancy and relieved to have the large rooms of his ancestral home filled with lively chatter once more. At other times Samuel's good intentions grated on him—largely because he no longer felt he needed to be looked after. And because his brother had not been there when he really had needed his care…during those darkest days when he'd wallowed, unwashed and undressed, drinking himself into oblivion.

Samuel must have seen something in his brother's expression to dissuade him from pursuing the matter of Isaac's heart, as when he finally spoke it was to change the subject.

'I'm glad you decided to come with me to Penrith. I know you have much to attend to on the estate, but I do believe it's done you the world of good.'

Isaac grunted, the temptation to offer one of his usual cutting retorts thwarted by the earnest look on Samuel's face. 'I suppose it did end up being something of an adventure,' he confessed, surprised to find himself thinking about the lady with the brown eyes and fair curls once more.

'Ah—you see!' Samuel declared, clapping his hands together. 'Even Sir Isaac Liddell is not immune to a bit of chivalry.'

'I wouldn't go that far,' Isaac retorted. 'As you said yourself, I barely acknowledged the lady.'

And he hadn't—not really. Noticing a pretty face was one thing, but his days of being a knight in shining armour to a fair maiden were long past. He was alone now; that was the cruel hand fate had dealt him, and that was how it was going to remain.

After being plied with tea, copious amounts of cake, and a conversation which bordered on an interrogation, it was with some relief and a very full stomach that Louisa made her way to her bedroom later that afternoon.

Aunt Clarissa had been horrified by the stagecoach accident, expressing her consternation that Louisa's parents had not seen fit to escort her on the long journey north. Louisa had protested mildly, informing her aunt that her family were all presently in London, and doing her best to ignore her nagging suspicions about exactly why her parents had left her to fend for herself. Why they were so keen for her to spend the summer here. What they thought it might teach her.

Her aunt's mood had mercifully lightened when the conversation had turned to Louisa's rescuers—or at least, the one she had seen.

'Mr Samuel Liddell,' she said, beaming. 'He has been away for some time, travelling in Europe, and has only recently returned to Hayton Hall. The Liddells are a distinguished family in this part of the country. You will recall that your grandfather was the rector of Hayton? He knew the family very well.'

'Yes, Mr Liddell spoke of my grandfather during the journey,' Louisa had replied. 'He said that he remembered him.'

'Mr Samuel would have been quite young back then. Your grandfather knew his father better. He passed away suddenly, years ago, before Mr Samuel came of age. I recall his mother followed not long afterwards. Mr Samuel's older brother inherited the baronetcy.'

The mention of Mr Liddell's brother had caused Louisa's stomach to lurch quite unexpectedly. Doubtless it was the memory of his sombre disposition and curt indifference which had vexed her.

'Sir Isaac Liddell was also travelling with us this afternoon,' she'd said, feeling duty-bound to report to her guardian the exact details of her rescue.

Her aunt's eyes had widened in surprise. 'Really? I did not see him.'

'He remained in the carriage when we arrived,' she'd explained, trying to suppress a fresh wave of irritation at his rudeness.

'I see. Well, my dear, you have had a rare introduction. Sir Isaac is almost never seen in town. Indeed, it is said that he seldom leaves his estate.'

Louisa had nodded, utterly unsurprised by her aunt's revelation. The gentleman she'd encountered earlier today had been inattentive and unsociable, and clearly had not wished to be in her company, so it was little wonder to her that he did not relish being in anyone else's.

On the other hand, she'd reflected, as she had sipped her tea, there were many good reasons to shut oneself away from society, as she knew only too well.

She'd been about to enquire what Sir Isaac's might be when her aunt had changed the subject.

'I'd suggest you don't mention the stagecoach accident or your subsequent rescue to your mother when you write to her,' she'd advised. 'I'm not sure that she would approve.'

Louisa had furrowed her brow at this. 'I've done nothing I should be ashamed of, surely? Nan was with me—and besides, I'm not sure what else I could have done. Mr Liddell was very kind, and Sir Isaac has insisted that their physician will call upon Nan and me, as a precaution.'

'I mean no criticism, my dear,' her aunt had replied, chuckling at her niece's defensive tone. 'Sometimes in life we find ourselves in difficult situations, and the choices offered to us are less than ideal. In those situations we are forced to trust our instincts. You should be reassured that, as an unmarried woman, you can rely upon yours. That's important—especially if this is the path you're set upon.'

Those words rang in Louisa's ears as she walked into her room to find Nan, still unpacking. The room Clarissa had given her was small, but well-appointed, tucked away at the rear of the house and overlooking a charming little courtyard. Beyond it were more houses, walls and courtyards; wherever she looked, there seemed only stone to be found.

It occurred to Louisa then that it had been a long time since she had looked out of a window and seen anything other than fields. Her last London season had been six years ago, and she'd seen nothing of any town since. Another aspect of the path she had embarked upon.

'Your books are on the table, miss,' Nan said as she bustled about. 'I know you'll be looking for them before you trouble yourself with your dresses.'

Louisa thanked her maid, moving to run her fingers over her most prized possessions as she gazed out of the window. The afternoon was ebbing away towards evening, but the light was still good, the early June sunshine warm and bright and uninhibited by cloud.

She wondered how often the room's previous inhabitant had stood there and enjoyed the view over the town. For years Aunt Clarissa had shared her home with another spinster, Miss Slater, until the woman had quite unexpectedly married at the age of five and fifty. The now Mrs Knight had subsequently relocated to Carlisle, with her husband, leaving Aunt Clarissa alone.

Louisa knew that this was partly what had prompted her mother to send her to Lowhaven—although she was not so naïve that she did not recognise the other motivations her parents were likely to have for wishing to remove her from Berkshire entirely.

'Have you told your aunt about what happened this afternoon?' Nan asked. 'I hope she is not too vexed by it.'

Louisa gave her maid a brisk nod. 'I have, and I must say she was only concerned that we might have been injured. The rest of the tale didn't seem to perturb her in the slightest.'

Nan stared at her mistress, her mouth agape. 'But, miss, your reputation—'

'In these parts I have no reputation, Nan. I am known to no one, so there is no one to discuss whether or not I should have got into that carriage, or to condemn me as silly, naïve or without virtue. And if I have my way that is how it shall remain. I am here to visit my aunt and to enjoy a pleasant summer before returning to Berkshire, and that is all.'

'I'm sorry, miss. I only worry for you, given what happened with your captain—'

Louisa held up a hand in protest and looked her maid directly in the eye. 'Nan, you will not mention any of that while we are here; I forbid it. You do not know who might be listening. I will not have my life become the subject of tittle-tattle between servants.'

Nan nodded meekly. 'Yes, of course, miss.'

Louisa's stern expression dissolved into a fond smile. She couldn't help it; she'd known Nan since she was a girl. At a little more than ten years her senior, her maid was not old enough to be a motherly figure, but nonetheless the pair shared a close bond which had only deepened as Louisa's life had taken increasingly difficult turns. Nan knew all of it, she'd seen everything, and yet she still cared.

Louisa retreated from the window once more, sitting down upon the bed which was situated in the centre of the room. She patted the sheets at her side, indicating that Nan should rest for a moment and join her.

'This is such a beautiful bedroom,' Louisa remarked, surveying her surroundings once more. 'I'm glad my aunt saw fit to put me at the back of the house. I'm not sure how well I would sleep with all the noise from the street outside. It was Miss Slater's room; my aunt told me so at tea.'

Nan's eyes widened at that. 'Well, I daresay that staying in this room is a good omen, miss. If its last occupant managed to find herself a husband in this town, perhaps you will, too.'

Louisa bristled. The words were kindly meant, but they stung her nonetheless. She closed her eyes for a moment, allowing herself the luxury of small remembered glimpses: his chestnut hair, his green eyes, his deep blue frock coat. The delicate feeling of his fingers caressing her face. The way that he always seemed to smell like the ocean, even though he'd been on land for months. The way he'd kissed her at their last meeting. The fearful urgency of it—as though he had already seen that a rising tide was coming and that it would part them for good.

Her thoughts darkened then, wandering to everything that had come after...everything she'd had to face alone. Everything that made finding a husband in a new town utterly impossible.

From beneath her lashes, a tear slipped out. 'You know that is out of the question, Nan. There is no one for me now, and that is an end to it.'

Then, before Nan could say anything further, Louisa fled from the room.

Chapter Three

Isaac whipped his horse, pushing the poor beast to gallop as fast as its legs could manage. The weather was as foul as his mood, having turned in these last few days from still and sunlit to blustery and beset with heavy grey cloud. It hadn't begun to rain yet, thank God. Like everyone else, he feared that if it did, it might never stop.

He might have little interaction with the world outside Hayton Hall these days, but he was not immune to its worries. They'd endured two of the worst summers he could remember, cold and endlessly wet, damaging crops and causing many a harvest to fail. What Cumberland and England prayed for was a long, hot summer.

He'd pray, too, if he could bring himself to speak to his maker any more.

Isaac growled, cracking his whip again as he sped towards the cliffs before turning to chart a rough path along their rugged edges. In front of him the land sloped down towards Lowhaven, its orderly buildings and busy port nestled into the bay. He wouldn't go as far as that; it was out of the question. It was difficult enough to slip away from Hayton unnoticed. He was almost guaranteed to be seen in town, to be remarked upon, and he despised being the subject of gossip.

Perhaps he ought to turn back now, before he got too close…

'You're a damnable coward, Isaac Liddell,' he muttered to himself.

Samuel would certainly agree. He'd more or less said it himself, a few nights ago at dinner. The evening had started well enough, with Samuel in high spirits after they'd gallantly rescued that lady from her overturned coach. His good cheer had eventually grown on Isaac, and after a pleasant meal and a few glasses of port he had found himself smiling, too. He'd relaxed, allowing himself to take comfort in his brother's company, to reflect that it was preferable to dining alone.

Samuel must have sensed that his guard was down, or perhaps he'd really been in his cups—either way, his words had not been gentle.

'You should go out more,' he'd said. 'Put on your best clothes. Go to a ball. Go to London! Find yourself a nice wife. Stop hiding yourself away, licking your wounds and hoping the world will forget that you exist.'

Isaac groaned at the memory of it, the pained sound mercifully carried away by the howling wind. The brothers had always been very different men, in both outlook and temperament, but these past couple of years seemed to have placed an unnavigable chasm between them. Samuel had travelled and Isaac had lost; one brother's horizons had expanded, whilst the other's world had shrunk.

Samuel would never understand that Isaac's life could not be repaired by embracing society or getting himself on to the dancing card of a beautiful lady.

'Watch out!'

He'd been so absorbed by his own thoughts that he hadn't seen the woman until the very last moment. In fact, his horse saw her first. The creature reared, letting out a high-pitched whinny as it drew to a sudden halt. Isaac clung hard to the reins; he was a good horseman, but not beyond being unseated by a startled beast.

'Hell and damnation!' he cried out, finally bringing his horse under control.

The woman stared up at him, wide-eyed and apparently frozen to the spot. Her terror was written all over her face, which had turned a ghastly shade of white. Despite the fright she'd given him, immediately he recognised the deep brown gaze, contrasting starkly with the fair curls which sprang at the edges of her bonnet.

The fair maiden they'd welcomed into their carriage on the way home from Penrith. The one travelling from Berkshire with her maid before falling victim to a careless driver and an overturned stagecoach. He watched as she furrowed her brow at him, giving him the same disapproving look he'd spied during that long journey to Lowhaven. Instead of stepping aside, the lady remained in his way, and inexplicably he felt the heat of irritation rise in his chest.

'What the blazes are you doing, walking into the path of my horse?' he snapped.

His accusing tone seemed to bring her to her senses. 'What am I doing?' she repeated. 'I am walking, sir. I might ask what you are doing, riding your horse in such a reckless manner, with no consideration for those whom you might encounter up here.'

Her question was a fair one; he had been riding with little care. With a sigh, he dismounted from his horse. 'I do not expect to see anyone up here. Not on a day like today, at least.' He drew closer to the woman. 'I am very sorry to have frightened you.'

'I wasn't frightened,' she answered him, taking a step back.

If he'd been in a better frame of mind he would have found her indignation amusing. Instead he found himself struck by the petite, pretty, but very stern figure standing in front of him, well turned out in a fetching pale blue dress and matching spencer, steadfastly holding her bonnet in place as the fierce wind threatened to carry it away.

A gentleman's daughter, Samuel had called her, and indeed there was no mistaking the air of gentility about her.

As he considered this, Isaac found himself regretting his coarse words. He gave her a small, belated bow. 'Forgive me,' he said. 'If I am not mistaken, I believe we have met before. My name is Isaac Liddell. We—that is my brother and I—escorted you to Lowhaven after that dreadful stagecoach accident. You may not recall… In fact…' He shook his head at himself, unable to comprehend his sudden lack of ability to speak coherently. 'That is to say, you may remember my brother better, as he made all the arrangements.'

The lady offered him a brisk nod. 'I remember you,' she said simply. 'Sir Isaac Liddell of Hayton Hall.'

He winced at the cool way with which she accorded him his proper title. 'Did our physician attend you? I asked my brother to arrange it.'

'He did, thank you.' For the first time, a small smile played upon her lips. 'I daresay Mr Liddell likes to arrange things.'

Isaac frowned. 'What makes you say that?'

She beheld him with a steely gaze he couldn't read.

'I was merely thinking about the day of the coach accident, and the way he took charge of the situation,' she replied.

Isaac tried not to feel the sting in her observation—tried not to consider the implication that, while Samuel had been something of a hero, he'd done nothing much at all. 'I suppose some people are good at fixing things,' he said. 'Or at least they like to believe that they are.'

'Indeed. But not everything can be fixed, can it?'

Such a knowing remark unsettled him, and he felt his breath catch in his throat. 'Fortunately, rescuing a fair maiden after a stagecoach accident and sending for a physician are skills well within Samuel's repertoire.' He kept his tone light, cheery, almost jovial. Everything he did not feel in that moment.

The woman frowned. 'Excuse me? A fair maiden?'

Isaac suppressed a groan, realising he'd said that aloud. Damn, it had been so long since he had spent time in company, and even longer since he'd spoken to a lady. It seemed that his sense of etiquette was something else he'd lost.

'Forgive me,' he said again. 'It was how my brother described you. He meant it kindly, but it was impolite of me to repeat it.'

'I see.' The woman raised her eyebrows at him, then pursed those pretty pink lips once more before adding, 'I'd wager you cannot even recall my name, sir.'

Such directness took him aback, and he felt an unusual heat rising from beneath his collar and creeping to his face. During their first fraught encounter on the road, some brief and extremely awkward introductions had been made. She had given her name then—of course she had—but he was damned if he could remember it. Ever since then, in his mind she had been the fair maiden. Samuel's name for her had well and truly stuck, and he hadn't needed another when conjuring the memory of her dark gaze or her disapproving glances. A memory, he realised now, that he'd conjured more than once.

'Indeed I do,' he replied, floundering as he grasped at the only name he knew. 'I do recall, Miss… Howarth.'

'Miss Howarth is my aunt,' she replied flatly, although something like amusement flickered across her face. 'My name is Miss Louisa Conrad,' she added, extending a hand towards him.

He accepted the gesture as the olive branch it was clearly intended to be, and took hold of her hand with as much grace as he could muster. Although they both wore gloves, he found himself struck by the feeling of her small, delicate fingers resting briefly in his.

'It's a pleasure to make your acquaintance again, Miss Conrad. Please accept my sincere apology. I meant no disrespect.'

Miss Conrad laughed. 'To be honest, I'm not sure which is worse—being referred to as a fair maiden, or having your name forgotten entirely.'

Isaac winced at her gentle teasing. 'Truly, I am sorry on both counts,' he replied. 'You have my solemn promise that I will never refer to you as a fair maiden ever again.'

'Do not fret, sir. I have been called worse, I'm sure,' she quipped.

'Really?' asked Isaac, disconcerted by the forthright remark. 'That I cannot believe. Although you will have been seen arriving in Lowhaven with my brother and me.

Such an event is certain to set tongues wagging around these parts.'

Isaac had made the observation in jest, but immediately he could see that he'd offended her all over again. The look on her face hardened, and those dark eyes blazed with something he couldn't quite name. Hotter than hurt, but cooler than anger.

He shook his head at himself, unable to believe his own impertinence. Truly, what had become of him?

'I'm sorry, Miss Conrad, I didn't mean—'

'Oh, I'm quite sure you did,' she replied, her tone scathing. She gave a brief, insincere curtsey. 'I think I'd best take my leave of you now, sir. I wouldn't wish my unchaperoned presence here to provide any further fodder for the gossips. Good day.'

She spun round, determinedly marching away from him and back towards Lowhaven. Isaac stared after her for a few moments, dumbstruck at his own stupidity. What on earth had possessed him to talk so loosely to a woman he barely knew?

He sighed, and found himself wondering what Samuel would say if he'd borne witness to all that had just occurred. It was just as well he'd no intention of marrying again. After two years of solitude, it was clear that all his charm had simply withered away.

As she walked back to her aunt's house, Louisa felt that she ought to question her sanity. Aunt Clarissa had expressed reservations about her taking long walks alone, making vague insinuations about the possible dangers to a young woman, and saying how she really ought to accompany her but she feared she could not walk so far. It turned out that her aunt had been right—although perhaps not in the way she would have imagined.

It had only been days since Louisa had arrived in Cumberland. Already she'd got into the carriage of two unknown gentlemen, and now she'd argued with one of them for good measure. She shook her head, berating herself as she hurried in the direction of Juniper Street. Why had she spoken to him in that way, and with such a careless tongue? It was bad enough that her actions on the day of the coach accident had shown her to be a foolish and improper young woman, but to then suggest that there might be some further stain on her character, that people might see fit to besmirch her reputation— that was unforgivable.

It was also true, she reminded herself. She knew well enough what Berkshire society said about her. She had, without doubt, been called far worse than a fair maiden.

'A fair maiden, indeed,' she muttered as she marched along.

She tried not to imagine how the brothers must have made fun of her—how they must have laughed as they talked of the silly southern lady they'd rescued on their journey home. Certainly, Sir Isaac had all but told her what he thought of her, hadn't he? That she was the sort of woman about whom people chattered, and therefore, by implication, the sort of woman whose behaviour was unbecoming of a gentleman's daughter. That had been the point of his impertinent remark, hadn't it?

'Such a rude, disagreeable gentleman,' she said aloud to herself.

He had been rude—there could be no question about that. A man of honour would have kept such thoughts to himself, even if provoked by her own ill-advised commentary. A man of honour would not have cursed in her presence, either, or tried to suggest that she was to blame for his bad horsemanship.

She reflected once more upon the sight of him, his wild hair and thunderous expression as he'd stared down at her from his horse. A man of honour would have concealed such anger, not indulged it.

No, she thought. There was something altogether very disagreeable about Sir Isaac Liddell. Tomorrow she would walk a different route and hope that their paths did not cross again. He was a man whose company ought to be avoided.

Chapter Four

Louisa's return to her aunt's house put a swift end to all thoughts of her unpleasant encounter. She was greeted in the hall by an agitated Nan, who was mumbling about how long she'd been away and where she'd got to, and how she had been beginning to worry. Like Aunt Clarissa, her maid did not approve of the long promenades she'd so quickly established as a habit.

Louisa tried not to show her irritation; she knew that they both had her best interests at heart. She couldn't possibly explain to them how free she felt, able to wander the countryside unburdened by the worry of who might see her and what they might say. She couldn't expect them to understand what these past years had been like for her, confined to her family's estate, unwilling to venture beyond their own land. It had been her choice, she knew that; she'd been her own gaoler. But here she was unknown; Cumberland was indifferent to her, and it was liberating.

She smiled as Nan took her spencer from her and gave her skirts a swift brush with her hand. 'I haven't been away all that long, Nan—and besides, what is the hurry? I have nothing I need to attend to.'

'You do today, miss. Your aunt has visitors in the parlour and you've some mud on the hem of this dress. Do you wish to change first?'

Louisa frowned. 'No, the dress will do. Who are the visitors, Nan?' she asked, curious now. She glanced at the long-case clock in the hall, realising it was past noon. Her long walk had indeed encroached upon calling hours.

'A Mrs Pearson and her daughter. I gather they are fairly new in town and only recently acquainted with your aunt.'

'I see,' she replied. 'Well, then, Nan, I think I'd best be introduced, hadn't I?'

Nan led her mistress to the parlour, where she opened the door for her before briefly bobbing a curtsey and taking her leave. Tentatively, Louisa walked into the room, feeling suddenly self-conscious as her aunt's two guests stared at her from across the table where they were enjoying cake and tea. She was not used to company...not used to making polite conversation. Briefly, the thought of her earlier walk returned to her. She'd already failed in one social encounter today. She hoped she wouldn't give a bad account of herself in another.

'Ah! There you are, my dear,' said Clarissa from her chair. 'Come, sit down and have some tea. I'd like you to meet Mrs Mary Pearson and her daughter, Miss Charlotte Pearson.' She turned back to her guests. 'This is my niece, Miss Louisa Conrad.'

Louisa gave them both a polite nod before taking a seat beside her aunt. 'It's nice to meet you both,' she said, pausing briefly to accept a cup of tea from her aunt's young maid, Cass, who had entered the parlour to wait upon her. 'I apologise for not being here sooner.'

'Oh, not at all, Miss Conrad,' said Mrs Pearson. 'Your aunt was just telling us how much the Lowhaven air is agreeing with you on your daily walks.'

'It is indeed,' Louisa replied. 'The surrounding country is beautiful, and walking by the sea suits me very well.'

'I am glad to hear it. Regrettably, my health doesn't permit me to venture far, but Charlotte likes to promenade—don't you?' Mrs Pearson addressed her daughter, who gave an assenting nod. 'Perhaps you might accompany one another.'

'Ah, that would be wonderful,' Clarissa declared. 'It is better if young ladies walk out together, I think. It is the proper way of things.'

'Yes, indeed,' Mrs Pearson agreed. 'The right and proper way.'

Charlotte gave Louisa a brief look of amusement which said that she had heard such a sentiment expressed at least a hundred times before. Louisa returned it, before allowing herself to make a discreet study of her new acquaintance. Her smooth, freckled face pronounced her youth, and Louisa suspected she could not be much older than twenty. She had the most striking red curls and bright blue eyes, which sat in direct contrast to her mother's ashen complexion, sunken features and greying brown hair. If Mrs Pearson had not already declared herself to be in poor health, Louisa should have easily supposed it.

'Have you ventured far on your walks, Miss Conrad?' Charlotte asked her, clearly determined to make some conversation.

'Just the environs of the town,' Louisa replied. 'Although I did wander a little along the coast today. The cliffs are magnificent.'

Charlotte nodded. 'That is indeed a pleasant walk. There is another I might show you, too, which takes you inland towards a village called Hayton.'

Louisa smiled, glancing at her aunt. 'My grandfather used to be the rector at Hayton. I have heard much about the place, although I confess I have not yet had the opportunity to visit.'

'Ah!' Charlotte exclaimed, clasping her hands together. 'Then we must go! It is very charming, and so quiet. Not at all like Lowhaven. I can show you the church and the rectory, and if time allows we can walk towards Hayton Hall. It is not far from the village, and it is the most spectacular-looking house. Indeed, I think it is the best in all of Cumberland.'

Clarissa smiled at the two young ladies. 'This sounds like a wonderful outing,' she said. 'If I was a younger woman, I might join you. I seldom visit Hayton these days, for all that it is only a few miles along the road. And Charlotte is right; Hayton Hall is very old, you know, and very fine.' Clarissa paused, stirring her tea. 'Although I believe these days it is best viewed from a distance.'

'Oh, Charlotte knows not to venture too close to the house—don't you, Charlotte?' her mother interjected.

Louisa sipped the tea thoughtfully. 'Of course. That is only polite, surely? The family must be afforded their privacy when in residence.'

Clarissa shifted a little in her chair. 'I think it would be fair to say that Hayton Hall has been closed to the outside world for some time.' She patted Louisa's hand. 'It is a sad story, I'm afraid, my dear. Two years ago

Sir Isaac suffered the loss of both his wife and his only child. Since then he has seldom been seen by anyone.'

Louisa felt her heart beat a little faster. 'That is terribly sad,' she said.

Aunt Clarissa nodded her agreement, giving Louisa a conspiratorial look. Neither of them was careless enough to mention that Louisa had met the reclusive baronet and risk revealing the circumstances in which this rare encounter had occurred. And Louisa, for her part, had no intention of telling anyone the sorry tale of their second meeting.

She dropped her gaze, staring into her empty cup and trying not to think of those deep blue eyes staring down at her from the horse. Trying not to think about how she'd failed to spot the sadness lurking behind the near-permanent scowl. A sadness which she, of all people, ought to have seen.

'I hear he has been seen a little more of late,' Mrs Pearson interjected. 'Since his brother returned to Hayton. Hopefully he can bring Sir Isaac some comfort.'

Clarissa gave her friend a grim smile. 'I think we ought to pray for it,' she replied. 'For that is what the poor man deserves—our prayers and our pity.'

Louisa retired to her room early that evening, not long after giving up on the dinner which she had pushed around her plate. She'd brushed off her aunt's professions of concern with an insistence that she was merely tired after an eventful day, explaining away her lack of appetite with the excuse that she'd eaten too heartily at tea that afternoon.

After changing into her bedclothes and dismissing Nan, she'd climbed between the sheets, intent upon reading her book for as long as the remaining daylight and the glow of a single candle would allow.

Hoping she would be able to take her mind somewhere else for a little while, Louisa picked up Mariana Starke's *Letters from Italy*. She might never venture beyond the confines of England, but she could indulge her desire to travel by seeing the continent through another's eyes until she fell asleep.

But, try as she might to fill her head with Mrs Starke's descriptions of vineyards, volcanoes and ancient towns buried by lava, her thoughts kept wandering back to the cliffs above Lowhaven. To the intensity of Sir Isaac's stare, the gentle touch of his gloved hand. To the way his dark hair had been made wild by the wind. To the unpleasant way their brief exchange had ended, and to the cross words she regretted now that she knew the nature of what pained him.

Words she ought to have regretted anyway, she thought as she slammed her book shut. Sir Isaac had been rude, but it shouldn't have been beyond her to meet his rudeness with some grace. Instead she'd been angry—and why? Because he'd spoken the truth, that was why.

She was reckless and improper. She made herself vulnerable to gossip and she bore the taint of scandal. Her reputation might not be known in Cumberland, but it followed her all the same, etching itself on every word she spoke, every decision she made. She was not free of it. She would never be free of it. She was fooling herself if she thought she could be at liberty here, or anywhere. She might as well lock herself away on her family's estate again—this time for good.

Louisa closed her eyes, pressing her lips together tight

as a single tear slipped down her cheek. It seemed she and Sir Isaac had more in common than she could have supposed. They had both loved and lost, and had chosen to shut themselves away, to hide their pain from the world. She wondered if solitude had been a salve for him or if, like her, he had found it only allowed the wounds to fester. She wondered if she would ever see him again, and if she'd find the courage to apologise to him, to acknowledge his suffering without betraying her own.

A knock at the door caused her to sit bolt upright, her eyes wide open now as the unexpected intrusion brushed all thoughts of Sir Isaac Liddell away. After a moment Aunt Clarissa peered round the door.

'I'm sorry to disturb you, dear,' she said, somewhat tentatively.

Louisa gave her a small smile. 'You're not, Aunt. I wasn't yet asleep. Is everything all right? Are you quite well?'

'Oh, yes, nothing is amiss,' Clarissa replied, coming into the room and closing the door behind her. 'It was just that I had meant to tell you at dinner that we have an engagement with the Pearsons on Friday evening.'

'I see. I'm sure that will be lovely. At their home?'

'No, not at their home.' Clarissa paused, seeming to hesitate. 'At the Assembly Rooms. There is to be a ball, it seems. I pay little heed to these events usually, but Mrs Pearson has asked if we will both come.'

Louisa gave a slow shake of her head. 'I'm not sure, Aunt. I...'

Clarissa gave her a pained look. 'I am sorry, my dear, but I have already accepted. Mrs Pearson asked me earlier today, just as she was leaving. In truth, I think she wishes you to attend as a companion for Miss Pearson.

I have not known Mrs Pearson for very long…to have refused her invitation would surely have seemed ungracious, wouldn't it?'

Louisa sighed. 'Indeed, I suppose it would. I regret that I will be rather poor company for Miss Pearson, though, after so long away from society.'

Clarissa reached over and patted her hand. 'You are a charming young lady, and I won't hear anything different said by anyone. Your only flaw is that you are too hard on yourself, my dear. The past is the past. This is a fresh start for you, Louisa. If you want my opinion, a new town, some new friends and a busy social calendar is exactly what you need.'

Louisa gave her aunt a knowing look. 'A friend like Charlotte Pearson, perhaps?'

Clarissa chuckled. 'I cannot deny that I have thought that Miss Pearson would make a suitable companion for you this summer. I simply want you to enjoy your time here, Louisa.'

Louisa shuffled under her sheets, suddenly discomfited. 'That is kind of you, Aunt. You are close to my mother, and I know she has told you much of what occurred several years ago. You have my deepest gratitude for welcoming me into your home in spite of it.'

Her aunt frowned. 'My dear, you speak as though you murdered someone! What happened to you is a tragedy, and if your Berkshire society chose to shun you for it then that reflects poorly on them, not you.'

'But I did not conduct myself as a young lady should…'

'You conducted yourself as many a young woman has and as many young women will continue to do whilst ever there are young men in the world to turn their heads. Your family approved of him, yes? And you were to marry, yes?'

Louisa nodded. 'We had an understanding.'

'Well, then, you were a victim of dreadful circumstance, Louisa, and that is all there is to be said.' Clarissa gave her a tender smile. 'Your mother has told me how these past years have been for you, and I pray that being here in Lowhaven will put an end to all of that. Starting with this ball at the Assembly Rooms on Friday.'

Aunt Clarissa bade her a swift goodnight, leaving Louisa to blow out her candle and settle down beneath her sheets. Oddly, she felt more peaceful now, her aunt's soothing words having replaced the more distressing thoughts she'd entertained earlier. Aunt Clarissa knew about her past and loved her despite it. Perhaps one day she could manage to love herself again, too.

She fell asleep quickly, dreaming not of windswept cliffs and heated conversations, nor of lost sea captains and promises unfulfilled. No, instead thoughts of candlelit rooms, country dances and beautiful gowns spread through her sleeping hours, and when she woke in the morning she wondered if her aunt might be right. Perhaps this truly was a new beginning, after all.

Chapter Five

Isaac gulped down the last of his brandy, wincing as it burned the back of his throat. He seldom took strong drink in the afternoon these days, but today he'd decided to allow himself a single glass. Around him the library was gloomy, the grey day outside providing little by way of either light or solace. With a heavy sigh he hauled himself out of his armchair and set about lighting a candle by which to read. If he could concentrate on a book. If he could concentrate on anything at all.

Beyond the library Hayton Hall was silent, except for the occasional footsteps of a servant going about his duties. Samuel had been out for most of the day, having given no indication as to when he was likely to return. And, although he was loath to admit it, Isaac found himself craving his brother's company, his merry demeanour and even his gentle teasing. Increasingly, it struck him just how much he hated being alone. Just how much he resented the life he'd been condemned to. It was not the sort of life he wanted at all.

Unfortunately for him, it was the only kind of life he was ever going to have. He'd made a vow once, to love and to cherish until death. He'd spoken those words in a church on a fine summer's day, never considering that death would come so soon. Never even contemplating that the years of loving and cherishing would be so painfully brief. Making such a vow again was completely out of the question. His heart had been shattered by his loss, and although it had now mended enough that he felt able to live again, he was not sure he was capable of loving again.

Not the way he'd loved Rosalind. Not how a woman deserved to be loved.

He missed Rosalind as he would miss his own skin. That was how losing her felt—as though someone had flayed the flesh from his bones and he'd been left to walk around raw and bleeding ever since. And the child, too. How he missed his long-awaited, much-beloved son.

In the months after their deaths, with enough darkness and enough drink, he had pretended that they were by his side, his liquor-addled mind conjuring a vision of his wife sitting just across from him, their little boy perched on her lap. He had heard her laughter, seen her brown curls shaking as she teased him about some trivial matter or other.

He'd always been so serious, but she'd been able to counter that with a kind of inherent, light-hearted joy that had made his soul burn for her. He'd loved marriage, loved the companionship of having a wife. He'd loved waking up beside her each day and embracing her before bed each night. Others might be cynical about getting wed, doing it for money or connections, but he had entered into it for neither reason.

He'd married for love.

By God, he had loved her.

'And now look at you…can't even talk properly to a woman, you damn fool,' he muttered to himself.

The incident on the cliffs had been preying on his mind ever since he'd returned home on his horse. He'd left the poor, weary animal with his groom and marched inside, reeling at how Miss Conrad had slighted him, how she'd walked away as though he was the most offensive creature on earth. A few clumsy words—that was all he'd uttered. He wasn't used to conversation any more, or to women, and for some unfathomable reason he had tried to compensate with a loose tongue and ill-judged humour.

She might have been more forgiving.

She might have tried to understand him.

She might have stayed and talked for a little longer.

Inside Hayton Hall he'd poured himself a brandy, just as he'd done today, and inside that glass his indignation had dissolved into regret. He had been rude, he knew that, and a young lady of impeccable character like Miss Louisa Conrad had been quite right to walk away in the face of such insult.

Miss Louisa Conrad… He had rehearsed that name over and over in his mind, so that he might never forget it. He'd promised never to call her a fair maiden again, and yet that was exactly what she was—all dark gaze and honey-coloured curls. Now, a day later, he knew he owed the fair maiden an apology.

This would be no easy task to accomplish. A note simply would not do, but neither could he just turn up on her doorstep. Going to Lowhaven and exposing himself to comment was inconceivable at the best of times, and seeking out a lovely young lady like Miss Conrad was all but guaranteed to send the town's gossips into a frenzy. Perhaps he could ride that same route again and hope to see her. But then he'd be leaving it all too much to chance, and...

'You're a damnable coward, Liddell,' he said, closing his eyes and dragging his fingers down his face.

'Brother, are you quite well?'

Across from him stood Samuel, a look of concern etched upon his face. He'd been so preoccupied with his quandary over the matter of Miss Conrad that he had not even heard his brother return. He looked up now, wondering how long Samuel had been standing there. How much of Isaac's self-critical monologue he'd heard.

'I'm fine,' he replied, forcing a smile. 'Just a little tired, that's all.'

'I see.' Samuel sat down opposite him, and Isaac watched as his brother's gaze shifted warily to the empty glass on the table. 'How many of those have you had?' he asked.

'Only one,' Isaac snapped. 'Why?'

'I'm just making sure you're not falling back into your old ways, brother.'

Isaac flinched at the memory of how he'd lived during those long months he'd spent lost to his grief. Festering in the darkness in his library, surrounded by empty glasses laced with the residue of day-old drink and crumpled newspapers, half-perused and then abandoned. He had tried futilely to numb the pain with so much brandy that it was a minor miracle that he hadn't been struck down with barrel fever.

He was aware that Samuel knew it all—that he'd interviewed the servants almost immediately upon his return to Hayton Hall, ensuring that he had sufficient insight into exactly how his older brother had been faring during his long absence.

'Such bad habits are far behind me,' Isaac replied, glaring at him. 'That was the case even before you dragged yourself home from your continental adventures. I am quite capable of looking after myself these days, Samuel.'

To his surprise, his brother held up his hands in a gesture of surrender. 'I know that. Believe me, I'm not trying to be a nursemaid to you. But I am trying to encourage you to do more, to go out a bit more—for your own good.'

'I do go out,' Isaac countered, sitting back in his chair, arms folded. 'I accompanied you to Penrith at your request, didn't I? And I am out most days on my horse. I went riding just yesterday, if you recall,' he added, his mind wandering immediately to the cliffs, to those dark eyes staring boldly up at him as he spat out his fury.

'I do recall that you went riding alone,' Samuel agreed. 'I recall too that you came back in the most foul temper. A mood which, dare I say, has persisted ever since. A black mood even by your standards, Isaac.'

Isaac curled his lip. 'As I said, I'm just a little tired.'

Samuel, however, was clearly not going to let the matter drop. Instead he sat forward, his elbows pressed against the arms of his chair. 'I regret that I was not here for you, you know. I regret that I did not return home as soon as the news about Rosalind and the baby reached me. I can offer no excuses.'

He drew a deep breath, and instinctively Isaac found himself dreading whatever was coming next.

'But I am here now,' he continued, 'and I think it is time that a few things changed at Hayton Hall.'

Isaac frowned. 'Such as?'

'You are Sir Isaac Liddell, Baronet. It's time you started to act like it again.'

'I do act like it,' Isaac protested. 'I care for my estate and always have. Even when I was at my lowest ebb I did not neglect my duties.'

'That is not all that your position in life involves, and you know it,' Samuel countered. He pointed at the window. 'It involves going out there, visiting your tenants and going into town. It involves being a part of society. You might not spend all day in your robe any more, drinking yourself to death, but you must surely see that you are still living a half-life.'

At this, Isaac groaned. Samuel was right—of course he was. In his widowhood he'd become sullen and reclusive. To such an extent that sometimes he wondered whether he knew how to hold a proper conversation any more. His encounter with Miss Conrad yesterday had shown him just how low he'd sunk. Hot-tempered and impertinent, he had undoubtedly caused great offence.

Rosalind wouldn't have looked at him twice if he'd behaved in such a manner with her. Not that he wanted any woman to look at him the way she had—of course not. But a small, suppressed part of him did desire to see the old Isaac return, to see the man his wife had loved stare back at him in the mirror once more.

'All right,' he said at length. 'I place myself wholly at your disposal, brother. What would you have me do?'

Samuel smiled. 'Quite simply, Isaac, I want you to start venturing into society once again. I want you to show your face in the village, and in Lowhaven, and I want you to go to the events that those in our society would expect you to attend.'

'You really want me to offer myself up as fodder for the gossips?' Isaac scoffed, shaking his head.

'People will simply take it as an indication that you have come out of mourning at last,' Samuel replied flatly. 'They will be glad of it, I am sure. You must stop believing that the world is somehow against you, because truly it is not. We will start by attending a ball at the Assembly Rooms in Lowhaven this Friday.'

'But that is only a few days from now, Samuel.' Isaac stared at him, aghast.

Samuel nodded. 'You must start somewhere, Isaac. Let this be your new beginning.'

'All right,' Isaac conceded with another groan.

'Good,' Samuel replied, rising from his seat. 'Because I am rather looking forward to this ball. A pleasant evening among friends and perhaps a dance or two with some of the young ladies will suit me very well.'

Isaac gave him a wry smile. 'Indeed, brother. I expect you'll find yourself on scores of ladies' dance cards before the night is over.'

'As might you,' Samuel answered him as he made his way to the library door. 'Even you are not immune to the charms of a pretty face.'

Isaac made no attempt to reply, but instead sat back in his chair, exhausted at the mere prospect of what the next few days would hold. Putting on his best clothes and going out in company for the evening was one thing, but dancing with a woman was quite another. Although, he reminded himself, there was one young lady with whom he did wish to speak, and if she happened to be there requesting a dance with her might be his only means of offering an apology.

His stomach churned at the thought of such an interaction, at the possibility of her rebuke. At the small chance of her acceptance and the pleasant prospect of being the recipient of that dark gaze once again.

Samuel was right, it seemed. He was not immune to a pretty woman's charms. Not in the least.

Chapter Six

The sun was still bestowing its pink-orange glow upon Lowhaven when the Pearsons' carriage drew to a halt outside the Assembly Rooms that Friday evening. The Pearsons had arrived to collect Louisa and her aunt a little early, which had thrown the household into brief disarray as Nan hurried to finish dressing her mistress while Aunt Clarissa cajoled them from downstairs.

'It seems that the Pearsons keep to their own time,' she'd said as Louisa had finally emerged, 'and we must keep to it, too, since they are good enough to take us in their carriage.'

Louisa had met the remark with silence. She was not oblivious to her aunt's humble circumstances—no carriage and only two servants in her household—but acknowledging the ageing woman's situation so directly made her uncomfortable. Perhaps, she realised, it was because this was the future that she imagined for herself: independent, but only so far as a small income might allow.

The journey in the carriage had been brief and lively, with the two older women complimenting the younger

women's gowns and speculating as to how full both
their dance cards might be.

Louisa had felt herself grow anxious at the latter remarks. While she was enjoying having an occasion to
wear the pretty rose-pink silk gown that Nan had selected for her, she was nonetheless adamant that dancing was out of the question. Her aunt had asked her to
come as Miss Pearson's companion, and she would fulfil her duty, but that was all.

She'd felt relieved when Mr Pearson, a stout man
with greying red hair, had changed the subject to ask if
she'd found Lowhaven agreeable so far. An easy question, she'd thought, at least for the most part. As long
as she did not include clifftop arguments with disagreeable baronets when determining her answer.

The scene which greeted Louisa as she stepped out of
the carriage was one of crowds and chaos, as it seemed
most of Lowhaven had descended upon the fine white
building to enjoy an evening of music and conversation. As she was jostled up the steps and towards the
entrance she found herself taking hold of Charlotte's
arm, more for her own reassurance than anything else,
but Charlotte accepted the gesture warmly.

'We shall be fine if we stay together, I think,' the
younger woman whispered to her. 'I promise I shall not
leave your side, Louisa.'

Louisa blinked, momentarily taken aback by Charlotte's familiarity in using her first name before deciding to embrace it. By her own admission Aunt Clarissa
had identified Charlotte as a suitable companion for her;
perhaps during the course of the summer they could become firm friends, too. It had been so long since Louisa
had enjoyed a friendship.

She smiled. 'Thank you, Charlotte,' she said.

The two young women made their way inside, trailing behind their older companions as they wove their way through the congregating masses towards the ballroom, from which they could already hear the cheerful sound of violins playing.

Halfway along the corridor Louisa heard Mr Pearson announce his intention to visit the card room and to leave the ladies to their own devices. She smiled, thinking of her own father, who would do much the same thing when out for the evening. Her face grew serious once more as she remembered how long it had been since she had enjoyed such times in the company of her parents.

'Do not worry,' Charlotte said to her, misinterpreting her countenance. 'We shall do quite well without Papa.'

The four ladies settled themselves in a spot at the edge of the ballroom, with Aunt Clarissa and Mrs Pearson fortunate enough to find two seats upon which to make themselves comfortable. Louisa and Charlotte, meanwhile, stood close together, sipping from the small cups of punch they'd each been offered by a passing waiter. The drink was strong, and Louisa resolved to take only a little of it. She would act as an unmarried woman in her position ought to act: with good deal of sense and restraint. She would be a charming and responsible companion to Charlotte, and would give Lowhaven society no reason to gossip on her account.

'Do you know many people here?' Louisa asked Charlotte.

Charlotte shook her head in reply. 'Not so many, no,' she replied. 'I'm afraid we may be standing here like wallflowers for some time.'

Louisa smiled reassuringly. In truth, she did not mind.

It was rather pleasant to stand to one side and watch others as they danced in the warm glow of the candlelight. Her days of hovering beside her mother, trying not to fidget as she waited for some young gentleman to request an introduction and thereafter a dance, were long past. She knew, however, that Charlotte would be experiencing such nervous anticipation right now, and that her hopes for the evening were altogether different from those of a woman settled upon spinsterhood.

'I am sure you will be dancing before too long,' Louisa whispered encouragingly.

At length, Louisa was correct. When one dance ended and before the next began Charlotte was approached by a young man of her acquaintance and swiftly whisked away to dance a lively cotillion. Conscious she was now alone, Louisa stepped back towards her aunt and Mrs Pearson, intent upon looking at ease in their company while standing quietly with her thoughts.

She had managed well so far, she believed, cultivating an air of serenity whilst drawing no attention to herself. Perhaps venturing into society as a stranger was not so bad, after all.

'I'm afraid you may see little of my daughter for the rest of the evening,' Mrs Pearson observed as she approached. 'I usually find that once she secures one dancing partner, she shortly thereafter secures a dozen.'

'I am glad of it,' Louisa replied. 'Although Miss Pearson seemed to suggest that she did not know many of the people here.'

'She knows plenty who are of consequence,' Mrs Pearson answered, giving her a sharp look.

Louisa glanced apologetically at her aunt, fearing she

had unwittingly overstepped the mark. 'Of course,' she replied with a conciliatory nod.

But neither Mrs Pearson nor Aunt Clarissa were paying any further heed to her faux pas, their attention instead captured by something beyond her. Something which had made her aunt's mouth fall open in disbelief.

'Well, I never...' Aunt Clarissa began.

Louisa spun round, watching as the crowd seemed to part like the Red Sea. Standing in the chasm they'd left were two gentlemen—both of them known to her, and both causing her to take a sharp breath, albeit for very different reasons.

The fair-haired gentleman was smiling broadly, his open, friendly expression taking her back to those hours she'd spent in his fine carriage, reeling from the ordeal of the overturned stagecoach. But it was the other gentleman standing by his side who had really captured her attention—and, indeed, the attention of everyone else in the room. The dark, wild-tempered man from the cliffs...the one who'd inflamed her with his insolence and preyed on her thoughts ever since.

She heard herself gasp as he turned and caught her gaze. Then she felt the earlier calm she'd relished simply ebb away.

Isaac ought to have been mortified by the scene his presence had created—by the gawping expressions and unsubtle whispers which welcomed him to his first social outing in more than two years. Indeed, it was exactly this reaction he had dreaded. He had been so reluctant to attend tonight that Samuel had had to all but drag him out of Hayton Hall and into his carriage.

Yet now, standing there, he could think of nothing

but one lady's face, wide-eyed and uncommonly beautiful, just as she had been the last time he'd seen her. He could think of nothing but speaking with her again, of finding some discreet way to deliver the apology which was due to her. The sight of her staring at him with that same aghast look in her eyes that he'd seen when he'd almost trampled her with his horse was enough to make him feel ashamed all over again. How wretched he had been. How uncouth.

'Well, brother, it seems we've caused quite a stir,' Samuel observed, an amused smile playing on his lips.

'Exactly why I did not want to come here,' Isaac replied, although his protest sounded hollow.

Samuel helped himself to a couple of glasses of punch from the tray of a passing waiter, handing one of them to his brother. Isaac took a long sip, savouring its sweetness and the way it warmed his throat, as every pair of eyes in the room seemed to remain intently upon him. At least the drink was strong, he thought. He would need plenty of it if he was going to survive the long evening ahead of him.

'Ah, I see Miss Conrad is here,' Samuel observed, with a polite nod in her direction.

'Miss Conrad?' Isaac asked, feigning ignorance.

'The fair maiden,' Samuel whispered. 'The one whose aid we came to on our way home from Penrith. Surely you cannot have forgotten her, brother?' He nudged Isaac firmly in the ribs, making him wince. 'Come, let us say hello. I am curious to know how she is enjoying her stay in Lowhaven.'

Dutifully, Isaac followed his brother. He hoped he looked sufficiently detached, and that no one would detect his heart hammering in his chest as he walked across the room towards her. As he drew closer, he noted that the two older ladies sitting down behind her had got to their feet. One of them looked familiar, although he could not recall why. He noted, too, how Miss Conrad's eyes seemed to widen even further, her posture so stiff and brittle that she looked as though she might break.

His stomach lurched at the realisation that it was his approach which had provoked such a response.

'Miss Conrad!' Samuel exclaimed, giving her an impeccable bow. 'It is very good to see you again.'

'Mr Liddell.' Miss Conrad met Samuel's enthusiasm with a brisk nod. 'And Sir Isaac, of course,' she added, although she barely lifted her dark eyes to acknowledge him.

Isaac watched as Miss Conrad gestured awkwardly towards her companions and hurriedly undertook the necessary introductions. Isaac bowed politely at the two older ladies, realising that the one with the familiar face was Miss Howarth, the old rector's daughter. The other lady, Mrs Pearson, he did not know, and nor did he warm to her as she stood there, her sharp gaze flitting between them all like a crow choosing its supper.

With the formality of introductions now complete, he found himself watching Miss Conrad once more, his gaze lingering upon her while Samuel gave an account of their meeting Miss Conrad to Mrs Pearson, who had enquired as to how they were acquainted.

He noted that his brother's tale was less than truthful, omitting all mention of taking the young lady and her maid into their carriage. Apparently protecting Miss Conrad's reputation meant more to Samuel than providing evidence of his own gallantry. Guilt surged through him as he compared his brother's gentlemanly behaviour with his own clumsy, brutish tongue that day on the cliffs.

'I daresay that must have been frightening, Miss Conrad,' Mrs Pearson observed. 'Coachmen these days can be so reckless. I am surprised that neither you nor your aunt mentioned it before. It is quite a story,' she added.

Isaac found himself raising an eyebrow at the cutting nature of the remark. It was as though the woman sensed there was a shared secret she was not being made privy to.

'Ah—yes, well, fortunately the coach was able to continue on its way and no harm was done,' Miss Howarth interjected smoothly. 'And my niece is very grateful to you both for stopping to retrieve the fallen luggage,' she added, giving both gentlemen a smile which told them that she appreciated their discretion.

Miss Conrad, however, appeared not to be listening, her eyes cast down, her thoughts elsewhere. Isaac wished he could read them…wished to know what had her so preoccupied. Wished to know if she could stand this latest meeting, or if she wanted to turn and walk away all over again.

Around them the music ceased, and the bustle of men and women changing dancing partners began. Before he could think about what he was doing, Isaac reached out and offered her his hand.

'Would you like to dance, Miss Conrad?' he asked her, and finally she lifted her gaze and those deep brown eyes met his once more.

Chapter Seven

Louisa felt the heat rise in her cheeks as Sir Isaac led her towards the centre of the ballroom. It seemed to her as though every pair of eyes was upon them—as though every person there had the same whispered questions on their lips. Who was this woman? And why had Sir Isaac chosen her for his first dance?

In truth, she desired to know the answer to the latter question herself. After their awful last meeting she had assumed he'd want no further association with her. He'd had to endure his brother's approach and the subsequent conversation—that had been a matter of politeness. But asking her to dance? There had been no requirement for him to do that.

She wished he hadn't asked her. She wished she hadn't felt obliged to accept. It had drawn attention to her, and that was the very last thing she wanted.

They lined up opposite each other and Louisa said a quick prayer, hoping she could remember the steps. She looked up at Sir Isaac, realising she must appear as anxious as she felt when he offered her a small, reassuring smile.

The candlelight seemed to illuminate his face, and her attention was drawn to the gentle creases around his eyes and the smattering of silver in his near-black hair. It struck her that he was older than she'd thought—but then she hadn't thought very much of him at their first or second meeting...at least, not much to his credit. Now, she couldn't seem to take her eyes off him. His countenance—indeed his entire appearance—was very different from that which she had witnessed on the cliffs. Tonight, he looked every inch an elegant gentleman, in his dark tailcoat and contrasting breeches, whilst his windswept hair had been tamed, and apparently so had his rough manners.

Realising she was staring at him, she lowered her gaze, instructing herself to be calm as the music began and they took their first steps towards one another. It was only one dance. It would be over soon enough.

'I fear I have made you uncomfortable, Miss Conrad,' Sir Isaac said in a low voice when they drew close enough to converse. 'I only wish to apologise to you for the way I spoke to you at our last meeting. I was unforgivably rude.'

'Thank you,' she replied softly. 'I appreciate the trouble you have gone to in order to convey your apology.'

'Trouble?'

'Asking me to dance when I am sure there are many others in this room whose company you would find more agreeable. I was not... I was not all that I should have been at our last meeting, either,' she added hesitantly, hoping he would grasp her meaning.

The demands of the dance separated them for a few moments. As she moved with as much grace as she could muster, Louisa found herself feeling impatient.

Why was it that a man and a woman could not have a straightforward conversation in company without any need for the ruse of dancing?

By the time they met again Louisa could barely keep command of her words as they burst forth. 'I was ungracious towards you,' she blurted. 'Truly, I am ashamed of it.'

Sir Isaac caught her gaze, offering her his hand again as the dance required. She accepted it delicately and together they turned, exchanging small smiles which seemed to express a mutual understanding that words could not.

'Then it seems we are both ashamed, Miss Conrad,' Sir Isaac said at last. 'Come, let us start afresh.'

Louisa gave a nod of agreement. Although she very much doubted that any acquaintance between them would be sustained, it eased her conscience to know that there was no animosity between them.

They spent the remainder of the dance largely in silence, punctuated only by Sir Isaac's polite enquiries into the length of her stay in Lowhaven and whether she was enjoying her summer sojourn. She allowed herself to relax, enjoying the dance and the company of a man who, she could not fail to observe, had both charm and handsome looks in abundance.

For this indulgence she chastised herself; her days of admiring a gentleman's appearance were as far behind her as she'd believed her dancing days to be. Occasionally, though, when the steps brought them close together or compelled them to go hand in hand, she felt a long-forgotten warmth spread through her limbs. And when she caught Sir Isaac looking at her, letting his deep blue eyes linger over her face, she remembered why dancing could be preferable to conversation.

Trouble. That was what she'd called it. *Trouble.*

Isaac sat back in the carriage, resting his head against the hard wooden side as he waited for Samuel to join him for their journey back to Hayton Hall. The hour was late and, given the evening's exertions, he knew he ought to be exhausted. But rest could not have been further from his mind. Instead, he found his thoughts revisiting certain memories, again and again.

Her dark eyes staring up at him. The soft feeling of her gloved hand. The arresting sensation of her nearness to him each time the dance commanded them to draw close. The touching sincerity of her apology. It had all caught him unaware and left him so overwrought that he'd managed only the barest amount of conversation. Truly, she must think him the most charmless man she'd ever met.

Trouble? Indeed, he was troubled.

'Well, brother, I do believe that tonight was a success.'

Samuel climbed into the carriage, sitting down opposite him with a satisfied sigh. His eyes were heavy and a little glazed, and Isaac noted the smell of strong liquor emanating from him. His encounter with Miss Conrad had left him feeling distracted for the rest of the night, and he had neither paid attention to his younger sibling's merrymaking nor indulged in the strong punch himself. Now, he found himself wishing he was in his cups, too. Some gentle inebriation might help to distance him from uncomfortable thoughts about a beautiful woman.

'It was not as bad as I feared,' Isaac conceded.

'You see! I was right that you should come,' Samuel declared, with a self-satisfied tap of his knee.

'Indeed… Although I am very weary now,' Isaac replied, suddenly desirous of a quiet journey home.

His brother, however, was not to be dissuaded from his chatter. 'I cannot see how! You barely danced, except with Miss Conrad. That was a surprise, I have to say… you whisking her away like that. I wondered what had come over you.'

'Nothing,' Isaac grunted. 'I merely thought it polite.'

'You were under no obligation. Mind you, she is remarkably handsome. I had thought to ask her myself, but…'

'But what?'

'She's very reserved. Dare I say a little cold, even? I recall thinking as much when we first met her. The way she sat in our carriage, stony-faced and hardly troubling herself to make conversation.'

Isaac felt his fists curl with irritation and he pressed them into the seat. 'She didn't know us, Samuel. She was forced by circumstances to accept our assistance. I think she can be forgiven for being a little wary.'

Samuel let out a wry chuckle. 'You've changed your tune. What was it you called her after we'd left her with her aunt? Reckless?'

'Damn you,' Isaac growled.

Samuel's face grew serious. 'You're quite taken with her, aren't you? I saw the way you were looking at her, you know. I'll bet most of the people in the ballroom did—including her. I've not seen you look at a woman like that since…'

'Don't say her name!' Isaac snapped. 'Don't you dare!' He sighed heavily, composing himself. 'I was not looking at Miss Conrad is any particular way. I was only…'

'Only what?' his brother challenged him, sitting up-right now.

'Only—only seeking to apologise to her,' he admitted finally, rubbing his forehead with his hands.

'Apologise?' Samuel frowned. 'What could you possibly need to apologise for?'

'I saw Miss Conrad again—after the day of the stage-coach accident.' Isaac made his admission quietly. 'I was riding up on the cliffs near Lowhaven. Miss Conrad was out for a walk. I nearly trampled the poor woman with my horse. I was in a foul temper and I spoke to her in a way that I had no business to. Asking her to dance with me was the only way I could offer an apology discreetly.'

Samuel raised his eyebrows. 'I see. And when was this?'

Isaac shrugged. 'Less than a week ago. Does it matter?'

'I suppose not.' Samuel slumped back, closing his eyes. 'And that's all there is to it, is there? You've made amends to her and have no intention of seeing her again?'

'Indeed,' Isaac replied. 'Miss Conrad is visiting her aunt for the summer. I doubt that our paths will cross again.'

The only answer Isaac received from his brother was the sound of his loud snores punctuating the air as their carriage rumbled slowly along the road back to Hayton Hall.

Just as well, Isaac thought, settling into his seat. The last thing he wanted was for Samuel to hear how forlorn he sounded, or to realise just how unsettled the evening, the dancing, and above all Miss Louisa Conrad had left him.

* * *

By the time the Pearsons' carriage delivered Louisa and her aunt back to Juniper Street, Louisa could barely keep her eyes open. The short journey home had been quiet, with the older members of the party all dozing and the younger two exchanging only brief whispers about the evening's events.

Charlotte evidently relished her near-constant dancing. Her cheeks were flushed, her face alight with a smile which no amount of weariness could remove. For Charlotte Pearson it had been a very successful night indeed.

Louisa, on the other hand, felt more conflicted about her first foray into Lowhaven society. She hadn't wished to dance at all, and had it not been for Sir Isaac Liddell's invitation she would have succeeded in that regard. Yet, try as she might, she could not bring herself to regret it.

Dancing with Sir Isaac had thrilled and discomfited her in equal measure. She had been pleased to make amends with him, but it was more than that—if she was honest with herself, she had enjoyed his attentions. She'd relished his proximity, and the sensation which had run through her each time he'd taken hold of her hand. She knew she shouldn't feel that way—the dance would have meant little to him, and he'd only asked her so that he could apologise. But still, she decided, there could be nothing wrong with her keeping the memory of it for herself and bringing it out on those occasions when she needed something to make her smile.

'Goodnight, Aunt,' she said, almost as soon as they walked through Clarissa's door, determining to go straight upstairs and to bed.

'Could you perhaps come into the parlour for a moment, my dear?' Clarissa asked her.

Louisa nodded, wordlessly following her aunt into the small room and closing the door. She felt her heart begin to beat faster as she wondered what was amiss. Aunt Clarissa's face was drawn and grey with tiredness; whatever it was must be serious if it could not keep until morning.

'I wanted to speak to you about Mrs Pearson, Louisa.'

'Oh?'

Aunt Clarissa shook her head, clearly troubled. 'Unfortunately I think Mrs Pearson was vexed not to have known that you'd met Sir Isaac and his brother before.'

'I rather think it's none of her business who I am acquainted with, Aunt,' Louisa replied.

'Indeed, but after we'd discussed Sir Isaac at tea…' Clarissa paused, then waved a dismissive hand. 'Oh, never mind about that. I wanted to speak to you about your remark…when you suggested that Miss Pearson did not know many people at the ball.'

'I was merely repeating what Charlotte had told me herself,' Louisa protested mildly.

In truth, her thoughts had been so preoccupied with Sir Isaac that she had quite forgotten the incident altogether.

'I'm sure you were, and I know you spoke in innocence. But I thought I ought to explain to you why I believe Mrs Pearson behaved the way she did.' Clarissa sighed, sitting down on one of the parlour chairs. 'The Pearsons only came to Lowhaven a few months ago. Mrs Pearson is a gentleman's daughter, from Northumberland, but Mr John Pearson's family have made their fortune in trade. From what I have heard, he has squandered it, and the family now find themselves in reduced circumstances. Since coming to town, I believe they've struggled to make good connections. That's what Miss Pearson will have been alluding to when she told you that she had not had all that many introductions.'

Louisa frowned. 'Charlotte seemed to manage well enough this evening. She had sufficient acquaintances to keep her dancing for most of the night.'

'Ah, yes, but I doubt that even one of those young men she danced with will be considered suitable by Mrs Pearson,' Clarissa countered, giving her niece a knowing smile. 'Even though I'm sure she knows well enough that the leading families in the area will want little to do with a hapless tradesman's daughter—especially since I doubt there is even a substantial dowry to tempt them.'

'It cannot be so bad, surely? They manage to keep a carriage and horses of their own.'

'They keep up appearances, my dear, but I believe it is bad enough. Mrs Pearson will want her daughter to marry soon, I think, and as well as possible.'

'I see,' replied Louisa, biting her lip. 'I am sorry, Aunt. I did not mean to offend Mrs Pearson.'

Clarissa got up from her chair, gently patting her niece on the arm. 'I wouldn't worry. I daresay you more than made up for it by securing her an introduction to Sir Isaac and his brother.'

The mention of Sir Isaac made Louisa's face grow warm. 'Oh, yes,' she replied.

Clarissa shook her head. 'I couldn't quite believe my eyes when they walked in together. And then for Sir Isaac to ask you to dance! You did well, my dear. Very well.'

'I'm quite sure Sir Isaac only asked me out of politeness, Aunt.'

At this, Clarissa laughed. 'I might be an old spinster, Louisa, but I know enough about the world to know that a gentleman never asks a lady to dance just to be polite. He did not dance with anyone else all night, you know. And from the way he looked at you, I was quite certain that he'd ask you to take a turn with him a second time.'

Now Louisa felt sure her cheeks must be glowing scarlet. 'Well, I am glad he did not, for I am convinced I could not have borne it,' she replied hotly. 'And now I am tired and must go to bed. Goodnight, Aunt.'

Before Clarissa could say anything further, Louisa opened the door and marched out of the room.

Chapter Eight

'You've done well today, brother.'

Samuel's patronising tone made Isaac flinch, although he knew the remark was well-intended. The day was fine and bright and the two brothers rode side by side, paying visits to the farms and cottages situated across the not inconsiderable swathe of Liddell land.

'I was never so melancholic that I ceased to have any regard for my tenants,' Isaac countered, glancing briefly over his shoulder at his steward, who rode a little further behind. 'Although I will concede that I always had the very best help.'

'I do believe your visits today were appreciated, nonetheless. It means a lot for you to be seen.'

Isaac nodded. 'Indeed. I regret that I have been so absent these past two years. In plentiful times it may have been forgivable, but...'

'You are not responsible for bad harvests, Isaac,' Samuel interjected. 'Only the damnable weather can be blamed for that.'

'No, I know that,' Isaac replied quietly. 'But, as you say, it's important that I'm seen, and while my tenants suffered I was very much invisible.'

Samuel offered his brother a sympathetic smile, and together they rode on in silence. They had one more visit to pay on the edge of the village, before returning to Hayton Hall for luncheon. The mere thought of food made Isaac's stomach growl; they had been out for hours, and he'd barely had time to eat even a small breakfast before meeting his steward at nine o'clock.

Despite his hunger, he had to admit that the busy morning had buoyed his spirits. He'd enjoyed seeing the families, many of whom had lived and worked on his family's land for generations. And, he had to admit, he'd liked having Samuel accompany him as much as he'd appreciated the support of his steward. Samuel's light-hearted, relaxed manner and ability to regale an audience with tales of his European travels had put Isaac at his ease and made him feel less under scrutiny.

Yes, he thought. The morning had been a success.

He'd even managed not to think so much about Miss Conrad.

Isaac sighed, inwardly cursing himself for allowing his thoughts to roam back to that evening once again. Truly, it was ridiculous to think so much about a woman he'd met only a handful of times and danced with once. It was nonsensical to wake in the morning and realise he'd been dreaming about her, twirling in that captivating pink dress she'd worn. It was alarming to realise that the quiet moments of his day were dominated by her—her smile, her large brown eyes, her perfectly curled fair hair.

He supposed this was to be expected—that after so long on his own even the brief company of a woman like Miss Louisa Conrad could prove overpowering. He found the way that she haunted his thoughts unsettling, but at the same time he was forced to admit that he did not want it to stop.

'Almost there,' Samuel called out to him.

Good, he thought. He needed distraction, and thereafter a hearty meal.

'Is it not the most charming little village, Louisa?'

Charlotte took hold of her companion's arm as they made their way along the dusty track which served as the main thoroughfare through Hayton. This was their first outing together since the ball and, as promised, Charlotte had determined that they would walk to Hayton, so that she could show Louisa around the village her family had once called their home.

Louisa found herself easily agreeing with her new friend's opinion—Hayton was indeed as picturesque as it was miniature, with a cluster of low stone cottages forming its centre, framed by trees and hedgerows in full leaf. At its furthest edge was the ancient church where, Charlotte had reliably informed her, the old rectory could be found.

As the two ladies made their way in this direction, Louisa considered what life in Hayton must have been like for her mother and her aunt. Quiet, certainly, with only a handful of neighbours and their parents for company—somewhat different from the life her aunt led now, in a bustling port town.

Rather idly, she wondered which she preferred, and wondered, too, if the isolation of small village life had been the reason she'd never married. For whilst Aunt Clarissa's siblings had sought opportunities in the larger towns or, in her own mother's case, been removed to London by benevolent relatives, Clarissa had remained faithfully at the rectory, at her parents' side. She wondered how much that had been of her own choosing, or whether it had simply been the only option left.

'It is very lovely,' Louisa agreed at last.

'When I marry, I should count myself very fortunate if I was able to live in a place like this,' Charlotte gushed. 'Life in a small country cottage would suit me very well indeed.'

'Perhaps you ought to marry a rector, then. A man with a rural parish to tend to. That should assure you of the quiet life you seek,' Louisa said, a note of gentle teasing in her voice.

Charlotte wrinkled her nose. 'I doubt that would do for Mama.'

'What? Your mother would not approve of a match with a man of the cloth? To a gentleman with a steady income? I do believe most mothers would seek exactly such marriages for their daughters,' Louisa replied.

'Alas, my mother is not "most mothers",' Charlotte countered quietly. 'She is most particular on the subject of whom I might marry.'

Louisa gave her friend's arm a sympathetic squeeze, but made no further remark. She reflected briefly on Aunt Clarissa's words about Mrs Pearson, and the high aspirations she believed she had for her daughter. High indeed, Louisa thought, if she would not give her over to marriage with a clergyman.

'Well, here we are, Louisa,' Charlotte said as they arrived at the gates to the church. 'Here is where your grandfather used to minister to his congregation, and over there is the rectory.'

Louisa stood still at length, admiring the old stone church, its spire reaching far above the humble dwell-

ings of the village. She looked, too, at the rectory, finding it to be a pleasing white house of considerable size.
She found herself thinking again about the years both
her mother and her aunt had spent here, and how little
she knew of it.

'It's strange to see it,' Louisa observed, speaking
some of her thoughts aloud. 'I cannot claim to have really known my grandparents. They sent my mother to
London to stay with relatives not long before she came
of age. I knew her family in the south far better.'

'But you are here now, with your aunt,' Charlotte replied. 'You must know her well enough to want to come
all this way to visit?'

'I had not seen Aunt Clarissa since I was a girl, but it
is true that we have written often.'

'And after all these years you wished to see her and
spend the summer here?' Charlotte asked.

Louisa gave a hesitant smile. 'Yes.'

'I wish you would not leave so soon…' Charlotte
groaned. 'I fear I will have only just got to know you and
you will be going back to Berkshire. Perhaps you will
find a reason to stay?' she added, her expression bright-
ening once more. 'Perhaps you will find a husband here.'

'Oh, no, I shall never marry,' Louisa replied, the in-
stinctive response rolling from her tongue before she
could think about it.

'Never?' Charlotte exclaimed. 'But how can you say
so?'

Louisa sighed, taking Charlotte's arm again as they
turned away from the church and began their return
journey through the village. Quietly she cursed herself
for being so careless with her words. Such a forthright
statement demanded some form of explanation.

'I was engaged once, to a captain in the navy. He died at sea during the war…before we were able to wed. I swore then that I would not marry.' She tried her best to sound matter-of-fact, not to betray her emotions. Not to betray all that she had left out.

'Oh, Louisa, that is very sad. I am sorry for you. But you are still young. I do not think your captain would wish for you to remain alone. Surely if he loved you as you loved him, he would not?'

Louisa offered her friend a small smile, wishing she could explain, but knowing she could not. If Charlotte knew the whole story she would understand. But if Charlotte knew the whole story she would not want to be associated with her at all.

'I'm sure he would not. But it is my wish, and I am very much settled upon it.'

'Mama says the life of a spinster is one that no woman should desire. I have to bite my tongue to stop myself from pointing out that one acquaintance she's made in Lowhaven is just such an unmarried woman, and that she seems to do perfectly well by herself.'

Louisa laughed at this. 'Indeed, my aunt is an example to us all.'

'I suppose that while you are here you might learn something from her about managing alone?'

'Yes, I suppose I might,' Louisa replied, wondering, not for the first time, if such motivation had informed her parents' enthusiasm for sending her here. Wondering, too, if they'd hoped seeing her aunt's life for herself might put her off spinsterhood entirely.

'Mama hopes I will learn from you,' Charlotte continued. 'She says you will be a welcome influence upon me…that you are a gentleman's daughter of good repute and great sensibility.'

But Louisa was no longer listening—which was just as well as she might have reddened at Mrs Pearson's overly generous characterisation of her. Instead, she was staring straight ahead, her eyes wide, at the two approaching men on horseback—both of whom she recognised, and one of whom she had not wished to see so soon.

She had barely managed to collect herself following that evening at the ball, never mind recover from that ill-tempered conversation with her aunt on the subject of her dancing. Truly, she was not sure she could face him again. And yet, she realised as he continued his approach, it seemed she must.

Isaac had known it was her from the moment he saw her in the distance, standing in front of the old church. He hadn't been able to see her clearly, or to recognise her pretty features with any precision, but he'd known. He'd known instinctively from the way his heart beat faster and his empty stomach seemed to tie itself in knots.

For a moment he'd thought about turning his horse around and galloping in the other direction, to put some distance between himself and Miss Louisa Conrad and how she flustered him. However, he'd known that would only cause more problems than it would solve—notably in the form of questions from his brother, who still rode at his side. Besides, he was beginning to suspect that mere miles would not be enough to stem the tide which threatened to overwhelm him when he so much as dared to think about her.

'Ah, look—there is Miss Conrad,' Samuel called. 'And who is that with her? A friend? I wonder what she is doing in Hayton. We should stop to say hello.'

'Huh…' Isaac grunted, trying his best to look uninterested.

He wished he could be uninterested. But as he drew closer and saw her looking up at him, those dark, inquisitive eyes staring into his, he realised his folly. This lady—who'd clambered into his carriage, who'd berated him on the clifftops, who'd danced with him—interested him. Now fate had put her in his path once more, and Isaac found himself feeling unfathomably anxious about speaking to her, about giving a good account of himself.

He swallowed hard. His mouth was as dry as a desert, and his mind seemed barren like one, too.

He dismounted his horse, trying to find the right words.

Damn you, Liddell, he said to himself. *What is the matter with you?*

Chapter Nine

'Good day, Miss Conrad. What a pleasant surprise to see you in Hayton.'

Samuel spoke first—of course he did—finding exactly the words which Isaac lacked. Isaac forced a smile and a courteous nod at the two young women, ignoring the prickle of resentment he felt at his brother's friendly, easy manner. Rosalind had always been better in social situations, too, but she'd been his helpmeet. He'd felt gratitude and admiration for her grace and charm. The superior qualities of a younger brother, by contrast, could only ever be irritating.

Samuel dismounted his horse and Isaac watched as Miss Conrad dropped her gaze and gave them both a polite curtsey.

'Sir Isaac, Mr Liddell…may I introduce my friend, Miss Charlotte Pearson?' she said, raising her eyes to meet his once more.

Realising he was staring, Isaac turned quickly to regard her companion, whose acquaintance Samuel was already making, going to great pains to stress his delight. She was a striking young lady, her fair complexion contrasting with the bright red curls which peered wildly from the edges of her bonnet. She seemed younger than Miss Conrad, and both her appearance and manner betrayed a giddiness over which she didn't seem to have mastered complete control.

He wondered then how old Miss Conrad was. Younger than him, certainly—he was nine-and-thirty, and she looked ten years his junior, at least. Yet there was something in those dark eyes of hers, something about the seriousness of her countenance, which suggested a maturity beyond her years. He ruminated on this observation for a moment, before a nudge from his brother forced him to return his mind to the conversation.

'We would be delighted to accompany you back through the village. It would be our pleasure—wouldn't it, Isaac?' Samuel was saying.

'Yes. Indeed—yes,' Isaac replied hastily, realising he'd missed much of the discussion.

He watched with a mix of delight and anxiety as Samuel and Miss Pearson led the way, leaving him in the company of Miss Conrad. Giving her another nod, he took hold of his horse and together they began to walk, slowly and silently at first, as though each one did not know what to say to the other.

'You have enjoyed your walk to Hayton, I hope?' Isaac began, settling upon what he believed would be an easy topic.

There were so many things he wished to say to her, so many things he wished to know—too much to convey and to discover in a short promenade through the tiny village. He would have to content himself with more mundane subjects.

'Yes, thank you,' she replied. 'As you know, my family used to live in the village. Miss Pearson offered to accompany me while I explored the area. She has been very kind.'

'Miss Pearson is related to the Mrs Pearson you were with at the Assembly Rooms?' Isaac asked.

She nodded. 'Yes, they are mother and daughter. They live in Lowhaven. Mrs Pearson is acquainted with my aunt.'

Isaac furrowed his brow a little. 'I do not think I know any Pearsons from Lowhaven.'

'They are fairly new in town, much like myself,' she replied. 'Although they reside now in Lowhaven, whereas I am only visiting.'

'For the summer,' Isaac said, the temporary nature of their acquaintance striking him again.

Miss Conrad smiled. 'Yes, as I think I told you when we danced. I am here only for the summer.'

He nodded briskly, hoping she wouldn't be able to detect the heat that had risen within him when she had made reference to their dancing. God, how his mind had lingered upon the memory of that night. She spoke of it so matter-of-factly; he knew he never could.

'And you enjoyed the ball?' he asked her, wilfully ignoring the way his instincts were crying out at him to avoid the subject altogether.

'Yes, very much. I confess that I was somewhat out of practice when it came to dancing. I hope I did not miss too many of the steps.'

'You were perfect, from what I could see,' he answered her, a little too forthrightly. Reining in his feelings, he added, 'Although I am no expert, since I am more than a little out of practice myself. In truth, I hadn't danced in a long time until I danced with you.'

She smiled again. 'Then I hope I was a worthy partner.'

Damn, he thought. Worthy? She had no idea.

They were approaching the end of the village, and ahead he could see Miss Pearson and his brother had stopped to wait for them. He felt his heart begin to beat faster; they were almost out of time together and all he'd managed was a conversation about trivialities.

'I don't see a lot of people,' he blurted out. 'Other than my brother, of course. What I mean to say is I don't venture much into society. But I do like to walk, and to ride. I often ride out to the cliffs where we met that time. If—if I was ever to see you there again, I should be very glad to continue our conversation.'

He glanced at her, wondering if she had understood his meaning—nay, hoping she had. She turned to meet his gaze, and for a moment he believed he might lose himself in the depths of those eyes.

'Thank you, Sir Isaac,' she replied demurely. 'On the next fine afternoon, after calling hours, I believe I will walk that way again, too.'

What had come over her? What had she done?

Those same two questions circled around Louisa's mind all the way back to Lowhaven. She barely absorbed a word of anything Charlotte said to her, peppering their very one-sided conversation with 'yes' and 'indeed' in the right places as her friend gushed excitedly about her encounter with Mr Liddell.

She could think of nothing else but Sir Isaac's words to her. The way he'd complimented her dancing, the way he'd made sure she knew the significance of it for him—his first dance in a long time. The way he'd asked to see her again, to meet with her...alone. That *was* what he'd meant, wasn't it? She hadn't imagined that, had she? She hadn't misinterpreted his meaning? No, she wasn't so naïve as to have misunderstood him. But she had been foolish enough to answer in the affirmative.

She had said she would meet him, even though she knew she should not.

She'd been reckless—again.

In truth, she'd felt so flustered throughout their conversation she'd hardly known what to say to him. One look into those bright blue eyes had been enough to render her mind utterly incapable of conjuring any suitable conversation. Thank goodness he had taken the lead, in the end. Their encounter, though polite, had been thick with undertones—layer upon layer of words and thoughts unexpressed. She'd felt it, and she sensed he had, too. She hadn't felt this way in the company of a man since…

No. She would not think of him now. It would not do any good.

'Are you all right, Louisa?' Charlotte asked her, apparently finally running out of things to say about the charming Mr Liddell.

'Yes, I am well…just a little tired,' she replied, offering her friend a small smile of reassurance and hoping it would be sufficient.

'You haven't said much about your promenade with Sir Isaac,' Charlotte remarked. 'I observed you dancing with him at the ball, you know. And Mama told me that you were already acquainted with both Sir Isaac and Mr Liddell.'

'Yes, I met them both on my journey to Lowhaven, and, yes, I did dance with Sir Isaac,' she said. 'Both seem to be very agreeable gentlemen,' she added.

'Agreeable—and handsome,' Charlotte said with a giggle.

'Charlotte!'

'Oh, Louisa, surely even a committed spinster like you can see all that both gentlemen have to recommend them. Good looks and a good deal of wealth, I should say. Especially Sir Isaac, given his rank.'

Louisa flinched, not enjoying the brazen tone Charlotte had adopted. 'These are not the only qualities a woman ought to consider in making a marriage, Charlotte,' she tried to advise her.

'Tell that to my mother,' Charlotte retorted. 'For her, they are the only qualities worth noting. Anyway, you have not yet told me—what did you and Sir Isaac discuss?'

'Nothing of any import,' Louisa replied with a small shrug. 'He asked if I had enjoyed seeing Hayton, and we spoke a little about the ball.'

Charlotte's eyes widened. 'About dancing together?'

'Not really,' Louisa lied, wanting to put an end to this conversation.

'Oh. Well, still… It is fortunate that we saw them here today. Mama has been disappointed that I missed out on an introduction at the ball. Mr Liddell said it was quite by chance that they were riding through the village today, as they had been visiting Sir Isaac's tenants.'

'I see,' Louisa replied, realising with a pang of guilt that she had neglected to enquire as to the reason for their visit to the village. In fact, she hadn't asked Sir Isaac any questions at all.

She wondered then what he must think of her. Reserved—aloof, even? Or merely dull and uninterested? On the other hand, he'd made it plain he wanted to see

her again, so she couldn't have done so badly. She bit
her lip, resolving to be a better conversationalist next
time they met. After all, there would be a next time. In a
moment of madness she'd agreed to it. She could hardly
go back on her word.

Isaac couldn't recall when he'd last been this hungry. As he tucked in to his plate of bread and cold meat,
washing it down with a small glass of wine, he smiled,
reflecting upon how well he felt. It had been good to
spend the morning outside, to be with his brother and
to ride in the warm summer air. It had been good, too,
to see his tenants. It had been another step along the
road out of mourning, and another way in which he had
signalled to the world that he was ready to re-join society. And he was—truly, he was.

But none of that was the reason he felt so exhilarated.

He'd behaved boldly with Miss Conrad—had been
far bolder than he'd thought himself capable of being.
It was hard to comprehend what had come over him,
but ever since that day on the cliffs that woman had
been on his mind. Today's encounter had been a coincidence, but even as they'd walked together he'd felt
keenly that he did not want to leave the next time they
saw each other to chance. He wanted to talk to her, to
get to know her. He wanted to see her alone.

God, he had all but asked her to come alone.

And she'd all but said that she would.

'Well, that was quite an unexpected pleasure,' Samuel said between mouthfuls of food.

Isaac had been so absorbed in his thoughts that he'd
almost forgotten his younger brother was sitting opposite. 'What was?'

'Seeing Miss Conrad today. And meeting her friend, the lovely Miss Pearson. A charming girl…very lively.'

Isaac nodded. 'Indeed, she gave that impression. I'm not sure she ever stopped smiling.'

Samuel buttered another slice of bread. 'I found her very agreeable.'

'She seemed very…young,' Isaac remarked, searching for the right words to describe the lady who had clearly caught his brother's attention.

'Not so much younger than me, I don't think,' Samuel retorted. 'Twenty, perhaps? I doubt I have more than ten years on her. Remember, I am much younger than you,' he added, with a grin.

'Huh…' Isaac grunted, occupying himself with his food once more. 'We know nothing of the girl's family other than that they are new to Lowhaven. Miss Conrad told me so.'

'Ah, yes. And how *was* the stoic Miss Conrad?'

'Well, I believe. I wish you would not mock her simply because she seems to be immune to your charms,' Isaac bit back, his tone sounding harsher than he'd intended.

'I don't think you're immune to hers, though,' Samuel replied, giving him a pointed look.

'Nonsense.'

Samuel sighed. 'There is no shame in it, Isaac. Rosalind would want you to be happy.'

Isaac felt the heat of anger flash through him. 'Don't you dare to presume what Rosalind would or would not have wanted!' he snapped.

His ire was directed at Samuel, but Isaac knew that in truth the only person he was frustrated with was himself. He was no naïve youth, ignorant of his growing infatuation with Miss Conrad. But neither was he deaf to that inner voice which niggled at him, suggesting that his preoccupation with her amounted to a betrayal of his dead wife, that it was utterly contrary to his commitment to remaining alone.

A mere two years had passed since Rosalind's death; how could he possibly contemplate moving on? How could he even think of allowing himself to love again when he knew only too well the pain it had brought him? That was if he was even capable of love, he reminded himself. Surely his heart bore too many scars for that.

'All right, all right,' Samuel said, holding his hands up. 'All I'm trying to say is if you like Miss Conrad then you should pursue her. Just be cautious. The last thing you need is some disappointment with a woman to send you back into hiding with a bottle of brandy.'

'Then you have nothing to fear. Because I have no intentions towards Miss Conrad, or any other woman of my acquaintance.'

Damn, how that lie stung his lips. He gave his brother a hard stare, hoping he would not manage to see through the façade. In truth, he barely understood his own intentions. Barely knew what he wanted. All he did know was that he was tired of grief and tired of being alone. He wanted companionship and conversation and joy. He wanted to sit beside a beautiful woman and make her smile, even if it was only for the summer.

He could only hope he would find some of those things next time he rode out to the cliffs.

Chapter Ten

In the days after her visit to Hayton it did nothing but rain. Louisa was forced to remain indoors, sitting often with her aunt in the parlour while she read or passed the time with light conversation.

Louisa had sensed some tension between Clarissa and herself, ever since the night of the ball. She knew it was her doing, that the way she'd spoken to her aunt about Sir Isaac had made the older woman wary. She regretted that this was the case, but she did not know how to remedy it. To bring up the subject would be uncomfortable, and might lead her aunt to begin the discussion about the master of Hayton Hall anew—which was the last thing she wanted. But to avoid it, as she had done thus far, allowed it to fester between them, making the memory of her cross words no doubt a source of mortification for them both.

Oh, how she wished she hadn't spoken out of turn.

How she wished she'd said nothing about Sir Isaac at all. Especially not a lie—and it was a lie. She knew she'd have enjoyed a second dance with him very much indeed.

Nan was driving her to distraction, too, fussing around

her as she tried to read a book or write a long-overdue letter to her mother, to whom she hadn't written since she'd
sent word of her safe arrival several weeks ago. She knew
her maid had found the adjustment to a smaller household difficult, and that having to assist with kitchen or
cleaning tasks did not suit her as well as keeping solely to
the duties of a lady's maid. Nonetheless, she found Nan's
frequent intrusions irritating; she didn't need anything
brought to her and she didn't desire company. If anything,
she wanted to be left alone: to think, to reflect and—dare
she admit it?—to daydream a little. It had been a long
time since she'd allowed herself a luxury such as that.

On the first fine day in almost a week Louisa ventured outdoors as soon as the calling hours were over.
She'd done her best to make it appear like an impromptu
walk, deflecting her aunt's suggestion that she send a
note to Charlotte by insisting throughout the morning
that she planned to stay at home, only to then change
her mind at the last possible moment. Such deceit had
left her feeling flustered, but she knew she couldn't
take Charlotte with her, or indeed anyone else. Nan
had made some vague overtures about accompanying
her, but had been easily put off when Louisa had let it
be known that she planned to walk up to the cliffs and
take the sea air.

'I'll come if you wish, miss,' she'd said, gesturing at
the sewing in her lap, 'but then this mending will need
to wait until later.'

'Oh, no, Nan,' Louisa had replied hastily. 'I don't
want to keep you from your work. Besides, I will only
be gone a short while.'

A short while—indeed, it would have to be.

As Lowhaven's busy streets increasingly gave way

to countryside, Louisa reflected upon the risk she was taking. Meeting a man, unchaperoned, was not something any young woman should do. She tried not to think about what Aunt Clarissa would say if she knew, how she would lecture her and insist she ought to know better.

She tried not to think about the rumour and gossip she would be subjected to if she was seen. Instead, she tried to calm her nerves, to retain some perspective. After all, she had already met Sir Isaac on the cliffs once, and she had been alone then, too. To a casual observer this might simply appear to be a chance encounter between two acquaintances. Besides, she reminded herself, he might not even come. He might be busy, or he might have reflected upon his own recklessness in suggesting it and thought better of it.

Louisa began the slow ascent along the rough track leading to the cliffs, her boots sliding on the muddy ground which had been saturated by days of rainfall. It wasn't too late for her to turn back, she considered. To return to her aunt's house and forget all about Sir Isaac Liddell and his unusual suggestion. Perhaps that would be wise. And yet, despite her reservations, she kept going, spurred on by an instinct, a sort of curiosity she could not quite name. God knew, wisdom had never been her strong suit…

Isaac arrived on the clifftops a little before four o'clock. For the first time in a while he was alone, which in itself was a luxury he permitted himself to enjoy after all the socialising he'd done recently.

He'd had to put on a convincing show for Samuel in order to escape without arousing his brother's suspicions. Freshly shaven and smartly dressed, he'd joined Samuel for a late luncheon. Halfway through his third piece of cold meat and his second cup of tea, he'd casually announced that he planned to take some air later, now that the weather had improved.

'Then I will gladly accompany you, brother,' Samuel had predictably replied.

Isaac had put on his best and most cheerful smile. 'In fact, if you don't mind, I would prefer to ride alone today. It is nothing untoward, I promise you. I merely feel the need for a little quiet contemplation. I've spent a lot of time in company of late.'

Samuel had seemed unconvinced, but not prepared to challenge his brother further on the matter.

As ever, the early afternoon had brought no callers to the door of Hayton Hall, and after several hours at his desk, attending to estate matters, Isaac had ridden out to that spot on the cliffs where he and Miss Conrad had first met. Now, as he sat on a rock and stared out at the vast blue sea, he contemplated what a fool he was. He had no idea if she would come today or not. She'd said she intended to walk here on the next fine day, but that had doubtless been a flustered response to his impertinence. It was entirely possible that she'd returned to her aunt after meeting him that morning in Hayton and thought better of it. Indeed, he would hardly blame her if she had.

'You should never have asked her, Liddell,' he muttered, giving the ground a swift kick with his left boot.

'Do you often talk to yourself?'

Isaac sprang to his feet, turning around as she approached him. The sight of her took his breath away, from the perfect blonde curls tamed into place by her bonnet to the casual spatter of mud along the bottom of her violet day dress.

He removed his hat, running a swift hand over his black hair. Thank God there was no strong wind to tousle it today. He wished to give her no occasion to remember the wild, dishevelled creature he'd been at their last clifftop meeting.

'Miss Conrad,' he mumbled, greeting her with an awkward bow.

She returned the gesture with a polite nod, before raising her eyebrows expectantly at him. 'Well?' she asked.

He frowned briefly, before her meaning dawned upon him. 'Oh!' he replied, laughing. 'Yes, I'm afraid I am guilty of giving myself a quiet lecture or two when the occasion demands it.'

'And does sitting by oneself on the cliffs require such a thing?' Her question seemed serious, but her eyes, he could see, were smiling.

He felt a flush of colour rise in his cheeks. 'Only if you're the sort of man who recklessly suggests that a woman meet him upon those cliffs alone,' he confessed. 'Forgive me, Miss Conrad. I am very glad you came, but truly I do not know what came over me when we met in Hayton. I know just as well as you do that we should not meet alone.'

She gave another small nod, her expression unreadable. 'I won't tell if you won't,' she replied.

He gave her a small smile. 'There is no one for me to tell—except my brother, perhaps. But I've always found confiding in Samuel to be unwise.'

'Oh?'

Isaac let out a wry chuckle. 'Samuel is younger than me by almost ten years. I find telling him anything usu-

ally leads to either teasing or a lecture—although recently it's been more of the latter than anything else.
He has become very insistent that I should make more
of an effort to go into society. I have not found it easy
to be in company since my wife's death.'

Isaac paused, realising he was saying far too much
already.

'Forgive me, Miss Conrad,' he continued after a moment. 'I do not know why I am telling you all this. Would
you like to walk? Or perhaps to sit awhile on the rocks?'

'We could walk a little,' she replied. 'Although I
promised my aunt that I would not be out for too long.'
She glanced at his horse, standing obediently at his side.
'Will he be all right to walk with us?'

Isaac had almost forgotten the poor creature was
there. 'What? Oh, him! Yes, it was not a long ride from
Hayton. He will not be tired yet.'

He gathered the reins tightly in his hand, and with
all the courage he could muster he offered Miss Conrad his free arm. His breath caught in his throat as he
watched her hesitate, her dark eyes seeming to search
his for something—he didn't know what. Then, before
he could retract the gesture and apologise once more,
she reached out and took it. Her nearness warmed him
like the sun could never hope to, and it alarmed him to
acknowledge how quickly his thoughts turned to letting
the damned horse go and enveloping her in his embrace.

Louisa's heart hammered in her chest as they took a
gentle stroll along the coast. She'd barely known what to
do or to say since she'd arrived here. The way he looked
at her, the way he spoke to her with such openness and
familiarity—she could not fathom it.

Why her? What had she ever done apart from be defensive or reserved or muted in his presence? Now, as she walked with her hand clutching his arm, she tried to focus on her surroundings—the squawking of the gulls, the sound of the waves crashing against the rocks far below. Anything but the heat of his arm against hers... anything but the proximity of him.

Those thoughts, she knew, led to other thoughts—brazen, forbidden thoughts. Not the thoughts of a spinster. No, she told herself, this would not do. She was allowing this tide to carry her along, but she had been here before, and she knew what it would cost her. She had to remember the vow she had made to herself. She had to remember what was at stake if she didn't.

'Why—why did you ask me to meet you, Sir Isaac?' she asked, rushing out the words before she could change her mind.

He turned to look at her, studying her face, and she realised he was trying to understand what had prompted her question. She pressed her lips together, trying to swallow down her turmoil. Then he looked away again, staring far into the horizon as he spoke.

'I am drawn to you, Miss Conrad, in a way that I have not been drawn to another human being for a long time. I mentioned my wife before... You must know I lost her, and my son—it is an oft-repeated tale around these parts.'

'Yes,' she interjected. 'My aunt told me not long after that last time we met here on the cliffs. I was sorry to hear of it. Losing those you love brings much suffering.' She felt the truth in those words with a tightening in her chest.

He drew a deep breath. 'Since their deaths I have

struggled. I have kept away from society, tried to protect myself by remaining alone. But that is a fool's errand which brings only misery. Then I met you, and I feel as though I'd like to get to know you.'

He turned his gaze to meet hers once again, and there was no mistaking the warmth in his eyes.

'I know you are not in Lowhaven for long, and I do not ask nor expect you to have the same interest in me. But, nonetheless, if you would consent to spending some time in my company, I believe I would enjoy that.'

'You seek my friendship?' Louisa asked him, desiring clarity.

He nodded. 'If you will give it.'

She smiled then. 'Readily I will give it, sir. You do yourself a disservice if you think I have no interest in you.'

'Even after the last time we met up here?'

She laughed. 'Well, perhaps not after that…but I will admit you redeemed yourself a little when we danced together at the ball.'

'Only a little?' he teased.

'All right, perhaps slightly more than a little,' she replied, still smiling.

He looked at her again, that azure gaze of his growing more serious now. 'You must call me Isaac. If we are to be friends, it is only right.'

She hesitated for a moment, remembering how easily she'd slipped into more familiar terms with Charlotte after only a brief acquaintance. But this felt different— more significant somehow. She wasn't sure she could countenance it—not yet.

'I shall call you Sir Isaac, for that is the name you properly deserve. But I will not object if you'd prefer to call me Louisa, and perhaps, in time, Isaac will do just as well on its own.'

'I will hope for it, Louisa,' he replied, and it didn't escape her notice how broad his smile had grown. 'Even the mere promise of it will do very well for me.'

Louisa drew a deep breath, averting her eyes to concentrate once more upon the seascape. She'd agreed to be his friend, and indeed she sensed that a good friend was something he needed as much as she did. Nevertheless, she knew she had to draw firm lines in their acquaintance—and if that meant maintaining some formality in addressing him, then so be it.

A friendship was all well and good, but any deepening of affection between them could not be permitted. It was clear that Sir Isaac had suffered a great deal, and although he did not know it, so had she. Nothing good could come of becoming too attached, for either of them. Anything beyond friendship was, quite simply, out of the question.

Chapter Eleven

On the day of their next clifftop meeting Isaac found himself gripped by a potent mix of good humour and crippling self-reproach—and he was not sure which feeling disconcerted him the most. He was not renowned for having a cheerful disposition—even before Rosalind's death a solemn countenance had always come easier to him than a smile—and although he'd been a contented spouse, he'd been ill at ease showing it.

He'd often considered it was the force of habit…that his position in life—eldest son, then landowner and baronet—and all the years of bearing so much responsibility had etched a profound seriousness upon his soul. The loss of Rosalind and his child had also meant the loss of his reasons to smile, and so he hadn't.

Not until this summer.

Not until he'd met Louisa.

Acknowledging how much he enjoyed the lady's company, however, came with a considerable amount of guilt. That inner voice which berated him for betraying Rosalind's memory seemed to grow louder, as though it sensed he was contemplating his own readiness to move on. And he was, wasn't he? He'd emerged from the worst of his grief some time ago, and slowly he'd begun to accept just how much he hated being alone.

That acceptance had now bred other feelings—feelings which he had never expected to experience again. The enjoyment of a lovely woman's company. The pleasure of her hand holding his arm. Bit by bit his resolve had weakened, his desire for companionship increasingly defeating his commitment to solitude.

But it was only companionship, he reminded himself. It was only friendship. Surely fostering a friendly acquaintance with a lady during the course of a summer was not such a terrible transgression? In any case, he doubted that Louisa would have any interest in anything more than friendship with an older, morose man such as him. She was young and beautiful, charming and refined. She was hardly likely to consider disagreeable and damaged Sir Isaac Liddell a catch.

Such murky thoughts continued to preoccupy him at breakfast, combining with his growing anticipation of his later clifftop meeting to make him feel quite sick. As he forced down several slices of toast in the company of his brother he made a concerted effort to appear nonchalant about his plans for the day ahead. Fortunately, Samuel made life easy for him in this regard, informing him that he would be detained all day in Lowhaven on matters of business, and that he would not return before dinnertime.

'I am sorry, brother,' Samuel said regretfully. 'It cannot be helped. I hope you will go out riding without me. I can see all the fresh air you've enjoyed recently has done you the world of good.'

Isaac nodded. 'Indeed, I do not mind some time by myself. In fact, I think I might take a long walk today.'

Samuel looked up from his newspaper. 'Oh?' he said. 'Anywhere in particular?'

Isaac shrugged. 'No,' he replied, pushing his empty plate away. 'I am happy to see where the wind carries me.'

Of course the strong sea breeze took him to the coast, and the afternoon sun was shining down from its high position in the sky by the time he reached their meeting place. To his surprise, Louisa was already there, and inwardly he chastised himself for not leaving earlier. Clearly walking to the cliffs had taken him much longer than he'd anticipated.

As he approached, he offered her a warm smile, feeling his mood lift once more as she smiled back at him. He could not help but notice how lovely she looked in a cream and cornflower-blue dress, its vertical stripes seeming to lengthen her petite frame and make her appear taller as she stood to greet him. He'd seen her wear blue more than once now, and thought the colour suited her very well—a thought he would keep to himself, he decided. He'd asked for a friendship, not a courtship, after all.

'I am sorry to have kept you waiting, Louisa,' he said as he reached her, tipping his hat in greeting.

'I have not been here long,' she answered him, glancing back towards the sea. 'Indeed, I have enjoyed watching the waves. It is nice to have a little peace and quiet now and then.' She turned back to him, frowning as she peered over his shoulder. 'You have not brought your horse today?'

'No, I felt like walking to meet you. Besides, he is a

grumpy creature—like his master. It is better not having him here, forced to follow us around.'

Louisa laughed at that. 'I do not think you are so very grumpy,' she countered.

He grinned appreciatively at this compliment of sorts, then offered her his arm, which she accepted without hesitation. Together they began to walk, sauntering slowly along the clifftops, neither of them apparently in any hurry to go anywhere in particular.

He stole a glance at her, spying her contented expression beneath her bonnet. She seemed more relaxed today…more at ease in his company. He wished then that he could be so calm. In truth, the closeness of her, the feeling of her hand resting in the crook of his arm—all of it had ruffled him again, made him think about things which mere friends were not meant to consider.

'So…peace and quiet,' he said, determined on some meaningful conversation. 'You do not have much of that in Lowhaven, I expect?'

She shook her head. 'Such is life in a busy port town, I believe. It is all very new to me. I am far more accustomed to living in the country.'

'And what is the country like in Berkshire?'

'Tranquil.' She smiled fondly. 'And very green. Although there I am without the pleasure of seeing the sea every day.' She gestured towards the vast expanse of water stretching to the horizon. 'I will miss this when I leave Cumberland. The coastal air here has agreed with me very well.'

He nodded, accepting the compliment on behalf of his county. 'Do you enjoy walking at home, too? Or riding, perhaps?'

'Oh, yes—both. Although walking is by far my favourite outdoor pursuit. Indeed, it's a habit I have continued here, much to my aunt's displeasure. She does not think it is right for a young woman to be out so much on her own.'

'Ah, well, of course your aunt's concern is entirely justified,' he replied, giving her a mischievous grin. 'The unchaperoned lady is vulnerable to approaches from all sorts of ruffians and scoundrels.'

She laughed as she looked up at him, giving his arm a squeeze. 'Indeed,' she said. 'As I know only too well.' Her smile faded, and those brown eyes seemed to darken as her face grew serious once more. 'Aunt Clarissa means well, but I do wish she would not make such a fuss. I have been of age for some years now, and I am very accustomed to taking care of myself.'

'You are?' Her declaration surprised him. 'Forgive me, Louisa,' he said, frowning, 'but I assumed you lived with your parents.'

She nodded. 'Yes, I do. Our home is a lovely country estate, and when my parents and brother are in town—which they frequently are—I do very well staying there by myself.'

'You do not go into town with them?'

He watched as she seemed to hesitate, as though his simple question was giving her pause for thought. 'No,' she said after a moment. 'Not usually.'

How odd, he thought. In his experience, unmarried young women were seldom permitted any respite from the watchful gaze of a parent or guardian. Seldom permitted even the semblance of a reprieve from society or from the task of securing a husband.

'And your mother? She is quite content with this arrangement?'

The question slipped out before he could properly consider it, and the moment he uttered the words, he could see that he had overstepped the mark. Immediately Louisa looked away from him, staring straight ahead, her pretty features hardening against what she doubtless perceived to be criticism.

Inwardly, he chastised himself. After avoiding society for so long, what right did he have to question her apparent preference for doing the same?

'Forgive me,' he began. 'I...' His voice faltered, and he found himself at a loss as to how to explain himself.

She glanced at him then. 'There is no need to apologise, Sir Isaac,' she said stiffly. 'My mother is as content as I am. While in residence alone I am properly cared for by my maid, and I send regular reports to my parents, who are always anxious to be reassured of my good health. So, you see, there is nothing for you to concern yourself with on my account.'

Her rebuke, though politely delivered, stung him. What a prying, interfering man he must have seemed to her. How insulting he must have appeared towards her family. He'd been so gripped by his curiosity, by his desire to get to know her, that he'd managed to offend her all over again.

His earlier buoyant mood all but evaporated, and in its place the mist of malaise began to settle once more.

'I see,' he replied, his expression grim. 'I am glad the arrangement suits you. I can only hope that your time in Cumberland will bring you similar joy.'

Louisa could see that she had upset him, but in truth she was at a loss as to how to repair the damage. The fault was undoubtedly hers—there had been no need to mention her self-sufficiency, or her unconventional familial arrangements, and yet for some reason she had. She'd been momentarily unguarded and had said too much about herself. She'd given Sir Isaac cause to wonder about her unusual manner of living. Indeed, was there a gentleman alive who would not have wondered at it?

Her father had only reluctantly accepted her wishes, and that was because he understood the reasons for the choice she'd made. To an outsider it must seem baffling, but she could hardly explain herself. She could hardly admit to her past, which had given her little option but to embrace a solitary existence.

She needed to make amends to her new friend—she knew that. However, she also needed to put a stop to any further discussion about her life in Berkshire. On that subject, she needed to be the closed book she'd promised herself she would be. Her past was hundreds of miles away, and for this summer, at least, that was where she was determined it would remain.

'Tell me about some of your favourite places here,' she said, resolving to change the subject. 'Where do you like to ride, or to walk?'

She was relieved to see his face light up at her question. 'Anywhere quiet. I avoid the town whenever possible—not that there is anything wrong with Lowhaven, of course, but such a busy place inevitably presents the possibility of being seen by an acquaintance and forced by duty to converse.' He paused, glancing at her. 'You must think me very dull, Louisa. Or very disagreeable. Or both.'

She shook her head. 'Not at all. I think you are none of those things. The point in being out riding or walking by oneself is to be alone, not to seek out company. I would avoid the town too, in your position.' She offered him an encouraging smile. 'Please, tell me about a place you like to go.'

'There is a village a little way down the coast called St Bees. Before you reach the village there is a headland which reaches out west. It is a stunning spot, and home to all kinds of sea birds. There is a legend that an Irish princess called St Bega was shipwrecked there in the ninth century, after fleeing from being forced to marry a Viking prince. She became an anchoress, devoting herself to a life of piety and solitude. The village is named after her, and the priory there is dedicated to her.'

'How fascinating,' Louisa replied. 'Does the legend say what became of her?'

'She lived in St Bees for some time, but fearing the pirates who were raiding along the coast she eventually went east, perhaps into Northumberland.' He grinned at her. 'She appears to have caught your imagination, just as she catches mine.'

Louisa felt her cheeks begin to colour, although she wasn't sure why. 'It's quite a story,' she replied, turning to look ahead and steadfastly avoiding his gaze. 'I wonder if it is true.'

'I often ponder the same question,' he replied, not seeming to notice her unfathomable discomfort. 'I must confess, over the past couple of years I have often found myself sitting on that headland, staring out across the sea towards Ireland and reflecting on her perilous escape and her decision, once safe, to remain alone. I've had solitude forced upon me by the unhappiest of circumstances, but she chose it.'

'As you said, it was a matter of religious devotion,'

Louisa countered. 'There are many good reasons why people choose to remain alone.'

She bit her lip, realising that once again she'd said more than she ought to. She felt the weight of his gaze on her as he considered her assertion, but still she avoided looking at him. Indeed, she did not dare, lest he read something in her expression which she did not want him to see.

'I wonder if you speak from experience,' he ventured, apparently not quite daring to ask the question.

Perhaps it was the fine day, or the sea air, or the note of earnest concern in Sir Isaac's voice, but something in that moment caused Louisa's resolve to soften. She looked up at him, her heart lurching at the sincerity of his intense blue gaze, just as it had when she'd first learned of all that he'd lost. When she'd first understood just how much they had in common.

'I lost someone once,' she began, the words falling from her lips before she could truly contemplate them. 'Someone I loved very much. He died in the war.'

She paused, trying to ignore her racing heart, trying to remind herself that she'd said nothing more to Sir Isaac than she'd confided in Charlotte. Yet as she stared up at him, watching the frown gather between his eyes as their shared understanding dawned upon him, she knew that this would be nothing like talking to Charlotte. Nothing at all.

Chapter Twelve

'His name was Richard. He was a captain in the navy.'

Instinctively Louisa drew closer to Isaac, glad of the comforting feeling of his arm holding hers. It had been a long time since she'd talked properly about Richard, and longer still since she'd said his name. She'd begun this story now, for reasons which seemed quite beyond her understanding, and she was committed to telling it. Or at least part of it.

The parts she would tell were painful enough. The parts she would omit were wholly unutterable.

'We met at a ball, at the home of some friends of my family, who live near Reading. Richard was a relation of theirs, and had come to stay with them in the country while recovering from an injury he'd sustained when his ship was badly damaged in a storm. I was young…only nineteen; Richard was a little older at six-and-twenty. Suffice to say we danced and we talked, and were quite taken with one another. Over the following few months I saw a lot of him; our affection grew, and before long we were engaged to marry. By this time Richard's injury had healed and he'd received word that he was to return to sea. He'd applied for a new ship, his old one having been declared unfit for service, and had been appointed to another command. I'm not sure why, but it all seemed to happen very quickly, and we agreed we would marry once he returned.'

Louisa paused, swallowing hard. Even after all this time, telling this story seemed to affect her physically. Her mouth was dry…a dull ache was spreading through her chest.

'However, it was not to be. A couple of months after he took command, Richard's ship was sunk in the English Channel by the French. None of the crew survived.'

Beside her, she heard Isaac draw a deep breath, and she found herself looking out towards the sea, a strange sort of weariness settling over her like mist. She'd parted with as much of the story as she was willing to, and even that had been a trial. She prayed he would accept the sorry tale, just as Charlotte had done. She prayed he would not ask too many questions of her.

'I am very sorry for your loss, Louisa,' he said, his voice grave and sincere. 'And I thank you for telling me. I am sorry if my remarks about your living arrangements in Berkshire caused you any distress. I understand perfectly now why you remain alone.'

She offered him a tight smile. 'It's not a story I tell very often,' she replied. 'At home, it's a story everyone knows, and here… Well, it's been nice that almost no one knows.'

'I can understand that,' Isaac replied. 'After Rosalind and our son died I wearied quickly of all the condolences, all the pity. I just wanted to escape. I couldn't do that, so I retreated instead.'

'It is surprisingly easy to hide on a country estate,' Louisa mused, half to herself.

She felt the pain of guilt grip her as she thought about all the reasons she'd been hiding. About all the things a man like Sir Isaac could never know.

'It seems we have more in common than I'd realised,' he observed. 'I am sorry that you have had your life marred by sadness at such a young age, and before you were even wed. I have always been grateful that at least Rosalind and I did have some years together.'

She nodded. 'Our time together was so very short. Sometimes it feels as though I dreamt him—as though he was never in my life at all.'

'I often think that about my son, since he was here so briefly,' Isaac replied, his voice almost a whisper. He shuddered, as though brushing off unwelcome thoughts. 'It's been two years since they died, you know, and sometimes I wonder if I will ever fully recover from my grief.'

'I don't believe you ever do,' she replied. 'I think you simply learn to live with it…that it becomes a part of who you are.'

'Indeed. As long as you do not let it consume your whole self,' he said pointedly. 'Grief cannot be allowed to govern your life, to dictate to you over every decision you make.'

Louisa bristled, feeling his insinuation sharply. In the wake of losing Richard her grief had been utterly consuming, but even then it had not exercised full control over her choices. She pressed her lips together, thankful that Sir Isaac did not know anything of the other circumstances she'd grappled with during those long, dark months.

Sir Isaac seemed to notice her discomfort, because

after a moment he smiled wryly at her and added, 'I realise that I have no business saying that. I've spent much of the last two years allowing my grief to do exactly that. But it a lesson which I think I am beginning to learn.'

Louisa found she could only answer him with a tight smile. The growing wind whipped at her face and she drew closer to him once more, as though the mere feel of him could ground her, could stop her from thinking too much. Her summer in Lowhaven was meant to be a reprieve, and this walk with Sir Isaac was meant to be an enjoyable interlude with a new friend. Thoughts of the past, of her reasons for being here and her choices, had no place here.

Clutching his arm ever tighter, she drew a deep breath, burying those thoughts in the back of her mind as she so often did.

For a brief moment she felt the muscles beneath her fingers tense, before he brought his other hand to rest over hers. It was a tender, reassuring gesture, and one which, despite her instincts, she allowed herself to appreciate. He had responded to her sorry tale with kindness and sincerity, and had related to her grief with something far deeper than mere sympathy. It was hard to believe that this gentleman, who spoke to her so gently and honestly, was the same sullen and disagreeable man she'd first met.

Sir Isaac was right; they did have much in common. She'd recognised that herself, when she'd first learned of all that he'd lost. But she also knew that their shared knowledge of grief, of pain and of self-imposed solitude was only the half of it. The other half—the unspeakable half—was something Sir Isaac could never know. The other half of her story, she reminded herself, was something which no gentleman in his position could countenance.

Isaac replayed her sorrowful story over and over, picking through its details and feeling his heart lurch at the knowledge of her pain. He understood it now. The serious countenance, the aloofness, the reserve. The stoicism, as Samuel had correctly called it.

At the time, Isaac had objected to his brother's remarks about Louisa's character, and yet he'd been right, hadn't he? She was all of those things, and for good reason. For the same reason, it transpired, he had for being solemn and reclusive. Indeed, they had both locked themselves away, both sought refuge from the prying eyes of the world in secluded country houses. They'd both nursed their grief alone.

He could never have imagined on that first day they'd met, when she'd stumbled into his carriage, that they'd have quite so much in common.

Isaac made himself comfortable in his library, sending for some tea to quench his growing thirst after walking home from the cliffs. As he sat back in his favourite armchair, he found himself wondering how Louisa felt about being alone now...if she was as weary of it as he was. He wondered what had brought her to Lowhaven—if it was more than a simple desire to visit her aunt. After all, since she'd been in town she'd evidently not hidden herself away, attending balls and befriending the likes of the Pearsons. Befriending him.

She hadn't hesitated to accept his offer of friendship, had she?

You do yourself a disservice, she'd said, *if you think I have no interest in you.*

How those words had warmed him since.

'Friendship is one thing, Liddell,' he muttered to himself. 'But anything else is out of the question.'

And it was—it had to be. During these past months he'd come far—much further than he could have imagined possible during those early dark days he'd spent shrouded in his grief. He was loath to admit it, but Samuel's insistence that he re-enter society had been good for him.

If he hadn't been in that carriage returning from Penrith that day he would not have met Louisa. If he hadn't attended the ball in Lowhaven he would not have danced with her. If he hadn't been visiting his tenants he would never have had the chance to boldly suggest that they begin to meet. He would not have begun a friendship with her. But no matter how lovely she was, or how much they had in common, he knew it could never be more than that. He'd learned to live with the past now—it no longer dictated to him. But it was still there, nonetheless.

It still weighed heavily upon his heart.

It still surrounded him in every room, every inch of Hayton Hall.

Louisa had said that Richard's presence in her life had been so fleeting that it felt like a dream. For Isaac, it was the opposite. Rosalind was still everywhere in his home—from the rooms she'd tastefully had modernised, with fresh paint and plasterwork, to the clothes and other personal effects which remained tucked within the ancient cupboards and drawers passed down to him by his ancestors.

He'd clung on to her possessions, unable to look at them, but equally unable to let them go.

Well, he reasoned, perhaps it was time to do either one or the other.

Isaac hauled himself out of his seat and walked over to the large walnut chest sitting solidly in the shadows. He pulled open the middle drawer, noticing immediately the musty smell which rose up, as though stale, years-old air had finally managed to escape the confines of that dark, disused space. It caught him off guard, and he felt the past begin to claw at him.

He paused then, before placing a tender hand upon the pretty blue shawl and lifting it carefully. As though it might break. As though the memories it contained might disintegrate as soon as the cloth met the cool library air. He unfolded it, grateful that after all this time it no longer smelled of her. The whiff of neglect which tainted it now was bad enough, but for it to have held on to even the merest hint of her perfume would have been unbearable.

The last time she'd worn this she'd been heavy with child, sitting in the library and poring over one of her favourite novels by Mrs Radcliffe. *The Italian*, probably, but now he thought about it he realised he couldn't recall.

He clutched the shawl against his chest, feeling the fragility of the soft silk beneath his fingers. He was still fragile, too, he realised. His heart, though mended, was scarred for ever. There was no point allowing his thoughts to linger upon just how much he and Louisa seemed to understand each other, or the way his heart skipped a beat as she took his arm, or the way he would lose himself in her deep brown gaze. He'd found solace in her friendship, but he should not imagine that there could ever be anything more between them than that.

He remained rooted to the spot as the door creaked open and a maid delivered his tea, still holding on to that shawl and, with it, all the reasons he knew he could never allow himself to love again even if he wanted to.

The problem was, he reflected as he poured himself some tea, increasingly he suspected that to love and to be loved was exactly what he wanted.

Chapter Thirteen

Louisa sat beside her aunt in the Pearsons' splendid parlour, trying her best to sit still and look interested in the conversation. Outside the sun shone brightly, and from within this dark room, dominated by a deep blue Chinese wallpaper and an over-indulgence in mahogany furnishings, Louisa felt its pull, as though the fine day itself demanded she get up and leave this place at once.

But of course she could not. She had been informed that morning by her aunt that they would be visiting the Pearsons' home for tea, and it had been made very clear to her that she was expected to attend.

'It will be nice for you to see their home. It's a rather fine house on the edge of town. It is a bit of a walk, but I am sure we can manage it together. Unless you have another commitment?' Aunt Clarissa had asked, her eyebrows raised in surprise at her niece's apparent reluctance.

'No, not at all, Aunt,' Louisa had replied, swiftly recovering herself. 'I had just hoped to walk more of the coast this afternoon.'

'I'm sure if the opportunity presents itself Miss Pearson will walk with you,' her aunt had responded. 'Walking with another young lady is preferable, Louisa. You walk too often by yourself. You must have gone out alone not less than four times this past week!'

Four times, indeed, and each time to meet Isaac at the cliffs. Neither of them had hesitated to take advantage of the dry, sunny days, to fill them with conversation and good company. For the past two days, however, she'd been prevented from seeing him. Yesterday, her aunt had asked her to accompany her into town to visit the linen drapers, and today it was what was turning into a lengthy social call.

She tried not to begrudge it, reminding herself that Aunt Clarissa generally made little imposition upon her time. Nonetheless, she found herself repeatedly gazing out of the window, her mind wandering to the cliffs, to the image of Sir Isaac sitting upon a rock, waiting for her. She hoped he would not wait too long. She wished she'd been able to send word, to let him know she would not come today.

She wished, above all, that she could have gone to see him.

He had been so humorous at their last meeting—so light of spirit. Sharing silly anecdotes with her about his childhood and his family. He'd told her some of his memories of her grandfather, the stern but kind village rector, who had enjoyed the respect and affection of his parishioners. His tales had breathed life into her family history, and for the first time since coming here she'd felt the strength of her connection to Hayton. It had dawned on her that this quiet little corner of Cumberland was a part of her story, too.

How they'd laughed at his recollections of his boyhood scrapes! How they had smiled. She had enjoyed seeing that more relaxed, more cheerful side of Isaac—enjoyed, too, the reprieve from the more difficult subjects they'd previously discussed. To her relief, Isaac had asked her nothing more about Richard, and nor had he spoken of Rosalind. It was as though he'd sensed a need to lift the mood between them. To relish the present, rather than dwell on the past.

Not that she regretted sharing something of her past with Isaac. Indeed, telling him about Richard had brought her a sort of solace she hadn't expected. She supposed that was because she'd shared part of her story with someone who understood loss, who'd known grief. She supposed it was because they were friends.

She did not allow herself to contemplate that Isaac was the only friend she had who could cause her stomach to perform somersaults at the merest touch or the briefest glance. There was, after all, no point in considering that.

'Are you quite well, Miss Conrad?' Mrs Pearson asked, interrupting her thoughts.

'Oh, yes, thank you,' she replied, offering her hostess a polite smile.

Mrs Pearson narrowed her eyes slightly, glancing at the window which had held Louisa's attention before returning her focus to her guest. 'Charlotte tells me she has not heard from you since your visit to Hayton. She wondered if you'd been ill.'

Louisa glanced at Charlotte, noting how she sipped her tea and steadfastly avoided her gaze. 'No, not ill,' she began. 'I…'

'You've been quite preoccupied with writing to your friends and family in Berkshire—haven't you, my dear?'

Aunt Clarissa interjected. 'And the weather has been so dreadful of late I don't think any of us will have ventured much outside of our homes.'

'Quite so,' Mrs Pearson agreed, still looking at Louisa. 'I have felt the damp air in every bone in my body. I believe I must ask my physician to strengthen my tincture. Still, the sun has shone a good deal during the past week. Hopefully it will last, and you two young ladies can take the benefit of it together.'

Charlotte gave an enthusiastic nod. 'We could walk to Hayton again, if you like,' she said, addressing Louisa. 'Last time we did not make it as far as Hayton Hall, and it would be a real pity if you did not see it. I suppose if we are fortunate we may even see Sir Isaac and Mr Liddell out riding again.'

Aunt Clarissa looked up, her teacup poised at her lips. 'Again?

'Oh, don't you know? Sir Isaac and Mr Liddell accompanied them back through the village,' Mrs Pearson explained. 'Charlotte tells me that she talked at length with Mr Liddell, but could not get a word in edgeways with Sir Isaac as Miss Conrad had him entirely under her spell.'

Aunt Clarissa looked squarely as Louisa, her eyebrows elevated in curiosity and surprise. 'Oh?'

'We really only saw them very briefly, as they were visiting Sir Isaac's tenants,' Louisa explained, as evenly as she could manage.

'We talked for as long as it takes to walk very slowly from one end of the village to the other,' Charlotte added with a giggle. 'I found Mr Liddell very agreeable. He was very charming and witty.'

'Younger sons often are,' Mrs Pearson replied, putting her teacup down. 'When the eldest son has the property and the title, wit and charm are the only currency their brothers have to trade.'

'We should go and see Hayton Hall tomorrow,' Charlotte suggested. 'Let's go while the weather remains fine. What do you say, Louisa?'

Louisa sipped her tea, buying herself a moment's thought. She felt the eyes of the room upon her, all three ladies waiting expectantly for her response. What could she say? She didn't have any plans for tomorrow. Only hopes. Only possibilities. She'd had to let those slip by her today, and she would have to do so again. To do anything other than that would appear odd, at best, and rude at worst. She could not risk causing offence.

'Of course,' she replied finally. 'That would be wonderful.'

She hadn't come. Again. As Isaac rode home, furiously whipping his horse, all the possible reasons for her absence whirred around his frenzied mind. Was she unwell? Had he offended her? Had some other commitments detained her for these past two days?

She had not mentioned anything at their last meeting. Indeed, she had smiled and nodded when he'd asked her if it was likely she'd be walking on the cliffs the next day. Nothing had seemed to be amiss when they'd parted. Their conversation had been agreeable. He'd regaled her with some family tales, which she'd seemed to appreciate, before indulging with her in a lengthy discussion about books they'd enjoyed.

She liked to read; he'd learned that. Travel diaries, especially. She yearned to visit the continent, she'd admitted rather bashfully, as though such a sense of adventure was to be berated rather than commended.

He'd held back from telling her that he'd never left England…that his younger brother was superior to him in first-hand knowledge of other countries and cultures. Instead, he'd told her about his love for *Waverley*, and the other novels by the same anonymous author, how he found himself swept to other times and places whenever he lost himself in their pages.

'I know that they are very famous,' she'd said. 'But I confess I have not read any of them.'

He'd thought about all the hours he'd spent in his library, devouring those stories, trying to distract himself from his grief.

'If you like, I can lend you my copy of *Waverley*,' he'd offered, to which she'd assented.

He still had to consider how he would get the book to her, as its three volumes were too large to fit in his pocket. Just as well, he thought. He'd have felt even more of a fool if he'd brought them with him.

Why hadn't she come?

Isaac whipped his poor horse again, riding hard as Hayton Hall came into view. All other possibilities exhausted, he allowed himself now to contemplate the worst. She was ill, or there had been some sort of accident. God, how he wanted to know! How he wanted to help if he could. But how could he? He could hardly turn up at her aunt's house unannounced.

Yet that was all he wanted to do, and it was all he could think of—going to her, summoning his physician to attend her. Anything. Anything that might help.

He shuddered, remembering how he'd sat beside a bed and watched the life of the woman he adored ebb away. He could still see the sickly pallor of her skin, still feel the cold clamminess of her face. Those memories, he knew, would haunt him for ever.

He could not bear to feel such helpless agony again.

He arrived back at his home, all but flinging the reins of his exhausted animal at his groom. He marched inside, the sound of his footsteps thudding on the wooden floor as he made his way down the corridor towards his library. Once inside, he shut the door firmly behind him, leaning his head against it for a moment, trying to gather his thoughts.

He breathed in deeply, perturbed to realise that today he found no comfort in the familiar smell of the old wooden shelves and leather-bound books. His library had for so long been his sanctuary, his place of retreat. Now he realised he no longer wished to be in hiding. He no longer wanted to be alone.

'What the devil is the matter with you, Liddell?' he muttered to himself.

His foolish desire for companionship had really started to get under his skin, conspiring with the worst of his fears and his memories to drive him quite mad. He was a widower almost in his middle years, not some hot-headed youth, and yet here he was, entertaining impulsive ideas about running to the bedside of a woman with whom he'd promenaded a handful of times.

He had to acknowledge that her friendship had come to mean a lot to him even in such a short space of time, that he enjoyed being with her and talking to her. That her company enlivened him in a way he'd believed he would never experience again. He felt as though she understood him. Yet friendship was all there was between them, he reminded himself. It was all there could ever be. Anything else would be a betrayal of Rosalind and a risk to his fragile heart.

He pulled himself up straight. Louisa was his friend, he told himself. Of course he had to know if she was all right. There was nothing more to it than that.

'Isaac?' Samuel's voice sounded muffled through the thick oak door. 'Is something amiss?'

Isaac sighed. The last thing he needed at this moment was an inquisition from his brother.

'I'm well, thank you,' he called back, stepping away from the door and walking over to his desk.

'May I come in?'

'Of course.'

Samuel entered, a deep frown etched on his face as he glanced around him, apparently—and not too subtly—surveying the room. Looking for clues, Isaac thought wryly.

'You came home in an awful hurry. I thought perhaps something might have happened,' his brother said tentatively.

Isaac picked up a handful of papers from his pile of correspondence. 'I was out riding and recalled I had a pressing matter to attend to,' he replied, waving the papers nonchalantly in his hand.

Samuel narrowed his eyes. 'A pressing matter?' he repeated.

'Yes,' Isaac laughed. 'You do not run the estate, Samuel. You do not see the volume of work I have to contend with, even with my steward's assistance.'

'And is that what you have been doing on so many afternoons recently? Attending to pressing estate business?' Samuel asked, clearly unconvinced.

'No, I have been riding, or walking—as you know.'

Isaac tried to maintain an even tone, but he could feel his patience beginning to wane. He did not have time for this.

'For hours on end?'

'I have been enjoying the scenery Cumberland has to offer, and it is a vast county. So, yes, for hours on end, brother.'

'I see,' Samuel answered, in a way which told Isaac that he didn't see at all. 'Well, if there is anything I can do to assist with this pressing matter, you know I am at your service.'

Isaac gave a tight smile, feigning interest in his paperwork once more. 'Thank you, brother. I will bear that in mind.'

Samuel gave a brief nod and took his leave. The moment the door shut behind him Isaac sat down at his desk and got to work. His explanation to Samuel had not entirely been a lie—he did have a pressing matter to attend to. And while his brother had been interrogating him he'd settled upon the only way he could conceive of to address it.

He wrote furiously, committing his words to paper before he could lose his nerve. Before he could think too much about what he said or how he said it. As soon as he had signed his name he folded the letter and enveloped it within another blank sheet, then rang for his butler.

Moments later, the man arrived.

'Yes, sir?'

'Smithson, I need this delivered to Miss Louisa Conrad in Lowhaven,' Isaac instructed, handing over the letter.

Smithson looked at the paper in his hand, upon which Isaac had hurriedly written Louisa's name and address. 'Right now, sir?'

'Yes. Please see to it that this reaches Miss Conrad

as soon as possible. I am anxious to know that the lady is in good health, Smithson,' Isaac added, 'so any information you manage to discover in this regard would be appreciated.'

The butler nodded. 'Very good, sir,' he replied, turning to leave.

'Oh, and Smithson?'

'Yes, sir?'

'Please ensure that this remains confidential. Particularly, that no word of this letter should reach my brother's ears.'

'Of course, sir.'

Isaac sat back in his chair as Smithson left the room, rubbing his face with his hands. The mix of weariness and agitation he felt following the day's exertions was potent, and he knew his judgement was not as sharp as it ought to have been. Writing to her and having her sought out in this manner was impulsive, and if discovered it would provoke comment and speculation.

But damn it all if he cared about that! All he cared about was knowing—knowing what had happened yesterday, knowing what had happened today, and knowing that she was all right. He would endure any amount of trouble for that.

Chapter Fourteen

Louisa knew her aunt had questions for her; she could almost see the words forming upon her lips the moment they left the Pearsons' home in the late afternoon. Their walk home was a quiet one, with little in the way of conversation to divert Louisa from observing the way Clarissa looked at her, with brief but unsubtle glances, as though she was trying to get the measure of her niece and decide upon the best line of enquiry.

Louisa did her best to ignore it, feigning interest in the town's busy streets as they passed along one and then the next. As they approached Juniper Street she noted, as she always did, how the sounds of the port grew louder. She could hear the clatter and shouts of the dockworkers as they loaded and unloaded cargo at its numerous quays.

She recalled how she'd remarked upon its ceaseless din to Isaac, who'd laughed wryly at the observation. It was one of the busiest ports in England, he had told her, with all manner of goods passing through it, from cocoa and sugar being brought in, to coal and lime being shipped out. She'd quite marvelled at the prospect of it, feeling suddenly worlds away from her home in quiet, rural Berkshire. It had been a liberating thought.

Now she found herself considering how frequently her thoughts turned to Isaac and how, in her mind, she called him only that: Isaac.

'Louisa, is there something between yourself and Sir Isaac Liddell?'

Aunt Clarissa put the question to her almost as soon as the door closed behind them. The young maid, Cass, who'd been busying herself with collecting their shawls, gave them both a quick curtsey, sensing the need to take her leave. The awkward moment offered Louisa a brief opportunity to steel herself. She had not expected her aunt to be quite so direct.

'I barely know the gentleman, Aunt,' she replied, as nonchalantly as she could manage.

Clarissa frowned. 'That is no answer, Louisa. Marriages have been made on the barest of acquaintances, and other associations between men and women on far less than that.'

'Aunt!' Louisa protested, feeling the heat rise in her cheeks.

'Do not give me your blushes, my dear. We are both women of the world. Your mother may have tiptoed around these matters with you, but I will not. What Mrs Pearson said today about you and Sir Isaac—she made it sound unseemly. I cannot bear for you to be subjected to such comments again. Not after all that you have endured.'

Louisa sighed, glancing down the corridor, mindful of who might be listening. 'Perhaps we should talk in the parlour, Aunt,' she suggested.

Clarissa nodded in agreement and they moved into

the little room, with Louisa closing the door behind
them. Together they sat down, and Louisa took a moment to collect herself. She did not wish to lie to her
aunt, but she couldn't bring herself to be entirely truthful, either. She did not wish to contemplate her aunt's
response if she knew about her secret clifftop meetings with Isaac. She did not want to consider the consequences of her reckless actions.

Above all, she did not want to consider whether there
was, in fact, something more than friendship forming
between herself and Sir Isaac Liddell. Something she
knew she could not countenance, no matter how their
heartfelt conversations and the tender feeling of her
hand holding his arm had made her feel.

'There is nothing unseemly or otherwise between
myself and Sir Isaac,' she said in the end. 'I will admit
that when I have seen him I have enjoyed his company
and conversation. He is very agreeable. But that is all.
Charlotte is merely being fanciful if she imagines anything else.'

Clarissa gave a tight smile. '"Fanciful" is certainly
a word I would apply to young Miss Pearson,' she replied. 'She ought to mind what she says. It's one thing
to speak like that to her mother, but what if she recounts
her stories in such a way to others?'

'We cannot control how others behave,' Louisa said
simply. 'We can only be responsible for our own actions.'

The truth in this last statement made her stomach
churn.

Clarissa exhaled deeply, reaching over and patting her
niece on the hand. 'I'm sorry, my dear. I feel as though I

have interrogated you. I was just so taken aback by Mrs Pearson's remarks.'

Louisa nodded. 'I will admit what she said managed to set me on edge. I fear I have not endeared myself to her of late. She made her displeasure with me plain enough when she alluded to me being remiss in keeping up my friendship with Charlotte.'

'Yes, I noted that. But you are going out with Miss Pearson tomorrow, which I am sure will placate them both.'

Relieved that their conversation had lightened, Louisa rose from the table. 'I think I will freshen up before dinner, Aunt, and perhaps read for a little while. I do find the bedroom you gave me so very peaceful.'

Clarissa gave her niece an appreciative smile. 'It is nice to hear you remark upon it,' she replied. 'Miss Slater used to say the same thing. Or rather, Mrs Knight, as she is now.'

Louisa nodded. 'Do you ever hear from Mrs Knight?' she asked gently.

'She writes to me occasionally, tells me of life in Carlisle. Her Mr Knight keeps her very busy.'

Clarissa was still smiling, but Louisa could not fail to notice the sadness that had crept into her eyes.

'Her marriage seemed to happen very quickly,' her aunt went on. 'But then at our age there is little time left to lose. I suppose she is a reminder that it is never too late.'

'Very true, Aunt.'

Clarissa got to her feet. 'It is true, Louisa, and certainly true in your case. I know you have determined upon spinsterhood, and I understand your reasons why. Nonetheless, I would caution you to think hard about your decision. Remaining alone is far from your only option. The way the likes of Sir Isaac Liddell regard you should be sufficient to remind you of that.'

'Aunt, you surely know that it is my only option,' Louisa replied. 'No gentleman could risk an association with me if he knew all about me. A gentleman like Sir Isaac would imperil his good name overnight. I could not countenance doing such harm to anyone.'

Clarissa sighed. 'As I've said to you before, my dear, you are too hard on yourself. You know that I have never condemned you for what happened, and neither have your parents. There will undoubtedly be gentlemen who would take the same view as I do. Perhaps Sir Isaac might be one of them,' she added meaningfully.

'Perhaps,' Louisa replied, unconvinced. 'Alas, it is a moot point, since there is nothing between Sir Isaac and me,' she reiterated quickly, trying to ignore how hard her heart was beating.

Clarissa gave her knowing look. 'Perhaps not on your part, but you cannot speak for him. He was obviously captivated by you at the ball, and I don't doubt that in essence what Charlotte told her mother about your encounter with him in Hayton was true. I can well imagine that he did not leave your side.'

'We enjoyed only a brief and very polite conversation,' Louisa countered, feeling her cheeks begin to burn as thoughts of their long walks and intense conversations returned to her once again.

'Oh, my dear! It is not so much what is said, but what is left unsaid, believe me.'

'You sound as though you speak from experience, Aunt.'

'I had a life before spinsterhood.' Clarissa's lined face

crumpled and she sat back down upon her chair. 'I was engaged once, you know. Goodness, we were young… and so much in love. His name was Frederick.'

Louisa took her seat again beside her aunt. 'What happened?'

'Frederick was a curate, but he had not yet managed to secure a living. Of course he needed an income, so that we could marry and begin our lives together. After our betrothal he joined the army as a chaplain and boarded a ship bound for the Caribbean. I heard nothing from him for several months. I remember being so worried… Then one day a letter came—not from him, but from his captain. In it, he told me that there had been some sort of epidemic and poor Frederick had perished, not many weeks after they had arrived.'

Louisa felt her eyes prick with tears and she tried furiously to blink them away. She felt every detail of her aunt's story keenly. Indeed, its resonance with her own could hardly be more acute.

'Oh, Aunt Clarissa…' was all she managed to say.

Clarissa gave her a watery smile. 'It was a long time ago. You see, my dear, we are really quite similar. Like you, I loved and lost, and I chose never to marry after that. It was a choice I was able to make as Frederick had left me a small inheritance in his will. Nothing extravagant, but it has helped to give me my independence.'

'And you have been happy all these years?' It was a searching question, but Louisa couldn't help but ask it.

'I have done well enough by myself,' her aunt replied. 'Although it is far from easy, being a woman in my position. You see for yourself how modestly I live, and keeping myself even in this manner has become more difficult since Mrs Knight's departure and the loss of her… Well, her contribution to the household. I find myself a little more reliant on the help of my family than I'm accustomed to—a fact which makes me uneasy.'

Louisa frowned. 'Your family? Do you mean my mother and father?'

Clarissa nodded, then quickly patted her niece reassuringly on the hand. 'But please do not consider that has anything to do with why you are here this summer. You know I would always gladly have you here with me, whatever the circumstances.'

Louisa gave her a meek smile. 'Do you ever wish you had married?' she asked quietly.

Clarissa sighed. 'In truth, I never met anyone after Frederick who could hold a candle to him, so the decision to remain unmarried was relatively easy in that regard. I can't say what I would have done had I found myself falling in love again,' she added, looking pointedly at her niece.

'I do not think I could bear to fall in love again. Not since losing…' Louisa bit her lip, unable to finish her sentence. Unable to say Richard's name. Unable, perhaps, to face contemplating just how close to falling in love again she might be.

'But one day you might, my dear, and if you do please heed my advice—follow your heart. Life is too short to hold yourself to solemn oaths made in the throes of grief.'

Louisa drew a swift breath, poised to argue. Ready to repeat that in her case it was about more than honouring her fiancé's memory. That it would be futile to fall in love again, for surely she could not marry. No gentleman would want her for a wife if he knew the truth.

Then she looked at her aunt's face, racked with the

pain of baring her soul, and she realised that she had not the heart to say any of it.

'Thank you, Aunt,' she answered instead, with a small and unconvincing smile.

All evening Aunt Clarissa's words preyed on Louisa's mind. After dinner she went straight up to her room, where she tried and failed to concentrate on the book perched on her lap. She'd known nothing of her aunt's story, nothing of the loss she'd experienced— a loss which bore such similarity to her own. In grief they were kindred spirits, a fact which made her aunt's words of caution about choosing to remain alone all the more discomfiting.

Louisa knew that for her marriage remained absolutely out of the question. Yet, despite this, the prospect of spinsterhood seemed more daunting than ever.

'A penny for them,' Nan said that night, apparently tiring of her mistress's prolonged silence as she unpinned her long blonde hair in readiness for bed.

'I learned something about my aunt today,' Louisa replied, giving in to the overwhelming need to confide in someone. Nan, she knew, could always be trusted with her secrets.

'Oh?'

'It turns out we have a lot in common. Like me, she lost the man she was meant to marry. He was an army chaplain, and he died in the Caribbean.'

'Your poor aunt,' Nan remarked. 'I wonder why your mother never told you.'

'I suspect she didn't regard it as her story to tell.'

Nan nodded at that. 'That's true, miss. She is very discreet. I suppose that explains why your aunt has never married…why she stayed up here with your grandparents rather than go off to London like your mother did.'

'Indeed.'

Louisa gazed absently into the mirror in front of her, considering her aunt's insistence that her choice had been straightforward because she had never met anyone else. It occurred to Louisa now that her aunt's decision to remain in rural Cumberland, to embrace quiet village life, had all but ensured that she could not fall in love again. This part of the world hardly teemed with eligible men the way London society did during the season.

Although, Louisa reminded herself, they weren't entirely absent.

She shook her head slightly, trying to brush off all thoughts of a certain gentleman standing before her on the clifftops, his thick black hair tousled by the wind and his deep blue eyes staring intently into hers. She spent too much time thinking about him, and it did her no good. She could not allow herself to form an attachment, to indulge in thoughts about anything more than a summer-long acquaintance. She could not allow her heart to rule over her head. She had done so once, long ago, and she knew what it had cost her. She would bear the scars of her choices for the rest of her days.

'Oh, miss, I almost forgot,' Nan said, reaching into the pocket of her apron. 'A note arrived for you today.'

Louisa turned round. 'A note?'

'Yes.' Nan passed a small folded paper to her. 'It was the strangest thing. The man who delivered it would not say on whose behalf he was calling. He would only say that I was to ensure this note reached you, and he enquired after your health.'

Louisa looked down, running her finger over the

letters of her name. She did not recognise the pristine
handwriting, but she knew instinctively who it must be
from. She felt her heart begin to beat a little faster, and
she hoped that in the candlelight Nan could not see the
colour creeping into her cheeks.

'And what did you say?' she asked.

'I told him you were well, but that I would not say
more without knowing who was asking.'

Louisa nodded, turning back and placing the note
upon her dressing table. 'All right. Thank you, Nan.'

In the mirror she could see her maid frown. 'Aren't
you going to read it, miss?'

'I will…in a little while.'

She could see immediately that Nan was not satisfied. She watched as her maid parted her lips, ready to
speak, before she pressed them together once again.
Clearly, out of respect for her mistress, she had decided
that she ought to hold her tongue.

She finished brushing and arranging Louisa's hair
quickly and in silence, perhaps not quite trusting herself not to say anything more on the subject.

Louisa thanked her quietly, then picked up the note,
clutching it in her palm as she climbed into bed. Once
Nan had left, she unfolded it, her heart hammering hard
in her chest as she found herself anticipating its possible content.

This was ridiculous, she told herself. It was just a
note. And yet as she held the paper in her hands and absorbed the words she felt a strange warmth spread from
her stomach all the way down to her toes.

My dearest Louisa,
Please forgive me for writing to you in this way,

but I find I am unable to prevent myself from being an utter fool.

I am sure there was a very good reason why I did not see you today, or yesterday, and of course you owe me no explanation for it. Indeed, you owe me nothing, since you have been so generous with your time already.

However, I cannot seem to rid myself of the feeling that something is amiss, that you are unwell or some other dreadful fate has befallen you.

I hope whoever accepted this note at your aunt's home will have been able to give my butler the assurance of your continued good health, which will help to ease my mind.

But, dearest Louisa, I must tell you that my mind is never so much at ease as it is when I am in your company. I hope we will be able to meet again soon.

Yours,
Isaac

Louisa read the note three or four times before sitting back and holding it against her chest. She closed her eyes for a moment and took a few deep breaths, trying to calm her racing thoughts.

Isaac's concern for her was as clear as it was endearing, although she hated to think that her absence had caused him such distress. But the manner in which he wrote told her more than that. His words hinted at a growing fondness for her, a tenderness which she knew she increasingly felt, too.

She had missed his company today. She knew she would have preferred an afternoon spent in the fresh air talking to Isaac over the confines of a stuffy parlour and polite conversation. Nonetheless, the strength of the feelings his note had provoked surprised her. Alarmed her, even. It was bad enough that she spent far more time thinking about him than she should. That she found her thoughts lingering on the sight of his deep blue eyes or the low sound of his laughter. That meeting him on the clifftops had been the best part of an otherwise pleasant but unremarkable week.

To be so overcome by a simple note was too much. It had been a long time since the words of a gentleman had affected her in such a way. It would not do at all. Not when she still bore the scars of the past. Not when she still bore the unmistakable taint of scandal. Not when there could never be any hope of anything more than friendship between them, no matter what her unruly heart might yearn for.

Louisa climbed out of bed and sat down at the writing desk, determined to respond. Indeed, time was of the essence. She was due to visit Hayton again the following day, with Charlotte, during which she felt certain she could contrive a way to call at Hayton Hall and deliver her reply herself.

She would assure him that all was well, but she could not allow him to form an attachment to her. It was quite obvious that their meetings had already sown the seeds of affection between them. She could not, in all good conscience, allow them to grow.

It would only end in heartbreak for them both.

Chapter Fifteen

After sending Smithson out with his instructions to deliver the note yesterday, Isaac had felt himself begin to sink. For the rest of that day he'd sat in his library, staring blankly at the volumes of books on his shelves, a black mood threatening to envelop him. He'd attempted to remedy it with a large brandy, but had managed no more than a sip before setting the glass aside, realising that he did not really want it.

Gone were the days when he'd wished to drown his feelings in the bottom of the decanter. Gone were the days of surrendering himself so completely to his melancholy. And so, with a resigned sigh and a few 'damnations' muttered under his breath, he'd rung for some tea and forced himself to confront what ailed him.

Louisa. Or, more precisely, Louisa's absence.

His anxiety had gnawed at him as he'd thought about the way he'd reached out to her, his mind reeling with the same handful of questions. Had Smithson been able to find her? Was she well? Had she read his note? And if she had, how had it been received?

This latter question had troubled him greatly. He

knew his words had been unguarded, and that he'd written in earnest about how her friendship had made him feel, what the time he'd spent in her company had meant to him. On reflection, his words had been too plain, perhaps, for either of them to countenance.

God, the wait for news had been unbearable.

Finally, just before dinner, Smithson had returned. By then Samuel had joined Isaac in the library, to peruse the newspapers and enjoy a small glass of port. Isaac had noted how his brother lowered the paper, peering curiously over it as Smithson approached his master. Isaac had got up from his chair then, steering the man towards his desk and away, he hoped, from Samuel's keen ears.

His butler, who was as discreet as he was loyal, had delivered his message in hushed, cryptic tones, but to Isaac his meaning was clear enough.

'I did as you asked, sir, and can confirm that all is well.'

It had taken a good deal of effort for Isaac to suppress his smile. 'Thank you, Smithson,' he'd replied, in the most businesslike voice he could muster. 'That will be all.'

'What was all that about?' Samuel had asked, almost as soon as the butler had left the room.

'Oh, just a household matter,' Isaac had lied. 'Nothing to concern yourself with.'

Knowing that she was in good health had buoyed Isaac's spirits, although he still worried about her reaction to the words his note had contained. He'd expressed himself hastily, and although not a word of it was untrue he feared she might be discouraged by his actions. He'd asked Louisa for her friendship, and yet he feared he was starting to behave as if he wanted far more than that.

Perhaps, he considered, he did want more than that. He knew he shouldn't, that there were scores of reasons why allowing himself to love again was a bad idea—not least the memory of his dead wife and the risk to his barely mended heart. Not least the risk of his love being rejected...a risk which was very real, given that he was neither young nor particularly agreeable.

Even Samuel, who had seemed to perceive the depth of Isaac's interest in Louisa before he did, had urged him to be cautious. And yet in sending that note he had been anything but cautious.

Damn, what had got into him?

Today that heavy feeling had returned, weighing him down in his chair as he sat in the library on a warm, sunny summer's day. He fidgeted uncomfortably, unbuttoning his collar in a vain attempt to combat the growing heat in the usually cool room, before shaking his head disapprovingly at himself.

His appearance today left much to be desired. After several hours of restless contemplation his shirt was badly crumpled, and his cravat hung loosely about his neck. He'd spent much of the morning staring wistfully out of the window, his mind returning repeatedly to the windswept cliffs. He'd briefly considered riding out there, just in case, but ultimately decided against it. She hadn't come to meet him yesterday for reasons which remained unknown to him, and in his note he had not asked to meet her there today.

He'd decided it was best to be patient...to await her reply. God, how he prayed that she would reply.

A knock at the door interrupted his spiralling thoughts.

'Come in,' he replied, rather impatiently. It was probably Samuel, he reasoned, coming to check on him, to ask why he wasn't going out riding, or to insist that Isaac accompany him to some place or other. Truly, there was never any end to Samuel's machinations.

To his surprise, however, it was Smithson. The man looked flushed and a little out of breath, as though he'd run down to the library in a great hurry.

'Forgive me for disturbing you, sir,' the butler panted. 'But I thought you'd want to know that there was a lady at the door just now. She was here to deliver a note.'

Louisa turned away from the front door of Hayton Hall and hurried back down its wide drive. At the gate stood Charlotte, waiting for her, and even from this distance she could see that she was put out: arms folded, lips pouting.

Louisa let out a sigh. Managing Charlotte had been trickier than she'd expected, and she'd almost tied herself in knots trying to explain to her companion why she needed to call here and deliver a note.

'It's a silly thing, really,' she'd said, as casually as she could manage. 'When we met in Hayton, Sir Isaac and I talked a little of the books we like to read. I told him of my love for travel literature and he said he knew of a book I must read, but he could not remember the title. He wrote to me later, to give me the details. Since we are here today, I thought I might drop off a little note to thank him for his kindness.'

Charlotte's eyes had widened. 'You're exchanging letters with Sir Isaac?'

'No.' Louisa had been emphatic. 'It is one note. To thank him. It is only polite.'

'If my mother found out I was writing to a gentleman she'd say I was being improper, even if it was only to converse about books,' Charlotte had retorted.

'Well, your mother is not my mother, and she doesn't need to know anything of this,' Louisa had replied, a little more sharply than she'd intended. 'If you wouldn't mind waiting for me at the gate? I will only be a moment.'

Charlotte had acquiesced, although Louisa wasn't sure she was convinced by her explanation. She'd felt her heart thudding rapidly in her chest as she'd made her way towards the house, and briefly she'd considered Charlotte's insinuation about the propriety of her behaviour. If Charlotte disapproved of her writing to a gentleman, Louisa did not wish to imagine what she would say if she knew she'd been meeting him, alone and in secret.

She'd pushed the thought from her mind, turning her attention instead to the large, grand house before her. It was very old, certainly—much older than she'd expected. It had many lattice windows, and a roofscape rising at several points, giving it a castle-like quality. She'd wondered about its history, and for a moment had yearned to ask Isaac to tell her about it. Then she'd remembered the note in her hand and what she must do.

It was the right course of action. For both their sakes.

At the front entrance she'd knocked hurriedly, before she could change her mind. When the door had been swiftly answered by a grey-haired butler with a kindly face, she'd pressed her note into his hands and mumbled something barely coherent about being grateful if he would ensure that it reached Sir Isaac.

The man had nodded, his mouth agape, as though caught completely by surprise. He'd recovered himself quickly, and had started to say something about fetching his master, but Louisa had all but fled from the door then. It was one thing to deliver this note—quite another to watch Isaac's face as he read it in front of her.

She was certain she could not bear it.

'All that trouble over a book,' Charlotte huffed now, as Louisa finally reached her at the gate. 'You should have let me accompany you. I might have been able to see Mr Liddell if he's at home.'

'A good book is worth any amount of trouble,' Louisa replied, deciding that humour was the best remedy for her friend's growing bad mood. 'And I did not ask if either Sir Isaac or his brother are at home, as I would not wish to disturb them.'

Charlotte sighed as they linked arms and began to walk. 'I do hope I see Mr Liddell again soon. Perhaps there will be another ball at the Assembly Rooms, and...'

'Miss Conrad! Miss Pearson!'

Both ladies spun round to see Samuel Liddell, running down the path towards them. Louisa watched as Charlotte's pout quickly dissolved into the broadest smile.

'It seems you're going to get your wish, Charlotte,' she observed, feeling her heart sink at the prospect of her swift retreat being thwarted.

'I saw you both from the window,' Mr Liddell puffed when he finally caught up with them. 'Did you call at the house? It looked as though you were coming back down the path.'

'Louisa called,' Charlotte answered, before Louisa could speak. 'She had a note for Sir Isaac—something to do with a book.'

Mr Liddell frowned. 'A book?'

Louisa nodded. 'Yes, a travel book,' she explained, trying her best to sound nonchalant. 'I shall not bore you both with the details.'

Her breath caught in her throat as behind Mr Liddell she saw Isaac emerge from the front door of the house. He marched briskly down the path, his eyes intent upon her even from this distance. As he drew closer she noticed he looked more dishevelled than the last time they'd met. His dark hair was untamed, and he wore neither a coat nor a waistcoat over his white shirt, which looked loose and crumpled next to the smooth lines of his pantaloons and Hessian boots.

She swallowed hard, wondering if he'd already read her note. Surely he was not going to speak to her about it now, in front of his brother and her friend, was he?

'Ah! Here he comes now, Miss Conrad,' Mr Liddell said, after briefly turning to follow her gaze. 'I'm sure he will be at your service regarding this book of yours.'

Louisa inclined her head, hoping she looked more serene than she felt. By the time Isaac reached them her heart was pounding so hard that she believed it would burst out of her chest. She stared up at him, locking eyes with that cool azure gaze of his. He looked strained, she realised. His face was pale and drawn, as though something was weighing heavily upon him.

Her stomach lurched as she considered that she might be the cause of his unrest.

'Miss Conrad brought a note for you, Isaac, concerning a book,' his brother informed him.

Isaac nodded in acknowledgement, although his eyes never once shifted from Louisa. 'Yes, I have received it, thank you.' He gave her a tight smile. 'Perhaps we might all step into my library for a few moments? I believe the book you seek is in there.'

Louisa's eyes widened at the suggestion. 'I'm not sure, sir,' she began, feeling increasingly flustered. 'Miss Pearson and I must—'

'Louisa?' Charlotte interrupted her, frowning. 'I thought Sir Isaac had already given you the details of the book and you'd merely written to express your gratitude?'

'She did,' Isaac replied quickly, not missing a beat. 'But there is another book we discussed too, if I recall. The one by the anonymous author. I had promised to lend it to her.'

'Splendid,' said Mr Liddell, clasping his hands together. 'Might I suggest that since you've come all this way we give you both a tour of Hayton Hall? It would be our pleasure.'

Louisa's heart descended into the pit of her stomach. 'No, really…' she tried again.

'That would be wonderful!' Charlotte spoke over her, all but squealing with delight and taking hold of Mr Liddell's arm as soon as he offered it. 'Come, Louisa, let's make haste.'

Louisa continued to stand there, dumbstruck, a wave of horror washing over her as the futility of any further objection dawned upon her. She'd come here today to draw a firm line under an acquaintance which was in danger of becoming far more than it could or should be. Going into Isaac's home, seeing where he worked and ate and read all those wonderful books they'd discussed, was not at all what she had intended.

Beside her, she felt Isaac draw nearer. He did not offer his arm, but simply walked by her side as they sauntered towards the house. No words passed between them. Nothing about her absence at the cliffs, or his note, or her reply. Just silence. Difficult silence.

Ahead of them she heard Charlotte, already deep in conversation with Mr Liddell. She wished then that she could feel so light-hearted, that this was simply an enjoyable tour of a gentleman's ancestral home. That her friendship with Sir Isaac Liddell had not grown so fraught and so complicated.

But as she drew nearer to his fine country house once more, she realised that nothing between herself and the master of Hayton Hall would ever be straightforward. No amount of wishful thinking could change that.

Chapter Sixteen

As they walked through the front door of Hayton Hall and towards his library Isaac wasn't sure what would drive him to madness first: his head or his heart.

His mind was still reeling at her unexpected presence here, and at the words in that damnable note she'd delivered—the one he'd read frantically before screwing it up and flinging it across the room, only narrowly missing poor Smithson's head.

His thoughts raced at the impulsive way he'd invited her into the library. He had meant to lend *Waverley* to her, that was true, but he could not deny that in that moment outside it had been a ruse to secure a few more moments of her company and an opportunity to speak to her. But how on earth was he going to speak in earnest with his brother and Miss Pearson present?

His heart, meanwhile, lurched from joy to despair, her company both lifting his mood and leaving him anxious that he might, in fact, never see her again. Certainly that was what her note suggested, wasn't it? That there would be no more clifftop walks, no more heartfelt conversations. That she would not, it seemed, permit a friendship between them any more.

In the library she seemed nervous, cutting herself adrift from him and pacing a little as she made a point of admiring the many shelves filled from floor to ceiling with his family's collection. He left his brother to attend to Miss Pearson, who lingered by the door with a bored expression on her face, and fetched the first volume of *Waverley* before taking it over to Louisa.

Her eyes seemed to widen as he approached, and her clear discomfort made his heart lurch. Had he really offended her so terribly by writing to her in the way he had? Was his admission that her company soothed him genuinely so distasteful to her?

'This is *Waverley*,' he said, loud enough for Samuel and Miss Pearson to hear. 'Well, the first volume, at least.'

Isaac held the book out to her, and Louisa's fingers brushed against his as she accepted it. Her unexpected touch jolted him, and his mind immediately returned to the clifftops...to the day she told him that she'd loved and lost, just as he had. To how he'd placed his hand over hers. To how deeply they'd seemed to understand one another. That day they'd drawn closer—a fact which he'd been grappling with ever since. Perhaps she had, too. Perhaps that was why his note had caused her to end their friendship so abruptly.

'Thank you,' she replied, offering him a tight smile but avoiding his gaze as she admired the fine leather cover.

'There are two more volumes,' he explained, 'if you will permit me to fetch them. They are not in their usual place, but I am sure they are here somewhere.'

A loud sigh punctuated their strained conversation. 'Forgive me, Sir Isaac, but I am feeling suddenly rather hot and thirsty after our walk,' Miss Pearson interjected, fanning her face with her hand. 'Could I trouble you for some tea?'

'It is rather too warm here in the library,' Samuel replied, before Isaac could utter a word. 'The small parlour is far more agreeable at this time of the day. Perhaps we might all retire there?'

Miss Pearson's face brightened at the suggestion. 'Oh, yes, let's! But do not trouble Sir Isaac and Louisa, Mr Liddell, if they are busy with their books. They can join us when they have finished fetching the rest of *Walpole*, or whatever it is.'

'*Waverley*,' Isaac muttered, raising his eyebrows at his brother.

Samuel, however, seemed helpless in the face of the young lady's machinations. 'Well…of course, Miss Pearson,' he began, looking uncharacteristically flustered. 'If you will be comfortable, then I'm sure we could…'

'Excellent!' Miss Pearson declared, seeming suddenly less fatigued as she took hold of Samuel's arm. 'I'm sure Sir Isaac and Louisa will do very well without us,' she added, casting the words carelessly over her shoulder as she all but dragged Samuel along with her and breezed out of the room.

The door slammed shut behind them and the library grew suddenly very silent. Isaac looked over at Louisa, offering her a smile and hoping it would convey his apology. He'd already noted her discomfort, and knew that being left alone with him would surely only make it worse.

'I will try to find the other two volumes as quickly as I can. Then we can join the others,' he said, returning his attention to his shelves.

'Thank you,' she said again, before adding, 'This is a lovely library, sir, and a lovely house. When was Hayton Hall built?'

'At the beginning of the seventeenth century, by the first baronet,' he replied, turning back to face her. 'My family has lived here ever since.'

'My goodness,' she replied, looking around once more. 'There is so much history here.'

Her expression of sheer wonder brought a smile to his face. 'I can show you the oldest book in the library, if you like.'

She nodded eagerly and, feeling that the ice between them had finally been breached, Isaac rolled up his sleeves and fetched the ladder, climbing up to retrieve the infamous volume without a moment's hesitation.

All the while he felt her hovering at the bottom of the ladder, her eyes upon him, following his swift movements up, then back down again. The observation intrigued him, and when his feet touched the ground once more he saw that she was blushing. *Blushing!* Whatever had he done to make her blush?

'The first book of *Don Quixote*,' he said, handing it to her. 'An early translation. It's about as old as the house.'

Louisa gasped, clutching it tenderly in her hands. 'I have never read it, have you?'

He shook his head. 'I must admit I have not. A book this old feels almost too precious to be read. You might like the story, though. I believe it's about an idealistic traveller,' he added, with a grin.

What on earth was wrong with him? She'd as much as told him that their friendship was over, and yet here he was, trying to tease her.

She smiled back, although he noticed that it didn't

reach her eyes. 'As much as I'd love to travel, I cannot admit to being idealistic,' she replied.

No, she wasn't—he knew that. Her life, like his, had brought her too much heartache for her to be quixotic.

Around them the library remained quiet. By now his brother and Miss Pearson would be enjoying their tea in the parlour on the other side of the house. For propriety's sake they had only a few more moments together. If he was going to speak honestly to her, then it was now or never.

'Have I offended you, Louisa?' he asked quietly, barely able to bring himself to do so.

She stepped back, just a little. 'No.'

'Your note said that we should not meet any more.'

'It is for the best,' she replied. 'We take a risk each time we meet alone.'

'Then we don't have to meet alone,' he answered. 'We can meet here, with my brother and Miss Pearson and even your aunt in attendance, if you wish. Invite the whole of Hayton, for all I care, if it means still spending time with you.'

She bit her lip, casting her eyes down, and he sensed that he was not winning the argument. 'But your note, Sir Isaac, the way you expressed yourself...'

'I was concerned when you didn't come to meet me. I had to know you were all right. And I felt that I must tell you what our time together has meant to me,' he said flatly. 'Please, Louisa, call me Isaac.'

Louisa looked back at him then. 'I had to go to the linen drapers with my aunt, and then to the Pearsons' house for tea,' she explained. 'That was why I didn't come. I am sorry to have worried you. I would not want you to fret on my account.'

Isaac smiled at her. 'I must admit I could not seem to help it,' he replied.

'Do you not think that is exactly why we must no longer meet?' she asked him.

'Why?' he challenged her. 'We are friends, are we not? Would you really wish for me not to care about you?' He sighed heavily, rubbing his forehead as the meaning of her objection suddenly dawned on him. 'You do not care for me,' he stated. 'I understand. I am too old for you, perhaps? Or too sombre. Indeed, I am well aware of my own shortcomings.'

'No.' He felt her hand upon his arm. 'You are neither of those things, Isaac. It is not that.'

His heart lifted at finally hearing her drop the damnable 'sir' from her address. Their eyes met, and before he could think about what he was doing he leaned towards her, his lips tentatively meeting hers.

He knew he shouldn't kiss her…that he ought to think of Rosalind…that he ought to remember the grief that love and loss had inflicted upon him. But, to his shame, those thoughts had flown from his mind, replaced by other, less familiar and more confusing ideas about the warm proximity of this woman, the orange sweetness of her lips.

His senses heightened as she drew closer, placing a gentle hand on his upper arm as she kissed him back. It was all the encouragement his foolish, impulsive heart needed. He wrapped an arm around her, pulling her close, then unfastened the ribbon of her bonnet and pushed it away. He ran his fingers through the loose curls of her hair, his lips trailing kisses from her mouth to her soft cheeks, her delicate jaw, and down her neck.

The taste of oranges combined with the scent of lavender as his senses were utterly overwhelmed by her. When their lips met again her tongue greeted his, and his mind began to entertain thoughts which he knew would be his undoing. *Their* undoing.

She pressed a hand against his chest, pushing him away. 'No, Isaac, we must stop.'

She was as breathless as he was—breathless and beautiful, her lips and cheeks made pink by his attentions. She stepped back from him, reaching down and picking up the bonnet which moments ago had been discarded on the floor.

He held up his hands, half defensive, half frustrated. 'I'm sorry,' he said. 'I should not have kissed you.'

He watched as she replaced her bonnet, noticed how her fingers shook as she tied the ribbon into an untidy bow. 'No, you should not,' she replied, her voice wavering. 'You must know I cannot—not after Richard...'

'Of course,' he replied grimly, his heart still racing, his mind still reeling from the taste of her lips, the feeling of her pressed against him.

What the hell had he been thinking? Had he gone completely out of his wits?

'Please, forgive me. I shall forget it ever happened, Louisa. You have my word.'

She nodded briskly. 'We should join your brother and Charlotte for tea. They will wonder what has become of us.'

'You go ahead,' he replied, giving her a thin smile. 'I will join you in a moment.'

He watched as she hurried from the room, then slumped down in his favourite armchair with a groan. He needed a few minutes to collect himself—and to chastise himself.

What a fool he was. There would be no more cliff-top walks, no more pleasant conversations now. Kissing her had sealed the fate of their friendship, and it was all his fault.

Worse still, he realised, was that for all he'd promised to forget their kiss, he believed that was the very last thing he was capable of doing.

'You're your own worst enemy, Liddell,' he muttered to himself.

It took Louisa a few minutes to locate Charlotte, following the trail of her giggles as they echoed around the ground floor of the house. In the end she found her in a cosy parlour, sitting far too close to Mr Liddell on a green velvet sofa and enjoying a cup of tea. Neither of them got to their feet when she walked in; they were far too deep in some whispered flirtation.

Even in her turmoil, it occurred to Louisa that they were as brazen as each other. She didn't wish to consider what Charlotte's mother would think of this scene, if she was here to witness it.

'Miss Conrad, do join us for some tea,' Mr Liddell said in the end, gesturing towards one of the seats opposite. 'Is my brother not with you?'

Louisa shook her head as she sat down. 'No... No— he has some business to attend to,' she lied. 'He will be here momentarily.'

Mr Liddell clicked his tongue disapprovingly as he poured her a cup of tea and handed it to her. 'That sounds like my brother—all business and no pleasure.'

That last word made Louisa's heart flutter, and she felt a sudden heat grow in her cheeks. 'I'm sure his tenants appreciate his endeavours,' she replied flatly.

'Are you all right, Louisa?' Charlotte asked. 'You look a little flushed.'

Louisa nodded, then sipped her tea, and was grateful when Charlotte and Mr Liddell's attentions returned to each other. She sat rigid in her seat, listening to the pair of them talk about nothing much, while her mind ran skittishly over everything that had occurred in the library.

Isaac had kissed her, and she had allowed it—more than allowed it, in fact, since she had kissed him in return. Her heart thrummed in her chest as she relived the moment: the soft touch of his lips against hers, the rough hint of stubble brushing her neck, the muscular solidity of his arm beneath her hand. She'd wanted to touch those arms ever since he'd rolled up his sleeves and set about fetching *Don Quixote*. A glimpse of his bare skin, sun-kissed and covered by a layer of fine dark hair, was all it had taken to send her mind to places it ought not to go.

She supposed it was little wonder that she'd surrendered herself so completely to his kiss, when even the mere sight of his flesh seemed to place her on the cusp of ruination.

All the more reason that they must no longer see each other.

At least she'd had the presence of mind to end their embrace. To be firm with him. To tell him that it should not have happened, and to remind him of her grief, of the man she'd loved and lost. That had been as much as she'd been able to say.

There was so much more she could never say to him—so much more he could not know. About her, about her past, about why she was not the sort of woman he should attach himself to. If she allowed a romance to blossom between them, she knew she would not be able to build it on lies. Sooner or later she would have to tell him everything, and she would have to endure the look in his eyes and the inevitable extinguishing of his affection for her. That would be too painful—for him and for her.

He'd already lost his wife and child; he had suffered enough. He needed someone who was worthy of him… someone who did not bear her scars.

It was kinder this way. Kinder to let him go.

And yet she'd made her attraction to him evident, hadn't she? She'd complicated matters with her blushes, and her kisses, and her protest that he was not too old, or too sombre, or indeed in any way disagreeable to her. She hadn't been able to feign dislike or uninterest; she could not have been so cruel. She had pushed him away—but not before indulging herself first. She'd allowed momentary passion to rule her head, to lead to her to go against her better judgement. It seemed she had learned no lessons from the past, after all…

'Are you sure you're all right, Louisa?' Charlotte asked, interrupting her thoughts. 'You look suddenly very pale.'

'I'm fine,' she replied, as smoothly as she could manage. 'However, I do think we ought to begin our walk back to Lowhaven. The afternoon grows late.'

She finished her tea and got to her feet, making her intention to leave clear.

Charlotte rose too, somewhat reluctantly, followed by Mr Liddell, who beamed at them both. Charlotte let out a little laugh at his light-hearted attentions and Louisa bristled, not sure which of them was irritating her more.

'I will have the carriage brought round and my driver will take you back to Lowhaven,' Mr Liddell said. 'Miss Conrad is right—we have detained you here for too long. It is the least we can do.'

'Oh, thank you, Mr Liddell, that is so very kind and thoughtful,' Charlotte gushed.

Louisa watched as her companion took hold of the gentleman's arm, trailing behind them both as they walked out of the warm parlour and back into the cool air of the wide, wood-panelled hall.

'It is a pity we did not have time to show you around Hayton Hall,' Mr Liddell said, glancing at her over his shoulder.

'Another time, I'm sure,' Louisa answered.

'Oh, yes, another time,' Charlotte interjected. 'Perhaps next time Sir Isaac and Louisa won't find themselves detained for quite so long in the library,' she added with a giggle.

Louisa bit her tongue, resolving to say nothing. The enjoyment Charlotte clearly derived from making scandalous remarks was beginning to grate on her nerves. Especially when, in this instance, her insinuations were not so far from the truth.

Finally they reached the front door, and inwardly Louisa breathed a sigh of relief. She had never been so glad to leave a place as she was at that moment.

'Miss Conrad!'

Isaac's deep voice echoed around the hall. Slowly Louisa turned around, felt panic creeping in at the prospect of facing him after all that had happened between them. What they both now had to forget.

Isaac strode up to her, clutching something against his chest. Her mind was so fraught that it took several moments before she realised it was a set of books. He held them up, giving her a broad smile, but she could not fail to see that it did not reach his eyes.

'Waverley,' he said, placing three leather-bound volumes in her hands. 'You almost forgot to take it with you. I hope you enjoy it.'

Louisa smiled back at him, conscious of their audience and the need to express a delight she didn't feel. 'Thank you, Sir Isaac,' she replied. 'I am sure that I will.'

Chapter Seventeen

'Come, my dear, we are going to be late.'

Louisa could hear Aunt Clarissa pacing at the bottom of the stairs as Nan hurried to finish pinning the last curls of her hair into place. She sighed wearily, displeased with the turn her day had taken.

She had been resting quietly in her room, engrossed in the third volume of *Waverley*, when her aunt had knocked on the door and informed her that Mrs Pearson had sent a note requesting the pleasure of their company for tea that afternoon. Louisa, unaccustomed to such last-minute demands on her time, had mildly protested about attending, but her aunt, as usual, had been resolute.

Louisa had known that there was little point in arguing, and Nan had been duly summoned to help her dress for the occasion. Now Louisa emerged from her room in a blue day dress, her hair pulled back into a gentle chignon with a handful of curls framing her face. She just about had time to grab her spencer before Aunt Clarissa hurried her out of the house and across town to the Pearsons' home.

They arrived a few moments after the appointed hour and were shown, somewhat breathlessly, into the parlour.

As Louisa walked through the door she felt suddenly as though she had been thrown into a lion's den. There, sitting on the other side of the small, oval table from Mrs Pearson and Charlotte, were Mr Liddell and Sir Isaac. She felt her breath catch in her throat as Sir Isaac put down his teacup and turned to look at her. Like his brother, he rose to his feet to greet them both, but his face was unsmiling and unreadable.

Beside her, Aunt Clarissa took a step back. 'Forgive me, Mrs Pearson, you have other company. I must have misread the day or perhaps the time on your invitation.'

'Not at all, my dear Miss Howarth,' Mrs Pearson replied with a smile. 'Why…did I not mention in my note that Sir Isaac and Mr Liddell would be joining us? How silly and forgetful of me. Please, do sit down.'

Both ladies did as they were bade, with Clarissa taking the seat nearest to Mrs Pearson, leaving Louisa to sit on the only other available chair, beside Isaac. The prospect of such close proximity to him made her heart beat faster, and she found herself thinking about being with him in the library all over again.

He looked well today, dressed for the occasion in a deep blue tailcoat with contrasting fawn waistcoat and pantaloons, his dark hair tamed into order and his face freshly shaven. Louisa felt his eyes upon her as she eased herself into the seat at his side. She did not look his way, but instead sat back as a maid poured her some tea, trying her best to concentrate on the conversation.

'So Charlotte and I were taken with the notion of a ride in the carriage through Hayton, and who should we see in the village but Mr Liddell? Such a happy co-incidence—and now to have you both here to take tea with us... Such a pleasure,' Mrs Pearson was saying.

Louisa glanced at Charlotte, noting the elated grin on her face, and her eyes darting between her mother and Mr Liddell. A coincidence indeed, thought Louisa.

'It is certainly very good to see you both,' Clarissa agreed. 'Until the ball I had not seen either of you for some time.' She looked apprehensively at Sir Isaac for a moment, then turned her attention back to Mr Liddell. 'I believe you have been travelling in Europe, sir?'

Louisa listened intently as Mr Liddell regaled his audience with tales of his continental travels. Like Mrs Starke, he could no doubt write a book describing his experiences of Paris, Geneva, Rome, Florence and Vienna. He spoke about the places he'd visited so vividly that Louisa could imagine them—although she found herself comparing his accounts with those committed to paper by Mrs Starke, which she had pored over many times.

When he mentioned his visit to Château de Voltaire in Ferney, on the French-Swiss border, she couldn't help but interject.

'Oh, yes, I know of Monsieur Voltaire's house. Mrs Starke wrote of it in her *Letters from Italy*. She says it is unchanged, and that those who have owned it since Voltaire's death have gone to some lengths to preserve it.'

Mr Liddell raised his eyebrows and smiled in delight at their shared enthusiasm for the subject. 'Quite so, Miss Conrad. Although I must tell you that there is one notable thing missing from Monsieur Voltaire's home, and that is his library. It was purchased in its entirety by Catherine, the Empress of Russia, and moved to St Petersburg.'

'Astonishing!' Mrs Pearson exclaimed. 'And you, Sir Isaac, have you travelled, like your brother?'

Isaac gave his hostess a grim smile. 'Unfortunately seeing all that Europe has to offer is not a luxury afforded to a gentleman with an estate to care for—especially when that estate becomes his responsibility at a tender age.'

'Indeed, indeed...' replied Mrs Pearson, apparently somewhat taken aback by Isaac's directness.

'Louisa would like to travel,' Aunt Clarissa said, nodding warmly at her niece. 'I do believe her mother told me that it was one of the reasons she wished to visit me for the summer. Lowhaven isn't quite Lausanne, I grant you, but it has been good for her to see another part of England, I think.'

'I'm not sure I am so keen on the idea of travel,' Charlotte interjected, wrinkling her nose slightly. 'I think I'd much rather remain in a pretty little English village like Hayton and hear all about Europe from Mr Liddell.'

'Of course, my dear,' Mrs Pearson cooed. 'Like Sir Isaac, you know that your responsibilities are here, in Cumberland. Sons and heirs must do their duty, and so must daughters.'

Isaac gave a polite nod. 'Indeed, madam.'

To Louisa's consternation, Charlotte blushed, and she watched as Mrs Pearson eyed her daughter and Isaac keenly. Then she dropped her gaze, occupying herself with drinking her tea and wishing that the ground itself would open up and swallow her whole.

What the devil had he wandered into this afternoon?

Isaac sipped his tea, quietly cursing his brother, who had been responsible for agreeing to this visit in the first place. It was bad enough that since the moment he'd arrived he'd had to endure Mrs Pearson's obvious attempts to place her daughter in front of him, making sure that he knew every detail of her accomplishments. Now the giddy young woman was blushing at nothing, and Louisa had joined them to witness the spectacle.

He wondered if she'd noticed Mrs Pearson's machinations. Certainly, she looked uncomfortable—but then that could be due to his presence more than anything else. For his part, he found it hard to be in the same room as her, drinking tea and knowing what it was like to taste her lips, to feel her pressed against him. He had not expected to see her again so soon; in some ways he had not wished to. Forgetting what had happened between them had been difficult enough, but one glance at her pretty face rendered it impossible.

Isaac fidgeted in his seat. If only he had not come today! He hadn't wished to come, but had felt duty-bound to do so when Samuel had informed him that he'd accepted the invitation on their behalf. He considered himself too honourable a gentleman to deliver such a snub, even to people like the Pearsons, about whom he had to admit to feeling rather wary even before he'd been treated to the mama's scheming.

His brother's growing interest in Miss Pearson had prompted him to make some enquiries about the family, and what he'd discovered was less than encouraging. A trail of bad debt seemed to follow the father, and they lived almost entirely at the whim of his creditors. He'd tried to speak to Samuel about what he'd learned, but he had rebuked him with a speech so well prepared that Isaac suspected his brother of being all too aware of the family's situation.

'If I was to marry Miss Pearson—and I daresay it's too soon to consider that—then the wealth of her family would matter not a jot to me. I have invested my inheritance wisely and I manage my own affairs. When the time comes, I will support my own household. Large dowries and heiresses are no inducement to me.'

Isaac had quickly dropped the subject, in the face of his brother's iron will, and submitted to attending the tea party with resignation. He'd had no idea that Louisa and her aunt would be in attendance also. He still could not decide if that knowledge would have made him more or less likely to attend. All he knew was that between the shock of Louisa's sudden appearance and Mrs Pearson's dreadful efforts to match him with her daughter under his brother's nose, a swift return to the sanctuary of his library felt more tempting than ever.

'Have you managed to read any of *Waverley*, Miss Conrad?' he asked, leaning towards her and speaking quietly in the hope that they might share a conversation.

Fate in the form of Mrs Pearson had forced them together, he reasoned. They might as well make the best of it.

He watched as she hesitated for a moment, as though astonished that he was speaking to her at all. Out of the corner of his eye he could see Miss Pearson observing them, no doubt seeking to include herself in their discussion. He wished then that she would return her attention to his brother, who was engaged in a lively exchange with Mrs Pearson and Miss Howarth.

'Yes,' Louisa replied, 'in fact, I am reading the third volume.' She gave him a reticent smile. 'I must thank you for lending it to me. I have very much enjoyed it.'

'Well, I am glad to hear that. Though I cannot believe

you are almost at the end already. You must have spent a good deal of time reading these past days.'

'I confess that at times I have been unable to tear myself away from the story. The way the author describes the Scottish Highlands is so precise and so vivid that I find myself wishing I could visit.'

Isaac found himself nodding vociferously in agreement. 'I will admit that I entertained the same notion.' He glanced at Miss Pearson, who had mercifully lost interest in their literary discussion and had now been engaged by Samuel on another topic. 'As I think I told you once, I very much lost myself in the pages of that book.'

He watched as Louisa's face coloured slightly at this reference to one of their clifftop conversations.

'I can understand that now that I have read it,' she replied.

She pressed her lips together and he found his eyes lingering on them, his mind wandering to that kiss in his library once again.

'Pray tell, what are the two of you whispering about over there?' Mrs Pearson asked loudly, giving them both a stern look.

'We are just discussing a novel which Sir Isaac has given me to read,' Louisa replied, before Isaac could answer. 'It is called *Waverley*, Mrs Pearson. Perhaps you know of it?'

'No, I don't believe I do.' Mrs Pearson shrank back into her seat. Clearly a conversation about a book was not what she had been expecting to uncover.

'Ah, yes, one of my brother's favourites,' Samuel interjected. 'Its author chooses anonymity, but his identity is a secret not very well kept. I have heard it said on more than one occasion that the poet Walter Scott is the author of *Waverley*.'

Isaac bristled as he observed Louisa's eyes widen in wonder. Trust Samuel to manage to impress with such an assertion, he thought.

To his surprise, Louisa turned to him for confirmation. 'Did you know this, Sir Isaac?'

He shrugged. 'It is mere London tittle-tattle. I would not give it any credence unless the poet acknowledges it to be the truth.'

His answer earned him a nod of agreement from her. 'Indeed,' she replied, 'I would not credit even half of what is said in society.'

He could not mistake the note of displeasure in her voice. He glanced at her, frowning. The impassive expression on her face revealed nothing, but he couldn't help but feel that she was talking about far more than the secret identity of a writer.

'Since we are all gathered here today,' Mrs Pearson interjected, clapping her hands together, 'I would like to extend an invitation to you all. Mr Pearson and I have recently considered how very nice it would be to spend a little of the summer away from Lowhaven. Shortly we intend to travel to our country home, Langdale Hall, and we would be honoured if you would join us there for a few days—perhaps on the Friday after next, if that is suitable?'

Isaac blinked, thoroughly taken aback by the invitation. It was bad enough that Samuel had dragged him here today, but now he faced the prospect of a prolonged social engagement—one which would take him away from his own estate. One which would involve spending several days in Louisa's company.

He stole a glance at her, observing how she stared at Mrs Pearson in apparent astonishment. Clearly she had not expected this either.

'Mrs Pearson, my brother and I would be delighted to accept your invitation—wouldn't we, Isaac?' Samuel said, in his usual flawless way.

'Wonderful,' Mrs Pearson declared, clasping her hands together. 'We will hold a dinner in honour of your visit—won't we, Charlotte?' she added, her keen gaze shifting to her daughter. 'We can invite our neighbours the Suttons and the Coles to join us.'

Miss Pearson gave a vigorous nod, clearly enthused by her mother's obvious machinations. 'With dancing, Mama,' she added. 'Surely we will have dancing?'

'Indeed,' Mrs Pearson replied, clapping her hands together once more. 'Then it is settled.' She turned to her other guests, who still sat, apparently dumbstruck. 'My dear Miss Howarth, Miss Conrad… I hope you will both attend as well?'

Isaac noticed how Louisa's gaze shifted towards her aunt, in the clear expectation that she would answer for them both. The older woman, meanwhile, seemed to take a moment to find her tongue.

'Oh, well…yes, Mrs P-Pearson,' she stammered. 'Indeed we would love to come. But I'm afraid that, as you know, we've… Well, we've no means by which to get ourselves to Langdale Hall.'

The way Clarissa Howarth's face reddened at that final admission made Isaac's heart lurch in sympathy for her, and he felt the heat of indignation rise in his chest at the difficult position Mrs Pearson had put her in. He hoped it was mere thoughtlessness, but he suspected it was not.

'We could take a stagecoach, Aunt,' Louisa interjected, trying to be helpful. 'That will at least get us to the nearest town.'

The thought of Louisa setting foot inside another damnable coach after what had happened to her earlier that summer set Isaac's teeth on edge.

'No,' he said, the word sounding more forceful than he'd intended. He paused momentarily, composing himself. 'It would be our pleasure to escort you. You shall travel with us in our carriage.'

Louisa looked at him then, her dark gaze guarded and unreadable, as somewhere in the background her aunt uttered hurried words of gratitude. In truth, Isaac wanted none of this: no tea parties, no visits to the Pearsons' country home, no long journeys with Louisa sitting in his carriage. But he was a gentleman. He had no choice but to accept invitations and offer his assistance to a fair maiden and her aunt when they needed it.

A fair maiden, he thought to himself. It had been some time since he'd called her that. Much had happened since then—much which could not be undone. Much which, if he was honest with himself, he did not wish to undo.

Isaac glanced at Louisa again as all around them excited chatter about the visit to Langdale Hall grew.

Several days away from Hayton Hall. Several days of seeing Louisa's face each morning. Several days of eating and sleeping under the same roof as her.

Could he bear it? He wasn't sure. One thing he did know, though, was that it would make forgetting that kiss all but impossible...

Chapter Eighteen

The journey to Langdale Hall took Louisa into the depths of Cumberland's hilly, rugged countryside and away from the sea for the first time in weeks.

For the first couple of hours, as the horses pulled them along at a gentle pace, Louisa gazed out of the window, half listening to her aunt and Mr Liddell make polite conversation, but mostly preoccupied by the increasingly dramatic scenery as it unfolded before her eyes. It was either that, she realised, or risk meeting the eye of the man sitting opposite. A man who sat as quietly as she did, but whose presence nonetheless seemed to fill the entire carriage as they rattled along the uneven country roads.

He had surpassed himself today. The deep blue of his frock coat contrasted sharply with a high white cravat and buff waistcoat, and his attire was completed with a smart pair of fitted grey pantaloons. The only aspect of him which was not agreeable was the expression he wore on his face. His brows were knitted together in a near-permanent frown, his lips pressed together in forbearance. It reminded her of that day, weeks ago, when he and his brother had come to her rescue in the aftermath of the stagecoach accident.

Despite herself, Louisa smiled at the memory. Back then she'd thought him so rude and disagreeable. Now she felt she understood him better. She understood his tendencies to solitude, his aversion to polite society. Indeed, in many ways she shared his feelings.

To her, the invitation to Langdale Hall had been as vexing as it had been unexpected. There was little doubt in her mind that Mrs Pearson had orchestrated this sojourn to further Charlotte's marriage prospects, and increasingly she suspected that Mrs Pearson wished to match Isaac with her daughter.

Charlotte might have spent much of the summer encouraging the attentions of Mr Samuel Liddell but, as Aunt Clarissa had once observed, the Pearsons' circumstances meant that Charlotte needed to marry as well as possible. For her mother, a younger son simply would not do.

The thought of spending several days witnessing Mrs Pearson manoeuvring to secure a baronet for her daughter during endless dinners and dances filled Louisa with dread. The idea of Isaac being betrothed to Charlotte made her stomach churn, as did the prospect of spending so much time in his company after that day in his library. After that kiss.

In truth, she was still reeling from it—from its tenderness, from her unguarded response to it. From the way she'd kissed him back. It brought colour to her cheeks each time she thought about it—which she was alarmed to concede was often. Seeing him every day at Langdale Hall would do nothing to help her forget about it.

The carriage jolted on the road, causing Louisa to start. She caught Isaac's eye, saw the sombre way he regarded her, his gaze holding hers for just a moment too long. It occurred to her then that perhaps the prospect of her presence at Langdale Hall was what vexed him, too.

Around noon they stopped at an inn for luncheon, and to change the horses. Louisa followed her aunt out of the carriage, determined to stay close beside her guardian as they went in search of a parlour and some refreshment. Yet Clarissa, it seemed, had other ideas, and before Louisa could intervene Isaac's brother had joined her aunt and they were striding together across the courtyard, leaving Louisa and Isaac behind.

Louisa couldn't help but wonder if that had been deliberate.

'I'm not sure who is livelier—your aunt or my brother,' Isaac said, moving to stand beside her. 'They barely stopped talking enough to draw breath all the way here.'

Louisa looked up at him, forcing a smile in an effort to seem cheerful and serene. She needed to be at her best, she reminded herself, even if she did not feel it. It was a simple matter of duty.

Isaac moved closer, offering his arm, and she felt herself hesitate—not because she did not want to hold on to him, but because she was frightened of what she would feel if she did.

Something in her demeanour must have betrayed her reluctance, because after a moment Isaac's expression darkened and he withdrew. 'Do you not wish to speak to me, Louisa?' he asked. 'Are we to travel in silence all the way to Langdale?'

His directness perturbed her, and she found herself looking away. 'I doubt that very much since, as you say, my aunt and Mr Liddell are both apt to converse. Besides,' she added, 'I have been enjoying the scenery. I seem to recall you did much the same thing yourself, the first time we travelled in a carriage together.'

Isaac grimaced at the recollection. 'Oh, please don't remind me. I must have seemed like the most disagreeable man on earth that day.'

Louisa nodded, sensing the ice between them breaking. 'You did, but it is all right. I know you much better now.'

Isaac grinned at her, apparently warming to her gentle teasing. 'Should I dare to imagine that I have gone up in Miss Louisa Conrad's estimation?'

She returned his smile. 'Well, you do have excellent taste in books,' she retorted playfully. 'What I mean to say is, I can imagine that a muddy, dishevelled woman and her maid clambering into your carriage was probably the very last thing you needed that day.'

'I was actually most concerned that you were injured,' he replied, his expression growing serious once more. 'Every time we hit a bump in the road you clutched at your side.'

She raised her eyebrows at that. Now she understood why he'd been so insistent about sending his physician to attend her. It seemed that Isaac had not been quite as uninterested as he'd appeared, after all.

'I am sorry if I am not an agreeable travelling companion today,' she said softly, slowly walking in the direction in which her aunt and Mr Liddell had headed. 'I am sorry if my aunt and me are an imposition.'

'I have hardly been talkative and full of cheer, have I?' he answered. 'But you must know that you could never be an imposition, Louisa. Contrary to what my sombre countenance might suggest, it is my pleasure to escort you and your aunt to Langdale Hall.'

'Thank you,' Louisa replied, inclining her head politely. 'And you must know that I understand if our visit to Langdale Hall is the reason you are not feeling so cheerful.'

She drew a sharp breath, poised to change the subject. Their brief conversation had been quite candid enough; she was not keen to know where else it might lead.

'Now, let us go and find my aunt and your brother and something to eat. I am very hungry.'

As his carriage made its way along the drive leading to Langdale Hall, Isaac almost found himself breathing a sigh of relief. The journey had been long enough, taking much of the day and leading them into the very heart of Cumberland with its enticing landscape of lakes and mountains.

Usually the sight of such wilderness would be sufficient to preoccupy him for the hours it took to pass along the web of winding, uneven roads, and he would be content to sit there, watching it unfold and admiring its beauty. Instead, he'd begun the journey in a terrible 'black mood', as Samuel would call it, and had barely noticed the scenery outside.

He was still annoyed with his brother for accepting this invitation and for leaving him no choice but to come. The idea of spending several days with the unsubtle Mrs Pearson and her giddy daughter was bad enough—and that was before he even considered how he felt about Louisa's presence there.

How *did* he feel, exactly? He wasn't sure. The sight

of her sitting across from him in his carriage, silent and steadfastly avoiding his gaze, had provoked him, although he was at a loss to explain why. After all, given the way he'd apparently lost his mind in his library that day, and given the way he'd kissed her, the lady could hardly be blamed for wishing to keep her distance from him. Yet despite knowing this he'd found himself craving a look, a glance, even the smallest interaction.

When they'd stopped for lunch and had that brief conversation he'd felt his bad mood begin to lift. He'd even managed to smile. He'd suggested to her that he was glad to escort her to Langdale Hall—a sentiment which he'd been unaware of until he'd put it into words.

It was all very disconcerting and confusing. Ever since that kiss, it was as though all his thoughts and feelings had been thrown up into the air. They were still falling like autumn leaves, and he was still gathering them up and trying to make sense of them. Trying to understand how he could both long for companionship and yet still feel compelled to remain alone. Trying to understand how to reconcile his grief and his loyalty to Rosalind's memory with his growing attraction to Louisa.

That was what it was, he realised—it was attraction. It was more than mere interest…more than friendship. Those things, he knew, did not lead a man such as him to kiss a woman, or to light up in her company the way that he did.

Louisa understood him—that much was clear. She'd observed his foul mood today and known the reason for it—and, what was more, she'd felt moved to tell him that she knew.

I understand, she'd said, *if our visit to Langdale Hall is the reason you are not feeling so cheerful.*

When he'd resumed his seat opposite her, after luncheon, he'd begun to wonder whether the prospect of their stay at Langdale discomfited her too. Feeling suddenly anxious to put her at ease, as well as craving more of her conversation, he'd decided to engage her on a topic he knew she would relish, given her love of the subject matter.

'Did you finish reading *Waverley*?' he'd asked.

'Oh, yes,' she'd enthused, a smile spreading across her lovely face. 'I did, and it was wonderful. I could hardly bear to tear myself away from it! I have brought the books with me. They are packed away in my portmanteau, and I will return them to you later.'

The visible joy those books had given her had stirred something deep within himself, and it had taken all the strength he'd been able to muster for him to acknowledge her intention with a serene nod.

Finally the carriage drew to a halt outside the entrance to Langdale Hall. It was an attractive house—too petite to be called a mansion, but nonetheless impressive, with its red brickwork and elegant embellishments around the windows and doorways.

He wondered how the Pearsons managed to maintain a home such as this, given what he knew about their financial circumstances. Then he reminded himself that it was really none of his business. It was his brother who was nursing a great interest in Charlotte Pearson, not him.

Isaac stepped out of the carriage, swiftly turning and offering his hand to Louisa, who he was heartened to see accepted it without any hesitation. He'd been perturbed when she hadn't taken his arm at the inn, as though she was signalling to him that things between them had changed, that they could never return to the easy familiarity they'd enjoyed before that kiss. That had saddened him—although, to his consternation, he'd realised that it did not lead him to regret embracing her that day in his library.

The Pearsons had come outside to greet them, and a whirlwind of pleasantries were exchanged as all four weary travellers disembarked.

Mr Pearson was briskly introduced to Isaac and Samuel. Isaac was amused to note that the portly, red-haired man looked unenthused, wearing the sort of expression a gentleman wore when he desired nothing more than a newspaper, a stiff brandy and some peace and quiet. Confirmation, if it was needed, that this sojourn had not been his idea.

'I do hope Langdale Hall will feel like a home away from home to you, Miss Conrad.'

Mrs Pearson's shrill voice pierced Isaac's thoughts as she addressed Louisa.

'From what your aunt tells me, you live on a large and very grand estate. Is that where you spend much of your time?'

He watched Louisa hesitate, pressing her lips together momentarily before answering. 'Yes, indeed, I prefer to be in the country,' she replied. 'And, as you say, my home is very lovely. I prefer to spend my time there.'

Mrs Pearson raised her eyebrows. 'But you must spend at least some time in town, surely?'

'I seldom go to town, madam,' Louisa answered her quietly.

'But if an unmarried woman does not go to town, how does she expect to find a husband?' Mrs Pearson continued. 'You must give your mother cause to fret.'

Isaac saw a discomfited look flicker across Louisa's face at such an interrogation, and he felt the temperature of his blood begin to rise in indignation. Clearly Mrs Pearson knew nothing of Louisa's bereavement, or if she did she was being unforgivably callous. He wondered why the older lady felt the need to raise the matter at all. What did she hope to gain, other than to make her guest feel uncomfortable?

'I daresay all ladies are entitled to keep their own counsel on such matters, Mrs Pearson,' he said, giving the woman a stern look.

'Indeed, sir, indeed…' Mrs Pearson stuttered, apparently thoroughly taken aback by his intervention. 'I was merely reflecting upon the concern of all mothers, which is to see their daughters married.'

'Hmm…' he responded, unable to quite trust himself to say anything further on the subject.

Certainly, marriage was foremost in Mrs Pearson's mind. He believed that this was why they'd been invited to Langdale Hall, and he suspected, too, that he was the gentleman Mrs Pearson intended to secure for her daughter, not his brother. Well, Mrs Pearson would have to be gravely disappointed in that regard. Frankly, there was more chance of Louisa kissing him again than there was of him marrying Charlotte Pearson.

Where the hell had that thought come from?

The grateful look Louisa gave him was unmistakable. Emboldened by it, he walked over to her, offering his arm once again. She took it, and as they walked together through the front door of Langdale Hall, he brought his other hand to rest ever so briefly over hers. It was a caring gesture, acknowledging her discomfort at Mrs Pearson's line of questioning. But more than that he hoped to convey how defensive he'd felt of her, and how much solidarity he felt with her.

Earlier today she'd let him know that she understood him. Now, more than ever, he wanted her to know that such understanding was mutual. They were, without doubt, kindred spirits—in grief, and in solitude. In the losses they'd borne, and in the terrible circumstances they'd both had to face.

Still, as he walked by her side he suspected that such an affinity could not begin to explain the way he'd felt when his lips had met hers...or, for that matter, what had possessed him to kiss her at all.

Chapter Nineteen

Dinner that evening was a trying affair, and to her own surprise Louisa began to look forward to the arrival of the other guests the day after next. At least the presence of some less familiar faces might bring fresh possibilities for mealtime conversation.

Tonight, she was seated at the end of the table, next to Mr Pearson, who had little enough to say to her beyond trivialities about the fine weather and the quality of the soup. Unsurprisingly, that well of superficial talk quickly ran dry, and before long Mr Pearson turned to Isaac, and the two men became engrossed in a discussion about business and investments.

Several times Isaac caught her eye, his expression unreadable, as Mr Pearson wittered on about the price of this or that commodity. If he was bored, he did not show it. Truly, he was every inch a gentleman.

Faced with subjects upon which she could hardly hope to converse, Louisa found herself observing the interactions taking place elsewhere. Directly across from her Charlotte looked flushed, the flirtation between her and Mr Liddell so relentless that Louisa felt almost embarrassed to witness their whispers and smiles. Not that they seemed to notice; they were so preoccupied with each other that they barely looked in her direction.

Still, she thought, at least her peripheral position spared her from participating in Mrs Pearson's topic of choice. Even from here she could hear her engaging Aunt Clarissa at length on the favoured subject of her poor health.

Fortunately, after dinner the evening and the opportunities for good conversation seemed to improve. The ladies retired to the drawing room, where they played several hands of whist, while the gentlemen remained in the dining room, no doubt nursing glasses of port.

For whist, Louisa partnered with Charlotte, who thankfully seemed more composed now she was separated from Mr Liddell, although she was as hopeless at the game as Louisa was. Nonetheless, the card game served to occupy her mind, and for the first time in a while Louisa found herself beginning to relax. Perhaps, she reasoned, this visit to Langdale Hall would not be so bad as she'd feared.

The journey earlier today had served to alleviate much of her discomfort about her forced proximity to Isaac. In fact, at the inn and during the final few miles of the carriage ride, she'd found herself remembering just how much she enjoyed his company and his conversation. Just how open and kind he could be.

Furthermore, she had not been able to help the feeling of admiration which had washed over her when he'd stepped in to defend her against Mrs Pearson's onslaught of questions about marriage. He'd done so with such ease and such tact, but he had known what it had meant to her—the way he'd touched her hand afterwards had told her he had. She could only hope that his intervention had been sufficient to ensure that Mrs Pearson would have no more difficult questions for her, although she suspected that was wishful thinking.

'Oh! We lost again!' Charlotte cried out, startling Louisa from her thoughts.

Louisa smiled bashfully. 'I did say I am no good at this game—whereas I happen to know my aunt is particularly skilled at it. Truly, we did not stand a chance, Charlotte.'

Aunt Clarissa clutched her hand to her chest in faux outrage. 'Me? Whatever do you mean, my dear?'

'I mean my mother told me you and she were an unbeatable partnership as young ladies, Aunt,' she replied with a grin.

'It is all about memory,' Mrs Pearson interjected. 'If you are the sort of person who never forgets a detail, then you can be very successful at whist.'

'Which explains why I am hopeless at it,' Charlotte retorted with a giggle. 'I forget everything.'

'Just as long as you remember to do your duty, Charlotte,' her mother replied, giving her a pointed look. 'We can forgive a lack of skill at cards.'

The sharpness of Mrs Pearson's words cut through the jovial atmosphere like a knife, and Louisa was relieved that at that moment the gentlemen walked in to join them. Instinctively she sought out Isaac among them, catching his eye and offering him a small smile in greeting as he approached their table. He smiled back, then quickly adjusted his cravat and smoothed a hand over his dark hair, which was threatening unruliness again.

She thought of the first time she'd seen him on the

cliffs, his clothing and hair thoroughly windswept. She reflected that, as handsome as he looked in evening attire, dishevelment came very easily to him, and she was alarmed to find herself pondering which version of him she preferred. Clearly she'd had too much wine at dinner.

'Shall we retire to the comfortable chairs?' Mrs Pearson suggested, rising from her seat before anyone could answer. 'I will ring for some tea.'

Louisa did as their hostess bade, sitting down beside her aunt on a well-cushioned sofa. It struck her that the drawing room, like the rest of Langdale Hall, was immaculately furnished and decorated. Nothing about the Pearsons' country home suggested that their circumstances were as dire as Aunt Clarissa believed them to be. In which case, Louisa thought, they had to be living far beyond their means…

'So, who won at whist, Miss Conrad?' Isaac asked her as he took a seat on the sofa opposite.

'My aunt and Mrs Pearson—resoundingly,' she replied, inclining her head towards Aunt Clarissa, who was by now engaged in conversation with Mr Pearson. 'I seldom play the game, so there was little hope for Charlotte and me, I'm afraid.'

Isaac nodded. 'I daresay you prefer to spend the evening reading.'

She let out a small laugh. 'You know me well, sir.'

'Indeed, Miss Conrad,' he replied, lowering his voice. 'I believe I do.'

Although the expression on his face was earnest, Louisa found herself colouring at all the possibilities that remark could contain. Of all that it might suggest. He did, after all, know her mind well. But he also knew the taste of her lips…the feel of her body pressed against his. She knew instinctively that he had not been referring to that, and yet somehow, for some reason, that was where her thoughts had taken her.

'That reminds me—I still have your books in my portmanteau,' she said, grasping at any subject to draw her errant mind back from places it ought not to wander. 'I will fetch them for you shortly.'

He smiled. 'There is no hurry. I know they are safe in your keeping, since you treasure the story as much as I do.'

Louisa inclined her head politely before lowering her gaze, realising to her great mortification that she was still blushing. Truly, what had come over her this evening?

'Miss Conrad,' Mrs Pearson called, interrupting her thoughts. 'I had meant to tell you earlier that it seems we have a mutual friend in Berkshire.'

Louisa looked up at her hostess. 'Oh?'

'Yes—one of the Gossamers. Their estate is not far from Reading. I do believe that you know them?'

Louisa's stomach churned at the mention of that familiar name. 'Indeed, we are acquainted.'

'Mrs Gossamer is an old friend from my youth—our family estates were next to each other in Northumberland. We still write to each other frequently. In fact, I mentioned you to her in my most recent letter…' Mrs Pearson paused, giving Louisa a pointed look. 'I received her reply just a few days ago. She sends you her warmest regards.'

Louisa's heart pounded so hard that she could hear its rhythm in her ears. She'd been blushing before, but now her face burned fiercely, and she was sure she must

appear crimson to everyone, even in the dim candlelight. A feeling of utter dread washed over her. Terror
at the possible nature of the enquiries Mrs Pearson had
made about her, and fear at what might have been contained within the reply.

She glanced at Isaac and saw that he was watching
her intently, a small frown betraying his concern. She
was sure that he'd read her reaction, that he'd seen her
horror. He must be wondering what on earth had provoked it.

She gave Mrs Pearson a polite smile, trying her best to
recover. 'Thank you,' she replied, relieved that she sounded
more serene than she felt. 'Please convey my best wishes
to Mrs Gossamer in return.'

Isaac stood on the terrace and drew in a lungful of
the cool night air. He stared out absently, barely noticing the moonlit gardens which sprawled before him. It
had been a long day and he was exhausted, his limbs
heavy and his senses dulled by tiredness and, he conceded, rather liberal quantities of port. Yet the night was
young, by polite society's standards, and as a gentleman
he could not retire just yet.

A few moments in the fresh air ought to be sufficient
to restore him before he returned to join the party. Although the thought of yet more company and conversation made him inwardly groan. He'd had quite enough
of Mr Pearson's talk of wild money-making schemes
over dinner—and after dinner, for that matter. It was
little wonder he'd indulged in more port than was sensible; it had been all he could do to get through it.

He'd have much preferred to talk to Louisa. He'd
sought opportunities to engage her at dinner, but Mr

Pearson's monopoly on his attention had made that all but impossible. That had irked him; he'd felt as though she'd been quite neglected. With a prickle of irritation towards their hostess, he'd had to observe that Louisa's peripheral position at the table was largely responsible for that.

After dinner the ladies had departed for the drawing room, and he'd found himself oddly impatient to join them. When finally he had, he'd been pleased to see that Louisa appeared to be enjoying herself, finding an endearing amount of amusement in being thoroughly beaten at whist. Grace in defeat, he'd thought with a smile. Her face had fallen, though, when Mrs Pearson had mentioned their mutual acquaintance.

That had been odd... It was a fairly innocuous topic, and yet Louisa had reacted like someone awaiting a dreaded punchline at their expense, her eyes widening and her cheeks glowing scarlet. Now that he thought about it, that entire brief interaction had been inexplicably strange...

'Ah! There he is, Miss Conrad.'

Hearing Louisa's name caused Isaac to start. He spun around to see his brother standing in the doorway, grinning, his eyes sparkling after an evening of merriment. Next to him stood Louisa, clutching something in her hands. She looked tired, mustering only a small smile as her eyes met his. He suspected that, like him, she'd had quite enough of being in company today.

'I was just taking the air,' Isaac explained, giving them both a polite nod.

'He's hiding, he means,' Samuel quipped, and let out a hearty chuckle.

Isaac flinched, acknowledging that there was some

truth in his brother's remark. It was all right for Samuel. Social situations always seemed to bring out the best in him, and tonight he was undoubtedly in high spirits. Isaac had not failed to notice that Miss Pearson had been very receptive to Samuel's wit and charm over dinner—a fact which had no doubt contributed to his brother's exuberant mood. Indeed, their flirtation had been so overt that everyone must have noted it… including Mrs Pearson.

Perhaps that would put an end to any ideas the young lady's mother might have about matching her daughter with the older brother.

Isaac could only hope.

'Miss Conrad was looking for you, brother,' Samuel continued. 'She has brought you your books.'

Louisa took a step towards him, holding out the three pristine volumes he'd lent to her that day she'd visited Hayton Hall. That day he'd kissed her.

He forced a smile as he moved to accept the books, pushing that particular memory from his mind.

'I am about to retire for the night, but I wanted to make sure you had these back in your possession first,' she explained.

He nodded. 'Thank you, Lou— Miss Conrad,' he replied, inwardly chastising himself for his accidental familiarity when his brother still stood nearby.

Without doubt Samuel had noticed Isaac's slip, flashing him a mischievous look before clearing his throat. 'Well, I am in very great need of some more tea before I retire. Please excuse me—and goodnight, Miss Conrad,' he added, before bowing and swiftly taking his leave.

'You are retiring?' Isaac asked, turning back to Louisa as Samuel disappeared from view. 'Is everything all right? Are you unwell?'

'I have a slight headache,' she replied, 'but it is nothing to worry about. I am sure I will feel restored in the morning.'

He nodded. 'I daresay sleep will help; you must be fatigued after the journey. Please, let me know if there is anything I can do to assist you.'

'Thank you, Isaac, you are always very kind.'

He watched as she hesitated briefly, before continuing.

'I wanted to thank you for intervening earlier today... when Mrs Pearson asked me about marriage.'

Isaac bristled at the recollection. 'I still cannot understand what possessed her to speak to you in such a way. Does she know about your bereavement?'

'I suspect she does,' Louisa replied quietly. 'Charlotte knows a little of the story. I would be surprised if she had not repeated it to her mother.'

Isaac grimaced. 'Then that is even worse.'

Louisa shrugged. 'I suppose not everyone views these matters in the same way. There is still an expectation in our society that gentlemen and women will go on to marry or remarry after such losses.'

'But not you—or me,' he mused, with a conviction he was discomfited to observe he did not feel quite so strongly as he once had.

'Indeed. Anyway,' she said with a slight shiver, 'it is best forgotten.'

She rubbed her arms, clearly beginning to feel the chill of the night air through the thin muslin of her cream evening dress. Without thinking, Isaac put down the books he was holding and removed his tailcoat, draping it over her shoulders before either of them had time to contemplate the intimacy of the gesture, or how the distance had suddenly closed between them. How, momentarily, his hands had come to rest on her shoulders.

Isaac stepped back, clearing his throat. 'You looked cold,' he explained, as though words were needed.

'Thank you.'

He watched as she ran a careful hand over the sturdy blue fabric.

'If ladies could wear these in the evenings, instead of flimsy gowns, we'd certainly be much warmer.'

'You could try doing that,' he suggested, 'although I daresay you really would provoke comment from Mrs Pearson then.'

She let out a soft laugh, her dark eyes alight with amusement. The sound of it, and the sight of her, did strange things to his heart.

Before he could really understand what he was doing, he stepped towards her again. 'We have never spoken about that day in my library,' he said quietly. 'When I kissed you.'

She looked up at him, her expression unreadable. If she was taken aback by his remark she did not show it.

'You promised you would forget about it,' she said. 'We both should.'

'I did promise to forget,' he replied. 'But I must confess that has proved to be difficult. You know how much I have come to value your company and your friendship, Louisa,' he continued, rubbing his forehead with his hand. 'But I find myself wondering if, perhaps, something more than friendship has started to grow between us.'

Louisa shook her head, just slightly. 'Isaac...' she began.

Behind them, the sound of doors opening and the din of voices intruded.

Louisa glanced nervously over her shoulder. 'We must not discuss this now,' she said, hastily removing his coat from her shoulders and handing it back to him. 'I should go. My aunt will expect that I have retired by now.'

She hurried away, leaving him staring after her, clutching his coat in his hand. What the devil had got into him? He had not meant to say those things—he had not meant to express feelings he was still grappling with himself. Yet in those snatched few moments alone with her he'd done exactly that. He could try to blame fatigue, or port, but he knew it was neither. He knew it was the truth.

Since that kiss he'd felt something shift between them, and within himself. Something he felt less and less able to resist.

As the lively chatter of the rest of the party drew nearer Isaac suppressed the urge to groan. What in damnation was he going to do?

Chapter Twenty

Isaac sat alone in the breakfast room, clutching a cup of tea in his hands. In front of him his plate sat barely touched as he stared out of the window, his thoughts far from the business of eating.

He'd risen late that morning, after a fitful night's sleep, and had come downstairs to discover that his hosts and the other guests had already breakfasted and gone out to enjoy the morning sunshine in the gardens. Quietly, he had been relieved; he was tired, and out of sorts, and some peace to collect his scattered thoughts was exactly what he needed.

Isaac breathed in deeply and picked up a slice of toast, resolving to eat. The way his conversation with Louisa had ended last night had sent his mind into a maelstrom. He still could not fathom what had possessed him to speak the way he had.

After retiring last night, he'd turned the words over and over in his mind, and somewhere during the small hours he'd confronted his own raw honesty about his deepening affection for a woman who'd wandered quite unexpectedly into his life. He'd never thought he'd feel this way again. His heart had been so broken by grief that he'd genuinely believed himself incapable of such feelings.

Now he realised how wrong he'd been. He had not been incapable, merely unwilling. He'd erected defences around his heart...he'd shrouded himself in solitude. He'd allowed that inner voice to rule him, telling him that to remain alone was to honour his wife's memory, that love was a risk too great and that allowing himself happiness was a betrayal. Over the course of a single summer, though, those defences were being eroded, and if last night was any indication there were not many left to fall.

But how did Louisa feel? That question had plagued him for the remainder of the night.

In the library she'd returned his kiss with an ardour she'd been unable to disguise, yet ultimately she'd ended the kiss, reminding him immediately of the impediment to her heart, of her loyalty to the memory of her dead captain. Last night she'd done little more than remind him of his promise to forget the kiss, said that they should both forget it. Did that mean that, like him, she was unable to quash the memory of it?

How he wished they had not been interrupted—that they had been able to talk for a little longer. How he wished to know what else she might have said, if given the chance.

'Good morning, sleepyhead.' Samuel's cheery voice intruded as he walked in, a merry spring notable in his step.

'Good morning, Samuel,' Isaac muttered, pushing away his plate.

'I regret to inform you that while you were slumbering you missed a truly lovely promenade in Mr and

Mrs Pearson's gardens.' Samuel's grin faded as he sat down opposite his brother. 'Isaac, what's amiss? You look wretched.'

'Nothing. I didn't sleep well that's all,' Isaac replied, getting to his feet and avoiding Samuel's scrutinising gaze. 'I suppose I ought to give my apologies for my tardiness. Is everyone still outside?'

Samuel nodded. 'They are. Come, they'll be pleased to see you. Perhaps you might even manage to rouse a smile from Miss Conrad. She looks about as happy as you this morning.'

Isaac ignored his brother's jibe, following him wordlessly into the fine formal gardens which sprawled at the rear of Langdale Hall. He wondered if Louisa was as tired as he was…if she had also had a restless night. His heart sank into the pit of his stomach as he contemplated that his words might have upset her, and that she might not share similar feelings to his at all.

'Oh, Sir Isaac, a very good morning to you!'

Isaac squinted in the bright light as Mrs Pearson made a beeline for him, her daughter following dutifully at her side. The fabric of their immaculate day dresses swished as they approached, parasols in hand to shade them from the glare of the near-midday sun. He had to admit that Miss Pearson looked very becoming in the soft blue she wore, with loose curls of her red hair framing her youthful face. She gave him a pretty smile, which seemed to illuminate the smattering of freckles on her nose. For all that he had never warmed to her giddy demeanour, he had to admit that it was not difficult to see why his brother was so utterly smitten with her.

He inclined his head politely at the two women. 'Mrs

Pearson, Miss Pearson... I do apologise for my lateness this morning.'

'Oh, do not fret, Sir Isaac,' protested Mrs Pearson. 'I trust you slept well?'

He nodded, offering a smile which he hoped would mask his lie. 'I hope you are well this morning, madam?'

'Oh, yes, very well—very well indeed,' gushed Mrs Pearson. 'I feel considerably restored today. Like you, I rose late. My delicate health requires that I sleep a good deal.'

Isaac looked about him. 'And Mr Pearson is also well?' he asked, noticing that the man was not present.

'Indeed, he has gone wandering in the woods,' Mrs Pearson informed him, waving a dismissive hand in the direction of the trees clustered beyond the gardens. Her eyes shifted briefly to her daughter. 'Charlotte wondered if she might give you a tour of the gardens—perhaps show you some of our prized plants.'

Isaac hesitated, glancing at Samuel. He saw a look of confusion flit across his brother's face before he quickly composed himself once more.

Beyond Samuel, and a short distance away, he spotted Louisa walking alongside her aunt. The two women were sauntering at a snail's pace along the path which led to a walled garden. Their backs were turned to him, but he could see from the gentle shake of her aunt's head and the movement of her hands that they were deep in conversation.

He suppressed a sigh, resigning himself to an invitation which politeness dictated he must accept. He thought about Louisa's observation last night, that society was quite content to see widowed gentlemen like him lining up next to eligible bachelors on the marriage mart. Quite frankly, the thought of spending the rest of his days being sought after by ambitious mamas like Mrs Pearson made his toes curl.

Swallowing his misgivings, he offered Miss Pearson his arm. 'I would like that very much,' he replied, forcing another smile.

The sweet fragrances of the flowerbeds combined with the woody scent of conifer hedges to give Louisa a welcome sense of peace. She'd forgotten how much gardens and greenery could soothe her…how she felt better able to cope with her cares and worries after spending time among plants and trees.

At home they had beautiful gardens, carefully planned and every bit as splendid as those at Langdale Hall. Over the past years she'd walked in them daily, in all seasons and weathers, sometimes with others but often alone. Those daily walks had steadied her, had been her anchor when she'd felt the tides of madness and despair trying to sweep her away.

She realised now that her coastal walks in Lowhaven had been a continuation of that habit, although when it came to the walks she'd taken with Isaac, she suspected they had been less about grounding herself and more about wishing to cast her cares away on a sea breeze. About longing to somehow wipe the slate clean and start anew. About enjoying the solace that friendship could bring.

Only somewhere along the line something more complicated than friendship had begun to flourish, hadn't it?

This morning she was neither losing her mind nor at her wits' end, but she was tired and still reeling from the whirlwind of yesterday. The journey to Langdale, the hours spent so close to Isaac, the way his company and conversation had been her favourite things of the day... The way Mrs Pearson had mentioned her friend in Reading, and how that fleeting piece of conversation had opened old wounds. How she'd worn her pain and her panic on her face.

And then the manner in which Isaac had spoken to her last night—his admission that he still thought of that kiss, that he was thinking about more than friend-ship. She'd been so lost for words that she'd been al-most relieved when they were interrupted by the rest of the party. She was all too aware that, despite herself, her feelings for Isaac had grown too, that she regarded him with an affection and an admiration which went far beyond a friendly acquaintance.

She could not deny that she was attracted to him—that he was capable of provoking desires within her that until this summer she'd believed she'd long since sup-pressed. However, she also knew that this—whatever it was—could go no further. There could be no future for them; her past had seen to that.

She had to talk to him. She had to find the right words to explain herself. She could not reveal any more about her past—telling him about losing Richard had been as far as she'd been prepared to go. But she could assure him of her friendship. She could appeal to their shared knowledge of grief and loss and ask him to un-derstand that, for her, marriage to any man was out of the question. She could make him see that although she cared for him she could not risk falling for him. Because she could only ever be a spinster, not a wife.

'Are you even listening to a word I say?'

Clarissa had turned to face her niece, raising an inquisitive eyebrow at her. Louisa averted her gaze, staring instead at the handful of sparrows pecking at the ground, hunting for their breakfast. Or was it luncheon? Truly, she'd lost all sense of the time.

After a moment the birds flew away; she listened to the gentle flutter of their wings, wishing she could join them. Right now she wanted to be hundreds of miles from here. She wanted to be in the Neapolitan countryside, or on the shores of Lake Geneva, or indeed anywhere but Cumberland or Berkshire.

Cumberland, she realised, had become as suffocating as her home. She'd absorbed too much of it, let it soak through her skin, allowed it to become familiar with her. She thought again about the pointed way that Mrs Pearson had told her they had a mutual acquaintance in Berkshire. The blessed anonymity she'd enjoyed was ebbing away, and the past had got her firmly in its clutches once more.

'Louisa?' her aunt prompted her. 'What is the matter? Are you unwell?'

Louisa shook her head, taking hold of her aunt's arm once more and leading her through the entrance to a pleasing walled garden bursting with floral displays.

'Last night, after dinner, did you hear Mrs Pearson ask me about the Mrs Gossamer?' she asked quietly, hoping the old stone walls surrounding them did not have ears.

'Yes, your mutual acquaintance—I do recall Mrs Pearson mentioning her. Sometimes it's a small world, is it not?' Clarissa's smile dissolved into a frown as she regarded Louisa once more. 'Why do you ask?'

'Mrs Pearson said she'd mentioned me in a letter to

Mrs Gossamer, and that Mrs Gossamer had replied, acknowledging our acquaintance. The Gossamers are related to…' she paused, struggling to form the words '…to Richard, the man I was to wed. He was their nephew. What if—what if Mrs Gossamer spoke of us in her letter?'

The furrow on Aunt Clarissa's brow deepened. 'I don't quite see the problem. Why would it matter if Mrs Pearson knew about your betrothal?'

Louisa huffed out a breath. 'It wouldn't. In fact, I daresay she's already been informed about it by Charlotte, who I rather foolishly confided in a little while ago. But what if Mrs Gossamer has said more than that?' She shot her aunt a meaningful look. 'They are Richard's relations, after all. We met at a ball they hosted, and he was staying with them at the time. They know far more than most about everything that happened between us.'

She watched as Clarissa chewed her lip thoughtfully. 'Perhaps… But, as his relatives, they will surely wish to guard his memory. Try not to fret, my dear. I doubt Mrs Gossamer has said anything in that letter beyond stating that she knows you.'

'I hope you are right.' Louisa sighed again. 'I wouldn't like to think that I've brought trouble to your door…that my reputation might tarnish yours.'

'I'm an old spinster and the daughter of a long-dead clergyman. No one cares a jot about me—which is exactly how I like it.' Clarissa gave her a knowing look. 'What you're really worried about is Sir Isaac knowing your story. That's what is troubling you.'

Louisa raised her eyebrows at her aunt's perceptiveness. 'Perhaps.'

Aunt Clarissa chuckled. 'There's no "perhaps" about it, my dear. I've observed the two of you often enough by now to see the affinity between you for myself.'

'Isaac knows some of my story,' Louisa admitted. 'He knows I was engaged, and he knows about Richard's death.'

'Ah, so the two of you have discussed more than your favourite books, then?' her aunt teased. She held up a defensive hand. 'Fear not. I don't intend to interrogate you again about the exact nature of your acquaintance with the master of Hayton Hall. You made yourself very clear the last time. I do still wonder about his feelings towards you, however. Certainly he seems to enjoy your company more than that of anyone else here.'

Louisa felt herself begin to crumple. 'He has admitted to me that he feels there could be more than friendship between us,' she blurted, feeling the sudden urge to confide in someone she knew she could trust.

Aunt Clarissa's expression grew serious. 'I see. And what did you say?'

'I did not say anything. I did not get an opportunity as our conversation was interrupted.'

Clarissa frowned. 'Well, you must say something, Louisa. What if he offers marriage?'

'You know I could not marry him, Aunt.'

'Then you must find a gentle way to tell him so—a way of explaining yourself which you can both live with. Do you think you can do that?'

Louisa swallowed hard. 'I hope so,' she replied.

'You don't sound sure.'

'I…'

Louisa's words caught in her throat as over Clarissa's shoulder she spied Isaac, walking up the path with Charlotte on his arm. She felt a strange twinge in the pit of her stomach as she observed the smiles on their faces, and in particular Charlotte's unmistakable giggles and admiring glances as he pointed—presumably to different items of horticultural interest around the vast gardens.

The most powerful heat coursed through her— flames of indignation at the sight of Charlotte walking at his side, clutching his arm and gazing admiringly into his eyes. The strength of the feelings the scene provoked in her were alarming, and not at all reasonable. She could never be anything more than his friend. She could never be his wife. She could not begrudge him if ultimately he sought happiness with another.

Clarissa glanced over her shoulder, following her niece's startled gaze. 'Ah, yes,' she said, taking her by the arm and turning her away as they began to walk once more. 'I hope you are certain of your decision, Louisa, because it seems to me that there might soon be someone else vying for Sir Isaac's affections. And I have the distinct feeling that a certain young woman's flirtatiousness paired with her mother's ambitions will be quite a formidable force.'

'Then let us hope that the end of the summer arrives soon,' Louisa replied, blinking away the sting from the tears which had begun to gather in her eyes. 'Because at least then I will not be here to see it.'

Chapter Twenty-One

Louisa struggled to eat much at luncheon, her stomach turning somersaults each time she caught Isaac's eye. She forced herself to make polite conversation with the rest of the party, even struggling through a lengthy discussion with Mr Pearson, who seemed keen to tell her all about the undulating fortunes of Lowhaven's port.

She listened as he wittered on, doing her best to look interested, although she'd learned much of what he told her already, from Isaac. She pretended to be thoroughly absorbed in the subject of imports and exports, ignoring the painful hammering of her heart in her chest each time her mind wandered to the conversation she knew that she and Isaac needed to have.

It was for the best, she told herself. She would find a way to be clear with him and then, in a day or two she would return to Lowhaven. Shortly thereafter she would travel home. Isaac would become a distant memory, and in time he would forget about her, too.

'So, you see, Glasgow is the place for tobacco now. It has completely taken that trade over from Lowhaven in every respect,' Mr Pearson continued.

'John, you must be thoroughly boring Miss Conrad with all that talk of trade.'

For once, Louisa was grateful for Mrs Pearson's interjection. She watched as her husband's already rosy cheeks deepened their colour, his head wobbling indignantly on his shoulders.

'I'm not sure what you mean,' he objected. 'These are matters which ought to greatly occupy us all. There can be few in this part of Cumberland who are not heavily invested in the fortunes of the port, and...'

'I wonder...' Isaac began, raising his voice above the ensuing argument.

His interjection caused the assembled party to fall silent, and he smiled appreciatively at them before beginning again.

'I wonder if anyone might wish to walk with me this afternoon? I find the country air is very agreeable on such a fine day.'

Louisa felt her breath hitch as those deep blue eyes of his rested on her, making it clear to whom his invitation was primarily directed. She felt her cheeks colour to match Mr Pearson's, then looked away.

'Charlotte will join you,' Mrs Pearson replied, patting her daughter on the hand.

Charlotte nodded her agreement, although Louisa could not help but note her uncharacteristic lack of enthusiasm for the suggestion. It was not at all like Charlotte Pearson to be so quiet.

Isaac smiled at Mrs Pearson, although Louisa noted that the warmth of it did not reach his eyes. 'Delightful, Mrs Pearson. In that case, I am sure my brother would be happy to accompany us also.'

'Indeed I would,' replied Mr Liddell, inclining his head politely at both ladies.

Charlotte uttered some polite words of acquiescence, fixing a less than convincing smile upon her face. Her mother, meanwhile, appeared thoroughly chastened; her lips pursed, her already pale face turning chalk-white.

Little wonder, really, thought Louisa. No one in the room could have failed to notice how adeptly Isaac had side-stepped her blatant attempt at matchmaking.

'In that case Louisa must go, too,' Clarissa interjected, regarding her niece. 'As a companion for Miss Pearson.'

'Of course,' Louisa replied quietly, accepting her duty to Charlotte as she knew she must.

She bristled as she caught Mrs Pearson glaring at her, clearly still displeased at her machinations being thwarted and apparently now regarding Louisa as an obstacle. That was hardly fair, Louisa thought. Her presence was required for propriety's sake, after all. She could hardly refuse, even if she wanted to.

Did she want to?

She was not sure.

For all that she knew she needed to speak to Isaac, she doubted she would get an opportunity with his brother and Charlotte both present. Perhaps, she reasoned, the walk would be good for her, nonetheless. A little fresh air always helped to restore her and to clarify her thoughts, and Louisa felt keenly the need to do both after last night.

'Excellent,' Clarissa replied, a little too enthusiastically, and Louisa suspected that offering her niece as a companion had been motivated by more than propriety. Indeed, it seemed that Mrs Pearson was not the only woman at the table who was intent upon meddling...

'That's settled then,' Isaac said, clasping his hands together and giving such a genuine smile that Louisa could not help but find it endearing.

Immediately she chastised herself for the thought. She needed to be a good deal more resistant to his charms than that if she was going to speak frankly with him. From now on, she reminded herself, it was her head which had to rule her, not her heart.

Isaac was delighted to discover that Miss Pearson was completely out of sorts. The party of four set out at a steady enough pace, but it was not long before the young woman fell behind, complaining that she had a sore ankle and that she was unable to keep up. Samuel, ever dutiful and attentive, stayed with her.

Isaac had to suppress a chuckle at hearing his genuine concern for her welfare, his pondering aloud if they ought to in fact turn back. Truly, his brother was smitten.

Louisa, on the other hand, seemed determined to march ahead. Together they walked along, side by side, the distance between them and the other two growing by the moment. For some time neither of them spoke, both apparently enjoying the pretty sprawl of the surrounding countryside as they made their way up a gentle incline and into the shadow of the mountains and hills beyond.

Isaac allowed himself to steal the occasional glance in her direction, watching as the wind whipped at her skirts and loosened her blonde curls from under her bonnet. As usual she was immaculately dressed, wearing the same patterned pink day dress she'd worn this morning and at luncheon, and protecting herself from any chill wind with a rose-pink spencer. He tried not to notice how the increasingly rocky, uneven path forced her to lift her skirt away from the ground, revealing a hint of the bare skin above her ankle boots.

With some difficulty he averted his eyes, focussing instead upon the horizon, although his mind remained on improper thoughts of what he had seen—and what he had not.

'I do not think Charlotte finds walking quite so agreeable today,' Louisa said, finally breaking the silence.

'Indeed. Although I believe the fresh air agrees with you very well,' he observed. 'You seem very content.'

She inclined her head politely. 'I'm not sure if I could ever be anything but content in surroundings such as these.' She paused, glancing briefly behind her. 'It seems our companions have turned back. Should we join them, do you think?'

Isaac shook his head, not turning around. 'My brother is more than equal to the task of assisting Miss Pearson.'

'It was clear that Mrs Pearson wished for you to accompany Charlotte. She seemed quite put out when you insisted that Mr Liddell would join you.'

'I was hardly going to promenade with Miss Pearson alone, whatever her mother may or may not wish,' Isaac countered with an amused laugh. 'Besides, it is my brother's duty to assist Miss Pearson, since it is he who wishes to court her.'

'I think Mrs Pearson wishes it to be you who is courting her daughter.'

Her directness took him aback. He looked at her, observing the obstinate way she set her jaw, half intent upon the path in front of her, half intent upon—what? Provoking him?

He thought again about their conversation last night…

the way he'd spoken of his feelings. The way that she'd remained silent about hers. Was she trying to tell him something about them now?

'Do you think that I should?' he asked, choosing to answer fire with more fire.

'I think that would hurt your brother, given his obvious attachment to her,' she replied.

'And what about how *you* feel, Louisa?'

Again, she clenched her jaw. She did not look at him. 'We are friends, are we not? I wish for you to be happy, Isaac. Just perhaps… Well, perhaps not with Charlotte Pearson.'

He raised his eyebrows in amusement at her assertion. 'Do you not regard Miss Pearson as being a suitable match for me?'

She glanced at him, a smile pulling at the corners of her mouth. 'With all due respect to Charlotte, I think her excitable nature would drive you to distraction.'

He gave a brisk nod. 'Very perceptive. Fear not, Louisa, my interest does not lie with Miss Pearson, but elsewhere. Indeed, I think I said as much to you last night.'

Isaac watched as she drew a deep breath, realising that his heart was thudding in anticipation of what she might say. He did not wish to vex her, but he had to speak with her honestly, had to understand how she felt. To understand if she might feel the same way as he did. And it had to be now—just the two of them, alone in the countryside, with Miss Pearson and his brother well and truly out of sight. It was possible that they might not get the opportunity to speak like this again.

'I do care for you, Isaac,' she said at length. 'But I cannot be anything more to you than a friend. I decided long ago that I would remain unwed. Surely you must understand why, given all that you have also lost?'

'I do understand,' he agreed, his heart at once sinking at the plain tone of her refusal whilst also being buoyed by her admission that she cared for him. 'I have spent much of the past two years convincing myself that I should remain alone, that love is something to be altogether avoided—feared, even. But nursing such convictions, I have discovered, brings much unhappiness.' He gave her a hopeful glance. 'If we both care for each other, then perhaps that is something we ought to embrace.'

She gave a slight shake of her head. 'It is not possible, Isaac. I came to Cumberland to visit my aunt for the summer, and I will be going home to Berkshire soon. We will be hundreds of miles apart. Indeed, we are unlikely to ever see each other again.'

'You do not have to go,' he ventured, his throat suddenly dry at the prospect of her departure. 'That day on the cliffs when you told me about Richard, you said how much you liked it that hardly anyone here knows your story. Perhaps that anonymity has afforded you the fresh start you needed. Perhaps the distance between you and Berkshire has liberated you. Perhaps it has helped you to move on.'

'But the past is always there, Isaac,' she replied. 'You know that as well as I do. Surely that was why you were content with my friendship? Because, like me, you could not truly countenance anything else?'

'Even asking for your friendship was a considerable step forward for me,' he admitted. 'After Rosalind died, for the longest time it was as though I had died, too. I wallowed in my library. I drank too much and ate too little. And I saw no one but my servants. But over time I began to remember that I am in fact alive, and moreover I began to want to live. This summer, for the first time in two years, I have lived a full and happy life. I have been dancing, I have visited my tenants, I have enjoyed tea and conversation in parlours and I have walked arm in arm on the clifftops with a captivating woman.'

He smiled bashfully at his own frankness.

'The past is always there,' he said. 'But so is the future. It seems to me that what has grown between us this summer represents another chance of happiness, if only we will take it.'

They halted as a stream crossed their path, its fast waters flowing noisily over the stones it had carried down from the nearby peaks. Isaac glanced up, noticing how heavy grey clouds had started to gather on the hilltops, and he wondered how much time they had left. He leapt over the stream before turning back and extending his hand towards Louisa, indicating that he would help her. He bristled to see her hesitate, glancing down first at the stream and then at her skirts, as if to assess the situation for herself.

After a moment, and apparently accepting that she had no viable alternative, she hitched up her skirt slightly with one hand and grasped his hand with the other, before leaping towards him. She reached the other side, narrowly missing the water's edge and losing her footing, causing her to stumble.

Instinctively Isaac caught her, and found duty dissolving quickly into pleasure as he grew conscious of his own hands upon her slim waist. Despite his better judgement he did not release her once he felt her feet become steady on the ground. Instead, he allowed his arms to encircle her, pulling her closer to him. To his surprise she did not resist. At first her hands pressed against his chest, before moving up on to his shoulders. Her dark eyes gazed into his, the tips of their noses touched, their lips were barely an inch apart…

'Isaac…' she began.

He pressed his mouth against hers, stemming the flow of her words. The kiss was as fierce as it was urgent, and the strength of his ardour surprised even himself. Even more disarming was the way Louisa responded in kind, looping her arms around his neck, her body clinging tightly to his.

Even through his frock coat he was aware of every detail of her petite, alluring form, from the legs he'd glimpsed earlier brushing his to the soft curve of her breasts pressed against his chest. His heart pounded as desirous thoughts ran unbidden through his mind, warming the blood in every part of him.

Around them the wind continued its frenzied dance, and behind them the stream continued its ceaseless babbling. Time marched on even as he willed it to stop, willed it to suspend them both in this perfect, delicious union. Alas, he knew it would not. He knew that words must be spoken…that questions must be answered.

'Please stay in Cumberland, if only for a while longer,' he breathed. 'Being with you this summer has made me see my life clearly—made me see that I've allowed my grief to cast its shadow over everything for too long. Being with you has made me confront what it is that I truly want, and it is not to be miserable and alone. I want laughter and conversation, companionship and affection. I do not want to forget the past. I want to live with it rather than allowing it to rule me. My brother once said to me that Rosalind would have wanted me to be happy. At the time he made me angry, but he was right—she would. And I believe Richard would have wanted only happiness for you, too.'

'It is not as simple as that...'

She pulled away from him, stepping back towards the water as though she might turn and flee at any moment. The look of horror on her face in response to his honesty made his heart lurch.

'I do not understand,' he began, shaking his head. 'You have said that you care for me. I did not realise that the admission of my feelings would be quite so unwelcome.'

'I do not mean to offend you...' She paused, her lip trembling as tears welled in her eyes. 'I do care for you, Isaac. Please believe that.'

He stepped towards her again. 'Then do not deny yourself happiness, Louisa. You deserve so much more than to do that.'

'I do not deserve anything,' she replied, tears running unabated down her cheeks. 'I care for you, but this...this affection between us—it must cease. I cannot allow myself to love you, Isaac, and for your own sake you cannot love me. I am not the sort of woman you should have in your life.'

He frowned. 'I do not understand. What does that mean? Are you trying to tell me that your objection to me is about more than your lost sea captain?'

She shook her head. 'I am sorry, Isaac. I cannot explain...'

'The devil you can't!' he replied, his frustration growing. 'Surely you must know by now that you can trust me, Louisa,' he continued, doing his best to soften his tone. 'If there is more to your story than I know, then please tell me. Tell me whatever it is, so that I can assure you that it makes no difference to how I feel.'

Those brown eyes stared into his, and he watched as she bit her trembling lip, trying to regain some modicum of control. 'I am sorry, Isaac, but I will never be able to bring myself to say those words to you.'

'I see,' he said, his voice grave. 'Then you are a coward, Louisa. Plain and simple.'

Overhead the sky had darkened further, and the thick clouds seemed to beckon the low but persistent rumbles which could be heard in the distance. Isaac let out a sigh of resignation, his mood blackening like the weather as he realised there was nothing more he could say to her. He cared for her, and she cared for him, and yet it seemed he was doomed to lose her without even understanding why.

'Come,' he said grimly. 'Let's make haste and return to Langdale. There is a storm brewing.'

Chapter Twenty-Two

Just as Isaac had predicted, a storm did indeed arrive, bringing heavy rain which battered Langdale Hall's windows, and thunderclaps loud enough to set everyone's nerves on edge during dinner. Not that the inclement weather was the only reason that tension hung in the air—as Louisa knew only too well.

Dinner was a torturous affair. The sight of Isaac seated across the table from her, immaculately dressed in his deep blue tailcoat, made Louisa's breath catch in her throat and her heart race.

She was far beyond the point of being able to deny her feelings for him, even to herself. She cared deeply for him and was hopelessly attracted to him. Her eyes sought him every time she entered a room. She craved his attention, his conversation. His embrace. Worse still, she now knew the depth of the regard he had for her. She'd heard it in his every word today, felt it in that kiss. And yet those feelings were all for nought. There could not be any future in what they felt for each other.

As she sat at that table, sipping her wine and wishing she could muster an appetite for the food in front of her, it occurred to Louisa how different this was from her attachment to Richard. Back then she'd been so youthful, so simplistic about love. She'd also been naïve, trusting in that affection as it carried her along, never thinking it would bring her such heartache. Now she knew better. Indeed, it was that awareness, that experience, which made her involvement with Isaac so complicated.

Standing by that stream, with the sky looming thunderously above them, she had so desperately wished she could tell him everything—that she could trust her feelings just as she had all those years ago. Knowing she could not…knowing how the truth would only serve to condemn her in his eyes and confirm that they were lost to each other…was as painful as refusing his affection had been.

There had been no good choices today—but then, Louisa reflected, that had been the case for her for a very long time.

After dinner, Louisa retired to the drawing room, occupying a window seat away from her aunt and the Pearson ladies and nursing a cup of tea. She watched absently as bolts of lightning lit up the black night sky, making a pretence of being fascinated by the spectacle so that she might remain undisturbed. She was not in the mood for light conversation tonight.

The gentlemen hadn't joined them yet, clearly preferring to remain around the table with their glasses of port—a fact which Charlotte had remarked upon several times in as many minutes, her head bobbing up and down to look at the door.

She'd seemed uncharacteristically on edge ever since returning from her walk, and Louisa had caught enough of the whispers exchanged between her and her mother to surmise that the outing had not proceeded according to either of their plans. If she'd been in a better state of mind Louisa might have tried to speak to Charlotte herself, to discover what was amiss. As it was, she found herself still consumed by the events of her own afternoon, replaying them over and over, tormenting herself with every last detail.

The way Isaac had spoken of his feelings for her. The way he'd kissed her. The way he'd insisted that whatever had happened in her past did not matter.

That final declaration had torn the ground from beneath her feet. How could he say that when he did not know the nature of what he so readily dismissed?

A gentleman like Sir Isaac Liddell could not love a woman like her; it was out of the question. Even if he could care for her in spite of her past, his association with her would taint him and his good name. The whiff of scandal would plague them for ever. It would destroy her. It would destroy them both.

No, she reminded herself. Of course she could not tell him. She could not risk ruining herself further, or seeing the light go out in his eyes when he regarded her. It was better this way, even if it meant Isaac thinking that she was a coward. Better that than him thinking she was a scandalous woman.

'Are you all right, my dear?'

The kindly face of Aunt Clarissa looking down at her startled Louisa from her thoughts. She nodded, forcing a smile for good measure as her aunt sat down beside her.

'Mrs Pearson and Miss Pearson are going to retire for the evening,' she said, as both ladies departed from the room with the briefest and, it seemed to Louisa, the most curt of farewells.

'Charlotte has not seemed happy this evening,' Louisa observed, once the door had closed behind them.

'Nor have you,' Clarissa countered.

Louisa inclined her head, deciding not to deny it. 'I daresay Charlotte's reasons are different from my own.'

'Or perhaps not, since I suspect both of you have reasons that are rooted in your feelings for a certain pair of brothers.' She patted her niece on the hand. 'Come, we are alone, and I think the gentlemen are unlikely to join us now. Tell me what happened.'

'I spoke to Sir Isaac earlier today. I made it clear that we could not be more than friends.'

Clarissa's eyes widened. 'Oh, I see. And what did he say?'

'He left me in no doubt about the depth of his feelings for me.' Louisa felt her lip begin to tremble, her fraught feelings bubbling to the surface once more. She tried to quash them, but to no avail. 'He spoke so honestly, Aunt, and I am afraid I said more than I wished to when I refused him.'

'Did you tell him about your…about all that happened?' Clarissa asked, lowering her voice to a whisper as she chose her words carefully.

Louisa shook her head. 'I could not bring myself to. He knows there is more to my past than losing Richard, but that is all. He told me that whatever happened doesn't matter to him, but surely that cannot be true?'

Clarissa frowned. 'Sir Isaac is no starry-eyed youth, Louisa. He is a respectable gentleman. If he has given his word to you, then what reason do you have to disbelieve him?'

'His respectability and status are the very reasons

why I would be entirely unsuitable for him, Aunt—you must see that.'

'Oh, my dear, perhaps it would have been better if you'd just told him and let him judge the situation for himself,' Clarissa replied.

'Please do not be angry with me, Aunt,' Louisa replied, sobbing. 'I could not do it. I could not bring myself to tell him. What possible good could come from him knowing? All it would do is serve to ruin me all over again—this time in his eyes.'

Clarissa placed a comforting hand on Louisa's shoulder. 'You have a lot of regard for the opinion of a gentleman you once claimed barely to know,' she observed, giving her niece a knowing look. 'I'm not angry with you, my dear. I am saddened, though. Your summer in Lowhaven has not turned out as I'd hoped. I wanted you to leave here with a lighter spirit and a spring in your step, not weighed down by more difficulties.'

'Oh, but I have enjoyed my time here with you,' Louisa said, sniffing as she finally brought her tears under control.

'Yes, but it has not been the respite that I wished for. I wanted Lowhaven to be an escape for you…to be somewhere you could feel free from the past, even if only for a month or two. And, rather selfishly, I had hoped you'd grow to love it so much that you might wish to stay.' Clarissa paused, a watery smile spreading across her thin face. 'Your company has brought me great comfort these past weeks. It is not an easy thing, to be on your own. That is something you will learn, Louisa,' she added pointedly.

'I admit I have much to learn when it comes to being independent. But if I have learned anything in Lowhaven it's that I cannot run from the past, no matter how much I might wish to, or how hard I might try. I will live with its consequences for the rest of my life. And the only way I can do that is on my own.'

'And in doing so you are prepared to deny yourself love?'

Louisa wiped her eyes with a firm and steady hand. She had shed enough tears today. 'Fate has denied me love, Aunt,' she replied. 'God has denied me love. Napoleon himself denied me love when he took Richard from me. I lost all hope of love a long time ago.'

'I'm the wrong brother, Isaac. That's the problem. I'm the wrong brother…'

Isaac sat at the dining table with Samuel, the pair of them finishing off what had once been a healthy decanter of brandy. Mr Pearson had departed a few moments earlier, summoned to bed by his wife, and, rescued from the need to sustain an interminable conversation about investments, or gambling, or some other gentlemanly pursuit, the brothers had seized the chance to speak frankly for the first time in days.

Samuel had started first, his tongue loosened by drink and his heart apparently sore after today's ill-fated promenade with Miss Pearson.

'She has as good as told me that I must end my pursuit of her,' Samuel said miserably. 'She's made it clear that her father will not permit any such courtship, and has declared she is not ready to marry. She said that her mother plans to take her to London soon, so that she might experience "proper society", and that it will be a long time before she will return.'

'This is the mother's doing,' Isaac replied, before

gulping down another generous measure of the strong drink. 'A typical ambitious mama, if ever I've seen one.'

'Indeed… Why have the younger brother when you could have the baronet?' Samuel replied, and the bitterness was unmistakable in his voice.

Isaac raised his eyebrows at that. 'Mrs Pearson's efforts to foist her daughter on me have not gone unnoticed, brother, but I can assure you I am completely indifferent to that young woman. Let them try their luck in London, for they shall have none here. I am bone-weary of the female heart,' he added sourly.

'Oh? Pray tell, brother, which female heart has so grievously wounded you? Dare I suppose that it is the heart of a certain Miss Conrad to which you are referring?'

Isaac groaned, rubbing his temples with his fingers. 'I have told Miss Conrad that I care for her,' he admitted.

Samuel sat bolt upright. 'Good heavens, why on earth did you do that?' A mischievous grin spread across his face. 'I knew there was something between the two of you—although I did not imagine for one moment that you'd reached the stage of professing your undying love.'

'I most certainly did not do that—and besides, there isn't anything between us,' Isaac replied, shaking his head. 'She told me that anything more than friendship is impossible.'

Samuel's face fell. 'Really? Why?'

Isaac hesitated. As miserable as Louisa had made him, he could not stop himself from feeling protective towards her. 'It transpires that a number of years ago she had a fiancé—a naval captain who was killed fighting

Napoleon. It seems that her grief still troubles her,' he explained, settling on telling half the story.

The half he knew, he reminded himself, since the rest remained mere conjecture. Mere imagination, since she had given nothing away.

Samuel frowned. 'But you are a widower, and you are clearly prepared to remarry.'

'Perhaps there is more to the story than Lou—than Miss Conrad is willing to say,' Isaac replied, feigning a nonchalant shrug. 'Or perhaps she really is quite content to be alone, whereas I am not. I quite despise it, if the truth be told.'

'Then let that be the lesson here, brother,' Samuel said, refilling both their glasses. 'If meeting Miss Conrad has made you realise that you want a wife, then a wife is what you must find.'

He paused, holding his glass up in front of him as though considering its contents.

'I have seen a change in you this summer, Isaac. And if some of that is because of Miss Conrad then, frankly, we ought to thank her. You must keep moving forward now. If you do not want to be alone, then do not remain alone. If Miss Conrad will not have you, then you must find a woman who will.'

He took an enormous gulp of brandy, almost draining the glass in one swift movement.

'But not Miss Pearson, because I would never forgive you.'

Isaac laughed. Despite the trials of the day, the brandy-fuelled conversation with his brother had somewhat lightened his spirit.

'You've clearly drunk too much of this, Samuel,' he said, waving his glass, 'if it is giving you wild ideas about Miss Pearson and me.' He drew a deep breath, not quite able to believe what he was about to say. 'You are right, though, about me finding a wife. I think it is time I made a concerted effort to remarry—for companionship, yes, but also to fulfil my duty to this family. I am not getting any younger, and we Liddells need sons and daughters if we are to survive.'

Samuel rested his chin on his hands, giving Isaac a considered look. 'And what about love?' he asked.

Love. Indeed, Isaac thought, what about it? Love had been the sight of Rosalind, dressed in white, walking down the aisle towards him. It had been the smile on her face as she'd patted her swollen belly. It had been the cold clamminess of her hands as she'd gripped the bedsheets and clung to the hope of living.

This summer he'd come to hope for love once more—only to have those hopes dashed in the midst of the Cumberland countryside by a woman who'd wept as she'd rejected him. A woman who cared for him but could not bring herself to tell him the truth about her past.

All love seemed to have done, Isaac thought, was break his heart.

He gulped down the last of his brandy. 'Perhaps, brother, I've had quite enough of love,' he replied.

Chapter Twenty-Three

Louisa sat beside her aunt in the drawing room, running her finger absentmindedly over the rim of her wine glass and paying little attention to the surrounding conversation. The party had assembled for dinner, dressed in their finest clothes as they awaited the arrival of the handful of further guests who would be attending for the evening. Two had just joined them—a Mr and Mrs Sutton of Ashwell Park—and a further three were apparently expected at any moment.

Louisa suppressed a shiver, feeling cold in the pale blue muslin gown Nan had packed for her. She leaned towards the fire, grateful for its heat. She'd declined to have much involvement in the selection of her dresses—a decision she now regretted. Sometimes, she reflected, she could be her own worst enemy.

The day had passed quickly, with most of the household preoccupied with preparations for the evening's festivities. Keen to keep out of the way, Louisa had embraced the excuse to keep to her room as much as possible, busying herself with her books until the appointed hour, at which time a maid had arrived to help her dress for dinner.

She had not spoken to Isaac since they'd returned from their walk yesterday, their interactions having been restricted to polite nods of acknowledgement at mealtimes. She had noticed his sombre countenance whenever their eyes met over the dining table, and she didn't doubt that she looked just as unhappy. Being in the same room with him had become such torture that she longed to return to Lowhaven. Except, she reminded herself, it was Isaac's carriage which would take her back tomorrow.

The very thought of spending so many hours sitting close to him, after all that had passed between them, made her chest tighten and her stomach churn. She had no idea how she was going to bear it.

'Miss Howarth, Miss Conrad…may I present Mr and Mrs Edmund Cole and their daughter, Miss Carolyn Cole?' Mr Pearson said, interrupting her thoughts.

Louisa got to her feet, inclining her head politely at the final guests to arrive. Mr and Mrs Cole acknowledged her stiffly, before turning back to be introduced to Isaac, who had now joined the party in the drawing room. Their daughter, however, gave her a warm and hopeful smile. She seemed young, perhaps even younger than Charlotte, her green eyes filled with the anxious wonder of a woman not long out in society.

Louisa smiled in return, musing on the composition of the assembled party. The small size of it struck her, as did the obvious omission of eligible young gentlemen. It was a clear indication that Mrs Pearson's schemes had indeed been focussed upon securing one of the Liddell brothers for her daughter, and Louisa had well-founded suspicions as to which one she preferred.

Her smile dissolved as she spotted Charlotte sitting

quietly beside her mother, looking unmistakably glum.
She wondered again what might have happened to provoke such a change in her, and felt a stab of guilt that
she had not tried to find out.

'Are you quite well, Miss Conrad?' Miss Cole asked
her. 'You look a little uncomfortable.'

'Oh, yes I am well…just a little cold in this dress,'
Louisa replied as smoothly as she could manage. 'It
seems I am not yet acclimatised to summer in Cumberland. I am visiting from Berkshire, you see.'

The young woman's eyes widened. 'Indeed! I daresay it is warmer in the south, though I have never been.
I should be so happy to go—especially to London. I
suppose you will have been to London many times?'

Louisa laughed, finding it hard not to be encouraged
by Miss Cole's enthusiasm. It was hard to remember
how exciting a prospect London had seemed to her at
one time. 'Yes, although these days I prefer life in the
country. It is possible to tire of town, after a while.'

'Oh, I don't believe that! Cumberland is so dull that I
hardly think I could be anything but merry in London,'
Miss Cole gushed.

Louisa smiled, and without even thinking found herself gazing over the young woman's shoulder towards
Isaac. She drank in the details of him, from his immaculate deep blue tailcoat and crisp white cravat to the
curl of his dark hair, which had been tamed into order.

As though sensing her looking, he turned his head,
and for a moment their eyes met. She watched as feigned
indifference melted into curiosity, and felt a familiar
heat rise in her belly as the hue of those blue eyes deepened with desire. She looked away, unable to bear the
intensity in them a moment longer. Unable to bear the

longing his stare had conveyed. Unable to bear know-ing just how much he cared for her when his affection was futile.

'I find that Cumberland could be described in many ways,' she replied, recovering herself, 'but in my expe-rience "dull" is most certainly not one of them.'

Dinner was announced, and the party made their way into the dining room to find their seats. Louisa found herself hoping that she might be seated near to Miss Cole. The young woman had a pleasant and easy manner about her, and the sort of light conversation she would doubtless offer would make this difficult final evening at Langdale Hall more bearable.

Alas she was not, and furthermore Louisa's bad luck was Charlotte's good fortune, since the young ladies had been placed opposite each other at one end of the table. Suppressing a sigh, she continued to peruse the name plates, hoping that at the very least she'd been placed near to her aunt. Heaven forbid that she should have to endure another meal beside Mr Pearson…

'You are at the other end, Miss Conrad, beside my brother,' Mr Liddell called over to her, with an unmis-takably mischievous smile.

Louisa nodded, trying to conceal her alarm at the placement. She watched as Samuel Liddell rested a hand upon his own seat, beside Charlotte, arching her eyebrows as Charlotte immediately turned away from him with a look of haughty indifference. It was quite a change from the ceaseless flirtation of recent days, and Louisa could not mistake the look of hurt as it flickered across Mr Liddell's face.

Something indeed was terribly amiss.

'Forgive me, Miss Conrad, I do believe my brother

has swapped the name plates.' Isaac spoke discreetly, his low voice behind her making her stomach flip. 'I am sure we can change it if you like.'

'It is fine,' Louisa replied, in an equally hushed tone. 'I daresay your brother has his reasons for the change, although I fear his suit does not fare well.'

'Indeed,' replied Isaac, his eyes momentarily shifting towards Mr Liddell. 'It seems that neither of us has had much recent success when it comes to matters of the heart.'

Louisa stared at him open-mouthed, unsure how to retort. It seemed that tonight she did not have the monopoly on forthright remarks.

She watched, dumbstruck, as Isaac turned his attention to Mrs Pearson, giving her the most magnanimous smile.

'I must compliment you on your table settings, madam,' he said.

Mrs Pearson beamed at him, although her smile quickly faded as she observed Louisa taking her seat at Isaac's side. A seat Louisa had not even wanted. And now, thanks to Mr Liddell's meddling, she had provoked Mrs Pearson's ire once more.

Louisa sipped her wine, trying to ignore how her senses were heightened with awareness at Isaac sitting so close to her. Trying not to remember the warm feeling of him as he'd wrapped her in his arms and kissed her beside that stream. Trying not to think about just how much she wished she could reach out now, touch his hand and tell him that she would be his.

Truly, she thought miserably, tomorrow could not come soon enough.

* * *

The sight of her in that sky-blue dress was positively arresting. From the moment he had spotted her coming down the stairs he had been unable to tear his eyes away from her. All the resolutions he'd made during his conversation with Samuel the previous night had immediately fled from his mind, his thoughts fixed instead upon the glow of her fair skin, bared by a plunging neckline and short sleeves, and the neat curve of her waist as the floaty fabric skimmed over it.

Unable to entirely trust himself, he'd not followed her into the drawing room, but lingered instead in the hall, feigning interest in the portraits on the wall. Now she sat beside him at dinner, her familiar lavender scent wafting beguilingly towards him, haunting his senses, provoking his memories. How foolish he'd been to think that he could simply set aside his feelings for her and seek someone else. How awful he'd been to consider a union without love.

If he could not have Louisa he would have no one else.

'The game is very good, is it not, Sir Isaac?' Louisa asked, nodding approvingly at her fork.

He agreed, then continued with his own meal. Conversation between them was stilted, at best, and he wondered if she too was trying to maintain her composure in the presence of so many listening ears. Certainly, Louisa's aunt seemed to be paying close attention whenever they spoke to each other. He wondered how much her guardian knew about their involvement this summer.

'I daresay that here in Cumberland we have the finest fare—wouldn't you agree, Miss Conrad?' Mrs Pearson asked, having clearly caught Louisa's remark.

'I would certainly agree, Mrs Pearson,' Louisa replied. 'There are many things I will miss about Cumberland when I return to Berkshire.'

'Chief among them are my cook's cakes, I should think,' her aunt interjected, provoking a few murmurs of amusement around the table.

'I imagine you will miss the beautiful scenery as well, Miss Conrad,' Mrs Pearson continued. 'Indeed, you must have spent a long while enjoying it yesterday, since I hear that neither you nor Sir Isaac returned to Langdale for some time after Mr Liddell escorted Charlotte home with her injured ankle.'

The woman paused, staring at Louisa, her expression impassive as she let the damning insinuation her words contained sink in around the table.

'Charlotte feared you had both become lost, after you continued walking. She said you were completely out of sight,' she added, apparently for good measure.

Isaac felt the heat of indignation rise in his chest. He could not believe what he had just heard—could not believe that Mrs Pearson had the audacity to sit at the dining table and make such thinly veiled scandalous accusations for all her guests to hear.

It was bad enough to hear such suggestions being made about *him*, to have *his* honour called into question, but as a gentleman he knew he would survive it. For a lady like Louisa reputation was everything—once ruined, it could never be recovered. Such was the cruelty and such was the difference in standards applied to men and women by so-called polite society.

Isaac glanced at Louisa, saw how her cheeks had reddened and her eyes had widened in horror. It was true that they had been alone together yesterday. They had talked of their feelings. They had embraced. But Mrs Pearson could not and would not know anything of that. He would make sure of it.

'I'm afraid you are mistaken, madam,' he replied, meeting her eye with a cool and steady gaze. 'Miss Conrad and I turned back immediately. However, Miss Conrad had twisted her ankle on the rocky path, and had to rest, which meant we returned to Langdale a few moments after my brother and Miss Pearson did.'

He watched as the older woman's nostrils flared. 'That is not what I was given to understand...' she began.

'Perhaps Miss Pearson's recollection is not complete, given she was in such discomfort. But I can assure you we never lost sight of either Miss Pearson or my brother.' Isaac turned to Samuel, who was regarding him carefully, his fork poised in his hand. 'Indeed, did I not wave to you several times, brother, to assure you we were just a little way behind?'

'Yes,' Samuel replied seamlessly. 'That is correct.'

Isaac gave Mrs Pearson a satisfied smile. 'I hope this eases your mind, madam. I'm sure that, as her guardian, Miss Howarth appreciates your concern for her niece.' He glanced at Louisa's aunt, who looked thoroughly dismayed at what was unfolding before her. 'It is regrettable that sometimes accidents happen...especially in the countryside. However, I can assure you both that Miss Conrad was appropriately attended throughout the entire short promenade. You have my word as a gentleman.'

Briefly he regarded Louisa. She acknowledged his explanation, inclining her head gracefully, and he felt another wave of protectiveness grip him as he noted the look of sheer relief in her eyes. How he wished he could reach out and place his hand over hers, reassure her that all was well, that he would always be there for her. That he would not allow the likes of Mrs Pearson and her spiteful tongue to harm her. That he wanted to care for her always, if only she would let him.

Around the table his final remarks were being met with murmurs of agreement about how dangerous the paths could be, and how regrettably commonplace such injuries were. Mrs Pearson, however, looked rather as if she had just swallowed a lemon. He watched as the woman exchanged a glance with her daughter. Whatever the look communicated, it seemed sufficient to wipe the small smile from the younger lady's face.

He suppressed a wave of irritation at their behaviour. How glad he would be to be away from these Pearsons and their scheming ways.

Hopefully Samuel's heartache concerning the daughter would be short-lived.

Hopefully, his own would be, too, although somehow he doubted it.

After their meal was finished, the party retired swiftly to the drawing room for drinks and dancing. It seemed that during dinner Louisa's aunt had been persuaded to do the honours on the pianoforte, and despite her mild protestations of being out of practice, before long she was delighting them all with a merry tune from her repertoire.

Isaac watched with some amusement as Samuel keenly assembled the dancers, persuading first the Suttons and then the Coles to participate in a dance. To his surprise, his brother then approached Miss Cole and requested a dance, and he watched as she accepted his hand with a shy smile. On the other side of the room the Pearsons had gathered, watching the festivities unfold, clutching glasses of wine as red as their faces.

It would have been an uncomfortable scene if it had not been so thoroughly deserved.

'Won't you dance, brother?' Samuel asked him.

'I hardly think Miss Pearson looks in the mood to take a turn,' he replied, making the observation quietly enough so as not to be overheard.

'What about Miss Conrad?' Samuel persisted.

'I believe she is turning the pages for her aunt,' he replied, inclining his head to where Louisa stood by the piano.

'I daresay someone else could do that,' Samuel said, raising his voice. 'What do you say, Miss Howarth? Could you spare your niece so that she may dance with my brother?'

'Gladly, sir,' Louisa's aunt replied. 'It is surely the duty of all young people to be dancing on such an occasion, is it not?'

Isaac did not miss the wily look the woman gave her niece, and nor did he miss the look of consternation Louisa gave her aunt in return. He strode towards her, holding out his hand and giving her the broadest smile.

Perhaps it was the wine, or perhaps it was the breathtaking sight of Louisa in that pale blue dress, but something emboldened him—made him determined to charm her once more. It was as though this summer, each clifftop walk, each conversation, each kiss, had led them to this dance. To spending a few final, fleeting moments in each other's arms, quietly acknowledging all that had passed between them and all that could never be.

'Pray tell us, brother, what dance would you have us perform?' Isaac asked, as Louisa accepted his hand.

Her touch seemed to set his fingers alight, and he found himself swallowing hard, grappling with the sudden tide of emotion which threatened to overwhelm him.

Samuel grinned at him, clearly enjoying himself. 'I had thought a country dance, but in truth I am now minded towards a waltz.'

Miss Cole's eyes widened, and Samuel smiled at her with what could only be described as rakish charm. For a moment Isaac almost pitied her. She was young, and only just entering society, and he hoped that his brother was not simply suggesting the performance of such an intimate dance in order to make Miss Pearson jealous.

Although if that was his intention it seemed to be working. Miss Pearson still hovered on the periphery of the room, looking completely put out, whilst her mother's pinched face had turned white with anger. Still, he thought, conscious again of Louisa's hand resting in his, he could not concern himself with his brother's romantic entanglements—not when he had such an insurmountable one of his own. How his heart would survive waltzing with her, he did not know.

Miss Howarth began to play, and the couples took their positions in the centre of the room. He smiled warmly at Louisa, trying his best to compose himself, to calm his racing heart. Louisa, however, looked worried, casting her eyes down and chewing intently upon her bottom lip.

Isaac felt his resolve begin to waver. 'What is the matter, Louisa?' he whispered.

'I don't believe I know the steps,' she admitted with a heavy sigh. 'It has been a long time since...'

Her voice faltered, but he knew her meaning well enough.

Isaac smiled again, taking his position at her side and holding her hands in his. The last time he had danced a waltz it had been with Rosalind. How many lifetimes ago that felt now.

'Please do not worry,' he said. 'Just follow my lead and all will be well.'

Tentatively he led her through the first few marching steps before turning to face her, their eyes meeting as he took one of her hands in his, above her head, and placed his other hand upon her waist. The feeling of her form curving below his fingers took his mind back to their country walk, and his blood heated with thoughts of the embrace they'd shared the previous day.

Louisa's hand came to rest on his shoulder, and if he'd been warm before, now his flesh was searing at the temptation offered by her touch. She looked up, those brown eyes bewitching him, daring him to hold her gaze, to be this close and yet not kiss her.

They turned and turned again, melded together, fixed on each other, not caring if the room around them was empty or full, not concerned about whether everyone or no one was watching. It had been a long time since Isaac had felt so light, so uncontrolled.

'Thank you for what you said earlier,' Louisa said quietly. 'To Mrs Pearson...about our walk. What she was suggesting...it was...'

'Let us not speak of her now,' Isaac murmured.

He felt her draw closer to him. 'I just want you to know what it meant to me. You defended my honour.'

'You must know by now that I would do anything for you, Louisa,' he replied. 'You can trust me.'

She nodded, her expression heavy with thoughts he could not read. 'I know.'

'You are the most beautiful lady in this room,' he whispered. 'I wish you knew how happy being with you makes me feel.'

Her dark eyes widened a little more, and her lips parted as she searched his face in earnest. 'I think about you all the time…' she breathed. 'I confess, I do not know what to do…'

The music stopped, ending the dance, breaking the spell. Louisa stepped back, taking her hand from his and smoothing it over her skirts as she cast her eyes about—first at the other dancers, then towards her aunt. He saw at once the rapidity of her breath, the flush of colour in her cheeks. She had felt it, too. Undeniably, she had felt it.

'Louisa, I…' he began, reaching towards her.

He had to say something, and yet at that very moment words seemed to fail him.

She took another step back, wrapping her arms around herself. 'Forgive me, Sir Isaac,' she said. 'I am a little cold. I need to fetch my shawl.'

Isaac blinked at her, as though startled, his arm still suspended awkwardly in the air. She had cut him adrift once more, and there was nothing he could do but watch as she turned away from him and hurried out of the drawing room.

Chapter Twenty-Four

The rules of etiquette forced Isaac to remain with the other guests, to keep a smile fixed upon his face and pretend that nothing was amiss.

The dancing continued, and mathematics conspired with politeness to ensure that he participated. With more ladies than gentlemen present, he could hardly decline—much as he wished to. Much as he wanted to run from that room and seek out Louisa. Much as he wanted to kiss her fiercely upon the lips and ask her all over again to stay in Cumberland, to stay with him.

At length he took two turns with Miss Pearson, after the sullen young woman's mother all but shoved her daughter towards him in the aftermath of Louisa's sudden departure. Fortunately that single waltz seemed to have sated Samuel's appetite for the borderline scandalous, and the party occupied themselves with a cotillion, followed by a lively country dance.

Still Louisa did not return, and Isaac found his gaze repeatedly drifting towards the door, wondering how it could take so long to retrieve a simple shawl.

'I am sure Louisa is quite well, Sir Isaac,' Miss Pearson insisted in the end, clearly trying to recapture his attention. 'She has always struck me as very…robust.'

Isaac forced a smile, not wishing to indulge her on this subject. 'An astute observation, Miss Pearson,' he replied, immediately regretting the note of sarcasm which had crept into his voice.

Thankfully, Miss Pearson did not seem to notice. 'Still,' she continued, 'if she does not return then you will have to dance with me for a third time! But I should not wish to hear us *talked* about,' she said, with laughably feigned concern. 'I should not wish anyone to think that we have formed an *attachment*.'

Isaac suppressed the urge to roll his eyes. The young woman was as ridiculous as her mother. What his brother saw in her, he could not fathom.

'Miss Pearson,' he replied, giving her a steely look, 'I do not think that anyone could look at the two of us and believe we are attached.'

Her nostrils flared, and to his eternal shame he felt no small measure of satisfaction at having provoked her.

'I daresay it is impossible to tell who has become attached to whom from mere observation,' she said smoothly. 'My mama says people will always surprise you—that those you dismiss are often the ones who remain constant, whilst those you pursue are most likely to trifle with your heart.'

He scoffed at that. 'You mean just as you did with my brother's?'

Miss Pearson's face flushed scarlet. 'I do not know what you mean, sir.'

Mercifully, at that moment Louisa's aunt stopped playing, signalling the end of the dance. Conscious of the sudden quiet in the room, Isaac checked himself, painting an insincere grin on his face as he bowed politely at his dancing partner, who gave him a furious curtsey in return.

'I am sure you do not, Miss Pearson,' he replied. 'Now, please, excuse me.'

With a reassuring nod in Samuel's direction, Isaac walked out of the drawing room as casually and confidently as he could manage. Once out in the hall he paused, taking a lungful of cool air. It was chilly tonight, he realised, and those light, fashionable gowns women wore were no match for the northern climate, even in summer. Little wonder Louisa had felt the need of her shawl.

But that did not explain why she had stayed away for so long. The reason for that, he expected, lay in what had passed between them during that waltz. It had enraptured him, and he was still in thrall to his feelings. Goodness knew what effect that dance must have had on a woman determined to deny herself love if she'd felt even half of what he had.

He made it across the hall and up the first half-dozen steps of the staircase before his thoughts forced him to pause again. What was his intention now, exactly? He could hardly burst into her bedroom, even to ask her if she was all right.

He took a deep breath, felt his heart rattling inside his ribcage. As improper as it was, he would knock on her bedroom door and ask to speak to her. He would not go in; he could say what he wished to say in the doorway. But he had to say it. This was likely the last chance he would get.

When he reached her door he knocked tentatively, his sense of honour rendering him uncertain about his chosen course. He was Sir Isaac Liddell, a baronet and a gentleman—not the sort of rapscallion who went about summoning women from their bedchambers. His means might be questionable, but his intentions were noble, he reminded himself. Noble and tender.

'Louisa?' he said softly. 'Louisa, it's Isaac. Are you all right?'

His words were met with silence. He stood still for a moment, his ear hovering close to the door, listening for any sound coming from within. But there was nothing—no answer, no footsteps…nothing.

'Louisa?' He tried again. 'I only wish to make sure you are well. I…' He faltered, trying to decide what to do. 'I will go,' he continued after a moment, 'but I will ask Mrs Pearson to send a maid to attend you.'

With a sigh he walked away, his footsteps heavy on the floor as he headed back along the corridor and down the stairs. He felt his mood shift from concern towards frustration. If she was not in her room, then where the devil was she? And if she *was* in her room, why had she ignored him? Why would she not simply speak to him? Tonight they'd found themselves in each other's arms once again, forced to confront all that had blossomed between them this summer, and she'd chosen to run from it.

She'd run from him.

Outside the drawing room he paused, feeling suddenly unable to face the party, to disguise his misery with a smile and bury his lovelorn heart beneath layers of obligatory merrymaking. Instead he turned away, making his way down towards the Pearsons' library. He would re-join the party in a little while, but right now he needed a few moments of sanctuary in the sort of place where he could always find solace.

He wandered in and shut the door, glad to be greeted by the same scent of leather-bound books that gave him such comfort at home.

Except that wasn't all that was there to greet him.

She was sitting in a wingback chair, a shawl wrapped around her shoulders, her legs curled up beneath her. She looked up at him, her dark eyes wide, surprised and unsmiling. As though he was intruding. As though he was the last person she'd expected to see.

That makes two of us, he thought to himself.

He had not expected this at all.

'Louisa,' he said, finally finding his voice. 'What are you doing in here?'

'I could ask you the same question.'

Louisa stared at him in something of a daze. She hadn't answered his question because she did not have an answer. She still wasn't sure what had possessed her to wander in here after fetching her shawl. Despair, perhaps. Desperation. The realisation that she could not return to the party and face everyone as if nothing had happened.

As if she hadn't just danced a waltz with a man whose gaze, whose touch, whose mere presence made the earth shift beneath her feet.

'I needed a few moments of peace,' he replied, both his expression and his tone remaining sombre. 'Do you mind if I join you?'

'It's not my library, Isaac,' she replied. 'Strictly speaking, we ought to ask Mr Pearson's permission to be in here.'

Strictly speaking, she thought, they ought not to be in here together and unchaperoned at all. She did not wish to imagine what Mrs Pearson would make of it if she caught them.

She watched as Isaac removed his tailcoat and sat down opposite her with a sigh. For several moments she continued to stare at him, drinking in the sheer deliciousness of those dark features against the sharp white linen he wore. His hair, threatening disobedience as always, had begun to curl on top, and she found herself dwelling on what it would feel like to run her fingers through it.

'I don't think I could live without the peace and quiet of a library to retreat to,' he said softly, casting his eye over the Pearsons' immaculate room.

'I could not live without books,' Louisa replied. 'Without being able to escape into the worlds they contain.'

He nodded. 'Hiding away in libraries and stories is a reliable way to avoid life's difficulties,' he said, looking at her pointedly.

He knew—of course he knew. He always did. He knew her. He understood her. He deserved to know everything, whatever the consequences.

'Isaac, I...'

She got to her feet, and so did he. They moved towards each other, drawing close. Through his shirt and waistcoat she could see the rapid rise and fall of his chest and instinctively she reached out, laying a hand over his heart, feeling its furious rhythm playing against her skin. She dropped her gaze, staring at the broad, solid frame hidden so tantalisingly beneath the fine fabric of his attire. He hooked a finger under her chin, lifting her eyes to meet his. Blue—so blue. Just like the ocean.

'Isaac...' she began again, searching his gaze, struggling to find the right words.

'Stay...' he breathed. 'Do not leave Cumberland. Stay here with me.'

Even as she began to shake her head she found herself pulling him towards her, running her hands over his shoulders and around to the back of his neck, her fingers finding those curls of dark hair. She pressed her mouth against his, revelling in the firm, muscular warmth of him, feeling the heat of passion rise in her as he wrapped both his arms around her waist and pulled her closer to him.

She knew she should not kiss him—that what she was about to tell him would likely break their bond for ever. That he would never look at her in the same way again. Perhaps that was why she kissed him—to feel his closeness, to feel his affection one final time before the truth parted them for good.

'Isaac.' She tried yet again. 'I have to tell you what happened—with Richard. I have to tell you everything...'

He shook his head. 'I do not need to know,' he replied, caressing her cheek. 'It is in the past. It can make no difference to this—to us.'

'You do not know that,' she replied, stepping back from him. 'When Richard and I were together, before he returned to sea, we...' She faltered again, the words sticking in her throat. Words she could hardly bear to speak. Words she'd have to live with from the moment they fell from her lips to the end of her days.

'I am sorry that I called you a coward yesterday,'

Isaac said quietly. 'I should not have said that. And I should not have asked you to tell me everything. I understand how much pain it causes you to speak of this; I can see it. Please, do not tell me.'

He placed a tender kiss on her forehead, and despite herself, despite all her better judgement and reason, Louisa pulled herself close to him once more.

He brushed the curls back from her face as his lips found hers, softly and gently, and the earlier passion she'd felt dissolved into an overwhelming need for comfort and solace. For reassurance. For a kiss to say everything that she had not been able to put into words. For it to tell him her secrets so that she might never have to speak them...

'Well, I daresay *this* will cause a scandal.'

A shrill voice intruded, causing them both to fly apart.

Louisa felt her cheeks begin to burn, the intimacy of a moment suddenly overcome by the sting of shame. She heard Isaac cough, saw him press his fist to his mouth, as though he too was struggling to compose himself. Her eyes flew towards the door, although she already knew from the voice she'd heard who had entered and caught them together.

Her heart sank as she met that familiar cold gaze and observed the self-satisfied curl of those thin lips. There was no doubt in her mind that this discovery would be her downfall.

'I am quite shocked,' Mrs Pearson continued, in a voice which did not sound very shocked at all. 'Although, given what I know about Miss Conrad, I cannot say I am altogether surprised that she has seduced you, Sir Isaac.'

Isaac took several steps towards her. 'She has not… What on earth can you mean, madam?'

Louisa bowed her head, feeling her heart and her stomach descend into her feet.

Mrs Pearson knew. She knew it all.

Mrs Pearson, meanwhile, was smiling. Louisa could not see it, but she could hear it, along with the note of something like triumph that was ringing in her voice.

'Oh, Sir Isaac, she hasn't told you, has she?' she continued, her tone honeyed even as her words bit like vipers. 'Then it is fortunate that I arrived when I did. I think there is something about Miss Conrad that you should know.'

Chapter Twenty-Five

Isaac glared at the spiteful older woman, challenging her to do her worst. He watched as she dallied towards them both, running a carefree hand over the back of a nearby armchair, her expression haughty and disapproving. Beside him, he sensed Louisa's frozen form. He glanced at her, beholding her ashen face and staring brown eyes. It was as if all of her was suspended in dread. Mrs Pearson, meanwhile, seemed to be relishing the moment, a smile twitching at the corners of her mouth as she turned to look at him once more.

'Well?' he demanded. 'You should know, Mrs Pearson, that I care little for idle gossip.'

'Oh, this is not gossip, Sir Isaac,' she replied, her tone irritatingly silken. 'You see, I have learned the truth about Miss Conrad from a very good authority on the matter.' She looked at Louisa, clicking her tongue disapprovingly. 'And to think, when she first arrived in Lowhaven I thought she would be an improving influence upon my dear Charlotte...'

He saw how Louisa visibly shuddered, and instinctively he reached for her hand. His heart sank as she drew herself away from him, retrieving her shawl, which had earlier fallen from her shoulders, and re placing it around her even tighter than before.

'I presume Mrs Gossamer did not spare any detail in her letter?' Louisa spoke quietly, her voice suddenly hoarse.

Mrs Pearson chuckled at that, which only served to rankle Isaac further. He frowned, his thoughts racing as he tried to make sense of what was unfolding.

He recalled Mrs Pearson's talk of an acquaintance she shared with Louisa, to whom she wrote. Her name was Gossamer, wasn't it? He thought about that dinner, and how perturbed Louisa had seemed when Mrs Pearson had raised the subject. At the time he found it strange. Now he was beginning to realise there had been an undertone to her words, a threat contained within them which he had not understood.

'Who is this Mrs Gossamer and why should I give a single damn what she says?' he asked, anger flashing through him now. Anger at Mrs Pearson—at her intrusion, her taunts.

At length, it was Louisa who answered him. 'Mrs Gossamer is…was Richard's aunt,' she whispered, venturing to look at him. 'You might recall that when I talked of him I told you that we'd met while he was staying with his relatives? Their family name is Gossamer.'

He nodded, holding her gaze, pained to observe how broken she looked. She had said that. He searched her dark eyes, as though he might be able to find answers in their depths. Mrs Pearson knew Richard's aunt— why was that significant? What on earth could the correspondence of two women contain that would leave Louisa looking so defeated?

Mrs Pearson, meanwhile, was not to be discouraged. 'Ah, but it seems to me, Miss Conrad, that you have not told Sir Isaac all that you ought to have told him about your dalliance with that young captain.'

'It was no dalliance, Mrs Pearson,' Louisa bit back. 'Had life dealt us a kinder hand he would still be here and we would be wed.'

'Life is cruel, to be sure,' Mrs Pearson answered her, just as sharply. 'Although a young woman can do much to protect herself against its evils if she is of good moral character. If she is not prone to wanton behaviour.'

Incensed, Isaac stepped forward. 'Mrs Pearson, I hope you are not suggesting...'

'Indeed, I am, Sir Isaac,' the woman spat. 'Imagine my horror to learn from a dear old friend that her poor dead nephew's memory has been sullied by his association with this strumpet! To this day, she remains so appalled by what was said that she could barely bring herself to write the details to me. Were it not for the duty she felt, to warn me against any association with such company, I doubt she would ever have mentioned any of it. To lose such a dearly beloved young man to war is bad enough, but then to hear society whispering about him leaving a woman behind, unwed and with child, is simply unthinkable.'

'A woman?' Isaac repeated. 'You cannot mean...?'

He turned to Louisa, searching her expression for something—he did not know what. A denial, perhaps? An explanation? Had he any right to ask for either? The colour had returned to her face now, and a hot fury was gathering in her cheeks to match the indignant look with which her eyes beheld Mrs Pearson.

The older woman, meanwhile, continued her dramatic remonstrations.

'Have you no shame, Miss Conrad?' she asked, her arms wildly outstretched. 'Have you no sympathy for the pain already borne by his grieving family?'

'I understand their pain well enough, Mrs Pearson,' she replied, her voice low but steady. 'Their loss was also mine. As for shame—I cannot own the portion you would give me, since I am not guilty of all that you have accused me of.'

'So, you were *not* with child?' Mrs Pearson rounded on her. 'You did *not* accuse that young man of going to war and leaving you in such a condition?'

For the longest moment Louisa just stood there, not answering, not even looking at her accuser but staring beyond her, her brown eyes eerily vacant and unmoved.

Isaac watched her intently, awaiting and dreading her answer in turn. So much made sense now—so much of what she had said to him over these past weeks and so much of what she'd left unspoken. Yet at the same time there was much still to be untangled—a good deal of rumour and insinuation which needed to be separated from the truth. Louisa's truth. The only truth, frankly, that he cared to hear.

'Louisa...' he prompted her gently.

Her eyes snapped back to Mrs Pearson then, but where that affronted expression had previously been, Isaac now saw only sadness.

'I was with child,' she replied, her voice trembling as her tears began to fall. 'Richard's child. The child did not live.'

Instinctively Isaac moved towards her, overwhelmed by the desire to comfort her, to wrap her in his arms and to never let her go. To make her understand just how profoundly he understood her sense of loss. To tell her just how little the opinions of society and its preoccupation with so-called scandal mattered to him.

But Louisa simply shook her head and stepped away. 'Now you see why I can never marry,' she sobbed, rushing past Mrs Pearson towards the door. 'Please forgive me. I should not be here.'

Then she left the library, leaving unanswered questions hanging in the air and, he realised, her dancing shoes abandoned on the rug.

She never allowed herself to think of the child. For these past years she'd made Richard the sole focus of her grief—a grief she'd worn like a shroud, owning it as a justification for her melancholy, her insistence upon solitude and her complete withdrawal from society.

She'd loved and lost, it was true, but she had not permitted herself to count those losses or to acknowledge the depth of them.

As she ran up the stairs and into her bedchamber it struck her that tonight was the first time she'd spoken of the child since he'd slipped from her body, limp and small, his tiny lungs not yet ready for breath.

Her child.

Her son.

Pressing herself against the door, she wept as she thought of the words that had been placed alongside him. Dalliance…wanton behaviour…strumpet. Shame. She had felt shame—shame for being swept away by passion, for her secret being discovered despite her efforts to conceal it. For all the things Berkshire society had said about her—some true, but most not. For not having the good sense to marry the man she had loved before taking him to her bed.

But she had not felt ashamed of the child. As she'd brought him into the world and watched him pass straight on to the next she'd felt overwhelming guilt and the deepest sorrow, but never shame. Perhaps that was why she could never bring herself to think of him. Because confronting that pain was hard enough without being reminded of what she was expected to feel but could not.

Feeling suddenly weak, she let her weight drop to the ground, slumping down on the cold, hard wooden floor. Isaac had known how she felt; she had seen it in his face—seen his own pain breaking through as he'd placed it next to hers. They'd long since realised that they shared an understanding; now they both knew just how deep it ran.

Except Isaac's was an acceptable sort of loss. Hers was not.

Not that any of it mattered now, of course. Isaac knew the truth about her, and whatever his feelings were for her he knew, just as she did, that any association between them was at an end. Cumberland, it seemed, had not been far enough away for her to outrun the past. It had got her in its grip once again. She could feel its pull, dragging her back to Berkshire, to loneliness and isolation, to daily reminders of all that had been and all that was gone.

It was time to go home.

Taking a deep, shuddery breath, Louisa forced herself off the floor and hauled herself to her feet. She glanced down at her flimsy gown in irritation, suppressing the memories it provoked—memories of tonight, of dancing, of Isaac holding her in his arms as they twirled.

Such dresses were no good to her now. She would have to change into some warmer clothes and put on some boots, since she realised now that she had nothing on her feet. Furiously, she pulled off her evening clothes and dressed herself in the plainest day dress she could find, along with the largest bonnet, the thickest shawl and the single pair of boots she'd brought.

Thank goodness Nan had had the good sense to include some items suitable for long country walks in her portmanteau. Her heart lurched as she thought of her loyal maid back in Lowhaven, blissfully unaware of her mistress's imminent departure as she retired for the night. How worried she would be when she learned of it. How worried Aunt Clarissa would be, too.

She hurried over to the little desk in the corner of the room, scribbling a brief note to her aunt. She would leave it on the hall table, just before she departed.

Louisa adjusted her bonnet and wiped her watering eyes, steeling herself. She retrieved her reticule, tucking the note she'd written into it and hoping that the money she'd brought with her to Langdale would be sufficient for her journey home. Not that there would be any coaches going south at this time of the night; she would have to wait until morning for that.

In the meantime she would have to find somewhere to hide—somewhere that no one would find her. Somewhere that Isaac would not find her. Quietly, she slipped out of the bedchamber, every step accompanied by a silent prayer that the solid floors of Langdale Hall would not betray her as she made her bid to find sanctuary and thereafter to get away unseen.

* * *

Isaac didn't know how long he'd been staring at those dancing slippers. Long after Mrs Pearson had departed, with a brisk nod and a muttered goodnight, he found himself still fixated upon them, as though a simple pair of shoes might hold the answer to what on earth had happened that evening.

Merely an hour or two ago he'd held that beautiful, beloved woman in his arms, losing himself in her gaze as they waltzed together. In the library he'd asked her to stay, he'd embraced her and told her that the past did not matter. But then Mrs Pearson had intruded, and she'd brought it all crashing down with her stories and her gossip.

How that dreadful woman had crowed over Louisa… how determined she had been to bring her low. Well, he told himself now, he was just as determined that she would not succeed. He cared nothing for scandals, for reputations. The only part of that sorry tale to affect him had been learning about all that Louisa had lost. He did not wish to condemn her, only to console her.

Only to love her.

That thought made his breath catch in his throat, but it was true. What he felt for her had ventured far beyond the friendship they'd begun earlier that summer. He loved her. He understood that now.

He picked the slippers up, holding them tightly in his hands as he hurried out of the library and up the stairs towards the bedrooms. He would go to Louisa and he would declare himself to her.

It had been a little while since she had left the library. He could only hope that sufficient time had passed for her to calm herself, that they might talk candidly now that they'd been freed from Mrs Pearson's poisonous presence.

He needed her to know that what he'd said was true—there was nothing in her past that could change his feelings towards her. If anything, knowing about her past had only served to deepen his affections. She had borne terrible losses and had been greeted not with the sympathy she deserved but with callousness and censure from those in society.

He understood now that she'd been all but forced into a life of solitude, robbed of the right to properly grieve as a widow and a bereft mother otherwise might. Her past was not a scandal; it was a tragedy.

'Louisa?' he said, knocking loudly on the door. 'Louisa, please—I need to speak to you.'

He waited for several moments but received no reply. Tentatively he placed his hand on the doorknob, in a quandary about what to do next. He ached to be with her, to speak to her, but bursting into her bedchamber was hardly the right or proper thing to do.

He listened at the door, trying to detect the smallest movement, the subtlest sound. He felt sure she must be in there. After all that had unfolded in the library, he could not imagine she had returned to the party. Perhaps, he reasoned, she'd been so exhausted and overwrought that she'd simply fallen asleep. Or perhaps she just could not bring herself to face him right now.

Either way, he decided he ought not to intrude. He let go of the doorknob, resolving to leave her in peace. He would speak to her in the morning. He would hope that in the light of a new day she would be able to see that all would be well. That his intentions and his affections remained steady and unchanged.

'Goodnight, Louisa,' he said softly. 'I will see you tomorrow. I want you to know that this changes nothing when it comes to how I feel about you.'

Isaac withdrew and walked towards his own bedchamber, his head swimming with the evening's events and his heart still yearning for her to change her mind and open her door to him. To see her face, to feel her embrace. To hear, at the very least, a 'goodnight' in reply.

Chapter Twenty-Six

Louisa slumped down against the wall of an old stone hut, listening to the wood pigeons as they cooed on the roof. She groaned, clutching her ankle as it throbbed painfully in her boot and chastising herself for not being more careful. She'd been sore enough already as it was, her legs aching after hours on her feet, and her back and neck stiff from spending the night in the cramped linen cupboard she'd found at Langdale Hall.

Not that she'd slept, she reminded herself. Indeed, each time she'd closed her eyes she'd revisited that scene in the Pearsons' library, from the condemnation in Mrs Pearson's words as she'd revealed Louisa's scandalous past to the sympathy and sadness Louisa had seen in Isaac's eyes.

In the early morning she'd crept out of the cupboard and then out of the house, leaving the note addressed to Aunt Clarissa on the hall table, before making her way to the stables. There she'd asked a bleary-eyed young groom for directions to the nearest coaching inn from which she might begin her long journey south. A look of confusion had flashed momentarily across his face, but he had imparted the necessary instructions, which had seemed straightforward enough.

In practice, however, she'd quickly lost her way, the seemingly endless woodland and lack of discernible landmarks leaving her disorientated. The burning heat of panic had begun to rise in her chest, clouding her thoughts, and moments ago she'd stumbled over a tree root, painfully twisting her ankle and falling to the ground with a thud.

Now she was filthy, and she was injured. She needed rest, but there was no time for that. She knew she had to carry on. It was either that, she realised, or return to Langdale Hall.

Going back, she knew, was not an option.

Wearily she hauled herself upright, gritting her teeth as she forced the injured leg to bear her weight. Tears pricked in the corners of her eyes as the overwhelming desire to escape which had driven her all morning began to give way to the harsh reality of the situation she faced. She had no idea where she was, or how far it was to the nearest inn, or indeed if she was heading in the right direction at all. She had some money, but no food or drink to sustain her. She had to find her way, and soon, otherwise she really would be in peril.

'Stop it,' she muttered to herself. 'Fretting will do no good at all.'

She swiped a hand across her watering eyes and forced her mind to focus. She had to get out of the woodland and on to a road—preferably one with inns and coaches, with other travellers and people who could tell her where she was. There was nothing else she could do; there were no other options. She had to keep going.

With renewed determination she began to limp along,

biting her lip at the pain which pulsed through her ankle. At least the day was fine and bright, with the sun streaming through the gaps in the trees. She inhaled deeply, filling her lungs with the crisp air as she forced herself to keep moving forward. Around her the pigeons sang their farewell, and although she was tired and sore she gave them a watery smile.

She would find the road, she told herself. She had to. Her life, as bleak and lonely as it was condemned to be, likely depended upon it.

'I've asked the groom to ready the horses. She cannot have got very far.'

Samuel's insistent words cut across the silent room. Isaac dragged his hands down his face, the shock of her sudden disappearance giving way to his sheer horror at the thought of her out in the countryside alone.

A myriad of thoughts raced through his mind. If only he had gone to her last night… If only he'd decided to walk into her bedchamber and offered his reassurance and his heart… If only he had not waited until morning to speak to her… If only he had not risen later than usual, after a fitful night's sleep…

Then he might have discovered her disappearance sooner. If only he'd been more impulsive and less gentlemanly, he might have been able to prevent her from fleeing at all.

'The young groom said that Miss Conrad approached him early this morning and asked where she could find the nearest coaching inn,' Samuel continued. 'However, she did not give him any indication as to where she might wish to travel from there.'

'And this groom did not think it odd? A lady like Miss

Conrad leaving Langdale alone shortly after dawn?'
Isaac snapped.

'He's a boy, Isaac,' Samuel replied. 'He was hardly
going to be disobliging.'

'You're right…forgive me,' Isaac said, rubbing his
forehead.

In truth, he did not know what to do with himself.
He could do nothing until he knew Louisa was safe and
well. Until he had her back here, with him.

'At least we know which coaching inn she is heading for,' Samuel continued. 'We also know that she is
on foot. On horseback, we should be able to catch up
with her.'

'Unless she reaches the inn before that and catches
a coach,' Isaac replied. 'If that is the case we will have
no idea where she is going.'

'I think I know.'

Louisa's aunt walked into the parlour, her lined face
drawn, her eyes red and swollen with tears. She had
been the one to discover Louisa's disappearance, having gone into Louisa's bedchamber after knocking and
receiving no reply. She had not stopped weeping since.

Miss Howarth held up a letter. 'One of the servants
just found this in the hall. It is from Louisa, and addressed to me. She thanks me for welcoming her into my
home, but says that she must return to Berkshire now,
and that…' The older woman paused, pressing her handkerchief against her mouth as she fought to suppress her
sobs. 'She says that now everything about her is known,
regrettably her time in Cumberland is at an end.'

'Please try not to fret, Miss Howarth,' Samuel said,
doing his utmost to comfort her. 'We will find her safe
and well, I'm sure of it.'

'She seemed troubled last night,' Louisa's aunt continued between sobs. 'I should have gone after her when she left the dancing. I should have spoken to her last night instead of waiting until this morning. I should have known, after all she's endured these past years...' She looked up at Isaac. 'This is my fault, sir. I suggested that it might be better if you knew all about her. I never imagined—' Her voice broke, her words faltering once again.

Isaac regarded her grimly. Such a remark, so laden with meaning, left him in little doubt that Miss Howarth knew the whole story of her niece's past. He drew a deep breath, knowing he had to say something. That he had to try to explain.

'Samuel, perhaps you could check on the horses,' he suggested, knowing that speaking with Miss Howarth about something so delicate could only conceivably be undertaken in private.

His brother gave him a look of surprise, but quickly caught on. 'Ah—yes, of course,' he acquiesced.

Isaac gave his brother a grateful nod as he left and closed the door behind him, before he turned back to Miss Howarth, who dabbed her eyes with her handkerchief.

'I know how profoundly your niece has suffered, Miss Howarth,' he began, speaking quietly. 'I know all of it. But I can assure you...'

'So that is why she has run away, then,' she sobbed, interrupting him. 'Oh, my poor Louisa! She never speaks of the baby, you know. Never. Telling you would have taken a deal of strength, and clearly she cannot bear it. Oh, my dear girl...'

Isaac's heart lurched at her assumption that Louisa

had confided in him. How he wished that she had. How he wished that he'd let her. How he wished that he'd heard the story in her own words, rather than from Mrs Pearson's venomous tongue.

He decided that he wouldn't tell Miss Howarth about Mrs Pearson's involvement in its revelation—at least not yet. Knowing about that right now would only cause her more grief.

'What a frightful journey for her to attempt…on the stagecoach alone!' Miss Howarth continued. 'Think of it—a young woman, unchaperoned, wandering about the inns…'

Isaac could not decipher the rest, since Miss Howarth had buried her face in her handkerchief, her words muffled then eventually overtaken entirely by a set of deep, racking sobs.

'I promise you, Miss Howarth, I will do all that I can to find your niece.' He spoke gently, in an effort to calm her. 'Please do not blame yourself. You must know that I care for her a great deal, and what I know now does not alter that. I will ride all the way to Berkshire for her, if necessary.'

The older woman nodded, composing herself as she attempted a watery smile. 'I believe you will, sir.'

A knock at the door startled them both, and before Isaac could answer it Samuel burst in. 'Sorry to disturb you, but I thought you'd want to know that the horses are ready.'

Isaac gave his brother a brisk nod, walking closer to where he stood in the doorway. 'We should leave immediately and go directly to the inn,' he said.

'Assuming she has found her way to the inn,' Samuel added. 'She cannot know this country well, given that she has been here for such a short time. She might just as easily be lost.'

'And if that is the case I will search every inch of Cumberland,' Isaac replied, rubbing his face with his hands.

He needed to wash, having had time only to change for riding. Alas, that was something else which would have to wait.

'I have to try everything, Samuel. I will not rest until I find her.'

His brother rested a sympathetic hand on his shoulder. 'I know,' he said.

Isaac sighed, glancing over his shoulder at Louisa's aunt. 'Before we leave, perhaps you could ask someone to come and sit with Miss Howarth.'

He sighed heavily, considering the options. The Coles and Suttons lived nearby and had left late last night in their carriages, before Louisa had disappeared. The Pearsons, meanwhile, had apparently not risen yet. Not that Isaac wanted to see any of them right now.

'Fetch a maid, perhaps,' he suggested, 'and ask her to bring some tea.'

Samuel nodded. 'I'm surprised Mrs Pearson has not been down to console Miss Howarth,' he mused. 'Where *are* the Pearsons, anyway? I have not seen any of them since last night.'

Isaac suppressed a growl at the mention of that family. He could not wait to be many miles from them—but he had to find Louisa first.

'Making themselves scarce, I hope,' Isaac replied. 'Mrs Pearson in particular.'

'Oh?' Samuel stared expectantly at his brother, frowning.

Isaac's gaze shifted briefly to Miss Howarth, who had begun to weep all over again. 'I will explain all while we ride,' he replied, his tone hushed. 'But believe me when I say that I wish never to lay my eyes upon that woman again.'

'I'm not sure which part of this I find most shocking,' Samuel remarked as they rode on to the turnpike road, having been apprised of all that had been revealed last night. 'That the sensible and serious Miss Conrad has a scandalous past, or that Mrs Pearson has the capacity for such ill behaviour. And to think I'd been considering pressing my suit with her daughter just days ago.'

'Indeed,' Isaac grunted, cantering alongside him. 'I'd say you had a lucky escape, brother.'

'I could say the same for you, Isaac, if all that Mrs Pearson has said is true. Miss Conrad has done you a good turn by refusing your affections.'

Isaac looked at his brother sharply. 'My feelings are unchanged, Samuel, and I intend to tell her so once we find her,' he said. 'Indeed, I wish to marry her if she will have me.'

Samuel looked aghast. 'But there will surely be a scandal. It does not sound as though Mrs Pearson can be relied upon to keep her own counsel on the subject. The news of Miss Conrad's disgrace will be the talk of Lowhaven soon enough.'

'What disgrace, Samuel? I should think it a terrible misfortune, not a disgrace, to lose the one you love to war.'

'But she was with child and unwed. You are no fool, Isaac. You understand how society views these things.'

'I knew Rosalind before we were wed,' Isaac said,

shooting him a meaningful look. 'If Rosalind had ended up with child, and I had died before the wedding could take place, she would have been left in the same situation. It is rank hypocrisy from so many among our society to condemn others for falling foul of risks that they themselves have often taken. And I would wager that you, brother, are no innocent, but are as yet unwed. Which means that...'

'Yes, all right, your point has been well made,' Samuel interrupted, screwing up his face in discomfort. Then he shook his head, smiling at Isaac in disbelief. 'You really have fallen for Miss Conrad, haven't you?'

Isaac looked straight ahead, not meeting his eye. 'I believe that I love her, Samuel. And I believe that she loves me, too.'

'Then you have my blessing. Not that you need it, of course.'

Isaac glanced at him then, offering a small smile. 'Thank you. I might not need it, but I do value it, brother.'

'Now, let's find this woman you wish to wed,' Samuel declared. 'We are not so far from the inn now, and look—there is a mail coach stopped ahead. We will ask the driver and guard if they've seen a woman walking along here.'

Before Isaac could say anything Samuel galloped ahead. Inwardly Isaac groaned. Its requirement for speed and efficiency meant that the postal service never took kindly to any imposition on its time. And if they were stopped here, and not at an inn, that meant they were already delayed. He was not keen to provoke an irritable guard, armed with pistols and a blunderbuss.

By the time he caught up with Samuel he saw that

his brother was already in conversation with the driver, an older man with a keen stare and a roughly shaven face. The red-coated guard, meanwhile, watched warily from his perch at the back.

'Thank you for your offer of assistance, sir,' the driver was saying. 'But we are about to be on our way. We hit some tree branches on the road a little further back; they got caught in the wheels and one of the horses seemed spooked. You can't be too careful.'

'Quite right,' Samuel agreed enthusiastically, effortlessly deploying that easy manner of his. 'Before you go, I wonder if you might have seen a young woman walking along this road? She has a very handsome face, brown eyes and fair hair. She might have seemed a little…distressed.'

The driver raised an eyebrow. 'I see, sir. Well, I daresay the course of true love never did run smooth for any of us.'

'It is not like that,' Isaac interjected, feeling suddenly defensive, although he wasn't sure why. 'The woman has had some bad news regarding a relative who lives some distance away,' he explained, the lie falling easily from his tongue. 'We fear she may try to catch a coach going south, and are gravely concerned about her making such a journey alone.'

'I see, sir,' the driver said again, although he looked far from convinced. 'Well, I'm afraid we haven't seen such a woman on the road.'

He inclined his head politely and began to ready his reins.

'There was that young lady at the last inn, John,' the guard reminded the driver. 'She looked much like the woman the gentleman has described.'

The driver nodded. 'Oh, aye—in a bit of a state, she was. Her dress looked all muddy and she was walking with a limp. She approached me just as we were leaving; she must have seen we'd nought but the mail on board and thought she'd try her luck. This last leg of our route can be quiet, as a lot of passengers leave us at Penrith. Anyway, she seemed tearful when I told her we were bound for Lowhaven.'

Isaac and Samuel exchanged a look, half hopeful, half fretful. If this woman was indeed Louisa, then she had already reached the inn. It also sounded as though she was injured.

Isaac felt his stomach lurch, a potent mix of anxiety and desperation gnawing at him. The need to find her was more pressing than ever.

'Thank you both,' Samuel said with an obliging nod. 'I think we will ride to the inn and make some enquiries.'

The driver began to ready his horses once more. 'You'd best make haste if you wish to find her there, sir. Many coaches pass through in the morning. She's bound to find a seat on one of them.'

Isaac did not need urging twice. With a brisk word of thanks he was off at a gallop, his brother speeding to catch him. Coaches be damned, he thought to himself. Let them all be filled. Let her be still stranded at the inn.

Quietly he appealed to his maker, casting out something like a prayer as his horse's hooves frantically churned dust on the road beneath. He hadn't prayed in a long time, but he would do so now. He prayed for Louisa, and for her safe return to Langdale Hall.

For her safe return to him.

Chapter Twenty-Seven

Louisa sat alone in the lowly kitchen, picking at an un-appetising meal of stale bread and cheese, accompanied by a sour-tasting watery beer. Moments ago the room had been a flurry of activity, with half a dozen travellers hurriedly helping themselves to the refreshments on offer while their stagecoaches changed horses outside.

All scruffily dressed and smelling ripe, they'd eyed her suspiciously as they'd shovelled bread and beer into their mouths before departing to take their seats once more—no doubt the cheapest ones, outside and atop the coach, exposed to all the elements.

Seats Louisa would have never contemplated occupying, until today.

Now she would take any seat, any means, to get where she wanted to go.

Upon arriving at the inn she'd received a hostile reception; travellers on foot, it seemed, were not particularly welcome. The portly, rosy-cheeked landlord had glared at her before pointing her wordlessly in the direction of a woman whom Louisa presumed to be his wife, a short and no less rotund individual, whose manner had been equally inhospitable. She'd pursed her lips as she'd looked Louisa up and down, no doubt noting the filthy fabric of her skirt.

Louisa had tried to enquire about coaches travelling south, but the woman had brushed her questions away with a brisk shake of her mob-capped head.

'You'll need to get to Penrith for that,' she'd said, her voice thick with the local accent. 'Penrith coaches do come through here, but you'll be lucky to get a seat on one.'

The woman had been right about that. After an hour or more of trying, Louisa had not managed to find a seat on any of the coaches travelling in the right direction. In the end, feeling faint with hunger and exhaustion, she had tearfully admitted defeat and approached the woman again, this time to ask if there was any possibility of a drink and a warm meal.

'There's the parlour,' she'd said, raising her eyebrows as she regarded her dirty clothing once again. 'Or there's bread and beer in the small kitchen, which you might prefer.'

Not wishing to make a spectacle of herself in the parlour, and conscious that she needed to keep most of her money for coach fares, Louisa had settled upon the cheaper option. The woman had directed her to this cramped, untidy room at the rear of the inn, and it was here that Louisa had sat ever since, forcing herself to eat the unappealing fare and trying to gather her strength for the long walk ahead. If she could not get a coach to Penrith, then she would have to get there on foot.

She shuddered, pulling her shawl tighter around her shoulders as she considered what lay ahead of her. Getting herself this far had been a trial. Her ankle had worsened, growing more painful and swollen with each mile, and conspiring with her growing fatigue to hinder her progress as she limped along. She wasn't sure how she was going to face more hours on her feet, enduring pain and lacking both sleep and proper sustenance. She did not even know if she would reach her destination before dark, or where she would rest if she did not.

'What is the alternative, Louisa?' she muttered to herself, shredding the dried bread with her fingers. 'You can hardly go back—not now.'

A tear slipped down her cheek as for a moment—the briefest moment—she allowed herself to despair. Last night, her life had seemed to unravel at such an over-whelming pace that she'd felt she had no other option but to flee. Yet her flight had not lightened her load; instead, it had only added further difficulties, which seemed to multiply and mount up by the hour. Running away, it turned out, had been no answer. It was self-destruction, plain and simple.

She wiped her eyes as a young maid flew in through the door, her small hands laden with dirty bowls which she dumped unceremoniously on the table in front of her. Servants had been to-ing and fro-ing like this ever since she'd been there, using this small area to abandon the used crockery that they had presumably collected from the parlour.

This maid, however, did not leave immediately; she lingered, her pretty emerald eyes regarding Louisa curi-ously for a moment. Normally Louisa would have found this impertinent, but she had no energy for such feel-ings today. Instead, she offered the maid a small smile, then filled the silence with another sip of the flavour-less beer.

'Is your name Louisa?' the maid asked after a moment.

'Y-yes,' Louisa stammered, taken aback at being so bluntly addressed. 'Why?'

'There's a fine-looking gentleman in the parlour asking about a young woman called Louisa something-or-other. The description he gave sounded like it might be you.'

Louisa felt her heart descend to the pit of her stomach. It was Isaac—it had to be. She ought to have realised he would come looking for her. Ought to have considered that, whatever he thought of her now, her sudden disappearance would grieve him.

'Oh,' she replied. 'And what did you say?'

'Nothing,' the maid scoffed. 'He didn't ask me—he asked Mrs Sym. She's keeping tight-lipped, of course. Doesn't like to get involved with runaways. We get a lot of that here, what with being close to the border. Mind you, if he offers her a few coins that'll likely loosen her tongue,' she added. 'Anyway, miss, you might want to slip out of here now—if you don't wish to see him, that is.'

Louisa nodded her thanks, but didn't move from the hard wooden stool upon which she was perched. She sipped her beer again, her heart still racing but her mind strangely blank. She was tired, and she was injured, and at that moment she realised that she had neither the will nor the energy to carry on.

The young maid regarded her carefully, her freckled face screwed up in confusion. 'Or perhaps you do wish to see him, after all?' she asked.

Louisa felt the heat of tears prickling in her eyes as she considered the question. 'Yes,' she whispered finally. 'But I cannot. It is better this way.'

The maid's brow furrowed deeper. 'With all due respect, miss, I don't see how moping in here is better than going out there to talk to him. If it makes any difference, the gentleman looks as miserable as you. Worried, too. I'll bet he's travelled miles, trying to find you. If I had a gentleman like that looking for me, I wouldn't be staying put in Mrs Sym's kitchen for a moment longer, that's for certain.'

Her spirited tone made Louisa smile. 'So, if you were me you'd go and see him?' she ventured to ask.

The maid grinned. 'I'd do more than see him. I would marry him and go to live in whatever grand house he's come from. Then I wouldn't have to work all hours in this place and give most of my pay over to my father just so he can spend it on ale. That's what I would do.'

Louisa sighed. 'I ought to have spoken to him last night, instead of running away from him. I was just so overwhelmed, and I got it into my mind that it would be best if I left.' She tugged at her skirt. 'Now look at me—all I've managed to do so far is injure myself, be a nuisance to every coach driver I've encountered today, and no doubt upset everyone who has ever loved me.'

'The gentleman must care very much about you,' said the maid thoughtfully. 'Whatever has happened, is it really so terrible that you must run away?'

Louisa grimaced, thoughts of last night's revelations flooding unbidden into her mind. 'Yes, it was terrible,' she replied, slowly getting up from her seat. 'However, I don't think I am running any more.'

'Are you going to see him, then?' the maid asked, raising an eyebrow. 'If you are, you'd best hurry.'

Louisa nodded, suppressing a groan at the pain that shot through her ankle as she began to walk. 'Thank you,' she said. 'If it wasn't for you I'd have never known that he was here.'

The maid shrugged. 'I just thought you had a right to know. That way, you could decide what you wanted to do about it.'

'I'm still not sure I have decided,' Louisa replied. 'I just know that I need to talk to him.'

'Then you *have* decided, in a way,' the maid answered her. 'Now, go on, miss—go and find him. But take care with that leg; you've turned very pale all of a sudden.'

Louisa smiled at her, her head feeling suddenly light as pain, nerves and anticipation potently mingled. Mustering the very last vestiges of her strength, she limped out of the room, trying to ignore the way the ground swayed beneath her feet and the world swam before her eyes.

Isaac made his way back across the courtyard to where Samuel was patiently waiting with the horses. Frustrated, he kicked at the dusty ground, cursing aloud and causing a couple of young grooms lingering nearby to cast him wary looks. The innkeeper's wife had been rude and evasive, and had all but refused to answer his questions.

'It's a busy place,' she'd kept telling him. There was no way to account for who passed through or when they might have been there.

Her unwillingness to look him in the eye had told him that she was lying, but there was precious little he could do in the face of such obfuscation.

'Did you not offer her a few coins for her trouble?' Samuel asked, when Isaac informed him that he'd failed to discover anything. 'Everything has a price in these

establishments—even information. She might have
been a bit more forthcoming with a shilling or two in
her pocket.'

'No. I hadn't thought of that,' Isaac replied, putting
his head in his hands. 'Perhaps I should have sent you in
there instead, brother, for it seems I am truly hopeless.
Louisa could be anywhere by now. What am I going to
say to her aunt? To her family?'

To his surprise, a slow smile spread across Samuel's
face as he looked over Isaac's shoulder. 'You can tell
them that you've found her. Look.'

Isaac spun round, his heart leaping into his throat as
he laid his eyes upon the slight young woman limping
towards him. For a moment he did not believe it could
be the same lady he'd waltzed with just a day earlier,
such was the extent of her transformation. Her bonnet
looked to be damaged, and some of her fair curls had escaped from it and come to rest on her shoulders, which
were adorned with a filthy shawl. Her dress was in an
equally ill condition, and as she drew closer he saw
that her pale face seemed almost grey, with pronounced
dark circles beneath her brown eyes. She looked up at
him, attempting a smile, but managing only a grimace.

'Good God, Louisa,' he said, darting towards her.
'What has happened to you?'

Without thinking he wrapped a supportive arm
around her. She looked fragile enough that one gust of
wind might blow her away.

'Please don't fret. I am quite well,' she said, but her
voice contained an odd, strained note which told him
that she was anything but fine. 'When I heard you were
here I realised I must see you. I needed to tell you I am
sorry…'

Isaac gathered her into his arms. 'No, *I* am sorry. Sorry for what happened last night. Sorry for everything that has happened to you. Sorry that you felt you had no choice but to leave Langdale. To leave me.'

Her lip trembled. 'I should not have run away. I should have spoken to you and…' She paused, a pained look flickering across her face as she leaned against him, grabbing hold of his coat and clinging on for dear life. 'I am sorry. My ankle…it's…'

She did not have to say another word. Without a moment's hesitation Isaac lifted her up, taking her into his arms and striding towards the inn. He carried her through the door and into the parlour, where a dozen or so gawping genteel faces awaited, with their wine glasses and their steaming bowls of soup.

He cared nothing for their whispers, nor their judgement. Propriety be damned, he thought. Society be damned. Society had brought Louisa nothing but condemnation and misery. It had left her feeling as though she deserved no happiness…as though she had no good choices left to make. If this was what society and its rules would do to a woman, then he wanted no part in it.

'Your best room, man—now!' Isaac bellowed to the ruby-faced innkeeper. 'With fresh sheets and a fire lit. And send for a physician immediately. Tell him that Sir Isaac Liddell of Hayton Hall requires his assistance. This lady is injured.'

'You're making a scene,' Louisa said quietly. 'You'll be the talk of Cumberland.'

He gave her a tender smile. 'Then so be it. Let them gossip. I care nothing for it as long as you are by my side.'

She searched his gaze, her brown eyes seeming to

darken further. 'You cannot mean that. Not now. Not after learning the truth about me.'

'I mean it more than ever,' he replied, as the inn-keeper beckoned them into a large and comfortable room. 'Indeed, Louisa Conrad,' he added, smiling at her once more, 'I mean to marry you, if you will have me.'

Chapter Twenty-Eight

He wanted to marry her.

As the young maid she'd met in the kitchen had fussed around her, and a physician had arrived to tend to her, Louisa had turned Isaac's words over and over in her mind. He cared nothing for gossip. He wanted her by his side.

He wanted to marry her.

She'd been unable to answer him at the time, such had been her shock at his declaration, and as propriety had required him to leave the room once the maid had come to help her remove her filthy dress and get into bed, he'd not had the opportunity to say anything further. Now, as the physician finished bandaging her ankle, she found herself wondering where he was. Wondering when she would be able to speak to him again and say all the things she knew needed to be said.

'It will heal,' the physician said brusquely, inclining his head towards her foot. 'With a few days of rest and a good deal of care there should be no lasting damage.'

Louisa offered him a meek smile and a nod of thanks before the maid escorted him to the door. The room she'd been given was comfortable and warm, with a low fire burning in the grate and the curtains drawn against the world outside. She sank back against the crisp bedlinen, trying to rest as she'd been instructed, but finding she could not relax.

Her mind raced, her thoughts scattering like leaves in the wind. He knew every detail of her scandalous past, and yet he wished to marry her. She'd run away from him like a reckless coward, and yet he wished to marry her. How was this possible?

A knock at the door startled her, and the maid flashed her a knowing smile. 'That'll be your gentleman, I expect.'

'He's not my gentleman,' Louisa said, sitting herself upright.

'He most certainly is,' the maid insisted. 'I'll let him in, shall I?'

Louisa nodded her agreement.

Inexplicably, she held her breath as the door creaked open and she caught sight of those familiar blue eyes, that dark, dishevelled hair with a will of its own. He was, without doubt, the most handsome man she knew. He was kind, and loving, and decent. And he wanted to marry her.

'Come in, sir,' the maid said. She gave Louisa another knowing look. 'I do believe Mrs Sym is looking for me, so I shall leave you both in peace.'

Hurriedly the maid departed, pulling the door shut behind her. For several moments neither of them spoke. Isaac busied himself by fetching a chair from the corner of the room and bringing it to her bedside. Louisa, meanwhile, found herself watching him, her eyes lazily wandering over his tall frame, over his broad shoulders.

He had removed his coat and wore only a shirt which had been rendered off-white, no doubt by his exertions. The sting of guilt rose in her stomach then, as she was reminded of all the grief her actions would have caused him.

'I have sent Samuel back to Langdale,' Isaac said, sitting down next to her. 'He will return in my carriage with your aunt and your portmanteau. The physician has advised that you would be best to rest here for a day or two, so you will need some provisions for that.'

Louisa nodded, lowering her gaze and feeling suddenly very conscious that she wore only her chemise beneath the bedsheets. 'Thank you, Isaac,' she replied. 'For everything. You must think me very foolish and reckless.'

'I do not think you are either of those things,' he countered. 'The way Mrs Pearson behaved towards you was unconscionable. It is little wonder that you felt you had to leave.'

She bit her lip, still not looking at him. 'I do not just mean that. What I did in the past...'

Isaac shifted in his seat, clearing his throat. 'What happened to you in the past is not your fault, Louisa. You were dealt a cruel hand, but neither you nor your fiancé did anything different from what scores of men and women have done since the beginning of time.'

She smiled. 'You sound like my aunt.'

'Well, your aunt is right.' He paused, as though searching for the right words. 'I just— I wish I had allowed you to tell me what happened. I wish I had not had to hear it from that dreadful Mrs Pearson.'

She felt her smile fade as her thoughts were overtaken by recollections of that scene.

'I think the satisfied look on her face will haunt me. Her version of events...the insinuations she made...' Louisa bit her lip, shaking her head in disbelief. 'I am not a strumpet. And I never accused Richard of anything. And I never—I never lay with anyone but him. By the time I discovered I was with child he was at sea. I told no one—not even my mother. Instead I waited, hoping beyond hope that he would return soon, that we could marry quickly and no one would be any the wiser. Then the news of his death reached me. It all... it all unravelled after that. I told my parents—I had to. But I told no one else. To this day I do not know how the rumours began—the careless talk of a maid, perhaps, or the prying eyes of a visitor who spotted my swollen belly. Being with child and unwed was scandalous enough, but some of the things which were said were appalling—that I had taken many lovers, that I was no better than a harlot. I've often wondered if it was Richard's family who said those things—to discredit me and to protect his memory, I suppose. It seems that the vitriol spouted by Mrs Pearson is some confirmation of that.'

Louisa sniffed, wiping crossly at the tears which had begun to form in the corners of her eyes. Isaac, meanwhile, got up, and to her surprise he perched on the bed next to her, taking her hand in his.

'You said yesterday that you lost the child,' he said. 'My son did not live for many hours after his birth... nor did Rosalind. She succumbed to fever a day later.' He paused, a pained expression briefly flashing across his face. 'I understand all too well the grief you feel. But I'm not sure I can put into words my anger at the way Mrs Pearson tried to shame you, or my sorrow for your loss. I am so sorry, Louisa.'

She gave him a watery smile. 'Thank you. You are the first person to say that to me. Even my parents, as kind as they were in the circumstances, never could bring themselves to say they were sorry.' She felt her face crumple as more tears began to fall. 'I wish I had confided in you, Isaac. I wish I'd trusted that you would understand.'

He squeezed her hand. 'Perhaps you would do me the honour of putting your trust in me now,' he said quietly, searching her gaze. 'Will you marry me, Louisa?'

She hesitated. Ever since he'd first uttered his intention as he'd carried her into this room, she'd been grappling with her answer. With what her heart desired and what her head still told her she could not have.

'You are a gentleman of impeccable repute, Isaac,' she said. 'Please consider what connecting yourself to me would mean for your name, for your family.'

'Reputations be damned,' he replied. 'I will not live my life for society's approval. I will be forty years of age soon, and I have endured quite enough pain in my life. I love you, Louisa. I wish to be happy, and I wish to make you happy. More than anything. Please, trust me. Trust that this is all that matters to me—not society, nor scandal. Just you. Just us.'

She nodded. 'I do trust you,' she replied, feeling the depth of truth in those words.

She could trust him—he had more than proved that to her. Over these past days he'd defended her, protected her, cared for her and sought to rescue her, even after learning her terrible truth. Now, when he said her past was no impediment to his heart, she trusted him. She believed him.

'Then the only question that remains is, what do you want, Louisa?'

His eyes continued to search hers and she knew he was glimpsing her answer, even if she had not yet put it into words.

She had spent so long fixed upon the past that she had never allowed herself to consider the future. Never permitted herself to contemplate being happy. Never dared to imagine loving and being loved in return. Yet the desire for those things had always been there, she realised now, lying dormant beneath layers of grief, sorrow and shame. This summer Isaac had awoken that desire—perhaps in the candlelight of the Assembly Rooms or on the breezy clifftops, or perhaps in his old library, when she'd first enjoyed his warm embrace.

She could not truly say. What she did know, however, was that this was a desire she must finally admit to.

She swallowed hard, holding his gaze. 'I want you,' she said. 'I will marry you, Isaac.'

By the time Louisa's aunt arrived with Samuel, Isaac felt as though he was ready to burst with joy. He wanted to rush downstairs and announce his news to his brother in the middle of the inn. He wanted to tell all of Cumberland that Louisa Conrad had accepted him. As it was, he tried his best to maintain his composure, reminding himself that there was a proper way to handle these matters. And as Louisa's guardian, Miss Howarth needed to be informed first.

After showing her to Louisa's room he tried to excuse himself, believing it was best to give the two ladies some time alone to reconcile, and for Louisa to deliver her news in her own way. However, Louisa would not permit it, insisting that he should remain. She seemed anxious about seeing her aunt again, and he suspected she was worried that the older woman would be angry with her for leaving the way she had. As it was, she need not have feared. More than anything, Miss Howarth seemed relieved to find her niece safe and well, except for an injured ankle.

Now that they were all happily far away from Langdale Hall, Isaac took the opportunity to inform Miss Howarth about Mrs Pearson's regrettable involvement in the revelation of Louisa's past. It was a task he did not relish, but he knew he had to do his duty.

Miss Howarth's mouth fell open in horror as the full extent of the woman's unpleasantness became apparent to her, and she turned back to her niece, regarding her tearfully.

'Oh, my dear, I am so sorry,' she said, shaking her head. 'I must admit that I was perturbed when I heard the suggestions Mrs Pearson made at dinner, about you and Sir Isaac promenading alone, but now I am truly horrified. I cannot believe she did that to you. It is no wonder that you ran away from Langdale.'

'Even so, I am sorry I caused you such distress, Aunt,' Louisa replied. 'I hope you can forgive me.'

'There is nothing to forgive,' Miss Howarth insisted. 'On the contrary, it is me who should be asking you for forgiveness. I regret the day that I ever introduced you to Mary and Charlotte Pearson. Please know that I will never welcome either of them into my home again. Our acquaintance is at an end.'

With that, Miss Howarth seemed to consider the matter of her callous former acquaintance closed, and their conversation turned to the future—specifically, the next few days.

In his elated state, Isaac had given little thought to

the practicalities of what lay beyond today, and he found himself rather taken aback to witness Louisa's aunt take charge of the situation. Neither he nor Louisa seemed to be able to get a word in edgeways as the older woman launched into listing all that needed to happen, and all that needed to be done.

'And Mr Liddell has been very attentive, and has secured me a very nice room here,' she continued, singing the praises of Isaac's younger brother. 'So I will stay while you convalesce, as is right and proper. Oh, and I will need to write to your mother. I know she is expecting you back in Berkshire by summer's end, but I will write to explain that there may be a delay on account of your injured ankle.'

'Aunt…' Louisa began, clearly trying her best to interject.

'Oh, but how shall we travel back to Lowhaven once you are well enough?' Miss Howarth began to fret. 'Sir Isaac and Mr Liddell will surely have departed by then.'

Louisa tried again. 'I doubt Sir Isaac will have gone, Aunt, since…'

'Oh! Well, then, sir, would you be so kind enough to take us back to Lowhaven in a day or two?'

Isaac glanced at Louisa, an amused smile twitching at the corners of his mouth to mirror the one she already wore. 'It would be my pleasure, Miss Howarth,' he said, beginning to chuckle.

Louisa's aunt furrowed her brow, regarding them both seriously as Louisa began to laugh, too. 'Pray tell, what is so funny?'

'I have been trying to tell you, Aunt,' Louisa replied, obviously composing herself. 'Sir Isaac has asked me to marry him, and I have accepted.'

The older woman clasped her hands together in delight. 'Oh! How wonderful!' she exclaimed. 'Why on earth did you not say anything before? I feel rather foolish now, talking of writing to your mother about your return to Berkshire. I shall have to write and tell her there is to be a wedding. Oh—and in your grandfather's old church, too. She will be delighted.'

He watched as Louisa sat bolt upright. 'The church in Hayton?' she repeated.

Miss Howarth nodded. 'Well, of course—the master of Hayton Hall can hardly get wed anywhere else, can he? I'm sure the whole village will turn out for it—and probably a good number of families from Lowhaven, too.'

Isaac saw Louisa's smile fade. She closed her eyes, a small frown gathering between them, as though she was trying to steady herself. His heart lurched as he realised something troubled her. Something that he sensed she was not prepared to reveal in front of her aunt.

'Miss Howarth, perhaps you would be so kind as to give me a moment or two alone with your niece?' he asked.

Perhaps noticing the sudden tension in the room, Louisa's aunt assented and swiftly departed, closing the door behind her.

Isaac sat down at Louisa's side, his heart thudding in his chest, his emotions swelling up into a lump in his throat. Dread. Anticipation. Agony. Hope.

'Is something the matter, Louisa?' he said softly. 'Do you not wish to marry me, after all?'

'Of course I wish to marry you,' she replied without a moment's hesitation. 'It is not that. It is...it is the thought of the banns, of church. Of the whole village watching us wed. Of what they will say.'

'You know I care nothing for any of that.'

'It is easy to say that you do not care when you have never been marred in scandal,' she countered. 'Besides, you are a gentleman, and a baronet—you will always command respect, even if tainted by your association with me. I, on the other hand, will always be considered a disgrace. I am not sure I can face the scrutiny... if I can manage to stand up in church in front of society and endure their whispers while making my vows.'

An idea dawned on him then, and he could not repress his smile. 'Then don't,' he said. 'Let's not marry in front of them at all. We don't have to marry in Hayton, and we don't have to wait until the banns are read. Indeed, I do not care for any of it as long as we are wed.'

She frowned. 'What do you mean?'

He took hold of her hands, clasping them in his. 'I mean, let's go to Scotland. Let's elope, Louisa, to Gretna Green. We can travel as soon as you are strong enough.'

Her eyes widened at the suggestion. 'An elopement? That will cause another scandal!'

He drew her fingers to his lips and kissed them. 'It might, but it will be our scandal. Together.'

She smiled. 'Sir Isaac Liddell, I do believe that you've lost your mind.'

'Oh, I have,' he answered her, laughing. 'Earlier this summer a beautiful woman climbed into my carriage after a stagecoach accident, and days later my horse almost collided with her on the clifftops near Lowhaven. My life has not been quite the same since.'

'Nor has mine,' she replied, stroking his rough, unshaven cheek. 'I'm not sure what I expected from my summer in Lowhaven, but I certainly did not expect this.'

'Well, you did once tell me that you wished to travel,' he said. 'And, since we both adored *Waverley*, Scotland seems as good a place as any to start.'

'To start?'

'Indeed,' Isaac answered with another smile. 'I think you and I have had our fill of hiding away. There's a world out there, and I'd like us to see it together.'

The look of utter joy on her face was a sight to behold. Isaac leaned over once more, enveloping her in his embrace and saying a quiet prayer that he would always manage to make her as happy as this.

Chapter Twenty-Nine

They were married not before an altar but an anvil, in a short ceremony conducted by the village blacksmith. Louisa did not take her eyes off Isaac throughout, and the words of the would-be priest washed over her as she assuredly made her vows.

The past few days had been strange and exciting, taking them across wild open countryside and into a succession of comfortable but often raucous inns as they made their way north.

Isaac had insisted that they take their time, travelling only as far as the horses could manage each day. She was still recovering, he'd pointed out, so a more leisurely pace would be better for her health. Louisa, in turn, had expressed her desire to be wed as soon as possible.

'I may have to reconsider my opinion that you are neither foolish nor reckless,' Isaac had teased.

She'd laughed and conceded the point, agreeing to be sensible just this once.

Their church on that fine summer's day was the blacksmith's shop, a humble building with whitewashed walls and a ceiling supported by exposed wooden beams. Their congregation comprised two witnesses tempted out of the nearby inn with a few coins for their trouble. For wedding clothes they'd made do with their country attire, although Louisa did not believe Isaac had ever looked a finer gentleman than he did now, in his dark frock coat, fawn pantaloons and black Hessian boots.

It was all very irregular, and far from sensible, and yet Louisa could not have been happier. Standing there in that little room, observed by no one who knew them as she committed herself to the man she loved, she realised that for the first time in a long time she felt truly free.

Isaac took hold of her hands as the blacksmith brought his hammer down on his anvil, sealing their union with the tools of his trade. Then he pulled her close, confirming it himself with a lingering kiss on her lips. She kissed him back ardently. Their first kiss as husband and wife.

'A very handsome couple,' one of the witnesses remarked. 'I wonder why they had to run away to get wed.'

'Let them wonder,' Isaac whispered in Louisa's ear. 'Although they are right,' he added, kissing her on the cheek. 'The bride in particular is a great beauty.'

Louisa blushed, glancing down at her plain cream day dress, conscious of the curls she'd struggled to tease into order that morning bouncing around her face. For all her delight at the way in which she'd been wed, she had missed the help of her maid.

Aunt Clarissa had assured her that Nan would remain at her home in Lowhaven until she could be reunited with Louisa when the new mistress of Hayton Hall returned. The thought of it caused Louisa to pause. That was what she was now: the new mistress of Hayton Hall. Isaac's wife. It was hard to believe the changes to her life which had been wrought by one summer sojourn to visit her aunt.

Aunt Clarissa, for her part, had been somewhat taken aback by their decision to elope. Ultimately, though, she had been supportive, understanding their reasons for doing so, albeit with some reservations about exactly what Louisa's parents would make of it.

Sharing her aunt's concern, Louisa had written to her mother directly before they departed for Gretna, explaining her decision and expressing her hope that her parents would be happy for her.

'We will invite them to visit once we return to Hayton,' Isaac had said when she'd broached the subject of how her parents might greet her news. 'I have no doubt that will allay any concerns they may have.'

'Are you telling me that the brooding Isaac Liddell plans to charm my parents?' Louisa had teased him.

'No, I thought I'd let Samuel do that,' he'd replied, grinning. 'For my part, I intend to impress them with my large estate and title.'

Smiling now at the memory, Louisa leaned against Isaac, steadying herself. Her ankle was slowly healing, but it still ached after any length of time spent on her feet.

'This has been quite an adventure, hasn't it?' she remarked, gazing up at him. 'Once we return to Hayton, I think it will feel like a dream.'

Isaac grinned at her. 'Alas, I have no plans for us to return to Hayton just yet.'

'You don't? But what about the estate?'

'I have written to Samuel, and I'm sure he will manage my affairs for a little while longer,' he said, wrapping his arm around her waist as together they walked outside to where their carriage was waiting.

'Poor Mr Liddell… I fear he has been rather put upon of late,' she remarked, referring to all the to-ing and fro-

ing the poor man had done across Cumberland, seeing
Aunt Clarissa home safely and bringing the eloping
couple provisions before returning to Hayton himself.

Isaac chuckled. 'He has enjoyed it. As a very beautiful and perceptive lady once told me, my brother likes
to arrange things. And, please, call him Samuel. You're
my wife now; hearing you call my brother "Mr Liddell"
sets my teeth on edge.'

'In that case, shall I expect to hear you calling my
aunt "Clarissa" when we next visit her for tea?' Louisa
asked, unable to suppress her smirk.

'Oh, heavens, no! She will be Miss Howarth until the
end of my days.'

They paused next to the carriage, and he pulled her
closer to him.

'Anyway,' he continued, his thumb caressing her
cheek, 'do you not wish to know where we are going,
if not back to Hayton?'

She gazed up at him. 'Indeed. Enlighten me.'

'It occurred to me on our journey to Gretna that I'd
like to see something of Scotland with my wife. How
does Edinburgh sound?'

'Edinburgh sounds wonderful,' she gushed, resting
her head against his chest. 'I love you, Sir Isaac.'

Isaac placed a tender kiss on top of her head as the
driver opened the carriage door, signalling the start of
their next journey together. Beyond the charming little border village were more miles of roads, more open
country, and eventually a city beckoned.

'I love you too, Lady Liddell,' he replied.

* * * * *

HISTORICAL

Your romantic escape to the past.

Available Next Month

The Countess's Forgotten Marriage Annie Burrows
A Housemaid To Redeem Him Laura Martin

....

A Proposal To Protect His Lady Elizabeth Beacon
The Secret She Kept From The Earl Sophia Williams

Keep reading for an excerpt of a new title
from the Historical series,
WEDDED TO HIS ENEMY DEBUTANTE
by Samanth Hastings

Chapter One

London, March 1815

'The London Season is abominably dull,' Lady Frederica Stringham said, to no one in particular.

Her mother had once again refused to let her go to the factory with her that morning. It was scandalous enough that a duchess owned a perfumery and actually oversaw its day-to-day dealings. But working there or at the fashionable shop on Bond Street was quite out of the question for an unmarried debutante of the *ton*.

Frederica stood next to a window as tall as a person and three times as wide. She stared at the rain pouring on the cobblestone street of the exclusive Berkley Square—brick and stone mansions in the best part of London. Wishing instead that she was in Greece with her sisters and their father. Papa had accompanied them on their journey, but only planned to stay for a month or two to get them established in a good place. Frederica had spent over a year with her married sister Mantheria in Italy, but Mama now insisted that she attend the London Season. She was one and twenty after all and *unmarried*.

Perish the thought.

And whilst flirting with dandies was delightful and playing cards with Corinthians was charming, no suitor had captured her heart. Although, she did enjoy kissing several of them. Another thing debutantes were *not* supposed to do.

Frederica yawned, walked back to the sofa, and slouched down in her seat. Stacked beside her on the side table were all the Maria Edgeworth books from the lending library. Picking them up, she saw the titles *Belinda*, *Castle Rackrent*, and *Tales of Fashionable Life*. She had read them all. If only she could return them and select more without her mother coming with her. Debutantes in London were guarded more closely than treasure. Listening to the raindrops pelt against the window, she let out another sigh.

A footman with a white-powdered wig opened the door for her mother, the Duchess of Hampford. Her mother was an older version of herself, with the same hazel eyes and brown hair, although showing some grey now. She was an inch or so shorter than her daughter, yet her figure was still trim where it ought to be and generous where she would wish it to be. The fragrant smell of lilacs and rock rose clung to her. She gave her favourite daughter a look of reproach.

'Lawson, you may shut the door,' the Duchess said majestically. 'Frederica, sit up at once. I will not have you slouching like a hoyden. You would think you were a chit out of the schoolroom, instead of a young lady in her twenties.'

Frederica sat up stiffly. All right then. This was going to be a business meeting. 'Yes, Mama.'

Her mother sat on a chair beside her and said in a

more coaxing tone, 'My nerves have been in shreds these last few weeks, but at last, all of my worries for you are over.'

Stretching out her arms, she smiled. 'I do not think I am about to die. In fact, I am in perfect health.'

'Stop it, Frederica,' Mama said in a sharp tone. 'This is no time for funning, Samuel is finally coming up to scratch.'

That wiped the smirk off her face and she lightly touched her throat. 'But his father only died less than a month ago.'

Mama brushed a finite piece of lint off her beautiful pink morning dress in what appeared to be silent frustration. 'Lord Pelford will be arriving this afternoon to make you an offer of marriage.'

Frederica's mouth fell open. 'I cannot believe it! He has not seen me in seven years and he did not like me much then. He was always criticising me and prosing on about proper behaviour.'

Her mother sighed and folded her arms. 'You are acting like this is a surprise. You were named after his mother and a union has been planned between our two families for years.'

Squeezing her hands into fists, Frederica stood up and walked to the window. Her heart palpitated and black spots blocked her vision. 'I thought… I thought after Mantheria's disastrous marriage to a duke, that you would have changed your mind. Glastonbury was not faithful to my sister for even six months.'

Dropping her eyes to her folded arms, her mother sniffed. 'Samuel is not like Glastonbury. I have known him his entire life and he is a steady, intelligent young man. He would never be unfaithful to you. Glastonbury was too old for Mantheria and I was too foolish to realise what a mismatch it would be. I admit that I was blinded to his many weaknesses by his wealth and position.'

'Including Lady Dutton?' Frederica asked, knowing full well that her mother knew about Glastonbury's long-time mistress before he married her sister.

Mama closed her eyes and inhaled sharply. 'We assumed wrongly that he would give her up. You have no idea how much both your father and I regret giving our consent to the match. We resolved to not bring out a daughter at seventeen again, deeming it too young to make a good choice for a spouse. You are more mature at one and twenty. You are well-educated and well-travelled. I believe you will make the right choice.'

Her blood boiling, Frederica threw her hands up in the air. 'But you are not giving me a choice! You are marrying me to a man who will disapprove of everything I say and do.'

'If you had found another young man who caught your fancy when you debuted at nineteen, we would have supported you,' she said slowly as if Frederica was still a small child. 'But after two years, you have not. And I will not attempt to deny that I did everything in my power to secure for my daughter a husband of the highest rank.'

Frederica's hands shook and fluttered. 'Have you bought me a husband?'

'I bought you a title—the husband comes with it.'

A giggle escaped Frederica's lips. Drat her mother for making her laugh when she was trying to throw a proper tantrum. 'It is all about town that Samuel inhcrited very little beside debts and mortgages from his father, besides a younger brother and mother to keep.'

Mama got up and walked to where Frederica stood by the windows. 'A union between our two families was planned almost from the day of your christening. Lady Pelford has been just as determined as myself for this day to come. She has invited us to stay countless times at Farleigh Palace to improve your acquaintance with her son.'

'Little good it has done either,' Frederica said, folding her arms across her chest. 'I was eight years of age and he eleven, when Samuel and I learned that we could not endure each other's company. And since then when forced together, we have done our very best to make each other miserable.'

'Well, I suggest that you stop trying to make him miserable when he is your husband.'

Frederica let out an airy laugh, but quelled it quickly. 'The last time I saw him, I was fourteen years old, when he stayed with us that summer at Hampford Castle. Samuel gave me a box of chocolates and told me I was immature and badly behaved.'

Mama put her hands on Frederica's shoulders. 'As I recall that summer, you and your little sisters put your papa's pet bear cub in his room in the middle of the night and scared the poor fellow out of his wits.'

Frederica grinned fondly at this memory. 'He didn't have many wits as I remember.'

'But you have both wits and talent,' her mother said, squeezing her daughter's shoulders lightly before releasing her hold. 'And I can think of no better person to leave my perfume company to.'

Her heartbeat raced in her chest as warmth radiated through her body. She grabbed her mother's arm and tugged it. 'You are leaving Duchess & Co. to me?'

Mama smiled like a lioness after a successful hunt. 'I am leaving Duchess & Co. to another duchess. Mantheria is not interested. Please tell me that you will accept Samuel and become a *duchess*.'

Frederica dropped her mother's arm and turned back to the window. She breathed in slowly and exhaled, but it did not slow down her racing pulse. There was nothing in the world she wanted more than her mother's company. She had always been afraid that Mama would leave it to Matthew, one of her elder brothers, who was a fine businessman. Frederica had little experience with running a company, but she had grown up practising languages and mathematics to prepare herself. She even planned to expand her mother's perfume business into red scented soaps with phenol. Adding phenol to the sodium tallowate, sodium cocoate, and glycerine had helped her scratches heal without infection. Three fragrances went well with it: camphor, rosemary, and eucalyptus. Trying different combinations, she had made at least one hundred cakes of them as she waited for something to happen during the early Season.

Gulping, she turned back to her mother. 'When do I get your company?'

The look on Mama's face was triumphant, she knew that she had won. 'I will deed half of it to you when you marry and the other half when I am dead. It is slightly less profitable currently, for I used a large portion of the savings to pay Lord Pelford's family debts.'

Frederica did not want her mother to die any time soon and she knew that she still had a lot to learn from

Mama about how to run her own business. She held out her hand. 'It's a bargain.'

Her mother shook her hand tightly, not letting go. 'You will dress in your blue sprigged muslin and have Wade thread flowers through your hair. Do not forget to put a dab of perfume on your inner wrist. And perhaps if you still look as pale as a ghost, tell Miss Wade that she has my permission to add some rouge on your cheeks.'

Her mother finally released her hand and Frederica threw her arms around her mother's neck, hugging her tightly. She kissed her cheek. 'I won't disappoint you, Mama.'

'With the business or with Samuel?'

Frederica laughed. 'Either.'

'I only met your father once before I married him,' she said, 'and we were not even alone. But any marriage can work, if both parties are committed to its success.'

She thought of Samuel and sobered. She was willing to commit, but she could not be certain that he would be. When they were younger, the harder she'd tried to get his attention, the more he'd ignored her. It had been infuriating. He'd had the unique ability to get underneath her thick skin. No person had ever aggravated her more.

'Yes, Mama.'

Her mother sighed. 'If you wish to love your husband, choose to, as I did. Love is not a feeling, but a choice.'

Frederica nodded again and left the room. She could try to love Samuel, but she doubted whether he would do the same. Was a perfume company worth a lifetime without love? Slumping, she walked up the grand staircase to the second floor. She opened the dark mahogany door to her room and found Wade waiting for her. The lady's maid had already laid out the sprigged muslin day dress that flattered Frederica's figure and colouring. Miss Wade was not yet thirty, but her thin face seemed older because of her perpetual frown. She wore her vibrant brown hair in a severe bun, and her plain dress emphasised her slender figure. She stood and executed a sharp curtsy to her mistress.

'I suppose Mama has already spoken with you.'

Wade curtsied again. 'Yes, my lady.'

'Well then, do your best to make me presentable,' Frederica said, sitting down heavily on the bed. 'For as you, and undoubtedly every other servant in the house, already knows, I am to be engaged to be married today.'

Wade assisted Frederica out of her morning gown and into her prettiest dress in the palest shade of blue. She added fresh white flowers to Frederica's coiffure and carefully added a bit of powder to her cheeks. Frederica held still as the lady's maid put on her gloves, silk stockings, and slippers that were dyed the same shade of blue.

'Thank you, Wade. That is all. I should like to be by myself for a little while.'

Once Wade closed the door, Frederica opened the top drawer of her dresser and pulled out her pistol and powder. It was time for some target practice in the garden.

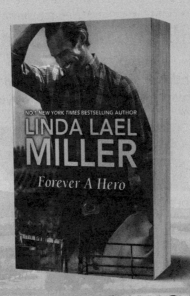

Subscribe and fall in love with a Mills & Boon series today!

You'll be among the first to read stories delivered to your door monthly and enjoy great savings.

WE SIMPLY LOVE ROMANCE

MILLS & BOON

JOIN US

Sign up to our newsletter to stay up to date with...

- Exclusive member discount codes
- Competitions
- New release book information
- All the latest news on your favourite authors

Plus...
get $10 off your first order.
What's not to love?

Sign up at **millsandboon.com.au/newsletter**